Victoria Moreton's Online Dating Diary

Elaine Yeatman

ISBN: 1502480182
ISBN-13: 978-1502480187

DEDICATION

To my mother and my daughter always in my heart and without whom this story would never have been told.

ACKNOWLEDGMENTS

Sue Nicholls whose support, tolerance and endless agony Aunt skills are much appreciated.

Joe Tippens a rare man of vision and determination.

Phil Taylor whose encouragement was boundless.

Martin Jones for being the first to read and laugh out loud.

Nico Tjarks for being the super guy he is and designing the book cover.

All the wonderful men in the World.

CONTENTS

Chapter 1

Deception

Victoria's first date of the 'project' was with a guy called Oliver. She'd spent a couple of weeks talking to him, and thirty others. By now, she had a system for calculating if she would call them back or not. One tick doubtful, two ticks maybe, three ticks yes, four ticks definitely! Oliver received three ticks and although she thought he would not be the 'one', he was very funny and she came to like him.

Victoria was excited to be meeting Oliver, so she dressed for the occasion. She was to have lunch with him in a restaurant she knew well from her many years in London. A sweet and very nice restaurant in Marylebone. She put on her tight Religion jeans and chose her favourite cream Dolce & Gabbana with blue and red trim. A classic jacket, a red string strapped top, a little of her lacy pink and red bra peeking over the edge. Much later to be dubbed the 'dating outfit'. It was very smart with just a hint of sexiness.

She stepped off the train with a little apprehension, but soon lost all her trepidation when snuggled in a taxi and breathing in the sights and sounds of her hometown. London always exhilarated her, and today was no different.

The taxi came to her destination, and she saw a man in a black coat straight ahead waiting on the pathway. Couldn't be him, as he was nothing like the description. Victoria had thought it impolite to ask for a photo. She paid the cabbie and he complimented her on the way she looked and how he enjoyed the conversation, and then wished her a good day.

'I hope so too,' she thought. Feeling a little butterfly inside. "Victoria!"

The man in the black coat was calling to her and by her name. But how could he possibly know her name? Oh No! He must be Oliver. Witty, amusing Oliver. Oliver who told her he did a hundred press-ups every morning but had evidently failed to explain that was *before* he woke up. She stood in amazement, nailed to the pavement.

He wasn't enormous. Just typically middle-aged, balding, overweight paunchy, very shabbily dressed, and ironically enough, holding a sports bag. He said he was a lawyer and looked like one straight from Dickens. Victoria did all she could to cover up her mixed feelings of disappointment and horror.

"Oliver… erm, Oliver?" she said, hoping against hope that she had got this wrong and was hallucinating.

"Hello! Victoria?"

Oliver was striding towards her with a huge smile on his face. He held out his hand and Victoria mumbled, "Oh you must be Oliver?" She was wide eyed and still searching for the six-pack he had said he owned. Obviously he must have been referring to the six cans of beer hidden in his sports bag.

"Yes, I *am*!" he proudly announced beaming at her.

'At least his teeth seem to be okay,' she thought. Victoria had a fixation with teeth, hands and toenails. They all had to be in great order for her to even think of touching a man.

He grabbed her hand and pulled her towards him wrapping his arm around her. She didn't know what to do - make her excuses and run, or take a deep breath and just get on with it. It was only a date after all.

'Berrie. Berrie where are you darling? Oh how he would just *not* understand,' she thought miserably as she was waltzed off to the nearby pub. It wasn't just Berrie who might have difficulty in understanding what she was doing, as she was having a great deal of difficulty understanding it herself.

Once in the pub, she rushed to the ladies powder room in order to calm herself. She was in no danger and he wasn't a gargoyle, she would just have to pull herself together, and gain perspective on the situation. This was her job and her first hurdle, so no problem. Let's have lunch and let's enjoy the moment, she told her image in the mirror. She refreshed her makeup and went to meet her first date.

'For God's sake! What on earth was he thinking? Doesn't a mirror give a reflection,' she thought, plonking herself on the barstool.

She had a passable time during lunch. Oliver was amusing. He lived four doors away from his ex-wife, and when he wasn't working he was looking after his teenaged children coaching them through their GCSEs. How 'funny' is that? Of course, it was good he was still friends with his ex-wife, and saw the children often, but where would he get time for Victoria? Even if she didn't want it. Oliver repeatedly burbled how lovely she was, and how he had been thinking of her all the time.

"I am so pleased to meet you. You are just like you described yourself. No, no better. Much better in fact, you are simply gorgeous," he sighed.

"Thank you Oliver, that's kind of you to say so." She stabbed at her salmon and thought, 'Why couldn't you have been just as honest, maybe he really doesn't have any mirrors in his house.'

They finished lunch and before she had even put her coat on, Oliver said he would accompany her to the station. Before she could protest, he had hailed a taxi, and was helping her inside.

What on earth possessed him to grapple her like a mad octopus, she would never know. She gave no indication that this sort of attention was welcome. In fact, she had told him that he was a nice man, but felt that she could only offer him friendship. He replied that he had enough friends, thanks! So where did he get from there, to believing flinging himself upon her and shoving his tongue down her throat would be something she would appreciate? Totally incomprehensible.

After scrabbling out of his grasp, her bottom almost on the floor in the tussle, she managed to prise herself free, and demanded from him, "What the bloody hell do you think you are you doing?"

Not surprisingly, he looked astonished and sheepishly sat back in his seat, and watched whilst she collected herself.

"Well really Oliver! What an amazing display of unwelcome attention. Just stay over there until we get to the station." She pointed to the other side of the taxi.

The taxi stopped. Victoria shot out like a greyhound from its trap.

She rushed as fast as her six-inch high heels would allow her, dodging the hordes of people at the station, attempting to find out what time her train to sanity and normality departed. She was in luck, only thirty minutes before her train took her back into the warmth and safety of her home. She even had enough time to get a coffee.

It wasn't until she was sitting by the roaring fire, sipping a glass of champagne, her lithe legs stretched out on the sofa, and her beautiful cats nestled by her side, that she started to feel comfortable and complete again.

She scrunched up her toes and wriggled into the yielding arms of the velvety, soft sofa listening to the crackle of the fire, and the gentle purring of Lady and Leander. She sipped her champagne again, closed her eyes, and put her head back to rest on the top of the sofa's arm.

"Mmmmm!" She licked her lips, sank deeper into the soft folds embracing her, and thought, 'Good Lord! What a terrible start to a new life. Not like entering a new world at all, more like entering a new kind of hell.' She giggled, and was slightly annoyed at the ringing of the telephone. Telephone? Wow! How long had she been there revelling in her own thoughts?

It was Beth, "Hi Victoria. Well, dish, darling how did it go?"

"Not according to plan and not according to description."

"Okay I want to hear it all, gore n' all," Beth laughed.

Victoria took another mouthful of champagne, got up from the sofa, sprinkling cats everywhere, and went to the kitchen. Whilst this may not be a 'bottle of wine story'. It was worth, at least two glasses of champagne.

"Hi Bethany. Well, firstly." She began to tell the story of dreaming Oliver. Little to her knowledge did she know that the coming events were to leave her with many far more bizarre and amusing tales to tell.

Oliver was just the beginning.

Chapter 2

How the 'Project' Began

"Why not?"

Emmaline sighed, totally frustrated with her mother. She placed herself nose to nose to demand her full attention. Her mother gently nuzzled her neck.

"Because, I am *not* that desperate. Okay? That's why. I am a lady and not the ugliest thing on the shelf either. Thank you." Victoria, released herself from the close-up stare of her determined daughter, and went into the kitchen. "I'm not on the shelf yet," Victoria muttered to herself, pulling pots and pans noisily from the cupboard, quite put out by Emmaline's suggestion.

"You don't understand," Emmaline said following hard on her mother's heels.

"Nothing to understand." She switched on the oven and began preparing their dinner for the evening. This was never a hard thing since Emmaline didn't really like much in the food department. She had a limited menu, which strangely enough was not reflected in her appetite for fashion. But Emmy loved her mother's cooking and Victoria loved cooking for her.

Emmaline didn't give up on her mother. She was eager to see her happy and settled with a loving, sweet guy - she had been through so much turmoil and heartache of late. Like so many kind and giving women, she didn't deserve the crap that her past relationships had delivered to her. She deserved a man who would love and cherish her.

Emmaline asked her mother which she thought the more important - running a successful business, or running a successful relationship?

Victoria replied, "Relationship."

"So why don't you approach finding someone to love as though it were a business project?" Emmy enquired, stirring her favourite bolognaise sauce. "Then you can make the most of it."

"A business project?"

"Yep. Straightforward. You know how," Emmy spooned a little of the bubbling sauce into her mouth.

"Oh be careful darling, that's hot." As she turned to stop her from burning her mouth, Victoria's mind was whirring away thinking of Emmy's idea.

"Mmmm, yummy." Emmy licked her lips and the spoon.

Victoria wasn't sure whether it was the comforting warmth and alluring smell of the kitchen, or Emmy's puppy dog eyes willing her to give in, that persuaded her to accept her daughter's idea: to join the world of online dating and dating agencies. But she did accept it, and decided to embrace it for all its worth.

'Mmm. Yes. Business-like appeals. She's got me there, and I must admit I am lonely sometimes. Nobody is going to knock on my door here in a tiny village in the back of beyond,' she mused to herself, arranging the spaghetti on the large floral-pattern bowls.

Chapter 3

The Beginning

Beautiful blonde damsel, has own castle wltm knight in very shiny armour to protect and play with. Sail blue seas and ski forbidden mountains. Financially independent essential.

There. That was done. This was the start of her quest. In fact it was her job, her new job. She placed the advert in the Encounters section of a Sunday Newspaper. Victoria had been persuaded by her teenage daughter to take on the intriguing task of finding 'The One'. She had made up her mind to treat the project like a business venture. To be precise, Victoria had begun an adventure searching for the love of her life.

She was a very striking woman, quite often described as a 'lovable beauty'. She was intelligent and had always been independent. She could be self-opinionated. It was true, she had the toughness that being in business often requires, but she was never too busy to help somebody, and was always thoughtful to those around her. She was generous with her time and money. She loved to make people happy, and would give the odd gift to her friends and family simply because she thought they would like it, or that it would suit them.

Victoria kept herself in shape. She worked out more to keep her mind tuned, than her body toned. This had been essential at one point in her life. Her ex-fiancé had treated her very badly. If not for Emmy, the help of the gym and bananas, she really thought she could have taken a warm bath accompanied by a couple of razor blades. There is nothing as great as the power of emotion. She had to fight herself to keep from total inertia and just fading away.

It is true you can die from a broken heart.

After placing the ad, she rang several dating agencies from the same section and made appointments to visit them. She hit the Internet and was shocked by just how many and quite how 'diverse' the sites were. There were sites for almost everything imaginable: sites for married people wanting to meet other married people; sites for gays wanting to meet gays; sites for straights wanting to meet gays. The list was long and complex.

She joined two internet dating sites that she thought would be suitable for her. WealthandHappiness.com, a dating site purporting to have just the right candidates for love and marriage, and sportingdates.eu, a dating site offering much the same. Harmonious matchmaking for people all over the world. Just a click away.

Victoria sat back from her PC and pondered what she was doing. Scepticism marbled with doubt, tinged with just a little hope, consuming her. She popped a pineapple-flavoured bonbon into her mouth. She was sucking hard and making loud munching noises, completely unaware she had been joined by her best friend Alberto.

He was half Italian. The good looking half. Seriously, he was the typical tall, dark and handsome, olive-skinned sex-on-legs, and a super lovely guy, just to put the cherry on the cake. His dress sense left something to be desired (his non-Italian half), but all in all just a wonderful man.

"What are you doing Lovely Lady?"

She jumped up in a mad panic not to let Berrie - her pet name for him - know what she was doing. She hadn't logged off the site for married people to have affairs with other married people.

"Jesus, Berrie! Don't do that to me! You've just taken ten years off my life." She was fumbling around on the keyboard (unsuccessfully) trying to seem nonchalant about the situation and searching to delete the site from the screen.

"Sorry," he said softly. "I did knock. And the door was open."

"Oh was it? Um yes, sorry, forgot, wondered where that draught was coming from. Humph." She hopped off her stool and hugged him.

He was the nicest person in the world and she loved him very much, as a dear and close friend. He was kind and gentle, which was a miracle under the circumstances. Berrie's wife had left him.

She had texted him, 'Sorry won't be back.'

Won't be back… for what? For dinner? The day? The night? A few days? No. As it turned out, she meant 'won't be back *ever*!' Remarkable. Leaving him with three children, adorable admittedly, but still children, and still three of them.

In spite of all that he remained gentle and kind. As his best friend, Victoria helped him with the children. They enjoyed each other's company and would often go out to dinner, or she would cook for him and the kids.

"What you doing?"

"Doing? Um. Yes. Doing? Think, think, for goodness sake." Her mind raced as she hugged him close to her.

"Um. Nothing. Nothing," she trilled. "Just emailing my brother. Yes, that's right," she paused. "What are you doing?" She pulled away trying to cover her embarrassment and stared at him.

"Taking you to dinner… Remember?"

"Omigod! Totally forgot. Sorry darling, give me ten and I'll be with you." She quickly closed her laptop, touched him lightly on the cheek with her nails and dashed up the stairs to her bedroom. She left him with a huge smile that could have split his face.

Chapter 4

Starting A New Business Is Never Easy

The next day she was straight back onto 'The Project' - finding Victoria a husband.

Focus. Focus. Focus.

She decided to take her best girlfriend on her first visit to a dating agency. Beth had had a dreadful time just lately. Her beloved husband had died two years ago and she was having great difficulty in getting back on the road. So an outing to London, lunch, shopping, and a visit to an upmarket dating agency would fit the bill to cheer her up. And of course it would also give a bit of moral support to Victoria while she was still getting into the swing of her new occupation.

Amanda, the proprietor of the Mayfair based dating agency, met them at the lift and invited them into a small, pleasant room. Victoria sat on the two-seater sofa and Beth took comfort in a matching, billowy pink and grey, flower-patterned armchair. Amanda offered them tea or coffee then posed herself very neatly on a dark blue, velvet upholstered chair.

"How very nice to see you both," she said smiling sweetly at them.

"Yes and you too," responded Victoria.

The interview/lecture/information talk went on for over an hour. Victoria was curious, but dubious.

She settled back into the soft, light blue, silken sofa, took a deep breath and said to her host, "Amanda, I accept what you say about your experience in this field and that you have at least thirty 'suitable men' for me already as members of your organisation. But I must tell you firstly that the man suitable for me - although I don't believe that man exists - let's just say *if* he did, then he probably wouldn't want me."

Amanda laughed and smiled her biggest, beamiest smile. Beth smiled and nodded. Amanda assured Victoria that she knew exactly the man for her and couldn't wait to introduce him. They bid their goodbyes and then quite suddenly Beth and Victoria found themselves outside, on the cold streets of Mayfair.

"Well I suppose it's just a gamble and you never know," said Beth. She offered Victoria her arm as they strolled down the street to find a celebratory glass of champagne.

The joining fee was eight thousand pounds! But if you are going to be a sucker you may as well do it properly, and Amanda did sound convincing. 'I'll just visit one other agency before making up my mind though,' Victoria reflected.

They were both quite excited by the prospect of meeting the one and only, special guy. You know - the one that doesn't exist, but a fairy godmother called Amanda was going to execute this task with no trouble at all, and in fact claimed to do so on a daily basis for anyone willing and able to part with eight thousand pounds. All sense had gone out of the window. The only sense now was Victoria's vulnerability.

Victoria slept well that night, dreaming of 'Mr Wonderful' and her new life with him. Sailing under blue skies in the summer and skiing forbidden mountains in the winter. Her breathing was soft and low, and she was smiling. She felt so content.

The week trailed along at a snail's pace just making selections and setting out some designs for her builder to follow. But the week took a meteoric lift when the time came to find out what sort of response had come from her newspaper advert. She was trembling with anticipation and excitement. She dialed in her pin number and when the nice lady told her she had fifteen replies in her voicemail, she nearly dropped the phone.

"Fifteen? Wow!" she said, clapping the air. This was a good idea after all. Hey! It was going to work. Of course it was all about money, so the process of retrieving these responses was slow, and depending on the respondent, quite tedious and repetitive. At least, it became that way, as ultimately she received over four hundred replies to her advertisement.

However, Victoria was very new to this job, and extremely naïve. She had no idea just how arduous her task was to become. But she certainly wasn't deterred. Picking up the phone, Victoria began retrieving the responses that she imagined would lead to the love of her life.

She listened to the first reply. "Hi. I am Roger and you sound like a very special person. Ummm! Your message is refreshing and very, err, funny and I really like the sound of you being an upside down pyramid. I like to ski. I am quite sporty and also like rugby. I travel a great deal and I love the theatre. Umm and I like your message, and I am in my early fifties, five-ten with blue eyes. Oh, I am very sorry, but you only mentioned this at the end of your message, but I do have a bald patch, but it is only a small one, and I do have all my own teeth, so I really hope you'll call me. Look forward to hearing from you Victoria."

He sounded okay, she supposed, and pressed seven to save his message. She leant over her desk and continued. She saved all fifteen, and resolved to phone all of them, after all, that was the polite thing to do. That evening she put aside an hour or so to call the men that answered her ad.

There were one or two that sounded very nice and interesting.

'Looks like Emmy is right. This is a great way to meet my Mr Wonderful,' she thought as she was dialling.

"Hello is that Roger?"

"Yes." There was a great deal of noise in the background. It sounded as if he was in a wine bar.

"This is Victoria. You very kindly answered my ad. If this is inconvenient I can call back?"

"Oh yes, err, well. No. Hang on. I'm just moving."

She soon learnt that about ninety percent of the men answering her advertisement would tend to act in an embarrassed fashion the first time she called them. At first it was endearing, but it quickly became irritating and boring.

"Hi. Yes I remember. How are you? Thanks for returning my call."

"No problem. Thank you for answering my ad. Would you like to know a little more about me?"

"Well, um, err, what do you look like?"

Nine out of ten men would start with that question. The other ten percent didn't ask it first because either they were a) Too shy and embarrassed or b) Downright petrified.

Chapter 5

This Little Piggy

She then found John. Or more accurately, John found her.

John. Sweet voiced. Sexy, beautiful voiced John. A veritable, hunky dream of a man. He seemed so exciting. He was charm personified and with a voice like that, he obviously had to be a seriously good looking man. And he couldn't wait to meet her.

They had been talking for ten days or so when he said, "I am sorry Victoria; I can no longer wait to meet you. You are the girl of my dreams." His voice sounded like warm, melted chocolate being poured over marshmallows.

"Well, what do you suggest?" she said, getting quite carried away with the mere thought of meeting this enigmatic man, who'd been blessed with the voice of an angel.

"Lunch. I know a super Italian restaurant in Richmond."

Now, Victoria lived in a charming village, and she much preferred the idea of John coming to collect her from home. However, her friends had warned her that it was not a good idea to have strange men come and visit her at home. They could be stalkers, rapists, murderers, maniacs, or all four.

Victoria scoffed at these foolish notions, as if by answering an ad, it automatically turned people into monsters. Absolute rubbish, but she thought she would listen to begin with, as she was still very new at this job.

"Well that would be wonderful. This Saturday? Two o'clock?" She was thinking what a drag the train journey would be, but she knew it would be so worthwhile. He sounded absolutely wonderful.

"Done," he lilted. "I'll meet you at the station."

"Great. Goodnight then. See you."

"Goodnight. See you. Sleep well," he moaned softly.

She was in seventh heaven. He just seemed such a nice man, and he sounded so good-looking. Sounded good-looking? If she could only hear herself 'sounded'? Only a woman would think like that. Saturday couldn't come quickly enough.

She dressed to kill in a favourite Thierry Mugler outfit. A classic navy tailored jacket with a white collar, nipped in at the waist, the collar tapering away just enough to show a little cleavage. The jacket was matched with a pencil skirt, so tailored that it forced the wearer to walk à la Marilyn Monroe.

"There," she said, admiring her reflection. "If this doesn't hook him nothing will." She primped herself, and smoothed down her skirt. "What do you think darling?"

Beth had come by for moral support and was equally excited for her friend. "You look stunning," she remarked, with a huge smile across her face, lips glimmering with baby pink lip gloss exposing her new dentistry, of which she was extremely proud.

Next to come for Beth was the breast reduction which she had been wanting for years, but which her dearly departed husband had refused to allow her. Her more than ample bosom measured 34HHH. Once when Victoria and Beth were in Venice, Victoria couldn't help but marvel at the bra left hanging on the bedstead. You could fit a football into each cup.

"Come on. I'll give you a lift to the station." Beth hugged her friend, and repeated how good she looked. "You'll knock him dead." She preened over Victoria like a very proud mother seeing her daughter off on her first date. Which is exactly how Victoria felt.

"Do you think so?" Victoria had a complex about how she looked. She was forever thinking this was wrong, and that was wrong, but the truth was, nothing was wrong except some past devilish manipulation, that had nearly broken her spirit. It had failed, but nevertheless it had left a few scars. One of which, was the ever-persistent lack of confidence, about her looks.

The journey was straightforward enough, even if she did feel a little conspicuous amongst the grinning, scruffy teenagers, and at least twenty, grey-haired, blue-rinsed, elderly women. One of the ladies was ginger, that had possibly been an attempt at auburn, which had gone miserably wrong, and had now left the poor thing with carroty, flyaway hair with white roots. They were all chattering away like a group of monkeys, whilst every now and then Victoria became a focus of their attention, as they made slight gestures toward her, and whispered to one another. It was a fair call. It wasn't every day, that a beautiful lady, dressed in an expensive suit, rode this particular commuter train. She really would have looked more at home riding in the back of a Bentley, but she wasn't. She was here and anyway she was going to meet the man of her dreams.

She tossed her hair aside and concentrated on the magazine she had brought with her, deciding to ignore all glares and stares. However out of place she appeared to be, she would put her best foot and face forward.

Memo to Victoria. Never, ever dress like this on a train again - well not unless I have an overcoat to cover me up.

At last, she arrived and headed for the taxi rank where John had said he would be waiting for her. She couldn't wait. She had refreshed her makeup on the train, and was here at last to meet with gorgeous John.

She spotted his car. Took a deep breath and wiggled over to it. She opened the door and looked in.

She almost fell into the car. What was sitting there resembled a photo from one of her daughter's picture books, *Charlotte's Web.* John, honey voiced John, unbelievably looked like Wilbur the pig.

"Oh Hi," she stuttered, her eyes were wide and wild. Flustered and horrified. There must be some mistake.

"Victoria, Victoria, darling do get in." He smiled a toothy grin at her.

So now she was in some horror movie scene where the 'Pig man' was glaring at her, his snout crinkled up grinning at her before eating her. 'Mercy! Lord have mercy on me,' she thought, as she managed to slide down into the seat of the sports car. 'However did he get in this car? Must have used a pig-sized shoehorn.'

"At last we meet. My beautiful Victoria. I knew you would be stunning." He drove off. Panic and nausea welled up in Victoria's throat.

"Yes, yes nice to meet you too. Where are we going?" She used all her courage and sensibilities to try not give away the revulsion she was feeling.

"To the restaurant I told you about." He patted her thigh very gently, but to her it seemed as though some greasy trotter had just slimed all over her.

"Oh great," she said, regaining her senses. Thank God that they would soon be at the restaurant and then she could exit through the toilet window, or back door, or something. Anything, but away from the 'Pig man'.

Once seated in the very nice restaurant, and having ordered a coupe de champagne, she started to relax, especially since she couldn't find a back door, and there was no window in the powder room.

'Okay, so he looks like Marvin the pig's ugly brother,' she said to herself. But I am here. It is a lovely day; the outside view of the river is nice, even if the view opposite me is not. I have come a long way, so let's be polite and have lunch. Also, he might just be a really nice guy.'

John warbled on about how great he was. He was a Managing Director of some car sales company. She sat and listened while he ordered a very nice bottle of white wine. The afternoon wore on, and much to Victoria's surprise John was quite good company. He was flirtatious and quite playful, but he still looked like a pig. Difficult just to be attracted to the personality, but she would try.

After some very pleasant interludes it was time to go. They had laughed a lot. The wine and the fact that Victoria hardly ever looked at him directly did help. It helped quite a lot in fact.

"Let's get you back home, young lady," John said.

"Thank you John," she replied, dreading the idea of the train again, but nevertheless she was looking forward to getting home, and putting the 'piggy dreamboat' experience behind her. She thanked him for a lovely time as he opened the door of the car for her.

"The pleasure is all mine," he said, with a slight slur. But the station was not that far away. John took this turn and that bend. Victoria was directionally dyslexic. She could get lost in a hotel, but she got the feeling that they should have reached the station by now. John was chatting merrily away to her. More stuff about how great he was, and how wonderful it was to meet somebody like her. Somebody with whom he could be soul mates. 'Must be a crazy man,' she thought, which would turn out not to be far off the truth.

"Here we are." He beamed at her.

"This is *not* the station!" she squealed.

"Observant as well as beautiful." The sarcasm was not appreciated. "I thought that as we will be seeing a lot of each other, you might like to see my house."

'Where the hell did he get that idea? Raving lunatic. No mirrors in his house either,' she thought, but wasn't going to stick around to find out. There was a Jaguar in the driveway.

"That is all yours," he smarmed.

"John. Now listen to me. It's very nice of you… um, err, to want to show me your house, but it is getting rather late, and well, I would like to leave that pleasure for another time." 'Like, 'never time',' she thought.

"Just a little while, a teensy, wincey glass of bubbly, and then I'll take you to the station. No wait, I have a better idea, I shall call my driver who will take you all the way home, how is that? Mmmmm? Pleeeease? It has been such a lovely day and David, my driver, is not far away."

Well put like that it seemed to be a very small request in return for a drive all the way home. 'No train,' she thought, Okay. The lure of a ride home overcame any reservations.

Okay? How much more idiotic could she be? Victoria was doing something at which she would go ballistic if Emmy even so much as thought of it. So, she wiggled into the Pig's house. The rooms were tiny.

Again, she thought, 'He must have trouble moving about in here, but then again, it doesn't look like he moves about too much at all.' She giggled at this thought, at which John said, "Nice to see you relaxing." He went into the kitchen and opened a bottle of Cristal. Well at least he had good taste in wines and champagne.

Victoria really wasn't thinking straight. She sat down on the sofa and took the glass of champagne from him. He sat down beside her, which, oddly for such a great hulk, he did it rather gracefully. Then he leaned forward and lunged at her. She avoided him by a hair's breadth as she rose up out of his reach.

"I want to go home, and I want to go home now," she said crisply, and stood iron rod straight.

"Oooohh, have mood swings do we?" He leaned back into the sofa.

At last, she realised the danger she was in. Her eyes darted around the room to find an exit.

"No need for your driver. Just give me the name of a taxi company, and I'll go from there." Victoria had no idea just how naïve that statement was.

"Taxi? Driver? Where do you think you are going? Oh no, my lovely, the only place you are going is up there." He pointed to the stairs.

She put the glass on the coffee table and said very stiffly, "I am a master of the Martial Arts! Do you honestly think I would put myself at risk if I could not protect myself?"

Suddenly John had the most bemused look on his face. He screwed up his piggy eyes and glared at her.

"Now! Kindly show me to the door before I change my mind and really hurt you." She stared directly and meaningfully into his eyes. "I mean it." She stomped her foot.

Something was whizzing about in John's mind. She could see him weighing the odds. She thought of tiny piglets circling his head. Odd, but it seemed fitting.

"There it is." He pointed with a chubby, short, sausage-like forefinger, leaning further back into the sofa, gulping in the sparkling liquid, then belching with a very menacing grin. He repeated, "Go on then. There you are. There is a taxi rank just to the right."

Victoria turned, stuck her nose so far in the air it was a wonder she could see where she was going and headed straight for the door. She found herself outside a strange house in a strange place. She turned right, but could not see the taxi rank, only something that looked like a shelter, so she walked towards it, and allowed herself a whimper. She looked back. One should never look back. There he was toasting her with his glass of champagne. Unbelievable! As she neared the shelter she saw it was a bus stop. She searched for her mobile inside her handbag. She dialled directories, and started looking for a street name or some sort of land mark.

"Hello. 110 110 how can I help you?" a voice at the other end droned.

"Oh, Hi yes. I need a taxi company I am in, umm, I am in… Where am I? Hang on. Please bear with me," she said, staring across the road at a street sign. "Well I know I am in Richmond. Yes a taxi company in Richmond please."

Silence. What! Victoria stared at her mobile phone. Oh no, please. It can't be! I charged it overnight. Tears welled up in her eyes and to put the cherry on the cake, she was dying for a pee as well.

It was no good, the phone was dead. How was she supposed to get to the station?

"That bastard. Pig! Pig! Pig!" she cried and hung her head in despair. What was she doing?

Reduced to walking the streets, looking completely stupid, lost, and degraded.

But help was on the way! A bus was coming, a beautiful, huge, wondrous red bus. There it was, all shiny and bright, with a wonderful golden glow surrounding it, like some great red carriage coming to take her to warmth and safety.

Once on board, which was a feat in itself, as it was one thing negotiating her way across a restaurant floor, but quite another climbing the steps of a bus, the conductor looked at her with a somewhat bewildered smile, which then turned to pity. Evidently she was quite lost, and didn't know where she was, or what she was doing, but she at least knew her destination.

After a very long journey she arrived home, bedraggled but very grateful to be there. If this was to be her new job, she had better learn the ropes a lot better than this. 'Maybe I should get some help,' she thought. 'Yep. Get some help, that's what I'll do.'

Chapter 6

The Going Is Tough

She joined the exclusive dating agency. Amanda was a godsend.

"So glad to have you as one of our elite members," she said, giving Victoria a toothy smile.

"That makes two of us," Victoria said, feeling sure that this was the right path to find her blissful partner. Hadn't Amanda already told her that she had at least thirty suitable members for her? She was going to have a ball. Put Mr Piggy behind her. He was obviously a one-off.

The responses from the newspaper advert kept pouring in. The tick system seemed to be working, but, boy oh boy, some of the replies were so, so dreary.

"Hello my name is Nick. You sound really nice I am in my early fifties (translate as sixty-something. In fact anyone who says early or late something as their age, add ten years). A very successful accountant (bean-counter for a small-time company). I live in Norwich (back of beyond, along with people of somewhat dubious sexual tendencies) and I am fit, as I walk every day with my dog Lucy (quite tubby and needy). I have my own house and I love gardening (left over from a leftover marriage, where his wife had probably left him).

Why do men whose wives leave them think they are a great catch? (If that was the case, then why would she have left?)

Nothing wrong with any of that, but not really the best self-description, and not even enthusiastically told. Usually said with as many 'umms' and 'errs' as those delicious coloured sweets that stick to ice creams, and chocolate buttons, but with a voice that could cure insomnia.

Victoria parked the ad responses, and waited for Amanda to perform her magic. It wasn't long before Amanda was on the phone describing the most amazing man to her. He was tall, in his late fifties, very successful. He had a mansion in Oxford, a house in the South of France, and a London penthouse. He was Chairman of several boards, and had time to play. The *pièce de résistance*, was that he badly wanted to get married again as he had been a widower for over five years and missed taking care of a lady, and having female company around him.

Why think of anybody else? Amanda was preening with sheer delight at this amazing find for Victoria. Amanda was so kind, and she definitely knew what she was doing.

"So Victoria, how does Edward sound to you?" Amanda's eyes were wide and she bit her lips.

"Perfect. He sounds perfect, but maybe he won't want me?" She was trembling a little, as this could really be the one.

"Nonsense. He will be bowled over. So shall I call him and give him your number?"

"Of course Amanda, don't tease. Oh, I am so excited. He seems just wonderful. And, his children are grown up, a son who is an explorer, and a daughter who is a famous actress. Emmy will be in seventh heaven. Don't waste any time, call him and let me know. Bye-bye and thank you Amanda. Thank you so much." She placed the receiver back in its cradle, and couldn't help but walk over to the mirror to inspect herself.

"Not bad," she whispered to herself, and then wandered off downstairs to celebrate with a glass of wine, but not the champagne she was saving for her birthday. Berrie was coming by later - she would have a glass with him as well. She mused about whether or not she would tell him what she had been doing. After all, he was her best friend, and she shared everything with him, didn't she?

She had just poured herself a glass when her mobile rang. "Hello is that Victoria?"

It was him. Edward. The one Amanda had just been telling her about. Edward the magnificent one. Edward the Great. Edward her true knight in shining armour.

"Yes… yes this is Victoria."

"Hi Victoria, I'm Edward. Amanda has asked me to call you." His voice was a little gravelly and very sexy. A flashback of the pig came to mind. Remember his voice was sexy too. She shook her head. 'No it's different, very different,' she thought.

"Oh, Hi Edward. Yes. Amanda was talking about you to me, not long ago actually."

"And what has the delicious Amanda been telling you?"

"Well not much really." She didn't want to divulge all that Amanda had told her. "What has she told you about me?" Victoria asked.

"Well not much either, apart from you are not particularly PC. Rather sassy, and a very special lady." He paused, and coughed lightly.

They chatted for a little over half an hour. Victoria laughing, and giggling at his jokes. Edward felt particularly taken with this new introduction.

"Say, Victoria," Edward stopped in mid-sentence. " I know this is a bit left field, but I am going to Cannes tomorrow. Did I tell you I had a place in the South of France? Erm. Anyway, I have to go as a friend of mine, who borrowed my Sunseeker, put petrol in it instead of diesel. The idiot! Anyhow it means I need to go and sort it out. Care to join me over there for a few days?"

"Umm, err, well? Mmm, I don't know."

"Well, you can always do a turnaround if we don't get on."

'As if that would happen,' Victoria thought. She made a lightning decision. Why not! Yes. Why ever not? It would be fun, and she could do with some sunshine, and he sounds so charming. Amanda had recommended him very highly.

"Well, it is a little unorthodox and slightly unconventional, but yes. Thank you. I would like to come. I am sure you are a gentleman, and at the very least, we could have a lot of fun."

"Great. Good. Well do you want to call me with the details, and I shall collect you from the airport?"

"Yes, of course."

He seemed marvellous, that was all that mattered. And, she was going to have a super weekend, with perhaps the love of her life.

"Look forward to seeing you Victoria." His voice was quite musical.

"You too Edward, thanks for calling."

"The pleasure is all mine. Call me as soon as you know your itinerary." He hung up.

She floated into the kitchen and made herself a cup of tea, wonderfully fruity, strawberry and blueberry. She placed the granules in a very thin china teacup, prettily decorated with raspberries around the edge. She collected a saucer to match it, and proceeded to go upstairs humming to herself. A very happy smile, on her very happy, shiny face.

She prepared to get ready for Berrie. Mmmm, such a nice warm thought crept into her mind. 'Looking forward, to seeing darling Berrie. I wonder where he'll take me? Mmmmmm, wonder what to wear?'

She showered, allowing the hot water and soft soap suds from her 'Sanctuary Spa' collection to caress her curves. She enjoyed soaping herself. Her hands travelled over her strong body, the water cascading down her back and over her firm, beautiful breasts. Her perfectly manicured nails tweaked her nipples, and then reached her laser smooth mound of Venus. A soft moan came from her bee-stung lips, and she found her clitoris begging for attention. The hot water crashed around and over her, her fingers gently played and stroked her pleasure bud. Her hand firmly squeezed her left buttock, and she thought of Berrie taking her from behind. Long, strong thrusts deep inside her. "Berrie ! Oooh Berrie! Please, please, fuck me baby." She shuddered in a delightful orgasm, arched her back, and shook her head from side to side, breaking the waterfall and sending droplets of soapy water flying up against the steamed glass panes.

She felt really good. All warm, soft and buzzing. Going to meet Berrie was a bonus. He really was a dish. A very fit, sculpted, tanned body, the lightest powder blue eyes you have ever seen, and a smile that made you feel quite giddy.

She decided to wear a turquoise, figure hugging, rather short, off the shoulder dress that she knew Berrie liked. And she knew she looked great in it. She never stopped to think why she liked to please Berrie. And knock him outta his socks when seeing him. He was just Berrie. Loving, lovely Berrie, the man who was not for her.

Berrie knocked on the door. Victoria rushed to the window, and called for him to use the key. Berrie had had the key to her home for some time now, but would never use it without her knowledge or permission even though she didn't mind a bit.

"Okay!" Berrie let himself in, and moved towards Victoria's living room, meeting Victoria walking down the stairs.

"You look lovely. Simply lovely, darling," he beamed and moved forward to hug her.

"Thank you sweetheart." She fell lightly into his embrace. At dinner, she decided to tell him what she had been doing.

Berrie knew all about Victoria's recent past, how she had been betrayed by her partners over the years. First by Matthew, who suppressed her and dragged her down, then Lutz. Neither men shared anything in common, other than Victoria herself. After discovering that her beloved Lutz had not only been unfaithful to her once, but when all the worms started to be uncovered, had done so on a regular basis. He had a penchant for black ladies - nothing wrong with that if you are single. But he was living with Victoria and they were engaged to be married. He used them for sex and used Victoria for social acceptability and money. Oh, and sex. Nice. It wasn't that what he was doing was unacceptable. Everybody has choices. It was just that if he had informed Victoria at the beginning of their relationship that he had these desires and asked whether she minded, she would have said, "Yes I do," and, "Goodbye Lutz." But that was exactly why he didn't inform her, of course.

Victoria had really been very much in love with Lutz. That was the fantasy that Lutz represented to her.

After a reality check, Victoria had returned home with a broken heart, shattered confidence, and a house that needed to be cared for after years of neglect. Her emotions took over. She found herself fighting with herself for her life. It was all she could do to get up in the morning, and put one foot in front of the other. Once it took her the best part of an hour to get from her bed to her bathroom, only ten metres away. But she was determined to survive, and beat the overwhelming desire to just curl up and die. The emotion was very strong. It wanted to take Victoria's life.

However, because she was Emmy's mother, she felt a duty towards her beautiful daughter to live and take care of her. Plus, it was through the bountiful, most wonderful properties contained in bananas, coupled with the amazing endorphins created by exercise that Victoria survived. It took a year and six months before she was properly whole again, but whole again she was, a new and probably better person for the experience.

In the comforting atmosphere of the local pub's restaurant, Victoria decided this was the time to tell Berrie about her new job.

"Berrie, you know how much you mean to me don't you?" Victoria sat across from Berrie, hands fidgeting with the cutlery, and moving the wine glasses around.

"Mmmm?" Berrie raised one eyebrow, and couldn't help wondering what the bloody hell was coming next. Victoria had always made it very clear that there would never be a 'romantic' relationship between them. He understood her reasons and respected them, but fell in love with her all the same. "No. I don't know how much I mean to you, so…?"

"Well, umm, and that we have been through the reasons why we are not an item?"

Berrie nodded solemnly.

Victoria winced a little. Better just to spit it out. "Well. I've joined a dating agency." She let out a long breath, her bosom rising, which distracted Berrie so much he paused a little longer than usual to respond. Victoria's heart was thumping.

"Oh good for you." He gave her a big smile, and squeezed her hand.

"Oh, erm, right, yes. Oh good… well, yes, yes it is good, isn't it?" She was stuttering, taken aback and to her great surprise wasn't very happy with his reaction. She withdrew her hand from under his.

"Good for you! Bloody good for you! Yeesh, right!" said Berrie with a broad smile.

'Well, I suppose it is, but…' she thought, and leant back in her chair, then hitched the chair forward, coughed and asked for the menu from the waitress who was then hovering over Berrie. Bloody cheek! She was almost in his lap.

"Certainly Madam and what would Sir be wanting?"

'Fuck off,' thought Victoria. 'For God's sake. Little hussy.'

"Some water from the tap, a glass of sauvignon blanc and a Magners please." He didn't even notice her overattentive gaze. Bless. Ahh. Either that, or he was really good at covering up. No. Berrie wasn't an actor, he didn't notice. Good. So you can shove off sweetie. Victoria gave the pretty waitress such a glare it would have split a rock in two.

Regaining some semblance of herself, she said to Berrie, "Well, I am glad you approve. I'll keep you posted."

"I didn't say I approve. I said 'good for you'. Can't really say anything else can I?" His mouth turned down, and he pushed his bottom lip out.

Victoria laughed and quickly changed the subject. "Did you see that waitress and did you see how much she was in your face?"

"No." Berrie's eyes widened and he leant back in his chair.

'Good,' she thought.

They chose their meal, and carried on chatting, and laughing throughout the evening.

Berrie dropped her off without going in for his usual cup of coffee. Victoria had a bit of a headache. Truth was, she was still puzzling why she was bothered by a) Berrie's pretty well laid back response to her 'bombshell' of joining a dating agency and b) Her response to that bloody waitress sniffing all around Berrie. Why should she care? She should feel good for him. Berrie needed a good woman with him. That was it, she concluded. That waitress, however, was *not* a good woman. Well, that explained one puzzle. Forget the other one. Nothing to wonder about really. After all, she had made it quite clear there would be nothing but a platonic friendship between them.

Victoria slept uneasily that night.

Chapter 7

Dating with Death

Next morning she went straight to the net and googled 'Cheap flights UK'. She needed a break and Edward's invitation of a few days in the South of France was just the thing. Edward sounded such a nice man and Amanda's 'write up' on him was extremely impressive. She smiled and mused on this as she surfed for a flight to heaven. It came in the guise of Easyjet.

She called Edward to let him know the details. "When are you returning, Edward?"

"Oh, I am there for six days."

"Well, why don't I come back with you? I am sure we will get on regardless of romance, or umm, whatever." She felt a warm flush all over her cheeks, and bit her lip.

"Mmmm. Of course. Good idea. You can always leave when you want to," he chuckled.

"I am sure it won't come to that, after all, we are both civilised creatures of the world." She smiled and didn't feel so embarrassed, but her face was red, and very warm.

"Okay then, meet you at Nice airport three thirty p.m. Easyjet isn't so bad and the flight goes very quickly it's only an hour and a half. Look forward to it." She clapped her hands in the air, and did a little hip swaying dance, lunging forward, shimmy-shammying, she laughed and laughed. What the bloody hell was she doing? For goodness sake. Flying off to see some guy she didn't know, with not even a photo!? Staying in a stranger's house in an unknown area. You wouldn't have to pick the bones out of that to think 'Bloody Barking Mad'. But she was going to do it. No harm, and it could change her life. She thought of the sweet smiling Amanda, and brushed all misgivings aside. Amanda had recommended him so highly. She would be a fool not to go.

She packed very carefully. Her favourite Herve Leger LBD. A silk Hermes. Extremely classy, it showed off her figure better than most outfits. She picked three swim suits, one sweet bikini, one shameless Miami bikini all strings and jewels, and a very classy, midnight blue swimsuit with a bejewelled anchor on the hip. Three luncheon outfits, very smart casual, for the Martinique, the Carlton, or at the very least Le Croisette. Probably all three. Tee hee. She tingled with the excitement of it all and hummed a little tune, as she put all her very necessary toiletries, (Victoria's bathroom looked like a cross between Selfridge's perfume and cosmetic departments) neatly in her Gucci bag. She was a makeup addict.

"There. That should do it. Oh Edward, please be as you seem and how Amanda describes you. I know we are going to hit it off." She heaved a sigh, went downstairs, made herself a cup of coffee, and sashayed from the kitchen to the open lounge, through to the snuggly TV area. She sat down on the cream, faux-fur covered sofa and pulled her legs up onto the exceptionally soft fabric, wriggling her toes in and out of the fibres. She leaned back on the sofa's arm, and sipped a mouthful of the dark milky, comforting liquid. She started to relax, and watched some TV. 'Friends', the sitcom, always had a beneficial effect on her, and would stop her mind racing that caused her to have one of her headaches.

Victoria slept well that evening.

Sean, her gardener, handyman and friend collected her early as usual. "You never know what may happen on the roads, better to be early than late," he would often say to her. Yeah, but this early? The roads would have to be dug up. But he was such a lovely man, and always meant the best for her. He took her suitcase and chivvied her into his car.

The whole trip was smooth and quite enjoyable. Especially the little retail therapy she enjoyed in the airport shops. An opportunity to top up her stock of perfumes. She would buy Edward a cologne and some Belgian chocolates, to enjoy with the champagne he'd mentioned.

At last, the plane landed. Once at baggage reclaim, she called Edward who told her he was waiting on the other side. She had a momentary feeling of nausea. What if he didn't find her attractive? Oh well, she couldn't help any of that. The worst that could happen was she would have a relaxing time with a wonderful charming man, in a wonderful charming part of the world. She loved Cannes. She looked ahead to search for her bag. Ah! There it was. She bent down and picked the case off the conveyor belt.

"Here we go," she mumbled to herself. "Ready or not!"

Once past customs, she surveyed the area for her wonderful Edward. No sign. She moved toward the information desk.

"Victoria?" Somebody touched her shoulder. She turned around. "Victoria?" the man said.

"Yes. Yes I am Victoria, and you must be Edward's, um, err, um…"

Before she could utter the word 'driver', the man said, "Yes, I'm Edward."

Good God! He was a skinny old thing with long, grey, dishevelled, greasy hair, wearing greying shorts and a tatty, old, sickly yellow polo shirt, with some kind of flip-flops, which had lost most of their flip, adorned his crinkly feet.

He took her bag, quite oblivious to the shocked expression on her face.

"This way," he said, smiling brightly, and showing teeth that matched the colour of his polo shirt. She followed meekly, not knowing what to do. Should she turn around now, grab her suitcase, stick her hand in the air screaming for help from the 'Wizened Old Man' police, or just go with the flow as she was here. He hadn't done anything, apart from die and come back as the walking dead. And by now he was quite a bit ahead of her, and if she didn't buck up she would lose him in the milling crowd. Her clothes were far too precious to lose and the sun was shining.

This was a decision she would later come to regret. She turned left, when she should have turned right, but Victoria's sense of direction wasn't everything it should be.

Victoria was still trying to hide her disbelief. There wasn't anything she could find that matched Amanda's description of Edward. Tall and slim build? Try 5'10. Well, he would be if didn't have such a hunch in his back. And 'rugged, cute looks'. Certainly, rug was in there somewhere, a face that looked like a beaten up old rug. And, as for smart dresser, where on earth was she coming from?

Victoria had a flashback to remember what Amanda was wearing. True, she was no fashion icon, but she was smart and had reasonable taste. Mmmmm. Maybe Amanda had a blind spot on the day she'd interviewed him. Goodness knew but this was *not* the Edward she had described to Victoria.

Oh well. Onwards and upwards. He was probably good fun, so she wouldn't judge this book by its cover, *but* this is one romance that was definitely *not* happening. The thought of even kissing him made Victoria want to gag.

She reached the car and tried to help Edward with her suitcase.

"No, my dear, just sit in the car and relax. I can see to all of this." She did as she was told, and thought, 'Yes. A gentleman. Probably eccentric, old-school English.' She began to relax and smiled a little to herself. Edward sat in the car and was preparing to drive off, when Victoria pointed out that it would be a lot easier if the luggage trolley was not directly in front of the car.

"What? Oh yes of course." He then faffed about looking for his glasses. "I am sure they were here before I left to collect you." His voice was a little shaky and agitated.

"Why don't you try the back of the car where you put my suitcase?" Victoria smiled sweetly at him.

"What! Err, in the boot? Couldn't be. Oh well, I'll check."

The spectacles were there, as Victoria had surmised. Edward got back in the car, but soon saw that the trolley was still in the way, so he leapt out again and pushed it away from the car.

'A very nervous gentleman,' she thought putting on her safety belt.

They left the car park. Brilliant sunshine hit the windscreen like a burst of yellow fireworks. Victoria placed her sunglasses on her pretty little nose, and settled back in her seat. Maybe this wasn't going to be so bad after all, especially when she looked out over the bluest sea she'd seen in a long while.

"Was the journey okay?" Edward suddenly piped up.

"Yes, fine thanks. How has it been down here? Have you fixed the Sunseeker?" She looked at him, side view on, of course, and sighed. 'Couldn't go there, but let's be nice and polite, as I am sure he is.'

"Weather's been superb for the time of the year." It was late September. "And, yes got the harbourmaster to help out. How can anyone put petrol in a diesel engine?" He shook his head and chuckled.

As they drove past Cannes, Victoria remarked on the fact.

"Oh, didn't I tell you?" Edward said. "My place is just outside. Closer to the sea."

"Oh, okay." she inclined her head. "So will we be going there tomorrow, or maybe this evening?"

"Cannes? Oh no. Not Cannes. Never can get parked." But it was late September, which meant that Victoria and Edward were probably the only people there. And, it was Cannes. The French descend 'en masse' at the beginning of August but, come the end of September, they more or less perform a mass exodus.

"Oh," she sighed and wondered just how long she would, or could stay.

The answer to her own question came like a lightning bolt when they drove through the barriers to Edward's 'place' in the South of France. It looked like something out of the Flintstones. She knew right then that she would be leaving as soon as she had the opportunity.

It was a complex! Where did the house go? All pink, and sandstone, and built over fifty years ago. It got worse. His apartment was more aged than Edward. The only thing lending to it anything of beauty was the view, but even then you had to climb up mouldy old tiled steps, only to be greeted with patio furniture that was ancient, tired and dirty. The barbeque looked as though it still had half a charred chicken and blackened hamburgers lying in it, and was all black and sooty. *Yuk*!

Edward took her suitcase upstairs to her room. Victoria followed. Once on the second floor, he led her to a room that was stark and had curtains even more threadbare than Edward's shorts.

"Here. Have this as your dressing room," he said while swinging her suitcase onto the bed. Her suitcase was almost as big as the bedroom, only much better looking and in much better condition.

"Thanks," Victoria mumbled.

Edward then led her through to another bare bedroom, picked at the covers, and declared, "Oh, doesn't look like it's made up."

'What! Doesn't look like it is made up! What does he mean for God's sake,' Victoria thought, now very alarmed.

Edward reversed out of the room, and went into what Victoria supposed could only be the master bedroom, as it was a little bigger than the other two and had more furniture. A chair, a bureau, and of course a bed, all in blue and gold, which was horrid and should have been redecorated years ago.

"So. Um, good then. Well, here we are. How about a glass of champagne? Only have rosé, I'm afraid." Edward clapped his hands.

"Um, err, yes. Well good. Yes, well I mean that's fine. Yes, good idea." Victoria made her way downstairs trying to calm herself. "It will be fine. Don't worry, it will be fine. Come on, buck up, just go back out onto the terrace," she told herself.

She then walked slowly up the outside stairs to the terrace. She was in a dilemma. What should she do? What could she do? She had no idea how to get a taxi, the night was drawing in, she was really stuck, and maybe she had just imagined that quip about the bed not being made up. She would be fine.

Just fine.

"Here we are." Victoria jumped back, startled as Edward handed her a glass of pink bubbly.

"Oh. Thanks." She took it from him and chinked glasses. "Cheers!"

"Cheers. Enjoying the view? Quite magnificent isn't it?"

"Yes it's lovely. Quite beautiful." 'At least it is a saving grace,' thought Victoria, sipping her champagne.

"Come. Come and sit down. Relax. Good to have you here!" Edward pulled up a chair for Victoria, and gestured to it.

She sat down and smiled at him. 'Oh well. If I get him drunk I guess I could make it through the night and just leave tomorrow.'

"It's absolutely stunning here." Victoria leant back, and placed her glass on the rusty, rickety table. "Mmmmm." She sighed rapidly followed by, "Aaarrgh! Get off. For God's sake, what do you think you are doing?" Victoria leapt off her chair, while Edward did all he could to stop himself falling off his.

Edward had made a lunge at her, grabbed her by her shoulders and attempted to kiss her.

"Edward? Edward! What are you doing? I have just got here. Good God man, are you a lunatic?"

"I thought it would help to break the ice."

"Ice? What ice? For goodness sake you've scared the living daylights out of me." She stepped further back, away from him.

"Well, you do look so yummy and kissable."

'My God! What have I done?' she thought. 'Keep calm, take control and then get out of here.'

"I am going to get changed for dinner," she declared.

"Let me help you." Edward started to get up.

"No. Don't you dare," she shouted. "You sit there. I am quite capable of changing by myself thank you. Stay here, and enjoy the view. I won't be long." Victoria marched away and up the stairs to the bedroom where her suitcase had been left.

"What the fuck is going on here! What's he like? Scrawny, dirty old man!

Fucking Amanda is due a real piece of tongue pie. I can't believe him. I mean, for God's sake, I am supposed to be here for six days. I haven't been here for ten minutes, so where did he get the idea I wanted him to kiss me?" She was talking to herself as she changed into her dressing gown. Then she suffered even more shock and horror. The shower room was horrendous. Absolutely, completely horrendous. It had been built in the seventies and it looked like not a single thing had been done since. Dull, slimy green tiles matched whatever she thought might be lurking in the shower waste outlet. The shelves and splash back above the hand basin were covered in toothpaste that had hardened into solid splats of black-lined white goo. Cracked mirrors accompanied what looked like some rags hanging from the towel rail.

'I think I'll miss out on a shower,' she thought, looking squeamishly around her. 'It will probably will make me feel more grubby than I do already.' She allowed herself a sarcastic laugh. She opened her makeup bag and attempted to freshen up.

She changed into an elegant, black, off the shoulder number, and wondered how she was going to handle this next little episode. Obviously, the 'ferrety' Edward wasn't a gentleman after all, and furthermore, however unbelievable, he wasn't aware of just how unattractive he was. What did other women do when he approached them in that way? Amazing, simply amazing! Well, at least she could knock him halfway across the room, if he tried anything again.

Now looking radiant, Victoria joined him on the terrace. Edward said nothing, except to ask if she would like her drink freshened.

She replied, "That would be nice." And he went off to bring the champagne.

She looked out over the view. "I won't be here for long, keep the situation calm, and everything will be just fine," she muttered to herself.

Edward returned with the champagne in a bucket full of ice. He put the bucket on the table and took out the bottle. Edward started toward her to pour the champagne and as he did so leant forward to kiss her again. This was too much.

Victoria screamed and pushed him forcefully away. "Edward stop it! Just bloody well stop it! Please!"

"Come on. You can't fool me. Why did you come here?"

"To see you, what else?"

"Yes of course, and to get fucked."

'What!' she thought. 'I can't believe I am hearing this.' "No! No! What are you talking about?"

Edward made towards her again.

"Stop! You have got this soooooo wrong."

"Oh! I have? Have I?" he said jauntily. "Why don't you want to be fucked? God!" he said. "You are so middle class."

What a fucking cheek this man had! She wanted to say, 'Actually, I wouldn't mind being fucked, but not by some scrawny old slimeball like you,' but it came out, "Actually, if wanting a deep and meaningful relationship is middle class, then good. I bloody well am middle class." She had moved toward the stairs, as she knew she had to get off that terrace. She was beginning to get really cheesed off with him.

Edward followed behind her and grabbed her shoulder to turn her around.

"For God's sake, you moron. Don't touch me," she screamed in his face.

"I am sorry, let's start again. Don't go, please." But all the time he was pleading, he didn't let go. Victoria tried to shake him off, but he held her tight, one hand on her shoulder, and another on her waist, pulling her to him.

"Get off. Gerr… off," she screeched. She twisted around and threw him away and off her. Edward swung around, lost his step and fell down the tiled stairs. Victoria fell back against the ivy hung wall, knees bent, holding tightly to the vine, as she watched with increasing horror as Edward went bouncy, bounce, bounce down the stairs. He came to a halt on the landing, looking for all the world like a broken marionette. One leg certainly looked as though it was bent back on itself.

She straightened herself, went to the top of the stairs, and whispered, "Edward, umm, err, Edward?"

There was no response. Everything was still. Deathly still. She timidly went down the stairs, one at a time, balancing herself against the wall.

"Edward," she repeated. "Edward." No response. No movement. "Edward, please stop messing about. It's not funny." Nothing. "Oh my God, what do I do?" she stood over him, motionless, her heart pounding in her chest.

'See if he has a pulse, go on. Check if he has a pulse,' she was telling herself, but her thoughts were not being transferred to her muscles and she just stood there, wide-eyed, staring at his limp, motionless body.

After what seemed like an eternity, she bent over and pulled his arm over to see his face. She saw blood. Lots of it, seeping from under his body. His head was in a very peculiar position. He was all limp and well, lifeless.

"Edward, come on Edward." Nothing. Absolutely nothing.

He was dead. Simple as that. Dead.

Why she just didn't call the police will remain a mystery to her for evermore, but she didn't. She panicked. She calmed. She panicked, she calmed, back and forth, even going up and down the stairs twice. Getting more and more flustered, until she had the idea. A crazy, mind numbingly witless, pointless idea, but she had it all the same.

She hadn't been there had she? No. Never got to the apartment. No one saw them. No one was there. The whole complex was deserted. She went back up to the terrace and picked up her glass. She needed to think. Yes, she needed a plan. Right. A good one.

He fell down the stairs. It was an accident. Call the police. What was wrong with that plan? It sounded like a good one to her and would be to just about 99.9% of the sane population. But, no, she continued down the path of absurdity, courting unnecessary danger. All reason now completely out of the window.

She went back down the stairs, grasping her glass. She was stepping very, very carefully, especially when she reached Edward's body. She moved slowly over his still and distorted body. Victoria halted once she had stepped over him and surveyed the lounge. Tired, so tired, it was as though the room had been halted in time decades ago. She took the glass to the kitchen and washed it thoroughly. So now she was Victoria the forensic expert.

What was she doing? She didn't know. Was she acting on some mad, primitive, survival instinct?

For some unfathomable reason, she thought the police would think she did it deliberately. In fact, as many millions of thoughts were crashing around her brain, it had actually occurred to her that maybe it wasn't just an accident after all, and pushing him down the stairs was deliberate. It wasn't as if he was brandishing a knife, or that the stairs were that close. Yes, perhaps it had been some deep, subliminal act, when she had finally reacted to all the whackos and boorish men that had crossed her path.

Victoria continued to erase any evidence of her presence in the duplex, including wiping down the patio windows, where she thought she had opened them wider when first going on to the terrace. She carried her suitcase down the stairs thinking all the time, her mind racing. She got to the door, hankie held tight in her hand. No prints, remember. The mere fact that the whole place would be covered with fingerprints of all types, and nature coupled with the fact that Victoria was whiter than white escaped her. In fact Snow White had probably committed more offences than Victoria ever had.

She opened the door with her handkerchief held against the door knob and peeked out to see if anyone was about. It was pitch black. The pokey old complex couldn't even get its act together to supply security lighting, but that was a bonus for her, providing she didn't trip over something and break her leg. She closed the door very softly and considered her situation. She was going to head for the local train station and get to the airport. She didn't know quite how far that was, but had seen it on the way in and knew its approximate location.

She walked across the road wishing her trolley suitcase didn't sound like a Roman chariot at the Coliseum. And now, just to add to the evening's events, she was dying for a pee. 'Best to go now,' she thought. 'No good bringing any attention to myself, either on the road, or worse still, at the station.'

She found some suitable bushes that were well out of sight, and peed the longest pee she could ever remember; she thought she was going to get cramp in her calves. *Christ, what am I doing?* This was the first time Victoria had any clarity of thought whatsoever, and it disappeared as quickly as it came, replaced by a huge drive to get home without being noticed. Nothing else was of any importance at all.

She arrived at the station all in one piece. There had been hardly any traffic on the road and she had taken the precaution to wrap her head in a silk pashmina scarf before she left.

Everything went from good to good. Plain sailing, or flying in this case. She boarded the train. No ticket inspector. She got off the train, straight into the airport, which was blissfully busy, and had a strong welcoming smell of burgers and air-conditioning. She made her way to the Easyjet ticket desk, and had a somewhat disjointed conversation with an assistant that couldn't care less. It would normally have irritated her, but on this occasion Victoria could have kissed her. The ticket clerk wouldn't remember the time of day, let alone a woman covered by a pashmina. She changed her ticket to the next flight to Gatwick. She wouldn't phone Sean to collect her, she would just get a taxi and soon be safely back home. Straight into the bathroom. Her beautiful clean bathroom, away from the hideous experience she had just been through.

Three hours later and that was exactly where she was, at home, lying in her bath, soft bubbles and candlelight all around her, vanilla and cinnamon aromas pervading the steamy air. She was so tired she couldn't think, she didn't want to think, she just wanted to get out of the bath, and slip into her cream, silk sheets and sleep, sleep forever. Every bone in her body ached, but she felt a slight tingling in her head. Her heart had a strange rhythm to it when she thought of Edward's body just lying there, dead. One minute the spindly creature was leching and lunging at her - she would never forget the lascivious look in his eyes. And the next… his tongue lolling out on his chin, spittle dribbling on to his shoulder. Yeeeow!

She slept an uneasy sleep. Fitful and fretful about what might happen to her.

Come the morning, she went straight to the TV and tuned to CNN, watching for anything on Edward. A little man hammered the inside of her head repeating, 'Murderer. Murderer.'

There wasn't anything about Edward. Nothing at all about France. Well, really! A man was dead, God dammit. She spent that day glued to CNN and the internet.

It was like that for another two days, but still nothing. Not a peep, not even the report of an accidental death.

'Good Lord what if nobody has found him yet?' The thought made her giggle, and she put her hand across her mouth in astonishment over the outburst. 'My God,' she thought. 'Imagine, laughing about the poor man.' Poor man be damned. Dirty, old, egotistical, delusional lecher more like!

As the days went on, Victoria didn't hear anything of Edward's fate. She finally picked up the phone, and called Amanda.

"Hello. Yes, Victoria Moreton here. I'd like to speak to Amanda." She kept blinking, and had to rub her eyes. "Keep calm. Keep calm, everything is going to be okay. Don't worry." Her heart was fluttering, and she felt a little nauseous.

"Hello there Victoria. How are you this fine and sunny day?" Amanda enquired.

'Fucking awful and worried sick,' Victoria thought, but replied, "Great, Amanda, I'm just great. I am calling…." 'Yes good idea, what are you calling for,' she asked herself. "I am calling to say that that Edward fellow gave me a call. He said he would call back after he had been to the South of France but I haven't heard a thing."

"Well, he is probably still there," Amanda replied.

'Yes, you bet your sweet life he is. I know he is still there, all bloody, cold and stiff, but not quite the stiff he had had in mind,' she was thinking.

"Yes, well he might be, but I am not, *and* I still haven't even had a date. Where are all those suitable men you told me about?" Victoria demanded. She then thought, 'Hopefully, they aren't all as 'suitable' as you thought Edward was, please God.'

"Ahh, yes, weeell, we are working on it." Amanda sounded a little sheepish.

'Bloody well should be, if she knew what I know,' Victoria thought. "What do you mean 'working on it'? You told me you had at least thirty of them. All suitable for me. What about that Jonathan, the musician with the Gulfstream? Or Michael? You remember, the city man, tall and devilishly handsome."

"Yes, weeell, Jonathan is now in a relationship and Michael is in Marbella on his yacht."

"Well, what's wrong in contacting Michael? He's not exactly in Outer Mongolia, is he?"

"Yes, well, he has asked to come off the scene for the moment whilst he's on holiday."

"Amanda, this isn't good enough," Victoria sighed.

"Now Victoria, not to worry. We have Peter, and he is such a nice man."

"Amanda we've been through all of this. I can meet 'nice' wherever I go."

"Yes I know that, but he is more than just nice. He is a self-made man. Very proud of his background, very adventurous, has sold his somewhat substantial business, and is ready to play with that special someone. Take care of her, have fun, travel the world. Your sort of man Victoria. Handsome, well dressed and tall."

'Okay, he sounds super,' she thought. 'I so wish I could tell smarty pants that I am not that convinced about her descriptions, but better let that go for now.' Victoria was surprised at how cool she was about the whole Edward 'incident'. It was, she thought, as though Cannes never happened and must have been a film. Oh well. Can't do anything about that now, and anyway the old fart had it coming to him. One way or another. How dare he say she was middle class in that derogatory fashion. Nothing wrong with class, but everything wrong with 'classless', Victoria mused.

"Shall I give him your number?" Amanda asked sweetly. "Victoria, Victoria Are you there?" Amanda turned her voice up an octave.

"What! Oh yes, yes I am here Amanda." Victoria had gone into a reverie, imagining the crooked, cold body of Edward all alone. Victoria wondered why she didn't feel anything. Neither sorry, nor regretful. Well I didn't do anything really, or did I? But not even worried about the police, or any consequence of the 'accident'.

Nothing. Mmmm, really nothing. How strange. She was especially curious to discover her lack of fear regarding the police, but of course she'd never been there, had she? So of course, she really didn't have anything to worry about. Nothing at all. The workings of the mind are most curious.

"Um, sorry you were saying. Peter. Well, he sounds good. Yes, please give him my number, I'll look forward to hearing from him." Victoria went into the lounge, and thought back on the experiences she had had on her journey to find love. True Love. Much more elusive than anyone could ever imagine.

Chapter 8

Bill and Beth

Billionaire Bill was the first to come to mind.

"Oh my," she grinned, remembering him with a mixture of affection and revulsion with the gravy sliding down his chin. She would never forget him. He answered the ad in the newspaper. His message stood out, as he spoke with deliberation. He had a sparkle in his voice, and told her that, from her ad and voicemail, she seemed just what he needed. He had a substantial manufacturing business in the South of England and was a widower. He gave the name of the business and told her to google it, and that he was looking forward to meeting her.

Victoria called him, spoke to him at length about all manner of things, from his love of Shepherd's Pie to his penchant for hunting. Not fishing though. They swapped notes on their beloved daughters, and he briefly explained he had taken care of his bedridden wife for over ten years, and it was now time for him to think of himself a little, and to find a new partner with whom to enjoy life. He sounded so sweet, grounded and more than a little fun.

They arranged to meet. Victoria couldn't wait. He rang and said he was coming with his driver because he would like to have a drink, and would the Phantom be okay? Victoria wasn't entirely sure what a 'phantom' was, but decided it had to be a car, and that he wasn't thinking of bringing his dearly departed wife.

"Of course, Bill. Please come in anything you like. Having your driver is a good idea so we can both enjoy a bottle of wine together and relax."

The day arrived. They were going to dinner at a local gastro-pub, where she was friends with Nicky the chef and owner. That way, she thought, she could tell her the situation, and everything would be perfect.

Bill arrived on time, early on the Summer eve. She watched a Porsche approach and come down the driveway.

'Didn't know Phantoms were Porsches,' she thought. She opened the front door with a flurry and a big smile, not knowing what to expect, but certain Bill was a nice guy, and he did say he was tall. Without being too materialistic, the car was beautiful, so he must have good taste.

She took a step backward, and her friend Beth's little dog escaped, yapping and barking at Bill as he emerged from the car. He was like the monster from the deep finally coming to get her. She flashed back to those bedtime stories of Jack and the Beanstalk, and the trolls in Grimm's fairy tales. Horrid images flashed by in a second. Fortunately, Beth came rushing past her, chasing Pebbles, her dog, and took the horrified look off Victoria's face.

Beth took over in any event. "Oh Hello. Good evening. You must be Bill." Beth addressed him warmly and did her smiley, smiley bit. "How do you do. Please excuse me. Pebbles, Pebbles here, come on darling there's a good girl."

Bill walked around the car looked at Beth longingly, and then at Victoria, not so longingly, and then back to Beth who was showing one of the nicest backsides ever, while bending down to retrieve Pebbles. Only Victoria saw this little episode. Well, well. There's a thing, maybe Bill should be taking Beth out his evening.

Bill was busy trying to coax Pebbles back into Beth's arms, but his eyes were busy on Beth's bottom, something that Beth was totally unaware of.

Victoria and Beth were great pals, best friends, crunch friends, members of the sisterhood. But they were as different as the proverbial chalk and cheese. They never looked like they should be together and, to tell the truth, most people who knew them both, or separately, were for the most part absolutely astonished at their friendship even existing, let alone the strength of it. They had very different looks. Both were attractive. Beth was older, a very striking fifty-something, and always struck a pose, which was what Bill was seeing now right before Victoria's eyes.

Pebbles barked and jumped into Beth's arms, she turned around, all smiles. Bill just stood there and smiled back.

"Victoria?" he said timidly.

'Oh boy,' thought Victoria. 'This is going to be good.'

"Victoria, err, no. Oh ! No, no, no. I'm Beth, Victoria's friend. There's Victoria." Beth pointed to a very confused but smiling Victoria.

Bill turned around, and really saw Victoria for the first time. Strikingly beautiful. Poised and elegant, but not Beth. Bill turned back and looked at Beth. Very attractive, very sexy, warm and cuddly with the most amazing breasts. It was evident that he would like to be in Pebbles' place right *now*! Squirming and settling down between Beth's bosoms.

"Hi Bill." Victoria waved. Pebbles barked, and there was a slight awkwardness hanging in the air. Bill came over, Victoria offered her hand. "Hi there. I'm Victoria."

"Oh! Right. Oh, sorry." Bill took her hand and Victoria smiled sweetly, but inside she was grimacing, as his hand was wet and clammy.

"Shall we go? It's not far."

Victoria went over to the car. "Are you going to be okay?" she said to Beth.

"Sure darling, no problem. Have a nice evening."

Victoria stood by the door of the car, and remained there. Bill didn't offer to open the door for her.

Bill shoehorned himself into the Porsche. He was tall, that much was true, but he was also huge. 'A very tall, very big man,' Victoria thought. 'At least as big as his car.' She gave up on any idea of normal run-of-the-mill manners, and simply opened the door. She gave Beth an exasperated look and sat in the car.

"Okay. Nice to meet you Bill. Shall we go?"

"Yes… yes, let's go." He started the engine which was music to Victoria's ears, as she loved cars. Simply loved them. For some unknown reason, she rarely thought of Edward, but right then a vision of him appeared to her, lying there, crumpled and crooked, and dead.

She had not heard a thing. Absolutely nothing. Not a sausage. Job done. She always felt a little giddy though, whenever he did fly into her mind. Giddy and a little tingly. Quite thrilling actually.

"Well young Lady, which way now?" Bill asked, snapping her out of her daydream.

"Oh, umm, yes. Sorry Bill, I went off the planet for a while there. Take the next left and straight on."

"Right Oh. An' Wot a lovely 'ome you 'av then, if I may say so?" Bill still felt nervous driving this lady, but thought he really ought to say something.

"Thank you. Yes, I like it. Turn left just there, and up the hill." She looked at him and couldn't help but smile to herself. It was like being driven by Shrek. He was billowing all over the car, but he had a nice smile and his teeth had been newly fixed. So let the evening begin.

They made their way to the table, only to discover that Nicky wasn't in that evening, and the staff hadn't a clue who Victoria was. The service turned out to be diabolically bad, which was only surpassed by the food.

Bill sat down and balanced on his chair. He must have been 6'4 and weighed twenty-four stones. A whale indeed. Whale in fortune and whale in virtual size. 'Blubber Bill' was the name that popped into her mind, and it set off a fit of the giggles.

"Wot's so funny luv?" Bill said, chomping on his T-bone steak.

Victoria looked up and saw the gravy running down his chin; she was fascinated as he made no attempt to stop it. Surely, it must have tickled? In fact, it just solidified and remained on his chin.

"Oh, sorry Bill. Just had a warped sense of humour moment. I chose here because I know the owner and the staff."

Bill gave her a quizzical look.

"Yes, I know. You wouldn't think so, would you? I know things have gone quite pear-shaped here. But that's probably because Nicky, the owner, isn't here and I don't know any of these people. The food certainly isn't Nicky's cooking, that's for sure. The funny thing is I wanted to come here so that things would run smoothly for us. And that's why I am laughing."

"Oh yeah, right Oh. Got it." Bill made a gurgling noise which she took to be laughter, and then he took a forkful of so much food, she wondered how it all stayed on, before managing to stuff it all in his mouth. She had a great deal of trouble not just staring at the man, open-mouthed, overawed and completely underwhelmed.

"Tell me Bill, what were you saying about your late wife, Gertrude?"

"Mmmmmm, grumph." There was a nod of Bill's head.

"Yes, Gertrude. Did she share your love of hunting and being out in the wide open spaces, fresh air, sailing, and all that?"

Bill laughed and wiped his sleeve across his mouth while still holding the fork although, thank God, it was now empty.

"Naah, that's so funny. Gert, yeah. Out in the open? Naaah luv. Gert's idea of fresh air was sitting in the Dorchester leaning back on her chair, opening the top winder, and putting 'er fag out. Haw, haw, haw, haw." Bill was shaking his head and grinning all over his face. "Naah Victoria, listen 'ere, Gert never did anyfing that was in the least bit 'ealthy. Now me, 'specially now she's gorn, well as I told yer, I 'ave me own gym and trainer."

'Oooh yes, I remember him telling me that. But oh boy what a waste,' she thought, looking aghast at Bill, and fixing her stare at the gravy that had run down his chin. She was itching to rub it off. 'Mmmmm. I would love to have my own gym and trainer,' Victoria thought wistfully.

"Naah," he continued. "She never even liked me yacht. Eric Clapton does tho, 'e rents it every year." He was mopping up the rest of his sauce with the bread. Victoria prayed he didn't want a dessert. She needed to get home and have a cigarette.

"Victoria, I don't mean to be impolite or anyfing, cos I mean, look at yer, yoo are bootiful, an all that, fer sure."

Victoria couldn't help, but purr and preen a little. "Mmm Bill, what is it?"

"Yes well, but it's that fren' o' yours."

"Who? Oh! You mean Beth?"

"Yeah, 'er. Is she wiv anyone?"

Bloody charming! Here she was in a restaurant that had seen better days, with a gigantic version of Mr Blobby, but in green not pink. And now, he was going to hit on her friend by proxy.

"Mmmm. No, err, umm. Not as far as I know, she isn't."

He grinned from ear to ear, revealing a little yellow stump of a tooth, which had a piece of the broccoli he had eaten dangling from it. Why hadn't the dentist fixed that tooth too? Sentimental value, she supposed. Mmmm, maybe no need for offence after all.

"Why Bill? Do you fancy her?"

He actually blushed, lowered his head a little, rubbed his eye and replied, "Well yeah, put like that it sounds a bit much, but I did sort o' like 'er. Yeah." He heaved a sigh, an embarrassed sigh, not for Victoria, but for himself. He acted as though Victoria was there merely for the task of introducing Beth to him. What happened to all the talk and texts of how Victoria was just the sort of woman he was looking for? Proof in the pudding.

And an enormous pudding at that, when it came to Bill.

Actually, this was to be a superb example of no matter how much you speak, text, email, or write to one another, the actual outcome would not be known until after the first meeting… when reality knocked at the door! Victoria took forever, or at least another forty encounters, before she realised this fact.

They left the restaurant with Victoria promising to let Beth know of Bill's interest in her.

"I'd show 'er a good time," were his parting words, as he poked his head out of the car window.

"It's okay Bill. I'll tell her." At which, Victoria turned on her heels and laughed to herself, as she watched him drive up the hill, wondering what on earth Beth would have to say about all of this.

She didn't have to wait long, as Beth had decided to stay at Victoria's to wait for her. She had thought that the big oaf who had come to take out Victoria might be dangerous, or at very least, dangerous to Victoria's ego. Well, she was right about that, more of a funny feeling really.

Beth didn't want her friend arriving home with only the cats to greet her.

"What! You mean what! He... Ha, ha, ha, you are kidding?" Beth doubled up on her stool.

They were sitting in Victoria's kitchen. Victoria was sipping a glass of wine, while Beth drank her usual herbal tea.

"Well, what's so funny? The Incredible Hulk fancying you, or the Incredible Hulk *not* fancying me?"

"No, no, no," Beth wheezed, her shoulders moving up and down, holding her tiny hand over her mouth. "No, no. Both. Neither. I mean. Oh come on, Victoria it *is* funny. I mean Bill, the Blobby Billionaire and that Gert thing. Oh Pleeease, too funny."

Well, yes. Of course, it had a certain amount of humour in it, but belly laughs? Not sure about that. He wasn't that bad. Beth coughed, and started to calm down.

"Okay, okay. He wasn't that bad."

Beth gave Victoria a very coy look. "So you are fed up that I could steal him from you then?"

"What? No. No, you know that Beth. I just mean, well, I don't think it's so funny, and oh well, maybe I am just a little tired of all this crappy stuff I keep doing?"

"Ahh baby." Beth moved around to hug her friend. "Come on, Victoria there's a good girl. You are right, he isn't so bad, and does seem like he has good taste. Ha, ha."

"Yeah right." Victoria hugged her in return. They looked at each other and both burst into peals of laughter. "Oh yes, I forgot to say his parting shot was that I was to be sure to tell you he would give you a good time, or 'I'll show 'er a good time,' to be precise."

"Oh, that clinches it then." Beth sat back down shaking her head.

"Wonders never cease. A man preferring me to you, oh Goddess of mine, and minted too. It's a dream come true." Sarcasm was never Beth's forte, but she was right, it was funny.

"Are you going to meet him then?" Victoria asked mischievously.

"Might do," Beth replied.

She never did.

Chapter 9

Personal Introductions Are The Best

Victoria was lying on the sofa and just curled up reminiscing. If she hadn't experienced it, she would never have believed it. A bit like everything that was happening to her regarding her new job.

In no particular order, there was Roger. Beaten up, washed up, old Roger. Turned up in a Jag older than he was. Granted, they went to a lovely restaurant, *but* he did bore her to tears. She actually lurched back away from him, when he went to kiss her. He rang the next day, and said he really thought they had had a connection. What? Another man with no radar. He called whilst she was in the supermarket, in between the nappies and toilet tissue aisles. An appropriate place, some might say.

"Umm, connection?" There was definitely a question in her voice.

He ignored it, and went straight on to say, "I am going to Majorca on Saturday. Business, but staying in super hotel. Thought it a waste to go by myself. Would you like to come?"

"Well that sounds nice, but obviously we will have separate rooms?"

"Good Lord, your directness takes my breath away."

'Well at least one of us has that feeling,' she thought, picking out the toilet tissue with the three rolls free offer. She never spoke to Roger again.

Next!

Bernard. Now Bernard, he did have potential. Irish Bernard. Great sense of humour. Self-made businessman. He had sold his business and wanted a lifetime partner to share the good life with. They arranged to meet. He was coming over to meet her. She booked a local boutique hotel for him. The night before he was due, Bernard rang and she mentioned that it was a shame he would be going straight past her en route to the hotel. He said no problem and he would pick her up. She said that taxis were difficult to get from the hotel he was staying in. He said no problem, she could stay. She said sex was not on the menu. He cancelled the following morning.

Next!

Then there was Alfred, dear, funny, sweet Alfred. Alfred was introduced to her by her friend Lauren. He was a client of hers. She rented aircraft and Alfred's company used her services from time to time. He was another blind date, but as Lauren gave him such a good write up, and he sounded so cute when she spoke with him, she decided to meet him, even though he was around sixty. Lauren said he was a true and utter gentleman.

The very worst that would happen was to have a nice evening out.

Alfred called again, and they spoke of this and that, nothing in particular, but promised to call each other again. Alfred texted her to ask if she would be free to go out that evening. She was, and wanted to see him, so called him.

That would be the last call she made on her mobile that day, as it broke and it wouldn't recharge. Goodness, how was she supposed to manage? Oh well, they had made precise arrangements. Everything would be fine. She would go to London and he would meet her at Canary Wharf as he lived close by. Victoria prepared for the evening. She dressed in a short 'Genny' black dress, with a pink inner slip, and a beautiful, hand-beaded, embroidered, black jacket. She deliberated over what stockings and shoes to wear in deference to his age and the fact that they hadn't met and so, instead of the bright pink House of Holland stockings and seven-inch black patent YSL heels, she chose a more sober ensemble, and went for the 'barely there' holdups and YSL crocodile court shoes. She looked fabulous. She was surprised to discover that she was getting excited to meet Alfred.

'Mmmm strange,' she thought. She set off with a bounce in her step.

Her journey was an absolute nightmare, the weather was atrocious, pouring icy rain, freezing winds, but 'No big deal,' she thought when she was on the train. Alfred would be picking her up at the station. It didn't turn out that way. Stratford station hadn't got its act together so she had to - yes, simply had to, as there were no taxis - take a bus to the tube, and then on to Canary Wharf.

It was horrible. The driving rain attacked her beautifully styled hair.

Fortunately, she had brought her long mohair scarf, and this protected her, at least for a while. But Canary Wharf was such a long way away, and she was late. No mobile, and going to meet a stranger.

Please, please don't go. Be a dear, Alfred, just as Lauren had described you.

She was walking and skipping, as fast as she could wearing seven-inch heels. The escalators were an obstacle course in their own right. In fact, the whole journey was one, a nightmare of an obstacle course.

At last, she arrived and only had a hundred steps to negotiate, before she met Alfred, where he said he would be.

"Please, please be there," she repeated, through clenched teeth, as she climbed the K2 of the Docklands.

"Oh, thank God." She gave a huge smile, and started to run towards the blue Aston Martin. Although she was splashing water over her legs, and stepped in a dirty puddle, she was just so happy that Alfred hadn't left. She was half an hour late and he had no way to contact her. She thought he may have decided that she wasn't coming, and so would have left, unknowingly leaving her stranded in London without anyone she could contact. So the relief was enormous. She opened the car door, and without really looking at the driver quickly got in, and started to tell Alfred her story.

"Thank God you are here. I was so, oh, so, oh, mmm, well scared that you might have left." She was now staring at Alfred. Well the guy in the car in any event, and her speech slowed as she spoke. She had gone through this before, but the other way around. "Oh, ummm, err, sorry you must be?"

"Alfred," the guy in the driver's seat said.

"Mmmm, yes, oh well, how nice. *You* are Alfred?" Victoria couldn't help herself, she was smiling, gave a little giggle, then immediately panicked that her hair was all rained on, and maybe her makeup had run.

"Yes, why, who were you expecting?" He gave her a small grin.

'Well, certainly no one like you, honey bear,' she thought. "Yes, of course I was expecting you, Alfred. Yes of course, Alfred, Lauren's friend." She coughed, felt slightly embarrassed, and squirmed in her seat, wrapping her coat around her legs, wondering what Lauren was talking about, or maybe that, she was very, very short-sighted, or blind even. He wasn't exactly George Clooney, far from it, but nowhere near how Lauren had described him.

She had told Victoria, "He isn't very good looking, but he is a gentleman and you never know whom he might know to introduce you to." Victoria was sure that was what she had said. But here was this rather presentable, good-looking man in his forties next to her.

"Why would I have left?" He turned his shoulder toward her, so he could see her more clearly.

Well! The mobile? The trains? Christ, the journey was hell, never again. "I was worried just sitting here that it occurred to me you didn't know what I looked like."

"No, I didn't and you don't look like anything Lauren described. I must have misunderstood or something." Although he did sound old on the phone, she thought.

"Well no, I didn't, but what a nice surprise. It's like a Christmas surprise." She beamed at him and he beamed back.

"I am never doing *that* journey again, never, but never. It was horrendous, but you are here, so well, shall we?"

"What? Oh yes." He was staring at Victoria and looked as surprised as she was.

"Let's go for a drink." He started the car.

"That would be lovely," she breathed.

He took her to a very modern luxury hotel. The valet helped her out, and she stepped into a massively high ceilinged entrance, adorned by heavy magnificent crystal chandeliers. There were huge vases everywhere, holding superbly arranged flowers. The highly polished marble floors were vast and spectacular.

"At last, someone with taste." Her head was spinning as she stepped timidly toward the lounge bar.

He found them a little alcove, and helped her off with her coat. After unwrapping herself from the long scarf, she shook herself, very aware that she must look like she had just been through Niagara Falls.

"You look terrific," Alfred said. He still had a surprised expression on his face, wide-eyed and with lots of pearly white teeth showing.

"Yes? Oh thanks, but I really must visit the powder room." She turned on her heels, and sashayed off to the Ladies' Room, aware that his eyes were totally fixed on her. Actually, more likely on her legs and bottom.

"Yay. Howzat!" She punched the air. "Well, he seems nice. Really nice," she said to herself once she had found sanctuary in the luxurious Ladies' Room. She quickly rearranged herself, and freshened her makeup. "Who knows what we may have here." She felt good, and was thankful that the weather hadn't entirely ruined her efforts to impress.

She left the room and walked down the corridor that led directly towards their table as if it were a catwalk, again fully aware that he was looking at her every step.

"What would you like to drink?" he had a waitress waiting to take the order.

"A glass of Sauvignon Blanc would be great."

"A bottle of the best Sauvignon Blanc you have," he said to the pretty redhead.

'Bottle? Not sure about that, but maybe he just wants a drink and then pack me off.' A very inaccurate and very naïve thought, but then that was Victoria. She babbled on for at least ten minutes, moaning about the dreadful journey. Alfred managed to get the odd sentence or two in, and rather charmingly told her that it was silly of him to suggest the meeting point, and that, next time, he would obviously collect her from the station directly.

Next time? Well charmed, I'm sure, but we will see Mr Smoothy, she was thinking.

Victoria was quite enamoured with him. They continued sipping the wine and engaging in light conversation. The banter was enjoyed by both parties. The atmosphere was electric.

"What would you like to do now?" said Alfred placing his glass back on the side table and picking up some cashews.

"Well, I am rather hungry," Victoria said, doing the same.

"Great. Do you like Chinese?" he said, cocking his head to one side, his dark brown eyes twinkling.

"Yes. I love Chinese," she mirrored him. The body language was hot.

"Good. Are you ready to go?" He gestured to her glass.

"Yes. I am. But I am afraid I can't glug wine back, just like that." She got up from her chair and he waved to the nearest waitress for the bill and coats.

It was still raining hard outside, the air was cold and hit Victoria in the face like a frozen dishcloth.

"Brrrr, aargghhhh." She pulled her coat tightly about her and stepped into the car. Alfred stared straight at her as she entered the car and looked deep into her eyes for a few moments before leaning back into his seat and driving off. The night was black and dank, yet Victoria felt all golden and warm, and it wasn't because of the wine.

They arrived at the beaten-up boat restaurant, bobbing up and down on the icy black water. Alfred had no manners to speak of and left Victoria feeling a bit stupid and a mite peeved, as he hadn't opened the door for her.

"Oh well, perhaps that's a bit too much to ask for?" She opened the door and, given the rain had let up a little, left her scarf in the car and ran after him.

"I've known this restaurant for some considerable time." He at least now held the door to the restaurant open for her to push up against him, into the welcoming warmth.

She instinctively knew he would take her to a restaurant where he was well known. This man hadn't a timid bone in his body. Quite the opposite. Alfred was quite the charismatic alpha male. He was basking in the reaction they received, as they weaved their way through the tables and chairs of the restaurant. Waiters nodding at him, stopping occasionally to have a quick conversation on football, or shaking the hand of another waiter, until they reached the table that was evidently HIS table.

No sooner were they seated, than he asked Victoria if she would mind changing wines to a Pinot Grigio. She said that would be fine, but secretly thought, 'Ah, not quite as sophisticated as I first thought.' At her assent he beckoned to a waiter and ordered the wine. He then did what Victoria considered 'the unthinkable'.

"I don't look at the menu here. I just order what I know I like." He was smiling and looking directly into her eyes. With his next breath, he said to her, "You do know how incredibly sexy you are?"

She was still reeling from him apparently thinking that it was a good idea to order for her, and now this crap statement. Good Lord. They don't change do they? If she only had ten pence for every man and boy - sometimes it was difficult to differentiate - that had said either that, or some derivative thereof. Welcome to the club Alfred, she was thinking, but Alfred heard.

"No that's fine. What do you like?" She had ignored his last comment.

"Duck and pancakes." He hadn't finished his sentence, when Victoria thought, 'With Sea Bass with ginger and spring onions.' She was correct, he ordered the Sea Bass. He finished his favourite menu. She suspected he had that every time he came here. Boring!

"Is the Sea Bass wild, or farmed?" she asked him demurely.

His eyes almost popped out of his head, and they were large enough without the help of surprise. She couldn't help, but give a little laugh.

"How the fuck should I know?" he replied, mirroring her joke.

The wine had arrived by then and he tasted the clear, crisp liquid. Nodding his approval he asked the waiter, "Is the Sea Bass wild, or what was that?"

"Is the Sea Bass wild, or farmed?" she asked the waiter directly. The look on the waiter's face was priceless. He didn't know either.

"Err, is very flesh from Birringsgate." He was nodding vigorously. Billingsgate was only around the corner, but at the same time she suspected it was farmed. Oh well, she was sure it will be delicious because of Prince Charming there.

"Thanks, that will be super," she said. 'That's a bit disappointing,' she thought.

All of the food duly arrived and it was very good, if not predictable. But the best thing was, that Alfred was proving to be quite an exciting dining partner. He warbled on about how he joined the business. Something in 'Music' about which he was unspecific, and how he was part Iranian, part Irish, part Jewish. He spoke of gangland meetings, and the kind of danger she had only known in films and books. He reminded her of an Iranian, Irish, Jewish Bruce Willis, except when Bruce had his own hair.

Quite an alluring combination. She was happy to listen to him bragging and boasting of his 'rather hard' background, maybe foreground, but he didn't speak much about the present, or the future. In fact, she got the feeling he was in some sort of trouble, perhaps a financial trouble with his business, whatever that was. He was very vague about it, preferring instead to chat about solo meetings with guys in deserted warehouses, guys who probably didn't floss.

The evening went roaring on, she was having a ball with him. He was enigmatic. Crude to be sure, but enigmatic nonetheless.

Suddenly she noticed the time. "Oh my. Sorry Alfred I have to go. The last train is at 12:07."

Alfred lost his smile, but acted at once. He called for the bill and they both got up from the table.

It was as they neared the car when he said, "Stay. Please stay. Don't go."

She was taken off guard by this request. It wasn't really how he had portrayed himself. She knew there was a softer side to him and actually felt very warm towards him. They had however discussed in a manner of sorts that she was going home. She wasn't that sort of girl and in any event she was far too old to be going home the next morning, whatever might or might not happen, in her clothes of the previous evening.

To which he fetchingly responded, "You would have to bring your bags with you next time."

Victoria just smiled, but inside she thought, 'Yes I would like to do that, I would like to see you again.'

"Victoria?" He had stopped ten metres in front of the car, as she was standing beside the passenger door.

"Why should I do that? I have already explained." She sighed.

He stayed exactly where he was and just said, "Because I don't want the evening to end."

She took a step backward and looked at him.

"Didn't expect that did you?" he said.

"No. *No*, quite frankly I didn't." It was the moment. A split second decision. She thought she was taking an inordinate amount of time to answer. But in reality it was just a few seconds. She really liked him, she could control the situation. She hadn't liked anybody this much in ages, years maybe? She would like to have a relationship with him. She said, "Okay." They sat in the car simultaneously.

He took her to his home on the river. It was only when she was sitting on the sofa in his nice minimalist lounge, once it was too late, that she began to think she hoped that she would not come to regret her decision. She did relationships, not one-night-stands, but it was okay. He had shown her a spare room on the way up. Granted it was horrible, littered with hundreds of wire hangers that sprawled all over the bed, with an ironing board standing up in the corner.

He had told her earlier that he had two housekeepers taking care of him. But just a once over glance told her they were very bad at their jobs. Evidently, he was great with the 'ard people, but completely useless with a couple of conniving old ladies. Mmmm, interesting.

He produced more wine, together with cigarettes. He had been smoking throughout the evening, going outside in the bitter cold. Victoria could never understand that, but she did smoke the odd cigarette or two. They sat and talked, and smoked and drank. They played truth or dare. She was very amused by this. He brought out some cocaine and asked her if she minded if he took some.

"No, why should I?" She said nonchalantly, adding, "It's your life."

The only time Victoria had ever taken drugs of any sort was with her dear friend Rowena. Hawaiian red, or Colombian gold, or the other way around. Anyway, dope. She hadn't taken dope, or anything else for that matter, in over twenty years. She had come to the conclusion that she was lethal enough without suffering the hallucinatory effects of narcotics. To be truthful she was frightened of them, as she thought she would like them too much, just like she was very fond of wine.

He got out a dish. She was to some extent disappointed that it was plain and ordinary and that the credit card was just ordinary too, with not even a fifty pound note to sniff it up. Whatever it was he was using looked like a tiny straw. How dull.

As they continued to play truth or dare, Alfred continued to return to the dish. Victoria was very curious and gathered enough pluck to ask, "Alfred, may I have a go at that," pointing to the dish.

"No," he said.

"Oh well, I don't mean to take it all from you. I was only curious as I've never had any before and well, it is here. What does it do anyway? I was told that it sobered you up and quite frankly," she giggled, "I could do with a bit of help in that area."

"Okay," he said quite coldly.

She wasn't sure, but went ahead anyway asking for instructions all the way. She tentatively snorted a small white line of powder up one nostril, pressing tightly to the other one. She really looked very comical.

"What now?" she asked.

"Put some on your gums." Alfred demonstrated.

"Aarghh! Phit! Phew! God it's awful. Tastes revolting. Yuk, Brrrr. Yeeeuk." She stuck her tongue out in disgust. "Mmmph. Where is my wine?" She gagged, and reached for her glass. This time she took a big gulp and Alfred just laughed. Victoria shook her head and laughed with him.

"Dare!" Victoria said.

"Take your top off." Alfred was sitting cross-legged on the sofa taking a drag on his cigarette.

"Umm! No. Can't do that," she replied, feeling just a little uncomfortable and for the first time since meeting him a little wary.

"Go on."

"No." She licked her lips.

"Okay. Wouldn't want you to do anything you were uncomfortable with." He dealt the cards.

"Good," she said. "I am glad about that, and I don't feel comfortable with it."

"No problem, beautiful. It's fine." They continued way into the early hours of the morning. Talking, drinking, smoking and playing with each other. Victoria liked Alfred a lot. He told her how much he liked her as well, and how much he would like to see her again. He said it frequently and with a softness, and directness she also liked a lot.

"It's time to go to bed," he announced. "I do have a meeting in the morning and it's late."

It was about half past three.

"Are you going to sleep in your room?" He said. It was a challenge.

The thought of the cold wire hanger bestrewn room, or the warmth of Alfred's body, made the choice simple.

"I think it would be churlish of me if I were to choose the other room," she said, leaning towards him and kissing him ever so softly on his lips. She held his neck in her hands, scraping her long nails over his cheek, while tracing her tongue over his lips.

"Mmmmmm, let's go," he said so softly that she could barely hear him.

They crashed through his bedroom door, panting, mouths locked together. Victoria pulled off her top, exposing beautiful, large, firm breasts, leading down to a slim waist and boy-like hips. He grabbed her around the waist and virtually threw her on to the bed. He couldn't believe his eyes, or his luck. He ripped off his shirt, buttons spraying everywhere, and fell on her. He continued kissing her whilst unzipping his trousers. A small miracle that he wasn't wearing socks.

"Victoria. God Victoria, you are beautiful." His tongue was sweeping over her teeth, and his hands gripping her tits, gently at first, then hard, his fingers pinching her nipples, harder and harder. They were tingling like crazy and she could feel herself wet and hot. He ran his hand down between her legs, caressed her thighs and slid his fingers gently and expertly around her pussy lips.

"Mmmmm. Alfred. Please, please," she moaned. He moved her up across the bed, the satin sheets helping to slide her into place. His fingers tweaked and stroked her clitoris.

"Do you like this babe?" he whispered in her ear, then continued stroking, and licking the inside of her ear.

'Like it?' she thought. 'I think I am going to explode right now.'

"Mmmm, darling it's heaven," she moved her hand down the bed, and found his pulsating, hard - extraordinarily hard, in fact - cock. Not huge thank God, and only just a little wet.

Victoria couldn't stand the dribbly ones. She must stop thinking, she told herself, and just go with the flow. The man didn't need a map, and was promising at least three, or four orgasms. Maybe not the 'wave', but that could come later when he really knew her body. Not that he was making a bad job of it so far. She closed her eyes and shuddered as he bit down on her nipples, sucking, and biting; they were on fire. She was on fire. Thank you Lauren, was the last thought that ran through her mind. He travelled down her stomach, and plunged his face into her soaking wet pussy. She was as smooth as summer cherries and he nibbled and licked all over her mound of Venus, still moving his fingers over her clit, and in and out of her vagina. She was dripping wet, and writhed in the pleasure that this man was giving to her.

Alfred slid his adept, long, soft tongue down, firstly into her vagina, and then sucked and licked her inner labia, pulling gently on her lady lips. Still using his fingers, he flicked across her beauty bean.

Her hips rose and she could feel the whole of her body. Her bottom, her thighs her shoulders, her finger tips, her lips, her very mind. She could feel her mind. He explored her pussy with his tongue, teeth and mouth completely and eloquently, with the adroitness of a prima ballerina, dancing in harmony with sweet wonderful music. His hands had moved up to her breasts again, holding them, squeezing hard, kneading them to their fullest sensation. She arched her back and immersed herself in the pleasure he was giving her. Alfred continued lapping at her clitoris and sucking it until it was like a stiff, tiny cock. She could feel him sucking on her. Sucking and flicking his tongue over her clitty. He traced one hand down her side, lightly scratching her soft skin with his fingernails, then placed his artful fingers back into her vagina. He moved them inside of her sliding up and down, up and down, probing for her 'G' spot.

It was too much, she had to let go. He took her higher and higher. It was as if his tongue could feel every nerve ending in her clitoris and knew when she would orgasm. He backed away and licked her inner thigh.

"Nooooo, no. Please! Dear God, Alfred pleeease. You mustn't go, dooon't leave me!"

Alfred grinned and licked his lips. He took his fingers out of her vagina and licked them. "Oooh! You taste sooo good my sweet. My darling girl. You are hot, so very hot my sweet baby."

"God! Alfred, pleeease! Don't tease me. I can't stand it."

"Shush, shush little one. Trust me. I won't let you go." He bit her inner thigh, and licked up her sweet juices from her hot, sweet flesh.

"Alfred. Pleeeease, please. Don't make me beg."

Alfred's eyes glinted in the dim light. Then he plunged his tongue as far as he could into her pulsating cunt.

"Aaahhhhh! AAHHH! Oh my God. Pleeease." He took her tiny cock between his lips, and sucked, using his tongue to flick over, and all around the tiny phallus. His fingers returned to their search, deep and soft inside her.

"Aaaaaah. Oh, aaaah, aaahhhhh, ahhhh, Oh, oh, oh, oh." Victoria's thighs clenched around Alfred's shoulders, her calves pulled him hard and strong into her as she erupted and gushed all over him. Her hips were high off the bed, her grip on him almost choking him, leaving a red raw mark.

She relaxed, and he climbed up her body, he reached over for a condom, and had it on his cock before Victoria could even blink. Then he thrust his very, very hard penis inside her.

"Uuuummmmm. My God! Good, God." Victoria embraced him and accepted all of his cock inside her tight and needy vagina. Her thighs wrapped around him and held him firmly against her, only allowing him to move in and out of her, slowly and precisely. This time he had her 'G' spot, and he knew it. Alfred was sinking into her cunt and feeling her pleasure. His hips were grinding against hers, his hands holding her buttocks, squeezing them hard, pulling her more and more onto him.

Victoria was lost. Completely lost in the folds of lust and absolute, abandoned pleasure. She held his sides and moaned with each lunge, urging her to climax again. She pulled him down to kiss her, and let go the full force of an orgasm she had never experienced before. Alfred could hold back no more and let a volcanic explosion force Victoria back up the bed. He continued to kiss her and squeeze one buttock, unyielding until his mouth travelled over to her neck, kissing it lightly.

Victoria lay there shaking. Alfred was still inside her.

"There, there, my sweet girl. Hush, now baby, hush. " He slid away from her and stroked her hair. He lay on one side, touching the side of Victoria's body with his. He gently caressed her body, stroking her arms, down over her hips and thighs, feeling her body vibrating lightly. Victoria was in heaven. She couldn't describe it any other way.

"Darling, you really are something else," she sighed, and placed a finger lightly on his lips.

"Couldn't do it without you babe." He smiled and gently kissed her nipple.

They fell into a tranquil sleep, only for Alfred to wake Victoria two hours later, gently prodding her bottom with his stiff cock. They were spooned together, one arm wrapped around her shoulders, his hand firmly locked onto her breast, teasing her nipple. He entered her from behind, sliding deep into her with his first penetration.

"Mmmmmm," she gasped. Her back arched stiffly, her vagina contracted onto his penis, pulling him even deeper inside her. Alfred pounded into her, turned her around so she was on her hands and knees. He put his hands on her strong toned shoulders, and just fucked her. His rock-hard cock sliding in and out of her wet pussy, his balls banging against her backside. He massaged her back with every stroke.

"Do you like this baby? You can have all you want of this honey. Say you're mine! You are mine now. All mine, my property."

Victoria would never be anybody's property, but right now she was all his.

"Baby, baby, say you're mine." He had taken a great mane of her hair and wrapped it around his hand. He gently yanked her head back.

"Alfred! Please, Alfred, let go, you are hurting me." She shook her head and her buttocks.

"Sorry babes. I don't mean to hurt you, but you must tell me. You *are* all mine." He let her hair swing back around her neck, and went back into pounding Victoria's wet pussy, sliding his hand down to massage her clitty.

"Oh yes, she needs attention. Do you like attention, hun? Soooo much attention. I want to make u cum and cum."

"Mmmmmm. Yes, yes. Mmmmm Alfred, just fuck me baby. Ooohh I love you doing this. Please dooon't stop babe, don't stop," Victoria moaned.

"I won't, you can have as much of this as you want. I want to take you every day, every way I can."

Victoria felt his cock rubbing against her 'G' spot and felt the heat rise in her entire body, alive, in rhythm with his body. She climaxed and at the same time held his balls.

"Now! Baby tell me, tell me!"

"Aaaah! I'm yours baby, I'm yours." Victoria found herself intoxicated, inhaling the pheromones, gulping the air.

Craaack! Alfred took his hand and smacked it hard against Victoria's bottom.

"Arrgh. Alfred!" Victoria tried to get away from his grasp.

Alfred's cock grew, and hardened even more at the sight of the reddening hand print sprawled across Victoria's smooth, lightly tanned, firm buttocks and he thrust again, his other hand grasping her hair, bringing her head back. Her long neck arched, her chin turned up to the mirror on the wall. She caught their reflection, Alfred holding her hair like reins in one hand. She watched him smack her across her marvellous bottom again and again. It was amazing, the pain transforming into an exquisite warm flood, flowing through her veins. Alfred smacked her, and fucked her harder and harder, holding her head in place with her hair.

"There, my baby, there. You are mine!" he screamed, and thrust into her for the last time, before slipping his cock out of her, spurting his hot semen over her lithesome back. This time he collapsed on her, making her fall to the bed. She grasped his buttock and breathed heavily. He writhed over her, the sweat dripping from him, his heart pounding against her back. Her heart felt like it had burst through her chest.

They slept on until morning. The sunlight trickling through the window blinds. Victoria raised herself up and looked out.

"Oh look. You have boats in your garden."

"Mmmmm. What, err. What are you saying?"

"Boats, boats. You have boats in your garden." she giggled and rustled his hair.

"Well here is a boat in your garden." He laughed and rolled on top of her.

"Alfred you are soo… well sooo… Mmmmmm." He kissed her and she returned his kiss, her tongue sucking his.

He was about to penetrate her when she cooed to him, "Oh baby, I think she needs a kiss from you."

"Oh yes. Yes. Darling I just love kissing your pussy. I love your taste. You can have as much as you want. I have lots of this for you," and he disappeared into her willing loins, bringing her back to heaven and sending her higher and higher. He pressed into her before she had finished her third orgasm and this was an out of - and inner - body experience. He made love to her, gently placing his fingers inside her mouth. She sucked gently on them whilst moving with him. They moved together as one.

He brought her to climax again and again her hips rose with the tremendous electric pleasure racing through her. He would have continued pounding into her, now squeezing her nipples so they were on fire and the size of her thumbs, but she stopped, panting, her mind and body coursing with pleasure, wanting to go on and on, crossing all barriers… she asked him if he would like her to suck him.

"Mmmmmmm babes that would be great."

She slid around and gripped his firm strong cock. She used her deft hands and fingers to arouse him even more, moving gently but firmly up and over, down and around his cock. She then bent down and gently flicked her tongue over the tip of his cock. She played with him like this for several seconds teasing licking and flicking her tongue all over the head of his penis and down his shaft. The veins of his tool stood out, she could feel the blood rushing through the whole of his member and then she went down on him deep, swallowing all of him, her throat soft wet and warm.

"Mmmmmm. Arghhhhhh. Thank you Victoria. Oohhhhhh. AAAhhhhh." Alfred had left the planet and was flying on a sea of pleasure. Victoria continued moving her tongue and lips slowly and softly up, down, around and over Alfred's cock.

Alfred gulped and turned his head moaning and murmuring. Victoria's hands were firmly on his cock, her mouth eagerly sucking and licking it harder and harder, now faster and faster. Hands and mouth, soft, bee stung lips playing and pleasuring his cock. She slid her hand down to cover his balls and squeezed them softly and firmly, alternating between the bottom of his cock and his balls, still sucking and pulling on his cock. She slid her tongue down between his anus and balls, lapping at his perineum. Her hands stroked his cock firmly and rapidly.

"Aarrrrgggghhh." Alfred's whole body was in another dimension. "Ooooooohh! Oh baby, baby, baby. Darling girl. Sooooo beautiful. Oh. Please, pleeeease. I'm coming baby. I'm cuuuming!"

Victoria did not desist, but instead she returned to the tip of his cock by way of sliding her tongue all the way up from his balls and shaft, and continued to lick the most sensitive part of his gland whilst he spurt out his hot semen. Alfred's body convulsed with absolute, pure pleasure. His breathing was fast and heavy. Victoria raised herself up on her knees her magnificent body glowing and her beautiful mouth full and smiling from ear to ear.

She fell down by his side and stroked his chest lightly with her fingers. She laughed quietly and contentedly. Alfred put his arm around her waist, turned to her and kissed her on the tip of her nose.

"Hello beautiful. Are you okay?"

"Mmm. Very okay thanks," she purred. She lay back and closed her eyes. Alfred leant over and looked at the alarm clock.

"Nine thirty. Not bad, but we'll have to get up in ten okay?" They lay in each other's arms for a while, basking in their sated pleasure, hearts beating in time with each other. Alfred got up and reached for his dressing gown. Victoria checked his bum. Solid and round. His belly would have to go and he definitely needed toning, but not a lot to get right. 'Mmmmm, yes,' she thought.

"So, am I your girlfriend?" she asked, smiling. She might as well have let off an atom bomb.

"I do want to see you again. Sure of course I do but..."

"Oh!" She sat up now, shaking off the soporific mood she was in. "You mean you wouldn't mind if I had sex with somebody else?"

Alfred turned around and said it wasn't any of his business what she did with her body. He wouldn't be so presumptuous.

Presumptuous! Pre-bloody-sumptuous.

"Err. So that would be okay then?" she asked quizzically.

"Well, not if we had a relationship." He turned and put on the gown.

'Relationship? What about all the 'must see you agains' and coming down to see me in the country? Hello. Hello!' All these thoughts went ricocheting through her mind. She thought that the last sixteen hours or so was just that. A relationship. Well the beginning of one in any event.

"Do you want to take a shower, while I go and have a cigarette?" he said, wandering off up the stairs.

"Mmmmmm, yes. Yes. Sure. Right." She moved off the bed and made her way to the bathroom. 'What the fuck does that all mean?' she thought wildly, whilst allowing the hot jets of water to pummel her body. 'I must have just thrown him with the 'girlfriend' word. Oh well, I'm sure we will see each other and go from there.' She soaped herself and massaged her hips and thighs.

His bathroom was small and tired, a bit like the rest of his home, but as he had mentioned to her last night, she would have great fun redesigning it for him.

She towelled herself dry and tidied her makeup as best she could. She looked for a new toothbrush in his cabinet. Moving things with her fingers, she came across a tiny prescription like bottle. She picked it up and peered at it. 'Viagra' it had written on the plastic, yellow bottle. Aha. That was why he always had such a hard cock.

"Thought it was me. Ha, ha," she giggled to herself.

Alfred entered and said, "Hey. You look great in the morning."

"I look terrible," she replied, quickly grabbing a toothbrush and replacing the bottle on the glass shelf. She turned and breezed past him.

"You have the body of death," he breathed in her ear, grabbing her by the waist and nuzzling the nape of her neck.

'Body of death?' she thought. 'Weird.'

Victoria dressed while Alfred showered. She went upstairs to see if she could make a cup of coffee for them both.

Alfred followed soon after. "What are you doing?"

"I'm searching for my earrings," she said, rummaging through her handbag. "Oh Alfred. Have we time for a coffee? I couldn't find anything in the kitchen."

"Sorry hun, the machine has broken."

"Huh… okay. Are you ready?"

"Yep. Thought I'd drop you off at the taxi rank is that okay?"

"Sure." She couldn't wait to get home now. The whole mood had changed.

Alfred went ahead of her. At the bottom of the stairs, he fished about in a dish and found her earrings.

"Oh. Thanks. That's great," she said.

"Want to wear them now?"

"No. Yeeeow!" They were very clearly evening earrings. "It's bad enough as it is already." She pointed to her attire. "Thank goodness my coat will cover most of me, so people won't notice I stayed out all night."

"Yes babes, but what a night." Alfred put his hand gently under her chin and kissed her cheek.

'Mmmm. He is lovely,' she thought, and returned the gesture.

In the car, he held her hand and occasionally lifted it up to his mouth and air kissed it. Victoria thought this gesture a little trite, and more importantly felt it to be somewhat false. They arrived at the side of a black cab. Alfred asked the cabbie if he would take her to the station. They kissed, said their goodbyes, and she stepped into the taxi.

That was the last she saw of him.

He texted her later on that day to enquire if she had arrived home safely. Victoria responded that she had, and further how thrilled she was to have met him. She was hoping to see him that weekend. Wanted him to come to see her in her house in the country. She thought she could have a wonderful relationship with Alfred.

She heard nothing for a few days more. She texted to ask where he had gone.

Nothing. Silence.

Victoria was just puzzled. Alfred contacted her later that week and apologised for his lack of contact, as he had some work issues, but that he wanted to see her soon. She texted back to say that would be great, but that she had family and work commitments for the next ten days, and so asked to see him after that.

No reply.

A few days later, she thought she might have been a bit too aloof. They had fucked and made love all night and now she was aloof? Playing hard to get. Wrong way around Victoria, men don't think like that.

Alfred was pissed off she had dared not to comply with his wishes.

She texted to say that, as they were sooo busy, perhaps he could send her some dates, so she could organise herself around them.

No reply.

Victoria often thought thereafter that his lack of interest was because she had sex with him on the first date. Old-fashioned as that may seem, it probably was right. Men don't really see that having sex on first night is a compliment, but after all, Victoria had not had sex for two or so years.

Alfred came up with the conclusion Victoria had lied to him about her lack of sexual activity, even though her story was true. Indeed Victoria didn't believe him. No sex for six months, so why did he have all those condoms? They were almost as if on a conveyor belt.

Alfred assumed Victoria had sex with everybody she met, assumptions which usually emanated from men with low self-esteem, and coupled with Victoria's idea that this was the beginning of a relationship, it had led to a dead end.

Victoria was beautiful and intelligent and had the body that Alfred desired, so what was wrong? Victoria was a handful for most men. They were terrified of her. She could never figure it out. She was one of the most caring and loving of people, but she did have her sharper side and she was often more than one step ahead. Hurt and bewildered, Victoria remained true to her cause of finding 'the one'. She really did like Alfred and thought that they would have made quite a team. But Victoria could be very green.

Chapter 10

What Are Friends For?

The men continued to stream in. Victoria had joined two more internet dating sites and had also decided to advertise once more in the newspaper. If a job was worth doing, it was worth doing well.

Phone calls. Texting. Texting. Men on-line like to text. Well, those that like to pretend; like to hide behind the internet that is. Those that have hidden agendas, those that lead double lives, and those that are really not of sound mind, and those that are simply delusional. There seemed to be a great deal of the latter. Broken biscuits. Damaged goods. Floating out there like so many barnacles waiting to clutch onto a rock.

Victoria made a date to see Beth for lunch. She was tired of it all and needed a good girly chat. Beth was always good at that. The Alfred incident had really knocked her for six.

"Hi Darling. How are you?" Beth got up from her seat to greet Victoria, who was in full flood hurtling towards her through the restaurant.

"Hellooo! Hello Darling." Victoria wrapped her arms around Beth's shoulders, and gave her a big kiss on both cheeks. "Ooooh! I have sooo missed you. So much to tell. How are you Beth?" Victoria sat down opposite Beth at the table.

"Well, I am just fine. It's you we are all worried about sweetheart. What is going on? You seemed quite down on the phone."

"Mmmm. Yes. Well, I am a bit. It's all this business to do with the man search. It's bloody exhausting. I wish I could say that the refurb of the house was at least keeping me sane, but Christ, well that's driving me around the bend as well."

"Jasmine tea please," Beth ordered from the waiter who had silently approached them.

"Yes thanks. I'll have a glass of sauvignon blanc and some tap water please." Victoria smiled up at the waiter, who nodded politely and left as quietly as he had arrived.

"Tell me Victoria, what has been going on?" Beth moved across the table and took Victoria's hand, gave it a squeeze, and leaned back in her chair.

"Shall we choose first, or else we shall never get to eat." Victoria coughed and giggled.

"Yes sure. I was thinking of the scallops and …"

"Thinking of dessert," Victoria interjected.

"Quite." Beth smiled. Beth adored puddings and she had such a sweet tooth that it wasn't past her to have two, or maybe even three desserts. Victoria recalled a time when they had been in a two star Michelin restaurant in France. They had agreed to share their desserts, and although Victoria was a more 'savouries' person, she enjoyed the odd spoonful of pudding and this restaurant was renowned for its amazing desserts. Well, the result was that apparently Beth had forgotten the agreement entirely, as on Victoria's return from the ladies, much to Victoria's astonishment both plates were clean. Beth had scoffed both of them. She hadn't even given Victoria a chance. They often used to giggle about this together. Victoria was still in wonder of her best friend.

Victoria proceeded to regale Beth about Alfred. Beth's attitude toward men was very different to Victoria's. Beth took them in her stride and used them every bit as much as they used her. Well Victoria wasn't entirely convinced of the stream being an equal one, but on the whole, she guessed it evened out. But now Beth had met Tom, she had quietened down much like a cat settling deep into the folds of a duvet. She was really quite content. As happy as Victoria had ever seen her.

Tom was such a nice man. Unassuming and it was difficult on sight to believe he had such an appetite in the bedroom.

"Quite insatiable, Darling," Beth would purr.

Victoria continued her story about Alfred and her amazement as to the outcome.

Having completed her narrative, and delicately nibbling on her bread she asked, "What was that all about Beth?"

"No idea, hunny. Who knows the way men's minds work? Could be anything, or nothing. But it's probably the usual… frightened silly of you."

Victoria never did understand this. Surely she had given all the right signals to Alfred. They had gotten on so well. Surely the odd comment about his house couldn't have put him off? She only said that the entrance to his apartment smelt funny and that his living space could do with some TLC, as it was tired and grungy. He even asked her to redesign it for him for goodness sake. Oh well. Not worth thinking, or bothering about anymore.

They ordered from the *plat du jour*, Victoria proceeded to give Beth an update on all of the men she called her side-lines. They were always in contact with her, but apart from the fact that none, including 'Mad Sam', were suitable for her, their behaviour was nothing less than weird and way out there! No rhythm, no rhythm, well none that she had discovered. Both she and Beth had their ideas and hunches but none were ever conclusive.

Chapter 11

The Sad Suitors

Victoria's 'SSs' or Sad Suitors, whom she'd called so, not because of their lack of humour, or because they were unhappy, but because they were just that: sad. One in particular was notably named Sam.

Victoria and Beth renamed him, 'Mad Sam'. And with due justification.

Sam had contacted Victoria about nine months prior to their first meeting. All in all his conversation, his photo and talking (well come to think of it, texting) seemed promising. Talking on the telephone was not one of Sam's strong points. But he panned out okay. He had responded to her profile on one of the internet dating sites she was using. He emailed her and appeared to be at least half sensible and truth be told, Victoria was very attracted to his appearance, which, as it turned out was the sole reason for tolerating his exceptionally strange behaviour and it was to add up to quite a lot. Victoria added two and two and made four. But Sam somehow was always able to persuade Victoria she had made it five!

"Hellllooooo." Victoria never liked the way he emphasized his Hellos.

"Hi Sam. How are you today?"

"I am just fine Victoria. When are we going to meet?"

"Why not lunch this Thursday?"

"I can do lunch, but it would be much easier for me to take you to dinner. I work in Southampton."

Southampton was a little difficult to negotiate from where she lived so she took a deep breath, and said, "Okay but, that's quite a journey there and back in the evening."

"Yes I know, but I am used to getting up early. I live in Oxford and so I have to leave at five in the morning during the week."

"Oh I am sorry Sam, but I can't let you stay here. We haven't even met and well err, umm you know. Not really in my remit, although there is a local restaurant with rooms. They are very nice. I am sure you would be welcome and comfortable there."

"Oh yes, of course. That will be fine."

"Oh yes, right then. Good, Thursday for dinner then?" Victoria was smiling and feeling quite good about Sam.

"I'll email you my address. Have you a satnav?"

"Of course. I'll arrange the hotel. Don't worry. Pick you up in the evening at seven thirty. I'll leave at four thirty so it should be fine."

"Great, see you then. Look forward to seeing you."

Well. That went well, and he said he looked like a better looking version of Gordon Ramsay.... could be worse. Actually, from his photo, she thought he looked a lot like The Kings of Leon's lead vocalist.

Victoria hardly ever had a crush on a celebrity, but Calib Willowfall and George Clooney were two exceptions to her rule. Either way Sam sounded nice and they did discuss that he was into the gym and worked out regularly. And he designed aircraft. Mmm, fascinating.

She began to get her hopes up again. It was all very well, but however much she girded herself against hope and success, based on her track record so far, there was always a glimmer of hope lacing its way through her mind and heart.

Sam texted her. 'I am just at junction 5. I'll be with you 10 minutes early. Is that okay?'

Unbeknown to Victoria there were going to be thousands of texts to follow.

'No problem. Looking forward to see you,' she texted back. She dressed smart casual, as they would just be going to the local pub. Stretch, black, soft leggings with small gold buttons down the side and a peasant style, raggedy hemmed, grey top, embroidered with a huge black and silver rose on the front. It clung tightly to her waist and fell wisplike around her hips. She decided that her black, stirruped D&G high-heeled boots, were best for this occasion, instead of her peep- toed blue and black Louboutins.

"Mmmmm," she said, looking at herself in the mirror. "Not bad." She made a twirl and was pleased. "I sure hope he likes this. Sure hope I like him," she mused. "I am so lonely," she sighed. She thought of Berrie, but quickly brushed it away as it made her sad, and slightly guilty. Not justified, but nonetheless...

There was a hard knock on the door, and her heart skipped a beat. She clapped her hand to her heart, took another quick check in the mirror, grabbed her coat and handbag, and went downstairs.

"Hello. Good evening." She opened the door to see Sam standing there one arm up against the wall, jacket draped over his shoulder, smiling through bright white teeth. The cowboy hat and a straw in his mouth was missing, but otherwise he could have been James Dean, straight in from the South.

'Cocky or what?' she thought. 'But nice, very nice. He does look a bit like Gordon Ramsay, but give him a beard and he'd be a dead ringer for Callib.'

"Hellllooo and good evening to you." He straightened, backed off the wall, and gave a little bow, raised his head, and gave her a cheeky grin.

"I'll just fetch my coat. Oh. Shall we go, or would you like to come in for a drink...?" The last few words got lost, as she was on her way to collect her coat, so they faded away, like lost notes from a flute. She made her way back, carrying her jacket and in quite a fluster.

"Pardon?" he said, as she looked him straight in the eye and said, "Pardon ehm! Pardon. Oh I am sorry, didn't mean to be rude. Would you like to come in for a drink before we go?"

Sam looked at her coat folded over her arm, smiled and said, "No, it's fine. Let's go. I'm hungry," he turned and led the way to his car. He opened the car door for her.

'At last manners,' she thought and gave him a big smile whilst gently lowering herself into the car seat.

He started the car and said, "Which way, beautiful?"

'Ahh, he likes me,' she thought.

"Top of the drive and turn left. We are going to a gourmet pub not far from Canterbury. Hope that's okay? I did explain it was another twenty minutes driving for you. But good food is hard to come by any closer." Victoria didn't want to use the local pub for her excursions and dates. Good Lord, the villagers didn't know what to make of her already, without all of this going on. So she chose a very good eating house for her 'dates'. It was quite funny, especially when Beth was doing the same.

Beth couldn't stand all the whispering and strange looks from the staff, so she explained that Victoria was on a quest for 'True Love', and she was on a quest for whatever came her way. Well before Tom came her way that is.

So, thanks to Beth, all the gossip had stopped and Victoria received support and guidance from the staff at The Old Brown Bull.

Victoria had lost count of just how many men she had taken there for their first date. Not in the hundreds, but definitely double figures. At a guess, it had been probably twenty or thirty. But Sam seemed different. Mostly because of his endearing looks, and he could string two sentences together without falling over his feet.

"Hi Victoria." Vanessa, the proprietor's wife, greeted her with a smile. It had taken Vanessa at least a year before Victoria had been privileged by this welcome. It wasn't that Vanessa didn't like her, or people for that matter, it was just that she generally had a rather negative view on life. That and the fact that her husband worked her like an ox in the fields. She always looked like she had been dragged through a hedge backwards, and had a face like a baby's smacked bottom.

"Hi Vanessa. This is Sam. Sam this is Vanessa. She runs a tight ship, but a good one. She even manages to serve some of the best food for miles around." Victoria slid onto a high stool showing her long thighs, which were wrapped tightly in soft, black velveteen.

Vanessa just rolled her eyes upward, and told Victoria that she had given her the table near the fire, as requested.

"What would you like to drink?" she asked Sam.

Memo to Victoria: Must stop that let go, he is the man, *not* you; fortunately, he seemed not to notice.

"Hi Victoria. How are you? What can I get you?" Natalie asked, all smiles and giggles, her pink t-shirt much too small for her rolls of fat, which were fighting with each other for comfort and attention.

"Sam?" Victoria cocked her head at him.

"I'll have a beer. Thanks," he said to Natalie.

"And I'll have a glass of sauvignon blanc, thanks Natalie," Victoria looked at Natalie and then turned all of her attention towards Sam.

"Well. Thank you for coming. How was the journey?" 'God how boring you sound darling,' she thought to herself.

"Thank you, for being here and much more attractive than your photos." He touched her cheek.

'Bloody hell, that's a bit much, but I like it,' she thought.

"Oh, it's nothing." She giggled and actually blushed. Victoria couldn't remember when she had last blushed in public. She felt the warmth travel up from her neck, past her eyes, right to the top of her forehead. "Gosh. I am blushing," she told Sam. Absolutely no need to point out the obvious, and with this further embarrassment, she felt her face get warmer and warmer.

Natalie arrived just in time, before Victoria felt sure she was going to slide off the stool, and sink through the floor. "Sauvignon blanc and one Orangeboom," she said, as she passed the drinks over the counter.

"Thanks Natalie." They both took their glasses, raised them in the air slightly toward one another smiled and Sam said, "To us," then, "No, no. silly of me. To you. A very beautiful lady." He leant forward and kissed her cheek.

She tingled all over and almost spilt her drink.

"Shall we look at the board?" The menu was on a blackboard. Victoria looked directly into his eyes and licked her lips. My God, she felt a tingle not only down the back of her spine, but also in between her legs. He was very attractive. He looked straight back into her eyes, moved a little on his stool. She didn't look, but could have sworn he was readjusting himself. She smiled and turned toward the board. The last thing on her mind was food. She would be lucky if she could get a few mouthfuls down, she was so wired up.

However, they managed to choose and sat down at the table. The electricity abated a little, well enough for them to order and converse with each other, even if it was small talk. Essential small talk like what did she both like, dislike and would she go with him to Dubai?

"Pardon?"

"Would you like to go to Dubai with me?" Sam was smiling, but looked very serious.

"Isn't that a little too soon? Sam, we have only just met." Victoria was excited, dubious and perplexed all in one. She didn't know whether she liked the feeling or not. She took a sip of wine.

Sam took her hand. "It's never too soon to take a beautiful lady away, spoil her, and pamper her."

"Well put like that, it must be worth considering," she giggled.

They finished their meal. Victoria was giddy with the very scent of Sam, and went all gooey just looking at him. She desired him so much. How was she going to say goodnight? Victoria felt herself slipping in love, or was it lust? Sam was very, very nice. A gentle handsome man. Tall, soft dark blonde hair. He looked like he did work out as he said he did. And the gobbledygook about engineering sounded authentic enough.

Designing aircraft was a very responsible position.

He called for the bill. Victoria watched to see if he would pay by credit card. Those that paid by cash always had something to hide, usually an overbearing mortgage, two kids and a wife. She was ever so pleased when he put an American Express card on the table. He didn't even look at the bottom line. Just placed the card into the crimson wallet and told Natalie to add fifteen percent.

"That was a very nice meal Natalie," he said, passing the wallet to her. She was all smiles of course, and Victoria had never seen her this happy before.

"I am just going to the ladies Sam, meet you at the door." Victoria got up and sashayed over to the restrooms. Sam's eyes never left her. Her long slender legs were pretty difficult not to watch. His eyes seared through her. Victoria could feel them on her.

"Oh my, oh my," Victoria leaned back against the toilet door clutching her side. "Slow, slow, breathe slowly," she said to herself. "Please God. Pleeeeease let him be for real." She composed herself and freshened her makeup. She was glowing. "Don't ruin this one Victoria. Go slow and cut the funnies. He doesn't want a comedienne, he wants a woman and you want a man. So stick to the rules. Just try to be girlie. You've seen it work a thousand times You can do it girl. You can do it," she commanded herself.

"Hi, everything okay?" she asked Sam, who was reading the newspaper that the restaurant provided for its customers.

"Absolutely. Here, let me help you." Sam moved forward to help her on with her coat. She breathed him in. Slightly salty, mixed with spices and tangy citrus. Like fresh sea air blowing through an orange tree. Very sexy. Very clean. Cutting through her senses, like a samurai warrior's sword slicing through a barrel full of apples. She was high, her adrenalin running freely, and rapidly through her veins. She really did feel as though she was walking on air.

They walked, well Victoria floated, to his car. Sam opened the door for her, but not before turning her around, lifting her chin toward him, and then firmly planting a kiss on her full and shiny lips.

"Mmmm. I have been wanting to that all evening." He moved away from her and gave that cocky grin again.

Victoria raised her hand to his face, and gently traced her nails across his jaw line. She said nothing, but gently sat down in the car seat. But she did think, 'Oh boy, oh boy. Could this be it?'

Sam came around and got in the car. He faced her again and said, "I am having such a good time, I hope you are as well Victoria, my lovely lady." Sam wanted to take her there and then. Victoria wanted him to take her there and then as well. Sam started the car and drove off, taking directions as they went.

They hardly said another word to each other, the air was so charged with their natural and perfumed aromas, mingling together, heightening their physical attraction to one another. Sam drove down Victoria's driveway and stopped the car. She didn't know whether to stay or flee.

"Well, thank you for one of the most amazing times I have had in a long time," Sam said as he turned off the engine and veered around to face her. A bit over the top, but what a nice thing to say.

"It has been a pleasure," she said. She had discovered at dinner that he had booked into a hotel not far away and was very impressed by that as well as the rest of the evening's frolics and fancies. Sam was very entertaining.

Sam turned right round, and opened the car door. Victoria followed. Sam approached her and escorted her to her door.

"I must see you again," he said placing an arm around her waist.

"Well, you would have to if we are going to Dubai," her body naturally responded to his familiarity, and she fell toward his firm torso.

"You'd come. You really would?" he asked with sincere surprise. Victoria was thrown a little by that, but what the hell. She supposed it was quite a thing to offer, let alone accept, after only one meeting.

"Why not! I can't think of a nicer way to get to know you, and we don't exactly live around the corner. So yes, I think it is a fabulous idea."

Sam pulled her tighter to his chest, and gave her a long lingering kiss.

"Errrgh um. Em Lovely," Victoria said, pulling away from him and licking her lips. She broke his grasp. "Sam, you are wonderful I really like you but…"

"I know, I know, you were perfectly clear about where you stand emotionally and physically and I respect that. Just one more kiss, pleeeeease, and then I shall be off. Look, no hands," he held up his hands in front of her.

"Oh really? Come here." Victoria reached out her arms for him.

Sam moved forward to meet her, held her face, kissed her softly, and licked her lips. She looked absolutely ravishing in the moonlight.

"Goodnight darling, I'll just stay here while I see you safe in the house," Sam breathed softly in her ear.

That night, Victoria couldn't sleep with sheer excitement. Sam could be the 'one'. He was so lovely.

In the morning, Sam texted her. 'Good morning gorgeous.'

She replied, 'Hi baby, have a nice day.'

They continued in this vein mainly texting and emailing a little until Victoria finally began to think Sam wasn't for real after all. No phone calls, and hardly ever any contact in the evening or weekends.

As they kept texting about visiting Dubai, Victoria asked Sam if he had booked the tickets. He said he had and was just waiting for his sister to confirm the hotel as she lived out there and worked for a one of the larger local airlines.

Whenever Victoria called him, she was directed straight to voicemail, or it was switched off. She asked Sam to call her. 'No problem, when's good for you?' he texted back.

'Doesn't anyone just call because they want to call and hope it's a good time to call anymore?' she thought whilst texting back and saying anytime that evening was great.

'Good. Speak to you then, then. Lol,' was his response.

Now, Sam was going slower than she'd anticipated. She had had dinner with him twice, discussed the Dubai vacation and was in the process of sex text. It was then that Victoria started to have grave doubts about Sam, but she found him very attractive. She kept making excuses for him and thought that perhaps she was making it difficult for him.

Memo to Victoria: If it has four legs and barks. It is a dog. Do not make excuses for anybody. If strange behaviour goes on for too long, you can bet your bottom dollar that there is something wrong. To be fair though it goes both ways.

However, Victoria hadn't learned that lesson yet.

It wasn't his fault she had had such untrustworthy partners, but meanwhile, nothing ventured, nothing gained. She would keep on cyber dating and continue her search. She didn't owe Sam anything and he was moving very slowly. Although she was looking forward to seeing him again, he had so far, not turned up to two Sunday lunch dates. She was so disappointed and bemused to say the least. They had both agreed that, as the distance was a problem. Well it was for Sam, as he worked far away from home and travelled quite a bit, so the mere idea of the M25 was an anathema to him.

"I've got M25-phobia," he joked with her. But they had further agreed at Sam's behest that they should discuss the possibility of a long term future together so. Oh and sex was pretty much on the menu as well.

Victoria had lost count of the amount of texts he had sent saying how much he wanted to make love to her. To take her in his arms. To cover her in soft, warm kisses. To take her from behind, holding her close to him, and so on, and so on. So the excuse of a crash on the motorway that first Sunday was a little daunting to say the least, especially as Victoria had just driven that way, that very morning, as she had agreed to drop Emmy at the meeting spot that she and Emmy's father used for such occasions.

Victoria had a feeling that something was wrong after saying goodbye to Emmy and driving like a lunatic to be home in time to change and be ready for adorable Sam. The excitement was too much, and the only thing travelling faster than Victoria was the adrenalin coursing through her veins.

She had it all worked out. What to wear: her tightly tailored DKNY cream skirt with her dark grey River Island strappy vest, mix and match couture with high street is sometimes unbeatable, plus Ralph Lauren three-inch wide silver patent belt. Her long tanned legs had no need for stockings and the weather was mild. She would wear her grey, open-toed Jimmy Choos and top off the whole thing with her tangerine, ostrich skin Hermes handbag. Knock out. Not that Sam would notice the details. Most men don't notice details, the bastards, but nevertheless the whole effect, he would notice something for sure, especially her glossy, tangerine lips, long, blonde, wavy hair, and let's not forget the legs, bottom and breasts going in and out in all the right places. They would have lunch at a wonderful little restaurant where she had taken some of her previous dates. She had told Sarah, the maître d', all about her mission. Sarah was a lovely Austrian lady and an understanding one at that. She sympathised with Victoria's quest and did everything she could to help her find a true love, so as may be imagined the service was impeccable, and Victoria always felt at ease. After lunch, they would go back to Victoria's and, while in the hot tub maybe have a glass of champagne from a bottle already chilling. They'd continue talking and making plans for their future together, just as Sam kept mentioning, and then Sam would take her upstairs to her beautiful bedroom. Satin sheets, candles everywhere, the scent of sweet roses, soon to be overtaken with the heady smell of unadulterated sex. Yes, it was going to be quite a day. One to remember and that would change her life forever. To be with sweet wonderful Sam for the rest of her life. Apparently, poor Victoria still had a lot to learn. She was still in love with being in love and had quite forgotten all her senses in her desperate need to find a mate.

Victoria called Sam, which had become a rare thing for her lately. Usually it was text, text and then more text. No answer. She called three times and on the third try, she at least was able to leave a message. It was now about 11.30, and she was due to meet him at one o'clock, in time for lunch at half past.

"Hi darling, I'm just checking that everything is okay, and you are on your way? I am so looking forward to seeing you." She received no reply and was a little fed up with herself for even have this nagging feeling that he wasn't coming. It beggared belief of course. He was coming. It was what they both wanted. They had discussed it. Well texted it at length over several months.

Victoria rushed around getting ready to be on time for Sam when her phone rang. She had a land line and had given the number to Sam some time back. She was quite surprised to hear it was Sam. He had never used it before.

"Victoria. Heeeelloo, Victoria." She really liked Sam, well she could have fallen in love with him, but for the way he had this false way of saying 'Hello'.

"Hi Sam, Yes it's me darling. Where are you baby?" Victoria was putting in her earrings in as they were speaking.

"Darling, I've been in a crash!"

"Crash what! What crash, are you okay?"

"Yes, Yes I am fine. I've been in a pileup. That's why I didn't answer your calls, I've been with the police."

"Oh! Oh well." Then Victoria saw red. In a lepton second, all her instincts and senses told her he was lying. She had just come down that very motorway. Sam wasn't to know that, as Victoria didn't tell him she was dropping Emmy off that morning.

"I don't believe you," she blurted out. Squeezing the telephone hard in her hand, her eyes wide and alarmed, her head shaking in disbelief. It was the 'Dubai' thing all over again, the no-show last week when Sam had said he was coming to dinner, but then changed and said he had to work late.

"Darling, I have just been in a crash."

"Okay, okay." A mixture of desire to believe him, panic and knowing, somehow knowing that he was lying, but none of this making sense. Why, why for goodness sake. Why?

"Where are you?"

"Junction nine."

That was impossible - she had entered the M25 at junction 8. Junction 9 was only a few miles up, so any pileup would have had an add-on effect and she surely would have been in traffic herself. She had breezed the whole journey. It had been almost like the world and his wife were staying home that morning.

"Well, are you okay?"

"Yes I'm fine."

"Good, good, but I don't believe you."

"Look. I've had enough. I've been in traffic and an accident now for over three hours. I'm going home." His voice was angry and tense. The temerity of him. He was angry? She was the only one that had the right to be angry. Going home? What did he mean he was going home? Her mind was skating all over the place. He was only one hour, if that, away from her and, if he was mobile, why not just pitch up? Better late than never.

'Poor idiot,' she thought later that evening sipping a glass of Chablis. How was he to know that she was on that same road at the time he professed to have had a crash. Of all the roads, in all the places? But for now, all she was experiencing was disbelief and anger.

The moron. The mad bastard. What was all this about? Her thoughts and emotions racing through her body, her hand now shaking holding the ringing phone. It was Sam.

"I don't believe you," she said, and before he had a chance to answer she hung up the phone.

Fuming with total disbelief and outrage, let alone amazing disappointment. She had so been looking forward to this day. She rang the AA road report. Maybe she could be wrong she told herself. The AA mentioned hold ups and crashes on the M25 alright, but none in the vicinity of junction 9!

She texted him. 'I am sorry darling, why don't you just turn around? You aren't far away and I can cook us something to eat. I so want to see you.'

Nothing.

She called him and left a message. "Sam, Sam baby. Come back, I am sure we can put the day back together." She was thinking, 'Well, if he has had a crash the car will be damaged. Proof I am wrong, so what's his problem?'

Sam did not respond. Victoria texted him again. 'AA report no hold ups M25 junction 9. Why are you lying? What is the matter with you? I am so disappointed. How could you do this to me?' She received no response. So after a few unsavoury texts later, which still resulted in no response, she gave up and decided to change into her trakkie pants and top. They were so soft against her skin and she looked great in them. She needed to look great right now, and feel comfortable, even though she wasn't going anywhere.

She wasn't going anywhere. Victoria was having a hard time getting her head around what had happened. She cancelled the reservation apologising profusely to Sarah, who charmingly said it didn't matter, but who was disappointed she wasn't going to see her.

"Another time, Sarah. Probably come later in the week and bring Beth with me."

"That would be great. Have a nice day Victoria."

'Yeah right,' Victoria thought. 'I was supposed to be having a great day I still can't work it out. Why didn't he want to come?' A small worm-like thought entered her mind. On the last date, she had noticed that Sam really did like a drink, but whatever. Surely not? He was staying away from her because he wanted a drink. Couldn't be, didn't make sense.

He could have all he wanted at lunch and after at her place.

Bizarre, totally bizarre.

Sam didn't relent in becoming more and more bizarre. Victoria later only played along for the hell of it, well not to begin with, but after his fourth or fifth no-show. He begged to see her and explain all. She finally gave in after being bombarded with many pitiful texts. He actually showed up and she was smitten again. Wary, of course, but smitten. He had lost more weight and had obviously been working out.

They talked over coffee at Victoria's place. He said he was sorry for not showing up. He still maintained his excuses which were totally potty, but Victoria listened. He said he had been far too tied up with work and perhaps it was a problem that he had been alone for so long. If he behaved like that with all the girls, no wonder he was alone. He told Victoria he loved her, and she told him she was very attracted to him, and so he should understand why she was so upset.

She was warming to his charm, and good looks, and thought they would have dinner, and Sam would stay that evening. Granted it wasn't discussed, but it seemed like a natural carry on from their meeting.

After a couple of hours of soul-baring, and discussing plans for the future, outline plans that he should move into hers, and that they should get to know each other by going away together as he had suggested such a long time ago.

"Yes darling, that is a good idea. We should go away. Dubai is too hot now, but we can go anywhere we like."

"Oh Sam. I have missed you," Victoria caressed his cheek and kissed him full on. Sam responded and held her tight.

"Darling, you never said how attracted you are to me before." Sam's eyes were a sparkling bright blue, and his smile almost split his face.

Jeez! Men! As if I would allow him here after what he has done, and contacted him as much, if I weren't attracted… Yeah I like Quasimodo's ugly brother, but he doesn't like me, so I'm settling for you as second best. Duh!

"Sam, oh Sam what am I going to do with you?" She got up to go to the kitchen. Sam followed puppy dog like still beaming from ear to ear.

"Would you like a glass?" she said opening a bottle of Mersault, as she thought a little celebration was called for.

"No, no thanks Victoria. I have to get back and the police stopped me the other day."

'Get back? Get the fucking hell back? What now? Strewth! God give me strength,' she thought, but said, "Okay darling of course. Another coffee? Shall we have an early supper? Perhaps you would like to stay and then you can have a drink, leave early in the morning?"

"I'd love to, but I really must be going."

"I hope you don't mind if I do then?" She gestured to the bottle, she sure needed a drink now, and a cigarette.

"No. Of course not."

"And I think I'll just have one of these." She reached for the packet of cigarettes lying on the top shelf above the sink. They talked a little more about absolutely nothing.

"I should go. Victoria It's a long run."

To this day, she had no idea why she didn't just ask the tosspot what the hell he was playing at. Pride and confusion probably.

"Sure, sure thing. Let me see you to the door."

Then he was gone. Gone into the night, taillights disappearing over the top of her drive.

"Bye-bye, see you," she said to herself, closing the heavy, black oak door behind her. She slumped against it, heaved a huge sigh and returned to the kitchen. "What a waste of a great bottle of wine," she said to the bottle. "Oh well. I'll cork it and put it in the fridge. Berrie is coming around tomorrow and it still should be okay. At least he deserves it."

Sam continued to text Victoria. They arranged to meet again, even though she hadn't seen him for two months or so. *One last time*, Victoria thought. He promised until he was blue in the face. Swore to God on high, swore on his life that there wasn't another woman, even though he failed to return her call one Sunday evening, professing he had no mobile signal. He was staying in a hotel. Did land lines mean anything to him? His reasoning? After being so used to using mobiles, he didn't even think to use a landline.

Yeah right! Poor dearest Victoria still allowed him one last chance. He couldn't do it again, could he? Surely not. What was his motivation for such bizarre behaviour?

So they made another date for Sunday lunch. A little later this time, so he had more time to get to her place. He agreed it would be easy for him to arrive at three thirty, and over lunch talk about their possible life together.

'I am so in love with you darling can't wait to c u.' He text her, 'Can't wait to see you too baby.'

Sunday arrived, and whilst she was wary, she was still excited to be seeing him, as he even texted her last thing Saturday night. 'CU tomorrow darling sleep tight gorgeous.'

Then, at eleven o'clock the following morning, he texted, 'Roads are looking dodgy will wait till they clear.'

Yet again Victoria had failed to see the dog. It did have four legs and it was barking, quite loud actually. It was a dog. Sam was that dog. 'What? No! No! No! No! Not happening. Not, not, not happening,' she thought.

Victoria called him. "What do you mean the roads are dodgy?"

"Haven't you seen the weather reports honey? It's snowing and here my road is blocked."

"No, it's not for goodness sake. You live in Oxford. First time I've heard Oxford has a microclimate. It's not that bad. A few flurries that's all. What *is* your problem? You could get here if you wanted to. You know you could. What's the matter?"

"Darling I can't. Don't you think I would if I could?" Sam sent her a picture of what she supposed was the road he lived in. A few centimetres of very light snow that a skateboard could ride through.

Victoria texted him. 'Forget it. you are mad. Absolutely insane. I am not playing your bloody cruel and awful games anymore. Get lost! DO NOT contact me ever again, you moron. Hope you and your friends have a great laugh well done. Just fuck off and don't contact me again.'

'It's NOT like that, I can't get out my road is blocked.'

'Then come later.'

'I'll wait and see how it pans out.'

'Leave ME alone, you basket case!'

'Babes don't be like that. Don't spoil such a good thing over nothing.'

'Nothing?' she thought. 'Nothing?' This creature says 'nothing', he has been having her over for God knows how long, and it's again 'nothing'. Not any more buddy boy.

She didn't respond, but instead rang Beth and they both laughed about mad Sam.

"What do you think of that Beth?" Victoria sighed, smiling at the madness of it all.

"I don't know honey, really I don't. All I can think is that he does have another woman, and he is being hampered each time. Good for her."

"Do you know, I don't think that is it. But there's something in the ether for sure though."

"I don't know Victoria. I am just so glad it's not affecting you like it would have three years ago."

"Yeah, I know. But however much I psyched myself up that it didn't matter, I am still disappointed. Even though I didn't believe he was going to show, it was counteracted by the fact that he knew this would be the last time I would ever entertain him, and well."

"I know sugar, but well, you have tolerated quite a lot of weird behaviour so far, so why wouldn't he not turn up yet again. How many times is it now? Perhaps he really is mad Victoria. I didn't really approve of you agreeing to see him this time, but you seemed so positive he would turn up, That and the fact you seem fixated with the 'Kings of Thingy' singer."

"You mean you thought he wouldn't turn up? And I am not obsessed with the Kings of Leon singer. For goodness sake Beth."

"Fifty percent of me thought he wouldn't show. Yes. He is one weird hombre."

"Mmmmm, that's for sure. Oh well hun, no real problem and no harm done. Actually, it's rather good, as I get to see Berrie and the kids instead."

"Oh, how nice. But I thought they were with their mother?"

"No. Back now. He is so wonderful."

"Yes, but Berrie is a *real* man darling." Beth heaved a sigh, and wondered for the thousandth time why Victoria just didn't get it. Oh well, she would have to get there by herself, if ever, she conceded to herself.

"Yes, yes. He is, isn't he? Just a darling beautiful man. Goodbye Beth. Catch you tomorrow."

"Bye darling, have a lovely time." Beth knew she would. Berrie was good for her best friend, and Victoria was good for Berrie and the kids.

Mad Sam didn't go away, but Victoria did have a great time playing with the maniac.

Victoria met Berrie and his lovely children that night. Mad Sam was a million miles away. She didn't think of him at all, just basked in the love and laughter she had with Berrie and his family.

Victoria slept very well that night.

Chapter 12

All About The Man

Victoria was quite hopeful about the 'actor', and was getting a teeny bit excited about 'Irish' Arnold. The juggling continued. Sometimes Victoria would receive between fifty to sixty texts a day, from being in contact with ten men at a time. She didn't meet all of the men who contacted her, but she was in contact with over fifty or so, during the time she was on her quest. It was taking so long, and nobody so far was right. They lied so much. Most were so delusional that they could have kept a whole team of psychiatrists busy for months.

Nonetheless, she pressed on regardless. After all she was learning a great deal about the male psyche, and was almost getting to understand 'Man Speak'. Apart from the tedium and repetition of having to go through the same stories, likes and dislikes etc. etc. She remarked to Beth, that now she had more of a handle on the whole scenario, she had nothing to lose. She was learning the ropes, and in most cases several steps ahead of the lunatics. In fact, she was having fun and she had everything to gain. *He* was out there somewhere.

Tim, the model come actor, was very cheeky and if his portfolio and the odd mobile image were anything to go by, pretty good eye-candy. He was a few years younger than Victoria, but not by so much that anybody would notice. He was based in Scotland, but had an apartment in South West London.

Tim did call. Once! He even usurped Sam and earned the title 'Top Text

Tim'. After they had been texting for a few weeks, and at which point they hadn't met, he asked her to go to Tenerife, saying that it would be a romantic way to get to know each other. She wondered if he'd met Sam and thought this could have been standard cyber-dating chat. She declined the offer, but said she would love to meet him on his return. Tim said it was the only thing he was looking forward to.

'Yeeeeeow,' she thought. 'But still he does seem sweet.'

Tim was dying to meet Victoria. This was the 'One', he just knew she would be great for him.

"Hi, Victoria?"

"Yes its Victoria."

"It's Tim. I am back from the Canaries. How are you darling?"

"Oh Hi Tim, I'm fine, but the weather's getting me down, fed up with the cold."

"I shall keep you warm. I shall keep you warm for the rest of your life baby." She could feel him smiling. She felt slightly on edge.

"I am in London this week, auditioning. When is a good time to come and see you?"

"Oh um, well, I am in London having dinner with my ex-business partner on Tuesday, nothing happens down here on Mondays, so why not Wednesday?" She breathed deeply and thought, 'Oh well, why not, we have to meet someday.' She was getting used to managing the many men that had, and still were contacting her from the various websites.

Nothing much was coming from Amanda and her agency, but she would get onto that later. Victoria had her hands full at the moment, but the time would come when Amanda had to deliver, or give Victoria her money back. Victoria had exchanged correspondence with Amanda, pointing out that the thirty suitable men Amanda had said she had as members of her organisation at the time of Victoria's joining this most illustrious, exclusive, and outrageously expensive company were strangely not forthcoming. This contravened most of the trading laws she could think of, or, colloquially speaking, Amanda and her agency were 'not doing what it said on the tin'. Unacceptable.

Victoria still didn't have a handle on Sam. She had heard absolutely nothing from him, for over two weeks. Most unusual. She guessed that Beth was right after all, and he did have a girlfriend, or she was right, and he thought Victoria was playing around and so, ergo, he could too. Or that Victoria's hairdresser, Andrew, was right, and Sam was bipolar and just plain mad. Definitely, Sam was in the 'Sad Suitor' category whoever was right.

Victoria felt a little uneasy about Tim coming to 'stay' with her, but they had been communicating, if you can call what seemed like a million texts communication, for a couple of months now, so hey-ho, the merry oh.

Nothing ventured, nothing gained.

Victoria texted Tim to confirm Wednesday evening would be fine, and that she would collect him from the station. He texted back to say how he couldn't wait to meet her, and see her beautiful face 'right up close and personal'.

'Strange phrase,' she thought.

She was in London, dining with her ex-business partner, Jonathan. They had known each other for seventeen years, and had had a successful business in PR and Marketing. Jonathan had been in love with Victoria for what seemed like forever, and she loved him as well, but not in the same way. Jonathan was another of the idiots she added to her list. Jonathan was now in his seventies, married and now a preacher come businessman? If ever there could be such a combination? Jonathan had propositioned her when they had met for dinner the previous week.

"Darling you know, I have always loved you." He went to hold her hand across the table.

"Jonathan," she sighed. "You are married. I know that sweetheart and I love you, but..."

"I know, but you know the status of my marriage," said Jonathan.

"Yes, it's called being married."

"Victoria. Let's go away somewhere, and just be together for a while."

"Jonathan. Please. Oh well, let me think about it." She excused herself and headed for the Ladies. Her mobile signalled that she'd received ten messages. She read Tim's first and, oh-oh, there he was mad Sam. Tim's message asked her to call him. So she did.

"Hi Tim. It's Victoria. How are you? How did the audition go today?"

"Hi Victoria, it went well, but you never know with these things they are so subjective. Victoria, I am in this flat and quite frankly it's really not me. It's dirty and bloody cold. I can't find out how to turn the central heating on!"

'What do you want me to do about it?' thought Victoria. "Oh, sorry about that. I don't understand. Why or how? It is your flat so surely..."

"Oh, didn't I say? It belongs to a friend of mine. I am renting from her while she is in the States and I am shocked as to the condition of the place... It's so not me. I am a clean and tidy person. I hate it here. Victoria, let me come home with you tonight."

"Good Lord." Victoria's eyebrows shot up. "We haven't met yet Tim."

"I know, I know, but don't you feel a connection? Meeting is only a formality."

"Mmmm, well I do feel that you are a super guy, but honestly Tim I don't feel comfortable with just meeting you at the station. Apart from that, it will be late. I'll probably catch the seven minutes past eleven, so I won't get in until a quarter to midnight, or thereabouts. No I am sorry, that would mean going straight home with a virtual stranger. Formality or no formality, I'd rather stick to the plan and see you tomorrow. Come around five if you can, and then we can have a lot of time together. We do need to talk and get to know each other better."

"Oh, okay. I guess you are right, but it's so horrible here."

'Ah bless,' she thought. 'Poor man, but too bad. He could always go to a hotel if it was that bad.'

"Got to go Tim. Too rude to keep Jon waiting for too long and the reception in the ladies isn't so good," she giggled.

"I love your laugh, beautiful. See you tomorrow then. Have a good evening."

"Yes, will do. You too. Well, as best you can under the circumstances. Be brave. Good luck for tomorrow. Break a leg, or whatever they say."

"Okay. Thanks. Bye."

She wandered back to Jonathan, who was waiting patiently for her. "Sorry to be so long. One of my suitors needed some attention."

"Mmm. I was going to mention that."

"What?"

"Well, it's what I want to say to you."

"Mmm? Go ahead. What is it?"

"I want you Victoria. You know I've always loved you."

"Has something happened to Katherine?" Katherine was Jonathan's poor, longsuffering wife. Well, she was poor and suffering, only because she was married to Jonathan who, apart from many other faults, was a workaholic. Victoria remembered, when they used to work together, the many late nights and weekends working to deadlines. She was single at the time, but Jonathan had a wife and a family. How he managed to get time to conceive children was always a mystery to her.

"No, nothing has happened to Katy."

"Well, what do you mean then?" She swallowed a mouthful of *foie gras* and savoured it. "Mmmmmmm, this is so good." Victoria looked straight into his eyes. Jonathan's eyes were a little watery. "It's just I miss you so much, and I want to spend more time with 'the most beautiful woman in the world'. A term by which Jonathan had always referred to her. Flattery would always do the trick.

"Jonathan. Of course I can spend more time with you. We could meet in London for dinner once a week. I would like that."

"That's good. But would you like to stay overnight. I always worry about you travelling late at night, and, well, you could be more relaxed. Have breakfast. Arrive a little earlier?" Jonathan's face was all shiny and pink, not at all attractive and he hadn't aged well either.

"Excuse me, if I am being a little dim here, but are you suggesting you would like to sleep with me, err, umm, have sex with me?" She sipped her wine.

"I can't remember when I haven't wanted to kiss you and make love to you darling." He squeezed her hand.

"Oh Jonathan," she sighed. It was a bloody sauce really. Here was yet another man with no mirrors in his house. Why on earth would she want to have an affair with Jonathan, she thought. Even more strange to her was why on earth he would think that she would want to have an affair with him! Madness, utter madness. She knew he didn't mean it as an insult, quite the contrary, she supposed. He probably thought she was getting a great deal. Jonathan wasn't paunchy, but neither did he have a six-pack. Plus, Jonathan had only ever once remembered her birthday.

"Jonathan," she repeated. "We have always been great friends, and you have always respected that, and Katherine. Why spoil that now?"

"It's because I can't bear the thought of not seeing you. One day you will meet someone and then, then I'll lose you forever."

You see Victoria's problem was this: Jonathan was not offering to look after her, marry her, and take care of her. Oh no. He was suggesting that they just 'upped' the relationship, so to speak, so that he could regain the control he once had over her. Victoria had adored him once upon a time, and was in awe of him, but that was a while back, and she deserved to be cared for, and adored in the first instance, not the second. How could Jonathan possibly believe that would be good for her?

Simple. This wasn't about Victoria. It was about Jonathan. Victoria came to learn that men rarely put their loved and desired women before themselves, despite how much they may try to convince otherwise. Depending at what stage the relationship was in, it usually got worse and she'd be lucky if they'd think about her at all.

They reminisced a little more, and laughed quite a lot. Victoria avoided the subject, while Jonathan did his best to reintroduce it.

"I really must be going, dear-heart," she told Jonathan, who was, at that moment, a very happy man. Victoria had never looked so lovely he thought. Her smile was quite infectious.

"I know it's not the last train home, but I'd like to catch the 11:07."

"Yes, yes. Of course. I'll just get the bill." Jonathan turned to attract the attention of the waiter who had been attending them all evening. Jonathan insisted on travelling with her in the taxi to the station. It wasn't far, but, if nothing else, he was forever gallant. He even walked her to the platform to ensure her safety.

On the way home, she thought over what Jonathan had said. Crazy really, better just put it down to good old lust and selfishness. Nothing new there then. Would she ever find this elusive guy she was so keen to meet? She heaved a sigh and fished in her bag for her mobile. A message from Berrie who always, always, wanted her to check in. His text read: 'Just need to know you are safe darling. Your business is your business, but I won't sleep if I don't know you are safe.'

'Hi Babes,' she replied. 'On train, should be home by 11.45; hope your evening was good. Mine was a little different lol.'

Berrie's immediate response was, 'Good thanks. Glad you are fine, let me know when you are indoors.'

'Will do.' She smiled, he was just lovely. She wondered how his children were, as Leo was being a little more than usually naughty at school. She would ask Berrie later. They chatted every night for at least an hour or so. They always had something to say to each other.

She drove onto her driveway, looking forward to her comfy bed and soft warm linen, snuggling up with her two cats. It didn't seem fair really, a hot blooded woman, like Victoria going to bed with her cats. Again!

But that was the deal. She promised herself she would rather stick pins in her eyes than be with the wrong man again. Impossible as her task might be, she was going to keep on 'going', until she dropped, if that was what it took. And anyway she loved her cats. The demands they made upon her were so insignificant to those of her latter day 'life partners'.

She washed and removed her makeup, which she did religiously, and quickly sent Berrie a text. 'Home safe. In bed. Good night and sweet dreams darling.'

'You too lovely lady Xxx'

A few more texts arrived that night from men in the States, Italy, Holland and France as well as the UK.

Chapter 13

Actors Will Be Actors

'I am at the station,' Tim texted her.

Bugger! She was late. She hadn't even left the house as she thought they'd agreed five and it was only a quarter to. She decided not to dress up in the whole razzmatazz this time, but simply in jeans and her favourite t-shirt.

'On my way. Be with you in 15 minutes,' she texted. She knew that she would be longer, but what the hell.

'Where are you?' tetchy Tim demanded.

'Five minutes away,' she texted while at the traffic lights. She was going as fast as the traffic would allow.

'Finally!' Tim thought. It was a fair thought, because it was very cold outside. But there was a coffee shop for goodness sake. She arrived and pulled up beside him. He opened the door and stuck his head through, deliberately staring straight at her. There was a two-second pause, enough time for eyes to transfer to brain.

'Great, she is as she described,' he thought. Followed by a very wide grin. He had a nice smile. Tim got in the car and leant over to kiss her. She moved sideways, and put the car into gear.

"Hi there, how have you been? Sorry to be late. Are you cold?" She put the heating up to full. The poor lamb did look a little frozen.

"Yes. I've been there for over half an hour."

"Why didn't you go into the coffee shop?"

"You said you were going to be fifteen minutes."

"Yes, so? Fifteen minutes *is* enough time to get a coffee and at least be warm." 'Our first row,' she thought, and laughed a little.

"I don't think it's funny," Tim growled.

"No, no, neither do I. I wasn't laughing at you and the cold, I just thought, oh well, never mind. Let's get you home, and have a drink by the fire." 'Sod him,' she thought.

"Now, that sounds more like it." He settled himself down in the seat of the car.

"The journey okay though?" she asked.

"Yes, great thanks. You were right. That high speed train is something else. And what did you tell me? You can get to Paris in less than two hours?"

"Yep, there or thereabouts. Good, isn't it?"

"Fantastic. It takes longer for me to get to London from Edinburgh. I like this village. Very pretty. Oh yes, I could happily live here." Tim's head was dodging all over the place, looking at the buildings on either side of the village's high street.

Happy living here? Hold on. Blimey this guy doesn't hang about. Good. He doesn't have an overnight bag, so he is expecting to go home. 'Thank goodness for that,' she thought, feeling relieved.

"Yes, it is a very lovely village. It only took me fourteen years of living here to be accepted." She gave him a big smile and thought, 'Take the bones out of that one, sweetie pie.'

She opened the door, walked into the hallway, and made way for Tim to follow her into the house. He moved ahead of her, into the open lounge and dining room.

"Very nice. Oh yes, this is very nice." He was taking his beaten-up old coat off and staring all around, up and down the room. Taking everything in, seemingly making a mental inventory.

Victoria draped her Shearling coat over the banisters. "Thank you. Yes, I like it. Pity you can't see the view I was telling you about but never mind."

"I can wait. I'll see it in the morning though," said Tim as he took off his student style scarf, warming his hands by the fire. "This is beautiful." Tim was admiring the enormous designer glass fireplace.

'See it in the morning?' she thought, walking towards the kitchen. 'See it in the morning!? The cheeky beggar!' Although she did think he was going to stay overnight. Just strange he hadn't brought a bag.

"Drink? Coffee? Glass of wine?" she called. Tim was still admiring the room, furnishings and especially the audio-visual kit. All Bang and Olufsen, he observed. Amazing cream sofas lined the walls of what he assumed was the TV area, largely because the TV was there.

"Have you any red?" he replied, almost skipping down the light oak polished steps into the kitchen.

"Yes. No problem. Is a Merlot okay?" She turned to the fridge, where a wine-rack had been created down the sides of the built-in pantry, and a huge American fridge. "Would you be a honey and get some wood? Sorry sweetie, I should have asked you before you took off your coat."

"No worries, I'd be glad to. Where is it?"

"Straight through the utility room, around the back, over by the tack room. I'll put the lights on for you. You will find the wheelbarrow just outside, and the wood inside," she laughed. He was cute and really quite good looking, even if he was the pushiest guy she had ever met.

Maybe he was just positive and outspoken. There's nothing wrong with that.

"Wait until I tell my mum about this," he said as he opened the utility room door.

Tell his mother? Tell his mother what? Why tell his mother at all? He was thirty-eight years old for heaven's sake, she thought as she opened the wine and poured it into the crystal glasses, the dark, ruby red liquid swirling around the glass as she did so.

Tim was back, but without the wood. "I'm sorry, I couldn't find the building you said where the wood is stored." He sounded sheepish. Well, at least he could be modest in some ways.

"Come on. I'll show you." She led the way outside. Bloody hell, it was freezing. "Quickly, it's around here. Brrrrr! This is really cold, I'll help you."

"I suppose this is where your husband comes out and ties me to the stable door." He gave a very nervous giggle.

"What? Oh yes, I see what you mean. But it's me that is supposed to be frightened of you. You could be a mad axe murderer." Victoria opened the old barn door, switched on the light, and pointed to the wood.

"Quick, its freezing. If we stay too long, we will be frozen to the floor."

"No, it's okay you go. I can do this." He gently pushed her toward the main house. "Go on. You're right, it's freezing. You'll catch your death."

"Okay. Only if you're sure." She didn't wait to be told again.

Victoria raced back into the house and immediately put a few more logs on the fire. He was really nice. Maybe she should put aside her suspicious feelings. Just a few days before Victoria had mentioned to Beth that she'd had the feeling that Tim was one of 'Those', the 'Predatory Piggies'. Albeit a handsome piggy, nevertheless, she had an idea Tim was looking for someone to fund him on his road to fame.

"But, for now, let's give him the benefit of the doubt, and enjoy the evening," she mused as she returned to the kitchen.

"Hi, where do I put these?" Tim was standing there hugging some logs, dirt streaked across his cheek. His dark brown hair framing his handsome face. The light caught his emerald green eyes and they sparkled just like jewels. His smile was white and wide. The sight of him stopped Victoria in her tracks.

"In the log basket near the fire. You can't miss it."

"Brrrr. Bloody freezing, won't be long and I'll be with you." He walked carrying the heavy logs, but still managed an attractive gait, which matched a very attractive bottom. His very tight jeans accented the round firmness of his buttocks.

'Hmmm nice arse,' she thought, as her gaze followed him into the lounge. And he was willing to help.

After Tim finished unloading the logs, he returned to the kitchen, his face all aglow, and smiling from ear to ear.

"Here, you deserve this." She handed him a glass of red wine. Tim took it from her, looking her straight in the eye.

"Cheers, to us." He chinked her glass as they drank to each other.

Victoria was feeling very high indeed. Could Tim be 'the one'? He was very charming, and handsome, with a very fit body. The night was young, and she thought it had all the makings of a good one. They continued chatting in the kitchen. She felt very comfortable and relaxed. They talked about their dating experiences.

"You are not the only one with mishaps you know," Tim laughed. "Your gender is also a nightmare." He drank the rest of his wine, and asked if he might pour some more for them both.

"Of course. Go ahead. Shall we eat about seven o'clock? There's a great Thai restaurant at the bottom of the road." Victoria was getting quite caught up on him.

"Yes, that sounds fab. I love Thai cooking, not bad at it myself either. I love to cook." He poured them some more wine.

"Go on then. Tell me some of your experiences." The atmosphere between them was charged. Laughing, smiling, gesturing towards one another, Victoria read his body language, and couldn't help having a little nagging feeling at the back of her head.

Mmmm. He seemed a little affected. Too much. But what the hell. Would I prefer some stiff cardboard cut-out? No, so just enjoy, she told herself.

"Well, let me see," Tim began to tell his story. "There was this woman, Anita. She sent me her photos and yeah she was a pretty and slim lady. We talked." Tim paused.

Victoria immediately thought, 'I bet you just used text ha ha. But don't pick,' she silently admonished herself.

"Well, and, then we decided to meet. It was quite a shock." Tim's head was cocked to one side, and he was smiling, eyebrows raised.

Victoria couldn't help but giggle to herself. "I am dying of curiosity. Did she have one leg?" Victoria had heard this before from David, one of the few 'dates' whom she had befriended.

"No, not that, but she could have had one or two hidden up her dress, and no one would have noticed." They burst into laughter.

"What?"

"She had told me she was a size ten, and she certainly looked in the photo, but she was at least size eighteen or twenty."

"No! Good Lord. What is all that about?" Victoria shook her head recalling Oliver and John the pig.

"Yes, right."

"So, what happened?"

"She said to me. You are disappointed aren't you? Well, I told her 'Yes, of course I am.' I asked her why she had done that, and had she done it before? You know, misrepresenting herself. She said that she had, but I was welcome to go back to her place to stay the night."

"What? No, I don't believe you. She said what?"

"Honestly. Straight up. She just stood there and said it was okay if it was only one night and that she was very good with her mouth."

Victoria almost spat out her wine. She held her hand across her mouth. "Get out of here." She just could not believe it, but he did seem to be telling it like it was. "Did you take up the offer?" Now, she looked Tim straight in the eye.

"No way! Not my scene." He finished his wine, head right back, and then put his glass on the kitchen counter. Somehow, Victoria didn't quite believe that final part of the story.

"Are you sure?" Victoria was really perplexed at this little story. It didn't seem to make sense.

"Yes, thank you Ma'am. I did not accept the lady's offer."

"No. I don't mean that, I mean are you sure she said that?"

"Of course I am."

"But why? I mean it's so degrading. It doesn't make sense."

"Oh yeah, sweet angel. Not all women are like you, you know. She just wanted to be fucked."

"And you didn't err, umm, err, want to then?" Victoria's head was tilted to one side with her chin resting on her hand, her full lips pouting at him. She knew she was taunting him, but couldn't help, challenging him.

"No, I didn't." Tim lowered his head and walked over to her. He took her glass from her and placed it on the counter next to his.

"Come on. I'm hungry. Let's go eat." He put his arms around her and turned her toward the kitchen door.

"Okay, Okay. I'm hungry too. Let's go."

Chapter 14

The Show Must Go On

The sweet, tiny Thai lady led them to a table. The restaurant was brightly lit and very colourful, with every single shade of yellow and orange you could think of.

"This is nice," Tim said sitting down.

"Yes, I like it. The food is good and the staff are excellent. I'd like to take her home in my handbag." She gave him a big smile, pointing to the waitress, and now Victoria's bright blue eyes were sparkling up at Tim.

"Oh, you aren't like that, are you?" his eyes were wide and inquisitive.

"Pardon, like what?" Victoria didn't get it.

"Do you like women as well?"

"Oh, oh yeah. No, I mean no, right yes of course. Sorry forgetting... you don't really know me, do you?" She was shaking her head, as she pulled the seat closer to the table.

"No. I don't like women in that way. Sorry to disappoint you. I do like and admire women though. I think we are all quite marvellous creatures." She stroked his fingers with her long nails.

"Well, I don't think they are all marvellous as you say, but certainly there are several of them out there."

Victoria was waiting for the obvious. You know something like especially the one in this room. Something like that, anything like that. But it didn't come. In fact Victoria couldn't recall if Tim ever did pay her a compliment. But what he did do, was spill his rather tatty and tawdry life story to her and mention several times all of the beautiful and stunning girlfriends he had been out with.

If only Victoria had a pound for every man who told her about all the stunning women they had either dated, married, lived with or met, she would have been a very wealthy woman indeed. A psychiatrist friend told her once, after she had complained about this habit men had with her, that it was a man's way of bringing control to a situation where he felt he had no control. It was his way of saying, 'You are beautiful, but I am not going to tell you up front, I want to let you know that I am desirable, so you must desire me too, like so many other beautiful women have and do.'

It did make some sense and certainly applied to Tim. God, he did go on. It was rare, but Victoria could hardly get a word in edgeways. She was amazed he managed to eat anything at all. But, apart from the chest- baring tales, his slight Scottish brogue was lovely to listen to.

"So, there you have it. My life story in a nutshell."

"Thank you. Interesting and thanks for your honesty," Victoria said, although she couldn't have meant it less. There was still that nagging feeling, but this time combined with a feeling like she had just been run over. Tim had quite exhausted her and she had hardly said more than a handful of words.

"That's no problem Victoria." Tim reached over, and held her hand. "I am honest, and I want to be totally honest with you, as we build our life together."

What! Whoa there buddy.

"Pardon, Tim?" Victoria's brow was all furrowed up and she crinkled her nose.

"I am fully committed to you." He smiled and brought his other hand over to cover hers.

She was really taken aback. What on earth had she got here, but decided to drop the subject, even though it gave her the creeps.

After all, this is what she wanted, a handsome, sensitive, honest guy to take care of, love and cherish her. Screech! Halt the show. 'Take care', that was the bit that was missing. Tim told her that, *if* he got the job, one of the commercials, it would be worth £70,000. Victoria suspected Tim may have been out of work for some time. She also strongly suspected Tim was looking for someone to care for him and he had found Victoria.

Hmmm. Still not absolutely sure, but nag, nag, nag.

Tim called for the bill, and they left smiling, arm in arm.

Once back at Victoria's home, Tim immediately went to the kitchen and opened another bottle of wine. Victoria was quite put out, and surprised. "Oh well, I'll put another log on the fire then," she called after him.

"Yes, that would be great. Be with you in a minute."

"Make yourself at home Tim," she mumbled to herself, putting three logs on the fire before taking off her coat.

They settled by the fire together.

"Do you mind if I have a cigarette? Only I noticed a pack of ciggies in the kitchen."

"No, not at all. Yes, I have the odd one every now and then. Help yourself." 'You have so far,' she thought. "The ashtray is in the kitchen."

Tim trooped off, happy as Larry. He thought all his birthdays and Christmases had come at once. Not only was Victoria beautiful, she had a fabulous body and Bingo! She was rich. He could become famous after all. He had so much talent, but the entertainment world was so competitive. He had just had a run of bad luck lately. How dare they say that he was too old. It was only a fucking car commercial for God's sake!

But never mind all that now. At last, he could be supported until he was rich and famous. Victoria seemed such a nice lady as well, unlike that fat old bag. Christ! Fancy having to fuck her and the things she made him do. Okay, so she was loaded, but her breath smelt of old cabbages as well as having to fight his way to her pussy. Yuk! It made him feel sick just to think of it. Oh boy! Oh yes, this was the jackpot, and she obviously fancied him. 'I'll check out the old bird in Stockholm though before I make my mind up for good, but even going on the premise of tonight and after I fuck her she will be mine, and I shall be hers. Divine. But I have bought tickets for Stockholm and the photo of Tatiana's pad did look like something else. Even so, Victoria's place is spectacular and I haven't seen the view yet. Oh I could be so happy here.' Tim skipped back to the lounge and offered Victoria a cigarette.

"Like one?" he lit a cigarette and offered it to her.

"No thanks, not right now. Come and sit down."

"You know you are very beautiful and look great for your age?" He leaned into her.

'So this is where the statement "in your face" comes from,' she thought. 'It's literal.' Victoria moved back a little and settled into the warm soft leather of the sofa.

"Thank you, and you are a very attractive man." She proffered her glass for a toast.

"To us," she said and immediately regretted it.

"Victoria, darling. I don't wish to embarrass you, but you know I'm in the business. Have you had any work done?" He was almost in her lap.

'Pardon?' she thought. Bloody cheek. 'Actually no, but I have been toying with the idea of botox, though the thought of injecting poison put's me off.' "No I haven't had any work. What makes you think that?" She was peeved.

"Well it's just that I've never seen anyone of your age look so good."

"Well! Thank you for nothing. I am a great believer in exercise, vitamins and at least a bottle of wine a day, if that's any good to you."

"Shush darling, take it as a compliment."

'Mmmm, backhanded one and that's the only one he had given to her,' she thought, but she said instead, "Okay. Thank you sugar."

Victoria then proceeded to rev up the complete and utter bollocks they were talking about until Tim said it was three in the morning, he really was tired, and had another audition the next day.

'Fair do's, I can only drivel on for so long,' thought Victoria. "Here is your room." She opened the door and Tim walked right past her.

"Oh no, this is my room." He made straight for Victoria's room and waltzed through the door.

"Err, um. No. No! I mean it. Tim, this is your room." Victoria went into her room and was pointing to the spare room. Too late. Tim had taken his shirt off, and oh well, the wine, the cold, the body, the smile, the body.

"Come here, baby doll." He held out his arms after back flipping onto the bed. Victoria capitulated and fell on the bed alongside him. He rolled over onto her and kissed her long and deeply, then started to undress her, mumbling little pleasure sounds as he did so. Oh well, this wasn't so bad. She writhed underneath him. Mmmm and such a good kisser.

Then Victoria woke from her revelry. "Uh Tim." She lifted herself onto her elbows, her long blonde hair swinging loose behind her.

"Hmmm, yes baby." Tim stopped sucking her nipples, gave a last lick and looked up at her.

"Hate to mention it but …condoms? Have you any condoms?"

"Why, is there something wrong with you?"

"Wrong? No, nothing wrong. I just haven't had sex for two years or so." she'd decided that Alfred didn't count.

"Well then that's fine then. I am fine and no, I don't have condoms because I don't need them."

"Erm!" she heard Beth's words ringing in her ears. It's not that you are just having sex with them, but you're having sex with all their other partners as well. Yeeeoow! Gross, but Victoria guessed she was right. However, she didn't have any condoms either and they were both naked now. Tim was kissing her neck and whispering for her to relax.

"Come on baby, come to me." He was rock hard and using his cock to masturbate her. He stopped almost as fast as he started and traced his tongue all the way up her side, and over her breasts, squeezing them hard. He nuzzled her neck and whispered to her, "Take him in your mouth hun. Give me a good sucking."

Whaaaatt! Now she was alarmed. Her very first, well maybe second lover had told her, 'Victoria, women are always willing and too quick to give men oral sex. Don't do it honey. Make sure they are willing and able to give you what they want for themselves first. Men just assume women are going to do that for them, no matter what. So don't do it, until they have pleasured you first.'

Victoria had always remembered that and thought it great advice. She had always had great lovers who gained more pleasure from pleasing her, rather than the other way around. So she stuck to the rule and ignored him. It didn't seem to matter and Tim carried on regardless. He turned out to be a pretty ordinary man in the sack. A bit disappointing, but Victoria thought she could get him right and, well, the Alfreds of this world don't grow on trees.

They fell asleep, but didn't curl up or spoon each other. Come the morning, Victoria washed off all of her makeup whilst Tim was still sleeping. She was never a fan of the 'panda' look. It had taken almost three months before she had allowed Matthew her first partner to see her *sans maquillage*, but she didn't care what Tim thought. She only wanted him out of the house.

She crept back to bed.

"What you doing?" Tim moved his arm over her back and gently massaged her shoulders. "MMmm, baby, you okay?"

"Yep. Sure thing." Victoria rolled around, and put her arms around him. Tim kissed her lightly on the lips.

Tim started to make love to her, but she wasn't too keen. Not only was it because of the two builders who were banging about the place, things hadn't finished in the loft conversion. That was not conducive to mad, passionate sex, or any kind of sex really, but also because she really didn't want him to. Well, not based on last night's performance anyway.

"Let's get you on the train so you are not late for your audition."

"But it's not until two this afternoon."

Tim did have a beautiful body. A very hard chest, a muscular back, and a fantastic bum, but Victoria didn't feel right about it, especially with the builders going up and down the stairs.

"Oh right, but well, Jeez hun, the guys going up and down the stairs, I know they won't come in the room, but… sorry, honey it just puts me off." She gave him a long and soft kiss.

"Yeah, see what you mean. Let's just lie here for a while then." He pulled her to him and she dropped down by his side. His arm was under her neck. She wasn't that happy about that either, but didn't want to be rude to him.

Tim began to stroke behind her ears. Victoria didn't like the sensation and also thought it a strange action. Stroking her breasts, buttocks, yes, but behind her ears? Odd.

All of a sudden it struck her. The toe rag was feeling for scars, to see if she'd had a face lift. What a fucking cheek!

"I am going to get up." She raised herself, leaning on his torso. "Hey look at me, no makeup. You are seeing me in the raw. Totally." She laughed and lightly kissed his nose.

"I noticed. I think you look younger than ever."

Victoria leapt out of bed and went to the bathroom. Her sanctuary. It was so feminine. It always smelt so good. She had fond memories of the art student who painted the murals. The head and shoulders of a man and a woman looking into each other's eyes. They almost seemed to be alive. The connection between the two of them was depicted very strongly. The student was in love at the time and he expressed it ingeniously in his paintings.

"Alright, I can take a hint. Okay if I take a shower?"

"Sure, help yourself. Here. Have some towels." She gave him a warm, fluffy, black bath sheet and bath towel. She looked him up and down. Nice. No doubt about it, but something's missing and he said he liked oral sex. When he said that he did, she hadn't thought he meant just for him.

"Hi sweetie." Tim came into her bathroom, one towel wrapped around his waist while drying his hair with the other. He grabbed her waist, his arms were muscly. Tim was over 6' 4 and only weighed in about eleven stone. He was in really in good shape. His hands quickly found her bum and he held her buttocks tightly.

"Mmm. You have such a great bottom," he said and kissed her. It did feel good. His hard chest against her soft, firm breasts.

"So, I'll cook for us this evening then?" Tim was nuzzling her neck again.

What? Oh no. She was seeing Berrie and then Christopher the criminal lawyer and Pocket Prince over the weekend. Tim obviously thought that he had his feet well and truly under the table. Outrageous really, as they hadn't discussed anything about finances and contributions. Actually, hadn't discussed anything that was important and now he was inviting himself everywhere.

"Umm. No. I am afraid not. I have made arrangements to see Berrie. You know. The friend I told you about." She left his grasp and stepped back against the basin.

"What? What? Are you sure this Berrie, this Berrie person, whoever he is, isn't your lover?" It was almost a snarl. His eyes were slits and his top lip curled upwards.

"No. No. I have explained Berrie to you. He is a great friend of mine. He is a good man and we are close as friends, nothing else I can assure you. Berrie is his own man and we are just friends. So back off." She gave him a slight push on his shoulder.

Tim seemed about to push her back, but instantly relaxed and leaned his hand on the bathroom wall. "Alright, alright. Just that you seem to think a lot of this man. Too much Maybe?" He was smiling and cupped her arm with his other hand. He gave it a gentle squeeze.

Victoria felt very uncomfortable. "I have explained to you and so can we drop it now? Your train leaves in forty minutes. Is that okay for you?"

"Yes sure. That's fine. Have you any deodorant? Hair gel? Tooth brush? Shaver?"

"No. No and then there's no. I live here alone. That's by myself, except when my daughter comes home from school. Why would I have those things here? Why didn't you bring an overnight bag?"

"Not even deodorant? I didn't want to appear presumptuous."

'Presumptuous! Jeez that's rich coming from him. He has been nothing but. Oh well,' she thought. 'Just get him on that train.'

"No, not even deodorant. I don't sweat," she said turning her nose up in the air. But she thought she might have a spare toothbrush and said so whilst she was ferreting through her cupboards.

"Okay. May I use some of your moisturiser then?" He popped a kiss on her naked shoulder.

He was really beginning to irritate her now. He was in her space, her inner sanctum, her bathroom. She had already told him where his bathroom was, which he'd simply ignored. Once she had found a toothbrush, she walked down to the guest bathroom, moving agilely down the glass staircase holding out the toothbrush as if it were bait. "Here is your toothbrush, and moisturiser, and your bath." she left both items on the shelf and returned to her bathroom, Tim passed her on the way down.

"Thanks sweetie."

'Mmm. What a pity he has to go. Nice looking guy, but!' she thought, brushing her teeth.

Finally, they were in the car on the way to the station. Tim started to talk about sex and his stunning ex-girlfriends.

'Here we go again,' she thought, raising her eyes to the roof of the car. He rambled on about how one was a tiny, beautiful girl with 32F size boobs, but had no interest in sex. For example, she would say to him things like, 'Would you like to have sex this evening?' Just like, 'Would you like pizza, or chicken tonight?' Not very sexy hey? She was a walking Trades Description Act.

'Do I really need to know this?' Victoria thought, praying they would get to the station on time.

"Sex with us was great, don't you think?" He didn't even look at her. She didn't even think he wanted an answer, so she left it as rhetorical, brushed her hair behind her ears, and then thought, 'What the hell. This guy has been bamboozling me since he arrived.'

"Well you did say you liked oral sex. Is that just a one way ticket?" She turned briefly to look at him. He was all huddled up in his seat. His scruffy scarf was wrapped around his neck and tucked into his coat. He looked like a student, or what he really was, an out of work actor.

"I love oral sex." He straightened up in his seat. "I love giving oral, just love it." He sounded amazed that she should ask such a thing.

"Oh, okay. That's great then," Victoria responded, but thought, 'Yeah right, love it, except with me, or actually not really interested. In that case why didn't you even attempt it with me last night?' she mused.

"Mmm. Here we are." She pulled into the station drop-off point. "I hope the journey is good."

"Yes, right I'll text you later." He leaned over to kiss her.

"Bye-bye honey. Mwah."

Tim walked off toward the ticket gates. Victoria drove off. She didn't wave goodbye or look back at him. She just gave a deep and heavy sigh. Oh well, it was worth a try. I just can't get the feeling out of my head that he is looking for a fund provider and I just can't go there again. I promised myself and I am sticking to it.

Tim texted her to say he was on the train and he would call her that evening. He had texted to say he would call before and had never done so. Tim was sitting on the high speed train to London, looking out of the window and thinking.

Well, she won't see me this evening and it doesn't look like she is the walkover I first thought. Actually I rather like her, but can't let an opportunity go if I can't button her down. So, Titania here I come. She had better pay me back the air fare as she said she would. Mmmm. I really liked being with Victoria though, and she has such a sweet, soft, very sexy body. But those tits and lips aren't hers. Who does she think she's trying to fool? It will serve her right if Titania gets me.

Chapter 15

Good Things Come in Small Packages

When Victoria arrived home, she picked up her mobile to answer the many texts she had received over the past thirty-six hours. Let's see. Ah! Pocket Prince with his usual, lengthy text of perhaps a hundred or more words, together with his outlook on life.

Victoria had met Charlie about two weeks ago now. They had been calling and texting each other for over three months. Charlie was different. Very, very different. He was the straightest gangster ever. By default, Charlie owned a club, as somebody who had owed him a lot of money couldn't repay. So instead, they just gave him a club in lieu. He ran a strip club and a weekend black, jazz, comedy club with his partner, Jameel. This was uncharted territory for Victoria. But she was fascinated.

She knew that Charlie was no Brad Pitt, but he was intelligent and didn't play games. He knew who he was and what he wanted. He had a rather disparaging view, not unlike herself, of the 'dating scene'. He had said a few times that most of the women who had contacted him, or whom he had contacted, as he had Victoria, were nothing but 'Broken Biscuits' or 'Hos'. Although Victoria had heard that quite a few dating sites were being used for those purposes, she thought that it wasn't any of her business, just like all of the other strange sites available.

They never discussed whether, or not he had met anybody else, but it took a long time for him to eventually meet Victoria. He was something of an enigma to her.

When Victoria answered the door to Charlie, she missed him by a foot or so, as at first, she'd looked directly in front of her, and then, not seeing anybody, she looked down. She had only seen a head and shoulders photo of him and, as their communication had been more cerebral than physical, they had not discussed their respective attributes, or indeed how tall or short he was.

Charlie had been aware of how Victoria had looked from the very beginning, as she had posted three photos of herself alongside her profile. Charlie had been very attracted to Victoria and became more and more so through their dialogue. He had a philosophical opinion on almost everything to do with human behaviour. He was an archetypal 'honour amongst thieves' type. At first, Victoria thought the whole gangster stuff was just an exaggeration. Just because one owns a strip club doesn't mean to say one is a hooligan. Does It?

"Oh Hi. Hi Charlie. Come in." She moved away from the door to let him in.

Charlie was about 5'6, slim and neatly put together, wearing one of the 'gayest' shirts she had ever seen.

Victoria was wearing her high heels which made her about 5'10. Charlie didn't even notice, or he certainly paid it no attention whatsoever, as he moved through the hallway.

"Thanks. Good to see you."

"Yes. It's been a long time in the making. I'll just get my coat and then shall we go?"

"Fine by me."

"You found me okay then? The directions were good?"

"Yeah great, and I have satnav anyway. Nice place." Well, at least he wasn't chewing gum and didn't have a New York accent. He spoke very well and had a gentle aura. Maybe an 'iron fist in a velvet glove'. Anyway, Victoria was fond of him already from the way he expressed himself in his texts, even if his opinion of the human race was very, very low indeed. Charlie was a moralistic gangster.

"Is the local pub okay? It's not far and the food is good."

"Absolutely fine."

His car was parked already to go. Usually, people who parked in the driveway had to turn around. Charlie had the forethought to do this, prior to knocking at the door. His car was enormous. A huge black Audi something or other. Convertible.

Victoria didn't think that he would open the door for her, which was just as well, because he didn't. Although later, when she asked him why he didn't, he answered, "Never met anyone that deserved it." Ever since, though, Charlie always opened the door of anything for her.

They sat at the bar, Charlie's eyes were round and shining, his pupils so big it made him seem as though he had black eyes. Charlie was in his element just sitting next to Victoria. He hadn't been able to get her out of his mind. He loved the way she talked with him. He loved the fact she was intelligent and articulate, and now he loved the way she had obviously told the truth about her looks. She had posted photos of herself as herself, and as she really looked as well as her house.

Charlie was totally smitten.

Victoria thought it was charming that this 'hard nut', little man who couldn't have weighed any more than nine stones, was sitting by her all dewy eyed and full of attention. The thought that they didn't exactly look like the perfect couple never crossed his mind. Charlie had more confidence than a river full of piranhas watching a horse drink at the water's edge.

Victoria was enjoying herself just hearing Charlie's stories about how his wife was a no good bitch, and after fifteen years of being suppressed by her, he had finally left. Victoria couldn't believe anybody could suppress Charlie, albeit most people thought the same about Victoria, and look at what had happened to her.

They were sitting in the restaurant now, and after having ordered, she asked him, "Why did you leave her? Another woman. Another man?"

"No. I just woke up one day and thought, I can't do this anymore. I don't love her, I don't think I ever loved her so, I thought, that's it, she can't manipulate me anymore, she's going."

"Pardon?" Victoria almost choked on her bread. "She's going?"

"Yes, that's right. She was always threatening to go. Old bag never did a day's work in her life. I provided everything."

'I know that feeling,' thought Victoria.

"So, I thought. Fuck her! The night before, she had left and gone to stay with her sister. Left the kids with me." Charlie had a son and daughter aged twelve and fourteen, respectively. "So that was it. I told her to come back, pack her stuff, and fuck off." Charlie took a mouthful of bread, and dutifully tasted the wine the waitress had poured for him.

"Just like that, after sixteen years?" Victoria marvelled.

"Yep. Just like that. She didn't believe me either. Cheers." Charlie picked up his glass and saluted her with it.

"Cheers," she responded, smiling. Victoria really liked her 'Pocket Prince'.

They chatted and laughed throughout their meal, obviously enjoying each other's company. Charlie had a little rat-like face, which Victoria came to find endearing but he was an interesting guy. They returned to Victoria's home and she invited him in for coffee.

"I'm not really much into coffee, thanks. But I would like to spend more time with you."

"That's fine by me." Victoria made to get out of the car.

Charlie gently touched her arm. "No wait. Please," Charlie opened his door, and whisked around to the other side of the car and opened the passenger door. Victoria was very happy to give Charlie her hand and stepped elegantly out of the car with his assistance.

"Thank you Charlie. Charmed, I am sure," she giggled and wiggled toward the front door.

She opened a bottle of Chablis and brought two glasses into the lounge where Charlie was sitting very much at home. Not in the arrogant way of Tim, but comfortable and easy. Charlie had a lovely aura about him.

"Here we are Charlie," she put the glasses and wine bottle on the thickly cut, glass coffee table.

"Thanks. Don't mind if I do. Your place is really nice Victoria. Really nice. Very tasteful. Did you bring in a designer?"

"No, I did it. It was a nightmare I have to say and wouldn't like to repeat the performance. The tales I could tell you about builders, and plumbers, and electricians and, and, and, the story goes on and on. No. I won't bore you with that, but thanks. I am glad you like it. It turned out well in the end. I am now an expert plumber and electrician, plus not a bad builder either. So, if you ever consider embarking on a mad adventure like an extension or bulldozing down your house, talk to me first." She beamed at him, and returned to the kitchen for her coffee.

They sat on the sofa almost all night and just talked non-stop, exchanging views from the running of a strip club, to the pros and cons of living like a gypsy, as Charlie had once done, and the benefits of anarchy, which Charlie largely approved of, not being that keen on authority. Well, starting out on life as a car radio thief didn't bring with it a respect for the law, particularly as Charlie said he had been a very successful one. Charlie still had the gypsy in him and a romantic one at that.

"Come away with me Victoria. I want to just grab a caravan and set off around the world." Charlie leant over to kiss her. He was so gentle. His lips were as soft as rose petals, and tasted of the wine. "You are so beautiful Victoria, so very beautiful. Your lips are soft and your eyes bright and kind. I love being with you." Charlie looked straight into her eyes, held her hand, and kissed her again.

This was no small praise coming from Charlie. His world was tough, 'dog, eat dog'. Compliments didn't come easily. More like a knuckle ringed fist between the eyes, than a bunch of flowers.

"Thank you Charlie. I like being with you too, but it's almost morning. I think you had better go. What time are you collecting your children?" She looked at her watch; it was four thirty and just beginning to get light. Apart from anything else, she was beginning to flag and further, even though she didn't think that Charlie would make the move to go to bed with her, he was a man and well it just seemed appropriate.

"Mmm. Yes, it's time to go, although I really don't want to. You are such good company." The sun was coming up now the faint light filled the room, Charlie did look like a rat. Oh well, she had nothing against rats, or rodents per se and it's said that rats are pretty intelligent creatures. Charlie was a gentleman and a bit of a scholar to boot. Something which Victoria found very attractive.

"Okay, let's make a move." Charlie got up from the sofa and helped Victoria up. She was only an inch or so taller than him in her stocking feet. He pulled her to him and pressed his lips to her cheek.

"Parting is such sweet sorrow," he whispered to her.

Shakespeare, hey? How about if 'Pocket Prince' turns out to be a Shakespeare quoting, gun-toting gangster.

"Yes it is, but getting some sleep seems a happier alternative to me at the moment. And you too, my little vampire."

Charlie's day was everyone else's night. He rarely got to bed before 4 a.m. So really Charlie was less of a rat and more like a bat.

"Well. I'll get an hour or two's sleep, before I collect the kids from her." Charlie lived about two hours' drive away.

"Come on then. Let me see you to the door," said Victoria. She opened the door for him.

He moved out to the porch, turned back to her and said, "Thanks for a lovely time. Well more than lovely, really. I didn't think I would ever meet anybody like you."

"You are pretty unusual for me too." She put her arms around his neck and planted a tiny kiss on the tip of his nose, she wrinkled up her nose, kissed him again, but this time on the lips.

"Bye-bye, sweet prince. Text me that you are safely home. Have a nice day."

"Will do. Probably go back to bed once I've taken the kids to school." He wandered over to the car, lit a cigarette, took a deep drag, opened the door, got in, and drove off. All in what appeared to be one movement. Seamless.

'Kids to school?' She thought, closing the door and yawning loudly. 'Why isn't their mother taking them?'

Victoria checked that all the lights were out and doors safely locked. She took the glass and debris of the night back into the kitchen and headed straight for her bed.

She said to herself, "I don't think I can take my makeup off. Sorry skin. I'll go to Fiona's for a special facial to make up for it. Okay?" Her skin didn't reply. It just felt sluggish and heavy. She stripped quickly, glancing at her shapely body in the mirror wardrobes, and flopped into bed. Thank God. No builders, or men tomorrow, well today, as it's morning. She closed her eyes and fell immediately into a deep, contented slumber.

Chapter 16

Trains Will Never Be The Same Again

Victoria woke up with her two cats wrapped around each side of her head like mufflers.

"Oh Leander, and you Lady, for goodness sake!" She moved and shoved her furry babies further down the bed. She got up and went downstairs taking each step carefully as she went. After making herself a cup of coffee, she went into what had now become her morning ritual.

Twenty messages on her mobile. Her own personal *army d'amour* were already on the march.

Oh look. One from Tim.

'Hi baby, off to Stockholm. Be back Tuesday, so coming to see you Wednesday and Thursday. Will book flights. Let you know when to pick me up xxxxxx.'

What a bloody cheek that guy had. Let's see, what am I doing Wednesday and Thursday? Mmm, nothing. Oh well, maybe I've got him completely wrong. He is just being positive, and going to Stockholm must mean he's there for a shoot, so he is earning money. I shouldn't be suspicious of everyone, should I?

Maybe she shouldn't, but she should by now have been learning to take notice of her instincts. So she texted him back.

'That's great. Take care and have a safe trip. Text me when you get there. I'd like to know you are safe xxxx.'

"Oh well, he does seem to be trying. I can't be like ice all the time," she said to herself. This really was contradictory. She'd met a guy once. He'd taken her out, explaining how well he would fit into her home and village. He'd further expressed in no uncertain terms how well he would get on with Emmaline and was absolutely certain Emmy would like him. Then he'd insisted on sleeping with her. Okay, true he didn't exactly force the situation, but then mediocre sex. She'd taken him to the station, dying to see the back of him because of his arrogant attitude. She had hardly been the 'ice maiden'. Perhaps it would be better if she really was like ice with him, instead of responding to him.

A text from Pocket Prince and one from Anthony, another man with no mirrors in his house. He constantly bombarded her with texts. She had met him at the Dorchester. He'd been nothing like his photo. Pleasant enough, but so un-kissable, although Anthony was the only person who thought he was.

Charlie was asking to see her at the coming weekend. She texted back to say she would love that. She had suffered selective amnesia about her new 'boyfriend', Tim.

Oliver, a Dutch International lawyer, texted his usual. 'Can't wait to see you… long soft kisses baby.' She texted back to say she couldn't wait to see him either. Actually, Oliver was down as one of her 'hopefuls', along with Simon. He was very, very hopeful. They had had long chats almost every evening. Simon was a 'talker', which as everybody knows is a good sign. He was tall, 6'5, good looking - well if that was a recent photo. He lived in Oxford, and hopefully he didn't know Sam. He was a 'gentleman farmer' and had two grown up sons. He was extremely interesting to talk to and was taking her out to lunch next Tuesday. He had no problem whatsoever with driving down to meet her. Talking of driving problems, there was a text from Sam.

"Hi gorgeous. How are you? I love you. Let's get married."

She had to read that one twice. 'Good Lord. Really. Totally mad,' she thought.

Scrolling down, she came to Christopher. Ah, Christopher. 'Hi babes, I can't wait to see you. Let me know when's a good time xxxx.'

She replied. 'Next Wednesday lunch okay? Will you collect me from home xxx.'

'It's a date. Look forward sweet lady. I have court at 12:30 near you xxxx.'

She hadn't seen a photo of Christopher, but had a good feeling about him.

Irish Arnold had also texted. 'Hi Victoria will call you this evening. Keep safe xxxx.' She had hopes for Arnold as well. They had had a few chats and he was just a sweet, sweet man. He was an economic consultant working for the European Union. From all accounts, a very powerful job. He told her he drove an Aston Martin, lived in Belfast, but had homes in Paris, somewhere in Poland and Prague. His father was very ill, but, along with the Sisters of Mercy, it appeared that Arnold took great care of him. He didn't have any children and the photo he had sent to her portrayed a tall, kind-looking man. He sent her the most beautiful flowers. She had had reservations about giving her address to him, but after a very long chat one night, she decided he wouldn't harm a fly and it was nice of him to offer to send her flowers.

"Victoria, I'd love to send you some flowers. Would you mind?" Arnold asked in his soft Irish brogue one evening.

Victoria was a little taken aback and then discussed the pros and cons of giving her address to him. Arnold convinced her it was fine, and he was a gentleman through and through. In the absence of seeing her, he wanted to do something nice for her. It didn't seem such a bad thing to do. They duly arrived. A huge bunch of lilies, gardenias and orchids all wrapped up in a translucent pink ribbon and reams of cellophane. They were stunning.

Gino had texted. 'Hi doll when you gonna do yourself a favour and come and see a real man? Xxxxx.' Gino was a tall, dark and handsome man, subject to the photo being true of course, and Italian by descent. A smooth talker, funny and very, very sexy. He spoke a great deal about how sorry he was that he had messed up his marriage, and almost lost his teenage daughter by being unfaithful and how much he regretted what he had done. He had vowed to never do such a thing again. And if he was ever lucky enough to find the right woman, how much he would love her and cherish her, never ever to cheat on her, and make her the happiest lady in the world. Gino would call from time to time to reiterate this spiel and was very cleverly weaving his well-worn story to lure Victoria into his web.

A text from Tim came whizzing across the airwaves. 'Will do sweetie, take care and be a good girl.'

"I think that boy is a little jealous and controlling," Victoria said to herself. She rang Beth.

"Hi Beth."

"Hi darling. How are you?"

"Good. I'm good. It's just… well, I think I've agreed to do a stupid thing."

"Not first time hun," Beth chuckled. She meant it kindly and treated

Victoria like a daughter.

"Yeah well. Remember Tim?"

"Mmm. Let me see. There are so many." Beth put her forefinger to her lips.

"Tim the Scottish *actoor* with the great bum."

"Oh yes. Got him. What's he done then?"

"Well it's not what he has done, but more like what he might do!" Victoria went on to tell Beth of her fears about Tim. He seemed to have mood swings and she felt he had an angry streak in him, let alone he was moving faster than a bullet with no apparent idea of how he was going to finance the plans he was making for them.

"It's not that I don't like him because I do. It's just well… I think he could get violent."

"Violent?" Beth shrieked.

"Well, not really violent, but slightly dodgy. You know… I am sure he isn't, but I do have a funny feeling about him," she sighed.

"Honestly Victoria. Do you really think it could go anywhere with him?"

"Weell, not really. No, not really." Victoria ran her fingers through her hair.

"Well. Then it's a no-brainer Victoria. If you just want to fuck him, then by all means do so, but he doesn't sound like he is too good at that either. I'd go with your instincts; he sounds like trouble."

"Yeah me too and no, I don't actually just want to fuck him, thanks. You know me Beth, I know I am having odd fantasies about 'Tom the Train', but well, we haven't even arranged that yet have I? And he is super scrumptious."

"Mmm. I know darling. You are such a vanilla. Ha ha. Drop him. He sounds like a scrounger and I certainly don't like you even mentioning the violent bit. Definitely a no-no."

"Yes will do. Thanks Beth. See you on Thursday for lunch then?"

"Yes, that's great. See you. Take care." They hung up and Victoria moved downstairs to the kitchen, musing on both Tom and Tim.

She texted Tim. 'Hi darling, How are you. How's everything in sunny Stockholm? hugs V xxxx.' Victoria was just giving him the final benefit of the doubt.

Her thoughts soon went back to yummy scrummy Tom the Train. So named because she'd met Tom on the train. He was so good-looking and Victoria had been feeling somewhat dismayed by her encounters so far that she couldn't help but do something she had never done before. Tom was sitting opposite her on the train. She was going home from London after her dinner with Jonathan and there he was. Just sitting there. Dark blonde, floppy hair, intense blue eyes and a smile to light up any room. Slim built, thirty-something and, she'd guessed, about 5'10 as he was sitting down. He'd kept glancing over at her. She smiled to herself as she was reading her book. He had no idea she knew that he was paying her an inordinate amount of attention.

Victoria kept thinking to herself: Great isn't it. I am seeing all these duds and just there opposite me is an Adonis, who appears to have the hots for me too. Bet he doesn't come over to me. Sigh.

"Hi. Great train isn't it?" She almost fainted, taking herself by surprise. She couldn't believe the words had come out of her mouth.

"Yes. Yes it is." She was startled by the power of his smile. He was even more handsome and he was staring at her. He put down the magazine he had been pretending to read.

"Are you going to Canterbury?" His voice was as gentle as he looked.

"No. I am off at the next stop," she'd replied.

"Oh." He seemed disappointed.

"You?"

"Yeah. I am going to Canterbury."

"Do you live there?"

"Yes and No. My family have a home there, but I live mainly in London. I'm just going for a weekend of R and R."

"Oh." They were smiling at each other, both wondering what would happen next.

The train was drawing to a stop. Victoria's stop.

She stood up to put her coat on. Tom's eyes devoured her. That was it. She wasn't going to let this be the last time she ever saw him. She picked up her handbag and moved toward where he was sitting. In a seamless movement he stood up as well, and came toward her, taking her in his arms and kissed her hard and full on her wanton mouth. The train came to a halt. They looked into each other's eyes, desire coursing through them.

Victoria said, "I'm sorry, but I have to go. Here is my card." She fumbled in her handbag, whilst moving toward the door and pressing the 'open' button. The door shushed open. Tom was standing by her. She found a card and quickly gave it to him. She stepped off the train, turned around and looked up at him.

"You are so beautiful," he said, holding out his hand to her.

"Call me. Make sure you call me." She blew him a kiss and then, quite overwhelmed, turned around and teetered off to the station exit. She didn't look back, but if she had, she would have seen Tom pressed up against the window watching her every movement.

'Wow. Where did she come from?' he thought looking at her card, scrambling to get his mobile out of his briefcase. Tom had been imagining what was underneath her elegant dress since she had sat down near him. He saw her get on and thought, 'Near me. Near me. Sit near me!'

And unwittingly she had. He just couldn't pluck up enough courage to talk to her, so when she'd said the immortal words, 'Great train', he couldn't believe it and now he had her number.

He dialled it immediately and texted her. 'Hi, it's Tom. Now you have my number.'

By the time she had reached home they had agreed to meet at Victoria's place the next day. Victoria had promised to wear high heels, fully fashioned, silk stockings, red and black, satin, waspy corset with matching panties and bra.

Victoria almost skipped up the stairs to bed.

Wow! My own Adonis. Such a lovely man. This time just sex. Sex and more sex, no complications and no fuss. Just pure unadulterated pleasure. She couldn't wait to get her hands on him.

Tom called her the next morning.

"Hi gorgeous. Just checking I wasn't dreaming and yesterday evening did happen?"

"Oh, hi Tom. Yes, it did happen and so will this evening. You know how to get here?"

"Sure do. I have satnav."

"Good. Call me if there is a problem and I'll talk you in."

"I want so much to fuck you. Oops sorry didn't mean to be so, well so…" He tapered off.

"That's fine Tom. Just fine. I am not planning to take you down the aisle you know," she giggled.

"No, no, of course not. Silly of me. Just, well, never done this before and got very excited."

"I know. I have never done this sort of thing before and quite frankly I am still not quite believing that I am, but you are so yummy." She sighed and bit her lip.

They chatted a little more about directions, and time, and lingerie and then continued with their day, both hyped up by the constant thought of having the most incredible sex together. They continued to keep up the hype by peppering the day with the most lurid sex texts that Victoria had either ever sent, or ever received.

Her favourite of the day was: 'I want to lift up your skirt and lick your sweet wet pussy until you beg me to stop and then I want to get my big hard cock up into you. Take you from behind and then fuck you up against the wall.' Tom actually sent her a photo of his beautiful, very big, hard manhood.

She texted him to ask if the photo was really him.

'Of course, who else's would it be?' he responded.

'Mmm. Heaven. Oh sweet Tom be gentle with me and then fuck the life out of me you beautiful boy,' she thought gently swaying and looking into the distant countryside view from her lounge windows.

Her mobile rang. It was Emmaline.

"Hello darling. How is my baby?" she crooned.

"Hello Mummy." Emmy sounded tearful.

"What's the matter, my baby? You sound upset."

"I am," she sniffed.

"What about sugar?"

"I am homesick. I want to come home Mummy. Pleeease. I want to come home now. I miss you and home so much," Emmy softly sobbed.

Whaaaat? No. No. Please, no. This isn't happening. Victoria's mind was whirling. "Pardon honey. You are homesick? Why baby?" Victoria sounded slightly choked.

"Don't know Mummy, I just am. I want to come home. Pleeease say 'Yes'. I miss you so much and I miss the cats, and I, oh well, I just miss home so much. I want to curl up with you on the sofa by the fire, and watch DVDs, and have your spaghetti bolognaise, and just snuggle. Pleeease." Emmaline did sound so sad. Poor thing.

Now, let me see. Snuggling up in their jimjams watching *Thumbelina*, or *Legend*, or *Legally Blonde* or more of Emmaline's favourites, drinking skinny cow, hot chocolate and eating Ben and Jerry's vanilla toffee crunch ice cream. Fire crackling and the beautiful smell of her baby's silky bright blonde hair in the air, or wild abandoned passionate unadulterated sex with a beautiful stranger? Another no-brainer.

"Of course darling. Are you okay to get the train?" Victoria gave a wry smile and shook her head slightly. She had a passing image of Tom's lovely cock inside her while up against a wall. Tom wearing only a pilot's hat holding her sides. "Oh dear." she sighed.

"Pardon Mummy? Are you okay?"

"What, erm, um. Yes, of course sweetheart." Victoria snapped out of her daydream.

"So that's fine then, is it? Will you inform the school?" Emmaline had cheered up substantially.

"Mmm, of course Emmy, baby. Can't wait to see you. Catch the high speed won't you darling? Let me know when you are on it and I'll collect you from the station." Victoria was rather wistful but resigned now to a very different sort of evening.

"Yes. Yes, I will. Love you. Can't wait to see you," Emmaline said in a singsong voice. She rushed off to her dorm to pack for the weekend. She was so happy to be going home. She had missed it so very much.

"Right. What do I do now?" Victoria said to herself. "Bloody hell. I do believe I am destined to have a sexless life. Fuck, fuck, fuck. Oh well *c'est la vie*. Poor Emmy did seem so sad. Odd for her to want to come home, but it will be wonderful to see her. Erm. What was I going to do? Oh yes. Turn off the promise of indescribable pleasure. But, fair enough, to be replaced with an equal yet different sort of pleasure." Victoria convinced herself, but had little effect on Tom.

"Pardon!" he said, cocking his head and scrunching up his aristocratic-like nose. He couldn't believe what he was hearing.

"I am so sorry. Believe me if it were anything else but my daughter I would say 'no'. I was so looking forward to seeing you. Believe me, I am so very, very sorry." Victoria sat on the stairs hanging her head. Tom sounded so disappointed. Not that she wasn't, but he also sounded as though he didn't believe her.

"No. no. It's quite alright." He sat down at his desk and slumped over the black, glass top, his elbow sliding over its smooth cold surface. But he was thinking, 'She's got cold feet, cold bloody feet. Bloody hell, I've had a permanent erection ever since I met her and I was going to have the most fantastic time with her, and now her daughter is coming home out of the blue. On the very night when I just know my sexual heaven was about to be reached. Right at my fingertips.'

"Tom, Tom. Are you there? Hello, hello. Tom?"

"Umm? Yes Victoria, I am here. Are you sure it's your daughter that's the problem, only I would rather know now."

"Are you kidding?" She gave a small laugh. "Oh Tom. Please, please. Emmaline is the only thing that would have… no, could have stopped me. I don't know where this sudden attack of homesickness has come from, but it's genuine and it's there. I could hardly refuse my daughter's request to come on home, could I?" Victoria had thought about it though, if just for a split second. Well look at what she was sacrificing. But another time. Certainly. "Are you in Canterbury next week?" she asked tentatively. Praying he would be.

"For you, I could be anywhere." Tom replied.

That perked her up. "Well, when we can meet? Tuesday? Wednesday?"

Tom wanted to say 'Tuesday', but he was back in London and had important meetings to attend.

"I am sorry Victoria, but I have to be in London then. What about we say next Friday? Same time, same place."

"Same lingerie?" she quipped.

Tom smiled. "Yep, same lingerie. That would be just great."

"Okay. That's good. Sorry again, but I shall think of you often. Be in touch."

"Send me a photo. Pleeeease," Tom pleaded, sitting up in his chair.

"Okay. Sure thing." She laughed and shook her head. She always, always took bad photos, but Emmaline had told her to 'get a life' about it and that her photos looked fine and really, really good. Alright for Emmy to say that was fair enough. She had to be one of the most photogenic kids on the planet.

Chapter 17

Aren't Daughters Wonderful

Victoria collected Emmaline from the station.

"Mummy, Mummeee, Helloooo." Emmaline came rushing at Victoria from the ticket gates and wrapped her arms around her mother's neck, almost squeezing the life from her, she hugged so hard.

Emmaline burrowed her head into Victoria's neck. "Oh I am so glad to see you," she said, straightening up and smiling the biggest, beamiest smile you ever saw. "You look wonderful Mummy."

"Darling, darling. Stop. You're squeezing the life out of me." Victoria held her daughter's hand, took her wheelie case with the other hand and strode over to the car. "It's so good to see you as well poppet."

They drove back home, stopping on the way to pick up some DVDs ready for the evening's lie-in. Victoria didn't hear another word from Tim all over the weekend. She had a wonderful time with Emmaline that was only punctuated by the ever increasing texts from her 'love army' of men.

"Let's go to the movies mother, then you can turn your mobile off and we can get some peace." Emmaline laughed and Victoria laughed with her. "How is the crazy search going Mummy?" She looked lovingly at her mum.

"Crazy darling, just that; Crazy. Although there are one, or two hopefuls."

"Not still seeing that 'Mad Sam' are you?"

"No, no. I am not! Haven't heard from him in a long while actually,"

Victoria lied as she thought it wasn't necessary for Emmy to know all about her love life. Even though, of course, it was absolutely essential that Victoria knew every minutiae about Emmy's.

Chapter 18

The Swedes Have Always Been Different

'Hiya Tim, I have been thinking about you and I have some reservations already, so I think it is best for both of us that we continue our search separately. Good luck with everything. I wish you well and take care.' Victoria texted him.

"There. Good. Done." She heaved a sigh. *And that will be the last of him,* she thought. She answered her door to Wednesday, her vivacious and eccentric cleaner. Wednesday, so-called because she was born on a Wednesday, was loyal yet nosy, but a pretty good cleaner. So what was the alternative?

But, most of all, she was completely honest. Everything was safe in Wednesday's hands, including Leander and Lady, who both adored her. She was a great help when Victoria travelled.

"Morning," Wednesday said, as she walked past Victoria. "And sorry to ring as I left my keys at the pub." Wednesday had several jobs and was always on the go.

"Morning. No problem." Victoria went upstairs as Wednesday headed into the kitchen.

Victoria heard her mobile that she had left downstairs in the kitchen making all kinds of noises. Messaging tones and ringing tones.

"Wednesday. Oh Wednesday." She shouted, "Wednesday WEDNESDAAAAY!"

"Yes, yes. What what's happened? Are the cats okay? I haven't seen Leander or Lady." Wednesday's face was screwed up in distress.

"They're fine Wednesday. They are fine. Would you be a doll and fetch me my mobile?"

"Oh. Oh Gawd. Don't do that to me. Thought my babies were hurt." At which, she trounced off and brought back Victoria's mobile.

Seven missed calls and twenty-seven messages. There was quite a build-up, especially since she had joined the American dating site. The American men were distinctly keen and all, so far, rather charming and apparently smitten with Victoria.

Apart from the Yanks, Charlie was there, as ever, having written his soliloquy for the night. This one surpassed all the others as it must have been at least ten pages long.

Several came from Anthony pleading with her to see him again. 'Once is enough,' thought Victoria. Anthony was an okay guy, but for some funny reason, maybe peripheral vision, or lack of mirrors, he saw himself as a really 'fit' man. However that was also true of Jonathan, who was also guilty of that same vice. A verse from Burns' poem 'To a Louse' sprang into Victoria's mind.

O wad some Power the giftie gie us

To see oursels as ithers see us!

It was frae mony a blunder free us,

An' foolish notion:

What airs in dress an' gait wad lea'e us,

An' e'en devotion!

Gino was unexpectedly there, as he would normally call. He was in hospital, with some sort of 'foot trouble' and wanted her to visit him, as he was fed up with all the other women that kept interrupting his rest. He was quite the Don Juan, or at least he was convinced he was. Victoria didn't think she would ever meet him, but was happy enough to play along, as he was quite amusing.

And there in large, bold capital letters, a text from Tim. Most unexpected. 'I thought I would receive a text like this. Well, I have cancelled my tickets and I'm glad I don't have to listen to your lies anymore.'

"What is he going on about?" She mumbled after reading over the text. "What lies?"

She texted back. 'What are you going on about? What Lies?' There then ensued what can only be described as a 'text spat'.

He replied, 'Your cosmetic work.'

'What cosmetic work?' Victoria had never had any cosmetic work. Acrylic nails, because she couldn't live without those and that's it.

'Your breasts and lips!'

This made Victoria laugh out loud. 'My breasts and lips? For goodness' sake. The buffoon,' she thought. However, Tim wasn't the only one to think Victoria had had breast implants and collagen injections in her lips. But it simply wasn't true. It was all in her genes. The top half of her body was from her mother, and her face was a kind cross of her mum and her dad. Her rear-end was a kind donation from her father, and the gazelle-like legs had been cloned straight from her mother. She had no stretch marks anywhere on her body and no cellulite either. 'Let's hear a loud cheer for crossbreeding,' she thought.

Her father was Dutch and mother Sicilian. Her grandmother on her maternal side was a Jewish lady while her paternal grandmother was a genuine Romany. This latter genetic link could also be why she had an unusual connection with Charlie.

She went on. 'They are all mine, as I told you. No lies and don't be so insulting. You didn't contact me for days.'

Tim was pissed off. Very pissed off. Titania may have had a great place to live, but it was hard for him, although it had turned out to be not so hard to want to have sex with her. Titania had seen better days and prior to moving to Sweden she had lived in California. The sun had done its dastardly work, along with the plastic surgeon. Poor Titania was a cosmetic surgery addict. She had had everything done. You name it and somebody had knifed it, tightened it, pulled it and screwed it. She did smile occasionally, but must have been fearful that she may split the skin on her face, because it had been pulled so much that it was now almost transparent. Her eyes had taken on a slant akin to those Egyptian beauties, but unfortunately they gave Titania a spiteful, scornful look. Tim had been quite shocked when he first saw her 'up close and personal', because the photo Titania had first forwarded to him had evidently been before she had sought the way of the knife and she had since sought several ways.

She had a fabulous home, very rich and luxurious. It was a Huf-Haus, all glass and timber. Titania was very enamoured with the lovely Tim. She had been through all of this before and she just adored handsome, younger men. She had arranged a candlelit dinner for him in her spectacular dining room. Furthermore, she had something else, quite particular, arranged for him after they had dined.

The dining room was huge, almost all glass, with panoramic views looking out to the snow covered hills and landscape. Titania had indulged in the most beautiful exterior lighting. She thought of herself as the 'Snow Queen', albeit Tim thought her more the 'Snow Hag'. But she was a rich Snow Hag, and bloody hell, he needed some help. He was here as he wasn't completely sure he could convince Victoria that she should take care of him.

Tim's worst nightmares came all in one when, after enjoying a sumptuous dinner, he woke up in a large, dimly lit room. Red and blue lights fought with each other. He was chained up. Spread-eagled upright. Chains and on his ankles were attached to the floor, while those on his wrists were attached to a large metal bar hanging from the ceiling.

Stark naked. He looked down in total disbelief. "Ahhh! Titania. Titania. Titaaaannnnniaaaaaa. Hello? Hello? Help, help. *Help*. Bloody hell is anybody there? HEEELLLP!" he shouted and moved his head left and right left and right in lockdown panic. Oh no. She had put a leash around his neck. What the hell was going on? The last thing he remembered was drinking a toast to Titania's beauty, whereas he'd been thinking 'wealth', while Titania was thinking about what she was going to do to that big, bad boy.

Titania had put a sleeping draft in his champagne. She knew the ropes.

She had lured many a young stud through her doors on the pretence that she was willing to 'take care of them'. Well, in a sense, this was true. She was very willing to take care of them.

Titania appeared from nowhere. Gone was the chic, ivory Chanel lounge suit and in its place she was wearing a black, shiny cat suit, including a tail and a cat mask. Bizarrely, Tim thought that this was good, in a way, as it hid her face. Titania's big, blue eyes sparkled through the eyeholes in the mask. The ears of the mask pointed up and had tufts of hair attached to them just like a real cat.

Her thigh-length boots had seven inch, very sharp heels.

To say that Tim was petrified is an understate of gross proportions.

"Titania. Titania," he shouted, but he already knew quite well who it was. "Titania is that you? What the fuck do you think you are doing, you bloody bitch? For God's sake, get me down from here," he screamed. The veins on his neck were protruding with the effort of trying to free himself. But he was chained up tight. All he did was rattle his captors.

"Titania, get me down from here. You can't do this, you old bag."

Yes, he really couldn't have been blamed. Tim was after all in a state of stress and panic, so it's understandable that he hadn't exactly got the power ratio correct. Run this by yourself again Tim. You are chained up in what appears to be a dungeon. You are stark-bollock naked and you can't move. You are in a strange country with a woman you have never met before who is now parading up and down in front of you in a shiny, black cat suit with a matching mask and, yes, you have just noticed she has a very shiny knife in one hand and a very snappy whip in the other and you are screaming insults and demands at her.

Not that bright really. He didn't have the right approach, but, then again, neither did Titania.

"Shhhusssh. Meowww. Purrrrrrr. My darling man," she whispered as she gently stroked the Japanese katana over his chest. The steel blade glistening in the eerie light.

"Aarrrrgh. Pleeeease, pleeease, Titania. What are you doing? What have I done? Pleeease let me down." His jaw was already aching from screaming with such force.

"Shhhhuuuuush my baby. Hush now sweet man, hush. You are going to enjoy every moment I promise. Queen Titania would not do this to you if she didn't think that…"

"Queen! Queen! What bloody Queen?" All sense of survival had now evaded Tim. Titania cracked her whip in the air and then laced it around Tim's torso.

"Pardon my love?" she hissed and then quickly bent down, nipping Tim's right inner-thigh and then the left with her strong, sharp teeth.

"Aarrrgh. For God's sake. Pleeease. What are you doing?" His voice had quietened a little. His eyes were darting all over the place, searching for a means of escape, but finding none.

He was captured and at the total mercy of Titania, the 'Snow Queen' of Sweden, also known as Gloria Workingsop, an ex-pole dancer and stripper from the English West Midlands. She had perfected her Swedish accent whilst being married to a businessman who had once seen her show, fell in love with her and took her off into a life of riches, and sex acts with a twist. It was Frank, her very own first husband, who first introduced her to the heady delights of S&M. He loved when she'd dance while spanking his behind. Ever since his tragic and premature death, she found herself not only going to the dungeon for succour and her own desires, but also to please her many clients and friends.

Tim was just another fly she had caught in her trap. Just another mouse to be played with by Titania the pussy cat.

Titania turned and clip-clopped her way over to a table which held an assortment of what looked like 'torture instruments', and in many ways that is exactly what they were. Tim was never going to forget this trip. All who found themselves at Titania's mercy never, ever forgot.

She clawed up a bespoke leather penis and testicles restraint and very slowly put it over her shoulder. She also collected two silver nipple clamps connected by wires, and placed them over her other shoulder. Finally she grasped a leather paddle that was resting against the table leg.

"Shush, shush my lovely," she purred, turning and smiling broadly. Tim was struggling to get free.

"Aargh! You mad cow. What are you doing? Let me out of here."

Titania cruised over to the tethered Tim and put the paddle down by his ankles.

"For Christ's sake, let me go! Please, please." With some sense of what was happening to him kicking in.

"Oh, but my precious. Why would I do that before all the fun begins?" She clipped one clamp to his left nipple and the other to his right. She then trailed the attached wires to an electrical wall socket close to his chest.

Tim strained to see what she was doing. "Titania. Please. Please," he panted. "I'm sorry. You are beautiful and I just want to be with you. I am committed to you. I was smitten as soon as I saw you…You… you are beautiful. Please let me go and let's talk. Pleeeease, let's talk."

"Oh, my dear, sweet baby. No, no, no, that will never do. I can't let you go. The game hasn't even begun. Relax my love and just enjoy."

She took the leather article from her shoulder. A carefully made, soft, strong, dark brown leather penis and testicle restraint designed to keep even the most flaccid cock harder than steel and to prevent ejaculation until 'Queen' Titania permitted.

Tim was gaping down as Titania stroked the restraint against her cheek and then crushed it gently in her hand and held it to her nose. She loved the smell of male pheromones and leather. Quite against his will, Tim felt himself getting hard.

" No, no, no. I don't want that." He struggled again to get free from his chains, but only managed to chafe his neck and become more uncomfortable.

"Now stop that. Bad boy!" she admonished him and sharply struck his penis with the restraint.

"Ouch! God. Please. Why, oh why is this happening?" he moaned and hung his head.

Titania moved closer to Tim. Her shiny, black patent rubber suit sculpted her body, tightening her waist to a tiny twenty-four inches and carving her breasts into large, pointed pyramids. Her thigh-length boots were shiny in the gloom. She bent her knees, made a growling noise and licked the tip of Tim's penis. He involuntarily shivered, his penis becoming erect. She held his huge balls in the palm of her hand and gently squeezed them, bringing up her other hand to grip the base of his cock. Holding tight and squeezing she thrust his cock down her soft wet throat.

Tim groaned. "Mmm. Aaaaahh!"

Titania continued to suck and lick, moving her hands up and down, curving around his now very erect, very large cock.

"Mmmmmm," she moaned and picked up the restraint. She moved like lightning, tacking up Tim's cock and balls in the restraint. She tightened the ball sack so it pressed his testicles together and strapped the penis restraint even tighter around the base of his shaft. When she had finished, Tim's cock was pulsating and almost bursting from the leather harness.

She raised herself up, but not before licking the tip of his cock, first hard then softly, she licked her own lips and squeezed Tim's encased balls.

"Arrrgh," Tim screamed, his body and mind confused with the mixture of pain and pleasure.

She moved swiftly to Tim's right side, picked up the paddle and spanked him hard on his firm, round buttocks. She repeated the spanking with irregular force, first soft, then hard, then harder, and then much harder, leaving great red welts across his flesh. His buttocks quivered after her administrations. His cock was now enormous the blood trapped within it making it as hard as iron. His whole body was tingling and zinging. Tim wanted to cum so very much, but she stopped.

"Oh no, my darling. Not yet. You aren't cumming until I say," she shrieked. She turned and flicked the switch on the wall. The electricity raced through Tim's nipples and chest.

"Oh dear God. Pleeease stop. Please don't." Titania turned off the current, leaving Tim's chest muscles contracting and his loins crazy with lust. His cock was bobbing up and down, straining against the taut leather. His body was on fire, pleasure and pain travelling together through his veins.

"Aaaah," he sobbed. His throat was dry. Instinctively Titania picked up a glass of cold white wine and put it to his lips, his head hanging down. He gulped the welcome, cool liquid. His body and mind buzzed. He thought he was going to go insane.

Titania unlaced the whip around his torso and cracked it smartly, alternately across his cock and thighs. Tim's body was crying out for release. She moved down to suck his cock again, licking very softly all over the head of his penis, scratching her nails up and down his thighs. Pleasure emanated from his moans and cries, his cock throbbing with each taunt that Titania forced him to receive.

"And now," she shouted. She had picked up the knife, turning it slowly with her fingers, sliding her long, red nails over the blade, the light bouncing off its bright steeliness. She moved slowly towards Tim, her walk was deliberate, exaggerating the movement of her hips and legs, as though she were on a catwalk.

Tim jerked his head back. "What the fuck?" he spat out. The light reflecting from the knife shone into his eyes. His head turned so that his chin now rested on his chest. He was resigned to whatever fate Titania had in store for him.

Putting the knife between her teeth she grasped his cock and deftly unstrapped the device that held his erection firm, rock hard, and thus prevented any relief and last surge of pleasure. She raked her nails across his right buttock, drawing blood as she dragged them over his flesh and down his inside thigh.

"Please. Please. Release me. I must cum," he screamed to some hidden God. His body was shaking and his huge hard cock had sprung up against his finely toned stomach. He was helpless, utterly helpless, humiliated, hurting and bursting with desire to spurt his semen that had been so cleverly trapped inside his balls. The veins in his cock were now bulbous and huge. Titania's eyes were sparkling and wide, she dropped the knife onto the floor near her left foot, placed her mouth over the top of Tim's cock and slid her hand and fingers up and down the length of his member, sucking. Her fingers played over the head of his cock in between her soft lips and tongue. She pulled hard and sucked down into her throat all of his penis and then deftly inserted her index finger into Tim's rectum, touching his prostate.

Tim's scream pierced the room. His semen shot over five metres. Titania then picked up the knife and moved behind him, as he was convulsing, lost deep in orgasm. Titania then completed her *pièce de résistance* on Tim's welted right buttock. There she carved, but only enough so that he would be scarred for life, the letter 'T'. He would never be able to forget the lesson that the 'Snow Queen' had taught him. So she left him, a little scarred both physically and mentally, but just enough to remind him to be a 'good boy' in future, a tad humiliated, and quite astonished at how much pleasure he had also gained from the whole experience. But this lesson would not be repeated, as Titania had arranged for him to be driven away to a hotel near the airport. She had paid for a night lodging, and the rest was up to Tim. She had done what she wanted with him, and now he had no more attraction for her than a bunch of withered grapes.

So much for Tim ruling the roost and thinking that the 'old bag' was just going to fall at his feet. Tim had to think again. And he was thinking, but this time it was of Victoria. That was just when he received her text. Now things were going from bad to worse. He was just getting used to the fact that he was going to settle down with the beautiful if awkward Victoria, and she sent him that bloody text.

I shall contact Victoria when I get back to Scotland. The best I can do now is have a hot bath and a cold beer, even if I have to take a mortgage out to buy one. I bet the old bag didn't include room service.

Actually, Titania had included room service. After all, she was a lady and she had kidnapped Tim, in a way, but nobody had complained to the police so far. No one would ever even try to explain the scenario. Who would believe them, and surely no one would feel any sympathy for them either? No. Titania was quite safe and Tim, as had all the others, would move on.

But Tim had begun a spiteful onslaught on Victoria as soon as he had reached the UK.

'I might as well insult her. I did detect a certain insecurity, so I should try and wind her up,' he thought to himself, walking toward the bus station from the airport.

He continued. 'And I suppose you couldn't come up with a decent explanation for Berrie if he eventually found out that I am your lover.'

Victoria was aghast with the low mentality of the man. 'I've explained all there is to explain regarding Berrie, so just be a good boy and I wish you luck,' she returned his text.

'Bet you are frightened that I know it's Berrie's house and you're just a pathetic lonely housewife.'

Victoria had steam coming out of her ears and her eyes had turned bright red, which was matching the colour her face was turning. He's an absolute nutcase. Berrie's house? Berrie my lover? The insulting bastard, she grimaced. 'Bloody insulting nutcase,' she typed. 'Where on earth did you get the idea this was anybody's house other than mine? None of my photos include a man and I didn't even have any deodorant for you.'

She sent the text only to have Tim return immediately with, 'I think you need to see a psychiatrist.'

Let's just leave it, shall we. It was simple, self-reflection, Victoria mused; accusers often do exactly what they accuse others of.

"Let it go, Victoria. Let it go." She breathed slowly and started to calm down, but still had to call Beth to let it all go.

Bloody insulting, cheeky bastard. Berrie's house indeed. Where in the aarrrgh, never mind. She really was very upset and didn't know why, which was even more upsetting.

Chapter 19

Love at First Sight

Tuesday came around very quickly. Victoria had completely forgotten her foray with Tim. Tim who? And was now fully concentrating on Simon. Lovely, tall, charming Simon. She had enjoyed their talks and was really looking forward to seeing him. She had butterflies in her tummy. She brought out the 'dating outfit', metallic dark grey jeans, bright red strappy top with the pink lacy, peekaboo bra, and the D&G jacket with cream, red and blue detail on the lapel and pockets. She looked lovely.

There were a few workmen hanging around, dealing with the plumbing and finishing the floor when Simon arrived, so the door was open.

"Hello."

She jumped a foot off the ground and fell backward onto the floor. "Arrgh."

"Oh my dear lady. Victoria, Victoria are you alright?" A very tall, gangly man rushed to her assistance. "Victoria, are you alright?" he repeated, helping her up from the floor.

"Yes. Yes, I think so. Oh so sorry. I didn't know you were there and I was miles away." She looked up into his eyes and had a close up view of his face. Once she had found her feet again and straightened her hair, she found herself flouncing, quite agitated, and, of course, embarrassed. Hardly the way you would want to meet your sweetheart for the first time.

"No, no. I am the one who should be sorry. Startling you like that. I am sorry. Please accept my apologies. I am only glad you are okay. It might have been nasty." He was smiling the biggest smile she had ever seen.

'Aaah. How sweet,' she thought and her eyes began to sparkle. 'Oh he isn't bad, not bad at all. Maybe at last?' She shivered involuntarily at the thought. "No, it's fine. No problem. Door shouldn't have been left open."

"Err, umm. I did call, but nobody answered, so I, err, um. Sorry. Just came in. Sorry it's all my fault." He looked down at the floor, overacting his apology. So the guy had a sense of humour as well. She had picked up on that through there many chats. But you never really know until you meet. And even then it's only the first step.

"Shall we go?" He held out his arm and gave her a big grin. In fact Simon never stopped grinning throughout the whole time she was to be with him. Victoria took his arm and just knew he was the 'one'. Never mind his perpetual grinning, which actually was only because he couldn't believe his luck in finding her. Well, either that, or because his face was slightly twisted. His nose was long, huge in fact and crooked. It must have been broken some time ago. He was overweight, his face was too red and last, but not least, although she hadn't yet seen his toenails, he needed some work on his teeth. She later found out that he had already started down the dental route. Anyway, all of these defects could be rectified without too much of a problem. Victoria was smitten.

Simon had a nice top of the range Mercedes. Nothing too flashy and nothing too trashy. He opened the door for her and off they went on their first step into heaven - the local gourmet pub. Once they arrived, he jumped out of the car and virtually skipped around the car to open the door for her.

Simon flashed his teeth, helped her out of the car and hardly let go of her all through lunch.

"I can't believe it," he repeated still grinning his grin. "You are just so beautiful. Just like your photos. And you are so intelligent. Where have you been all my life?" He squeezed her hand and just stared into her eyes.

She actually lowered her eyes in a very coy manner. Victoria commented on her coyness.

"I don't think I've ever done that before," she said. They laughed and giggled throughout the meal, neither of them eating much at all. They were completely enraptured with one another.

Wendy, the proprietor, had never seen Victoria like this before. She was normally quite formal with whomever she was lunching, but now she looked all starry-eyed and was flirting outrageously with the man. She seemed very happy, but not as happy as he was. Good Lord. If he got any closer he would be sitting on her lap. Victoria didn't seem to mind a bit.

Simon asked for the bill and they set off to the car. Victoria looked tiny next to his great height. He said he was 6'5, but he seemed much taller to her. He slid his hand down her arm and held her hand. He squeezed it slightly and bent down to plant a light kiss on her cheek.

"Thank you for being you. You look a million dollars and you are worth far more than that," he whispered in her ear.

"You're most welcome and thank you for saying so. You are lovely. Thank you for being you as well." She beamed back up at him.

They held hands all the way back in the car.

"Distance won't be a problem to this relationship, you know." Simon patted her hand.

"Well, that's nice to know. I am very glad to hear it."

Simon pulled her hand up to his lips to kiss it. "What colour are your nails?"

"Midnight blue."

"My favourite colour," he announced and very gently kissed her hand, replacing it on her thigh.

'What a wag he is,' she thought, smiling to herself.

When they arrived back at Victoria's house, Simon had no sooner stopped the car than he was on her.

He kissed her hard on the lips. Passionately and quite forcefully. This presumption would normally have put Victoria into a frenzy of anger, but this time she yielded and went with the moment. She returned his kisses just as passionately. The car windows steamed up, but both of them were oblivious to anything or anyone, as one of the builders walked by and, while rubbernecking them, tripped over.

"Shhimon. Shimon." She tried to call his name and shoved at his chest to regain semblance of decorum. They were really getting hot. It wasn't Victoria's style, and later Simon explained it wasn't his usual behaviour either. It was just that the moment had both caught them and the attraction was irresistible.

Mmmph. Yes, yes. Sorry. So sorry. Getting carried away like that terrible really. Like a schoolboy," Simon mumbled as he sat back in his seat, smoothing down his jacket.

Victoria sat upright in her seat. "It's fine. Wonderful actually, but I do think we are frightening the workmen." She giggled.

"Oh you are so sweet." He caressed her cheek. "Look. Look here. I have something for you to look at." Simon produced some photographs. "Here please." He pointed. "This is my villa in Portugal. Quinta da Lago to be precise. The one I mentioned to you. And this is Andrew my son."

"Where is this?"

"Well actually it's a little hamlet outside Oxford called Matching Tye."

"Gosh. There's a place not far from here called that."

"I know. I saw it on the map. The only two in the UK. How about that? We live in the same place. Ha, ha."

"What a coincidence."

"A sign my dear. A good sign."

"Yes, yes. It seems that way, doesn't it?"

"What do you think of my son?"

"Handsome. They are both handsome, like their father." she held her hand to his cheek and gave him a very soft kiss, her lips were now even bigger and redder with all the kissing. She returned to look at the photos he had given to her. The villa was huge and although painted pink, which wasn't Victoria's favourite colour, the architecture was good enough, and the gates were impressive. His house in Matching Tye was enormous. It couldn't be described as a house really. 'Mansion' would be more accurate.

"They are all very handsome." She smiled, handing back the photos.

"Thank you. Architecture is my hobby. I buy and refurbish buildings, or have them built. I see a building I like and then replicate it, either here or in Portugal."

"Mmm. Very interesting."

"Mmm darling. And you are such a darling." He took both her hands and looked into her eyes. "I don't want to alarm you, and I hope you don't mind me saying, and I am going home right after I see you to the door But…"

'Oh don't ruin it,' Victoria thought. 'Don't ruin it, you big beluga.' "Yes. What is it? Go on," she said cocking her head.

"Well. Sex is very important to me. It's not the whole relationship I know, but it is a very important part."

"Oh! Oh my." She withdrew her hands and started to laugh. "Is that all? Of course it's important. Very important. I love sex. Good sex that is."

"Is there any other?" He grinned and replaced her hands in his.

"Well I have had my moments, but of course I agree and I am so glad you think that way. Darling Simon. How very glad I am to meet you." She smiled warmly at him and blew him a kiss.

"Oh and you can bet all the tea in China that I am so glad to meet you too. Can't wait until next time. What do you think?" he said lowering his window to get rid of the condensation.

"Absolutely. When and where? I've shown you mine. Will you show me yours?" Victoria opened the car door and got out.

"Great. Yes. No problem." Simon followed.

When they reached the front door of the house, she placed the key in the lock and turned to him. "Are you sure you don't want a coffee?" she lowered her head and then turned back and gave him a coy smile.

"Tempting, but no. I must get back. My farm manager will be waiting for me. So would you like to come and visit me next week sometime?" It was now his turn to cock his head.

She opened the door and stepped inside, turning around and leaving Simon in the porch.

"Well, let me see. I don't know if I fancy driving all that way in my little motorcar." She was just about to ask how long the train journey would be and how complicated when Simon just piped up.

"You can have one of my cars. I'll buy you one."

Victoria stepped back in surprise. "Well thank you, but I was going to ask about the trains."

"Yes, yes. The train. Well I think there is a direct one from Paddington. Why don't you come for the weekend, or at very least come Friday evening and return Sunday morning? In fact, don't worry, I'll bring you back."

"Well that's great. How lovely. I would like that very much."

"Anything. Anything for you Victoria. I've always thought I was a kind of special guy and deserved a special lady and you are definitely very special Victoria. Very special." He took a deep breath and straightened his tie.

"Oh Simon. You are a special guy. Mmm." She leant forward and kissed him. "I would love to do that. I'll check train times. Which station is it?"

"Oxford. Go to Oxford, it's easy that way and I shall collect you. See. Eeasy-peasy pie." He touched the tip of her nose. "I'll text you when I get home and call you later this evening if that's okay?"

Victoria suddenly remembered that she was going to dinner with Berrie that evening and furthermore that she had arranged to see Tom on Friday night, and Charlie on Saturday evening. Simon was heading toward the car.

"I'm out this evening darling. Do you want to call me about eleven o'clock?"

"No, no. That's okay. I'm up early tomorrow. I have a shoot. No problem. I'll call you tomorrow." He blew her a kiss and saluted her. Funny guy.

Yes, this was it. She felt sure Simon would be the 'one'. And he seemed very kind and very upfront, no games. Just a really, really nice man. Totally smitten with her and she not very far off the same either. She stayed and watched until the car had left the drive. He beeped twice and she could just see his hand waving near the roof of the car.

She closed the door and bolted it. Wow and wow. A nice guy. A genuine man at last.

Victoria reminded herself that she also had lunch with Christopher her one and only personal criminal lawyer. Now, how did she feel about that?

Well it had only been one date with Simon, however enchanting and positive. She would rearrange Tom and Charlie. She might not even see them if things were what she hoped from Simon. Seeing Christopher tomorrow would do no harm though. Everybody needs a little insurance and one never knows when one might need a criminal lawyer. So that's what she did.

Obviously she would never cancel Berrie. She was looking forward to seeing him that evening. It never occurred to Victoria that it was slightly unusual thinking. Smitten with one man only to be looking forward to seeing another?

Simon texted her as he said he would. Reliable, as well as generous. Offering to buy her a car. How kind and thoughtful. 'He is perfect. Yep the man is perfect,' she thought and sat down to check the builder's inventory. It wouldn't take her long to freshen up for Berrie.

Her evening with Berrie was as usual charming, relaxing, funny, and altogether thoroughly enjoyable. She hardly referred to her dating activity on the grounds that Berrie had started to have a strange reaction to her stories and it tended to put a dampener on the evening. Besides, it wasn't really any of Berrie's business. She hated upsetting him in any way whatsoever and no one she had met, or spoken to so far was worth pissing off her best friend.

When the time was right and when the man was right, she would let him know. Of course, she would have to let him know. Berrie and the children would always be in her life and she in theirs. Berrie would want to be friends with her new man.

Chapter 20

Does Crime Really Pay?

'All on time just leaving the court,' the text from Christopher read.

'That's great, do you have satnav?' she responded.

'Yes, I have your postcode. Looking forward to seeing you lovely lady.'

'You too,' she replied. He did sound nice when he called and has an interesting job. After suffering a few pangs of guilt over Simon, she told herself that just having lunch would do no harm. They hadn't promised a life together yet, had they? Anyway, it was too late now. Christopher was on his way and it would be too rude to cancel at such a late stage.

Simon texted her to wish her a nice day. Does it get any better? And the car thing. Mmm too cute. The man is perfect. An absolute star.

Charlie texted her a reminder of Saturday and so did Tom confirming Friday. Arnold and Anthony also sent her a message.

'Flowers should be delivered today. Keep safe.' So Arnold meant what he'd said about the flowers. All that Anthony said was, 'Hello Gorgeous how is your day going? Xxxx'

She finished getting ready, deciding to dress in her tightest, blue skinny jeans, which showed off her fabulous bottom, together with a white capped sleeve t-shirt and a short, tailored, navy-blue jacket with huge midnight blue buttons. She put on her red heart, Swarovski necklace with matching earrings. She looked lovely.

There was a knock on the door.

"He is here and early," she gasped, running to the other side of the house to look out of the window. A little trick she had learned as time had gone by. She was fed up with opening the door to the blind dates, only to be the best actress in the world at feigning joy and happiness. This way at least she got ahead of the game a little, and found it easier to give a genuine smile whatever they looked like.

"Hi. Oh. Hello Christopher," she called. "Helloooo. I am here."

Christopher followed the voice around to the side of the house and looked up.

"Hi. Hi there. Be with you in a moment." She waved at him.

He shielded his eyes from the sun. "Hi Victoria. Yeah. Sure. Wow you have one helluva view here, don't you?"

Victoria had already disappeared skipping down the stairs. "Oooooh, he is handsome and driving a lovely car. I do believe I am on a roll," she said to herself.

"Hi Christopher." She opened the door and stood there; hot body, hot looks, her eyes smouldering at Christopher, who was a walking sex God.

Tall. Nice shoulders. Almost blue-black hair. Emerald green eyes. Cheekbones that were chiselled by Michael Angelo and dressed in a cool, silver-grey, mohair suit and black, plain shoes that definitely had a Gucci look about them, topped off with a beautiful Cartier watch.

His tie was raffishly loose around his neck. A stripy, three shades of blue, Ferragamo that matched perfectly with his ice-blue shirt.

"Hi Victoria. Hi. Mmmmmmm. Well, well, well." He gave her a great big smile. White, perfectly formed teeth.

"Well, well, well, to you too. Shall we go? The pub's only in the village. You may have passed it on the way up. I know you don't have much time, so I've chosen somewhere to eat that's close by. The food is quite good and it's a nice place really."

"Fine by me. Sounds great. Oh and the case has been adjourned, so I no longer have to go back to court this afternoon." He walked alongside her to the car and opened the door for her. She got in and he closed the door with a maverick swipe of his hand.

'Oh yes. Oh boy. Oh yes. Thank you Lord. At last a Goddess. Don't know how many toadettes I have kissed to get here, but oh yes! Okay! Now here she is. Wo, wo, wo. Way to go,' he thought whilst walking around to the driver's door.

"Okay?" he turned to her and started the car.

"Yes thanks. Up the drive and turn left." She smiled back at him and looked down. Mmmmm his hands were yummy as well. Long fingers, immaculately manicured, light pink nails with white moons and smooth skin. This boy definitely took care of himself. That's good, she thought. That's very good. They drove off. The sun was shining through the tree tops and the air was clear and crisp.

Victoria liked the car, but unequivocally preferred the driver. He smelt so good as well. Musk and ginger notes with herb overtones. She breathed him in and felt quite heady.

The air was bursting with their pheromones, mixing together. The pub was only a ten-minute drive away, but everything seemed to be going in slow-motion. They both knew what the other was feeling. Christopher wanted to turn around there and then, take her back to the house and rip her clothes off - although experience told him that her sprayed on jeans could be tricky - and just take her against the wall, on the stairs, on the table, in bed, in the bathroom, bedroom, or just anywhere and everywhere. Lunch was so unnecessary.

Victoria wanted all of the above, and she would have helped with the jeans, but lunch was so necessary. Or was it? Yes it was, she told herself. It sure was. This guy would have women falling at his feet, hanging onto his knees and begging him to fuck them. Victoria was different. She had always been different and this was no exception, even if her pheromones were giving it all away. Anyway, his weren't keeping themselves to themselves either.

Once inside the pub they went to the bar.

"What would you like to drink beautiful?" he said, his eyes sparkling and dazzling like the jewels in Aladdin's cave.

"A glass of sauvignon blanc please." Her eyes met his and Victoria swore she heard a crackle in the air.

"A sauvignon blanc and a light beer please." He turned to the barmaid who also seemed to wake up.

"Of course. Are you eating with us?" she asked.

"Yes. I've booked, Serena. Just the two of us. We'll go through to the restaurant in a minute. Would you be kind enough to bring the menus?"

'Wow. Looks like she has cracked it this time,' thought Serena, who couldn't wait to go and tell Kristina, the proprietor's daughter. She brought them their drinks and the menus. "Everything is on the menu and on the board over there." Serena pointed.

"Thanks," they both said in unison.

"Oh, make a wish." Victoria giggled. "It's supposed to come true if two people say the same thing at the same time. But be quick."

"Right. Okay." Christopher wished that he could be back at Victoria's later that day, tearing off her panties with his teeth and fucking the daylights out of her.

Victoria closed her eyes and wished, I do hope he is genuine. He is so good-looking and obviously has a good and fascinating job. Pleeeease, pleeeease, let him be legit. She opened her eyes and they toasted each other.

"To us." They chinked their glasses. And both set about reading the menus although neither of them wanted to eat, well not that kind of eating anyway.

"What are you going to have?" she said. She had noticed that it was invariably her who would enquire as to what favoured on the menu.

"Errmm. Don't know really, apart from you." Christopher sipped his beer and licked the froth from his lips. "Well I think I will have the duck confit." She ignored his flagrant gesture with his tongue, but giggled inside nonetheless. 'Mmm,' she thought. 'He certainly is interesting and so very, very sexy. Not that he doesn't know it!'

"Shall we go in?" She slipped off the stool, picked up her handbag off the floor, slung it over her shoulder, and moved toward the restaurant.

'What an ass! My God, that's good. She is so very, very sexy,' Christopher thought following her like a puppy dog, but a puppy dog with an erection. Christ! Not now, for God's sake. Down boy, down. Don't frighten the little lady off now. A mental picture of a Japanese car manual came to him. It was a little trick he often used whilst having sex, if he thought he was going to suffer premature ejaculation. Oh yes. Christopher may be a womanizer, or whatever you may want to call, it but he was here to be a ladies' man. The lady comes first.

As they sat down, Kristina seemed to appear from nowhere at the table as if by magic, before Victoria's tush touched down on the chair.

"Hi Victoria." She did a tiny dip, more of a little dance or shuffle, smiling clownishly, her eyes moving back and forth toward Christopher.

"Hi Kristina. How are you?"

Kristina was a pretty little thing and although she didn't possess the same aura as Victoria, she was catching all the same. Petite, long blonde hair, blue eyes. A sexy little number with quite a cheeky, sassy personality.

She had certainly been a handful when she was a teenager and was now about twenty-five.

"I'm fine just fine. Things are going really well." She nodded towards Christopher who, at this juncture, had taken no notice of Kristina as he was still ogling Victoria.

"Christopher."

"Mmmm. Yes." Christopher came out of his trance. "Christopher. This is Kristina. Kristina, this is Christopher."

Christopher looked up and was surprised to see yet another delicious female in his presence. "Hi Kristina. Nice to meet you."

"Hi. Yes, nice to meet you too."

Throughout the whole lunch Kristina flitted in and out of the restaurant, stopping here and there to make small talk. Victoria noticed that Christopher, whilst trying to engage Victoria's attention, was also flirting quite blatantly with Kristina.

'Get the fuck out of here,' Victoria thought, but decided to ignore it although parked it very firmly in her mind. It was true that Kristina did her bit to attract his attention, but, in essence, it didn't take much for her to get it. First downer, first loss of a brownie point Christopher.

Christopher told Victoria that he was separated from his wife.

"Oh. For how long?" She hoped that she was affecting a nonchalant attitude.

"Six months. It's been a bit hard on the kids."

Children. Children? she thought. Victoria could have sworn that when she was talking with Christopher there was no mention of children or a wife for that matter. But in fairness that could have been down to her. She really hadn't honed her enquiry technique.

"Yeah, I agree. How many have you got?"

"Twin boys."

"How old?" Here it comes, she thought the deal breaker. I bet they are no more than two years old.

"Eight."

Eight. Bloody eight. Twins and eight. Could be two years old. Not much in it really, she thought, but instead said, "Oh that's sad."

Sensing that he was losing Victoria, Christopher then explained that he had known his wife for over twenty-five years. She was his childhood sweetheart and they had just grown apart. His wife was in total agreement with the separation, and, of course, they were friendly with each other, plus the kids, whilst being upset about it, weren't being torn apart by the two of them.

Well that was nice to know. Ordinarily, Victoria would have walked away immediately at this 'accident waiting to happen'. Red Alert Victoria!

But Christopher was one great looking and charming guy. And it was difficult for Victoria to resist a Jonny Depp lookalike. And, Oh well, he was amicably separated, and he would stop that flirting, which was probably harmless anyway, as soon as he got to know Victoria better.

Victoria was not alone in telling herself all of this rubbish, it is just a fact of the female psyche that many women do it all of the time. And it was just the tip of the iceberg. Making thousands of excuses and reasons for men not calling, working late, their passion for football and, and, and. Actually, they don't call because they don't want to, not because they have lost the woman's number. For regular late working, he is likely to be having an affair with a co-worker. Passionate about football and he's lost that passion about his lover. Simple and true, so why don't women take notice of this?

So, whilst Victoria didn't invite Christopher in for a coffee. She was taking a little time out to consider where she was with Christopher and if she would see him again, but enough for now. Christopher couldn't believe she hadn't asked him in, and started to chew his bottom lip in anxiety.

'I can't lose her now. I am as horny as a ram that's been locked up for a fortnight and just been told it's his turn,' he thought, his brain going into meltdown.

"May I come in and look at your handiwork with the house? The outside looks amazing and I really would like to know what the inside looks like. Especially as its not been the easiest project you have been involved with."

Victoria had told him quite a bit about her house refurbishment and all the trouble it had caused, so in a way she felt obliged. Well that's what she told herself anyway.

"Mmmmm?" She hesitated. Should I let him go for now? There will always be another time, but what came out was, "Sure. No problem."

Although Victoria didn't see, or didn't want to see, Christopher gave a sigh of relief. 'Phew. Close one!' he thought, getting out of the car.

Victoria gave him a tour of the house explaining, the horror stories of the glass curtains, the fire, the stairs ad nauseam. Christopher was most attentive and made the right noises, in the right places.

They stopped in Victoria's bedroom. The view was spectacular and the room itself very 'Hollywood', as Beth had once commented.

"Well it all looks as though it was worth it. It looks fantastic. You certainly have an eye." Christopher grabbed her around her waist.

"Why thank you, kind sir," she giggled. Christopher saw his moment and kissed her full and hard. It wasn't difficult for her to respond. He was holding her neck with both hands and unbuckling her bra the next. She felt her breasts floating free from their constraints.

Christopher slid his hand under her top and squeezed one breast very gently. He started to knead the firm, soft flesh and fondled her nipple.

"Mmmmm. Oh baby, your tits are just fabulous," he breathed into her neck, whilst bringing his other hand up and under her t-shirt, gaining access to her other breast. He proceeded to knead and squeeze both breasts at the same time.

Victoria's mind was fighting with her body. He felt so good, but no, no. She didn't do this sort of thing. He was a complete stranger. Her heart was thumping through her chest and she could feel her wetness had soaked through her jeans.

Christopher kissed her hard again, exploring her mouth and soft tongue then running the tip of his tongue over her bottom lip and then he bit it just hard enough to send a charged shiver down her spine and through into her loins. My God, this man was such a turn-on.

"Come on my baby." Christopher started to manoeuvre her towards the bed.

There was a loud knocking. Somebody was knocking at her door. It shocked Victoria and immediately brought her out of her passion.

"Christopher!" she exclaimed pulling away from him. "Someone is at the door." She stepped back and saw how dishevelled she was.

"Yeeow! Look at me. No, no. Don't look at me." She was waving her hands at him. "I've got to see who it is." She was disorientated and flustered. The adrenalin and hormones taking their part.

"Baby you are beautiful." Christopher stepped toward her with his arms held out. "Leave whoever it is. It's not important. Please honey, come to me."

She felt like a rabbit trapped in the headlights of a car. She couldn't move.

"Trust me beautiful, baby. Please." He caressed her cheek. The knocking began again. Rap. Rap. Rap, only louder this time. She didn't know what to do. There he was, one of the best looking men she had ever seen. All suntanned, with a hard chest and stomach, and a very hard cock to put the cherry on the cake. Standing in front of her, lusting after her. But she didn't know him. It wasn't right. It felt right, but it was wrong. It wasn't her style.

"No I have to go." She pushed past him, doing up her bra as she went.

"Don't be long darling. I am so hot for you."

Victoria ran downstairs, not wanting whoever it was to leave. There was something wrong with all of this. She ran to the same window from which she had first called to Christopher.

"Hello. Hellooo?" she shouted. "Who is it?"

"Delivery." A huge red van was parked in the drive.

"Okay. Fine. Thanks. Be down in a minute." She dragged her head back through the window and went down another flight of stairs to open the door.

"Hi."

"Sign here please." the delivery man gave her a small electronic pad that she could never write a recognizable signature on. 'Might just as well write an X,' she thought.

"Thank you." He handed her a massive bunch of beautiful flowers.

"Someone's a lucky lady." The man grinned, his teeth all yellow and broken.

"Lucky man, I'd say," she quipped, taking the flowers.

The delivery man looked her up and down and cheekily said, "Reckon you're right there. Have a nice day."

"You too." She held the flowers, which had a tropical touch to them and were quite light considering their quantity and size. She looked for the card.

It read, 'To the most beautiful lady. Hope to see you soon. Keep safe. xxxx'

It was Arnold again, Sweet, dear Arnold. Maybe she should consider him more seriously. She loved the Irish.

Now what do I do about Don Juan up there. Please God, don't let him be naked, she thought. Placing the bouquet on the sideboard, she went up the stairs with great trepidation.

"Christopher? Christopher, come here. Come down and have a cup of coffee, I need to speak to you," she shouted up the stairway.

"What! What's she saying?" Christopher said to himself.

"Christopher. Christopher can you hear me?" Oh God, she thought, what have I done?

"Yes. Hi Victoria." Christopher went to the bedroom door, his shirt and belt undone and socks off. He always preferred to take off his own socks.

"Christopher come down here and have a cup of coffee with me. I need to talk to you," she repeated.

I don't believe it, he thought shrugging his head shoulders and hanging his head. I haven't wanted to fuck a woman as much as this one for as long as I can remember. And she wants me to, so what the fuck is she up to?

"What?" he shouted back. "But I thought we were, you know…" His voice faded away. She had gotten away. His experience told him that he was lucky enough to get Victoria in the position he had earlier, but now there was no chance of starting again from where they had left off. He resigned himself to another time. "Drag, and fuck and bugger," he quietly mouthed and hit the wall with his fist.

"Coming, I'm coming. Be right there," he shouted back. "Yeah. Right coming, not cumming," he muttered, while he shook his head in disbelief and disappointment and started to dress himself.

Christopher found Victoria in the kitchen. She had put her hair up and taken off her jacket. She looked so kissable, so fuckable, so sweet. He would never force himself on her. The last time he'd done that, it had caused one hell of an uproar. Lydia, his wife, almost didn't forgive him and his office strongly disapproved. What was wrong with these chicks? They come on to him and then change their minds, so what gives with them? Anyway, the good thing was that the silly tart didn't file charges. Yeah absolutely because she knew, didn't she? Yep. She knew she was encouraging him all the way.

Anyway Victoria was different. She was a lady and, oh well, another time.

"Hiya. How are you doing?" Victoria said brightly, putting a cup under the espresso machine.

'How am I doing? How the bloody hell am I doing? Blue balls frustrated like I've never known, and she asks how am I doing? She must be kidding,' he thought, but replied, "I'm fine. Just fine," giving her one of his sweetest smiles.

"Milk? Sugar?" She looked over to him. He looked so cute. A rakish handsome man.

"Mmmm. Thanks. Both. Two sugars."

"Why don't you take a seat?" Victoria pointed to the stools set up around the kitchen breakfast bar. She had it built in stainless-steel and wood. It was cosy and comfortable, whilst also being exceptionally modern and streamlined. She loved this room and spent a great deal of her time in it.

She took the coffee over to him.

"Sorry about that." She sat beside him and crinkled her nose.

"Sorry about what?" He smiled and took her hand. "No need to be sorry babes. If you're not ready, you're not ready. No problem. Forget about it. It's me. I just couldn't resist," is what he said, but he thought, 'Yeah. Right. And so you should be Victoria, feel where my balls are hun.' But he knew then he would lose forever, and Victoria was a prize worth waiting for, even if it did involve a bit of pain.

"Whoa. They are lovely. Another admirer?" Christopher had noticed the flowers lying on the kitchen counter.

"Yes they are, aren't they? And yes they are from an admirer. So are you one as well?" she teased, squeezing his hands and having some regret that she hadn't just gone upstairs and started from where they left off.

"Oh yes definitely most definitely. Big time. You are simply gorgeous." He leaned over and kissed her lightly on the lips.

"Well the thing is Christopher, it's like I said on the phone. I am looking for a long term relationship."

They all say that, he thought, but resisted, rolling his eyes upward. "I know darling and I am too."

"Yes, but I guess I should have enquired more than I did before I met you. Six months' separation isn't, in all honesty, that long." She emphasised 'that'. "And well, there are the children."

'I know all about the children. There isn't a day goes by that Lydia doesn't remind me,' Christopher thought, exasperated with the memory of it all. Flashbacks of Lydia running at him with the lawnmower as he sunbathed one day last summer left him feeling quite giddy. "You mother fucking bastard," she had screamed at him. Apparently, she had made the classic discovery taking his clothes to the cleaners and had found restaurant receipts. Several of them. She had turned a blind eye yet again, but maybe it was the heat of the sun, or the fact that he was sunbathing and she was mowing the lawn, or a combination of both. But she snapped and ran at him with the lawnmower, fully intending to mow right over his beautiful torso. She failed of course, because yelling 'Geronimo' at your sleeping victim was a good way to warn him or her. It had frightened the living daylights out of him though, and for some time after the incident, he did stop trawling the 'encounters' column of newspapers in the hope of finding unhappy housewives.

But now, after meeting Victoria, he was so glad he'd started again.

Victoria really was a gem. I might even take this one seriously and leave Lydia for real this time, he liked that thought.

"Christopher, Christopher." Victoria jogged him.

"Yes. Oh what? Sorry, went off there for a moment."

"Thinking of the children?" she said softly.

"Children? No, not the children. Well, yes. In a way. Yes."

"You know that I think you are such a lovely man. Almost everything I've ever wanted in a guy, but six months is untenable. I can't work with that. Not really and feel good about myself. And have you thought about the divorce settlement? Someone you have known for so long and the children. Pretty expensive I think."

"Oh no. Lydia isn't like that." He thought of the whirring of the lawnmower and how she had chased him so hard until he sought safety in the family swimming pool.

"Well, she might not be like that at the moment, but as soon as she knows another woman is on the scene, I suspect she would become quite murderous and take you to the cleaners. I've heard of such stories." She sipped her coffee and crossed her legs.

Christopher drank the rest of his espresso, got up from his stool and put his arms around Victoria's back, breathing her in. She smelt wonderful.

"Well young lady. I had better be going now," he sighed.

"Okay. Shall I call you this evening? See you next week maybe?"

"Yes. Next week is a good idea, but I don't think you should call me this evening."

"Oh, why not? Busy with work?"

"Weeell, you could put it like that. You see, I haven't left home yet."

Victoria shot off her stool. "Pardon? I beg your pardon? You haven't left home yet? What do you mean, you haven't left home yet?"

"Errm. Well I have started to look for a place. Lydia is quite calm about it though." The reality made even Christopher wince, which didn't go unnoticed by Victoria. All of a sudden, it dawned on her. She blinked her eyes and stood back from him.

"Have you forgotten to tell your wife that you are separated?" she asked incredulously.

"Ermmm, well, sort of." He bit his lip and looked to the floor.

"What part of 'sort of' am I to understand? Please give me a clue?" She was still trying to cope with this revelation, not wanting to believe there was any truth in it, and not wanting to hear her own words.

"Weeell, it's not like it hasn't been discussed before." Well that part was true. Lydia raised the question of him leaving at least once a month, but why should he leave everything he had worked so hard for? Just so she could have the beautiful house they lived in, plus he would also miss the kids a bit too. It wasn't his fault he didn't fancy Lydia anymore. She was the one who'd turned all 'Mummsy'.

Discussed? Just talked about? Victoria was having a hard time getting her head around this one. Her mind was telling her, 'Yes dear, he is still married, not separated. Except he is the only one with the knowledge that he is separated. He hasn't informed his wife of the situation.'

"You had better go." She made to move away from him. He went to stop her and knocked over the stool.

"Sorry, sorry," he said, picking it up.

"Yes, you ought to be sorry. Bloody, seriously sorry, but not about the stool. Quite frankly, you are sick. I don't believe I am hearing what I am hearing. What was the idea? Just to take me home, and God knows how many times you play this one, but anyway, take me home, fuck me, say cheerio, 'San Fairy Ann', and that's it. Based on that, if I was willing to let you fuck me the first time I have met you, serve me right. Is that it? Is that the way it goes?" Victoria was extremely agitated now and had raised her voice.

Christopher said nothing, but thought, 'Yeah. Actually, that is the way it goes. When are you women going to wake up?' but he thought better of saying it, as she was looking a little on the angry side, and, like she said, she was an expert in the martial arts and she looked fit enough to land him one right between the eyes.

"Christopher!" she shouted. "Answer me."

"Um. No, no. That's not the way it goes. I am very attracted to you. You are one sexy woman. I mean lovely. All round intelligent and well I want to see you again. Of course, I do."

Memories of Alfred came swimming back into her mind. Yeah right. Jeeez, she thought. I almost fell for it again.

"Well that won't be happening and I think you should go right now. Have a lovely day and go and take care of your wife. She is the one you should be fucking, not fucking her off." She walked out of the kitchen, shaking her head. Men. For God's sake. Why do I want one at all? Christopher followed hard on her heels, after considering that offering to take her to dinner probably wasn't a good idea. He had arranged that, if the date was any good, he would be working late that day. He also knew that if the date wasn't any good, then he could just call Roger and have dinner with him, arriving home a little earlier than if he had been shagging his date all day and evening long.

Victoria opened the door for him. "And goodbye to you." She wanted to call him an 'arsehole', but felt that would not undignified. She was just relieved to have uncovered the 'real' Christopher so quickly.

"I'm, err. I'm sorry Victoria. I really like you. I would leave my wife for you."

Now she felt it quite appropriate to call him an arsehole and did so, pointing to the door. "Don't dare contact me again, you idiot. Think yourself lucky I am in a good mood, or I would have kicked your sorry ass down the road."

He walked out onto the porch and she slammed the door, bolted it, and strode down to the kitchen. She needed a drink.

Chapter 21

The soft and the Hard

Her mobile rang. It was Arnold asking if she had received the flowers.

"Oh Hi Arnold, how are you? Yes, I have received the flowers and they are just beautiful. Thank you so much. They really make me happy," which was true, looking at them now, after such an episode with Christopher and definitely cheered her up. At least there was always good, old, trustworthy Arnold. What a dear, sweet man. He wouldn't let her down, she felt sure about that. He had a darling, attractive accent and was charm personified. Always very polite and very complimentary in a gentlemanly way.

"How are you Victoria?" Arnold would generally ask that question at least three times during a conversation. Highly irritating, but Victoria was pleased to hear from him, so they chatted on about Arnold's father and Arnold's job. He was going away to Warsaw the next day and would be back Wednesday week.

"I have been invited over to Paris by an introduction from the agency. I thought I would go and I could also visit a friend who lives there at the same time," she told him, whilst sipping on her glass of Chablis. She poured more of the soft, honey coloured liquid into one of her crystal glasses, just to make her feel better. Arnold and Victoria had agreed to keep their relationship platonic, so she used to tell him about her trysts, although she was going to leave out Christopher, and the less said about Alfred the better!

"Is that right now? Well How nice for you. Victoria, I could invite you to come with me to Warsaw, or Prague, or what about my place in

Donegal? It's beautiful there." The invitation took her by surprise. She didn't think that timid Arnold would ever have the gumption to ask her on a date, let alone to another country.

"Why Arnold, how nice. I don't think I want to go to Warsaw, but I love Ireland, so it would be great to visit you over there. Thanks, I'd love to come."

"You would? Well that's marvellous. I'll get the flights sorted as soon as I return from Warsaw. When can you come?"

"Well I don't know right now. Let's speak when you get back to Ireland. Okay?" There was too much going on, both in her head and in her life, to make any long term dates, but it pleased her to speak to sweet Arnold.

"Yes, yes. Of course. That's okay." Arnold almost wet his pants thinking that the beautiful Victoria would want to meet him. And to visit him in his own country, amazing! He'd keep smiling away to himself all week long. "I'll call you on my return. Is that okay?"

"Of course it is sweetheart."

He loved it when she called him that. It just sent him spinning into whirls of heavenly delight.

They said goodbye. Arnold ended the conversation with his usual, 'Keep safe.' Maybe it was all of the bombings and fighting that caused him to repeat that whenever he spoke to her. Arnold was from Belfast and so she thought it probable that he bore some scars.

Now she would have to prepare to make some changes and answer the many texts that had been coming in throughout the day.

Pocket Prince first. Victoria really had a soft spot for Charlie and didn't want to dismiss him out of hand just because he was short, and she was fascinated by the twilight world in which he lived. She knew he would be disappointed and would feel very let down by her change of plans. 'Good God,' she thought. 'This doesn't sit that well with me at all. But what am I to do? I am looking for the "one", which doesn't necessarily mean just "blind love". I've been there, done that, and look where that got me. Ten years up the swanny. Well I know not all of it. But if nothing else, I have learned a lot from it, which brings me back to the beginning: I must have other factors in a relationship. I want whoever it is to look after me, as well as I take care of him, and, well, that takes time to work out, and, umm, err, as I am not having sex with any of the guys I am dating. It's a little like Victorian times when the ladies had suitors. Yes, that's it suitors, as in "not one". This sex business has really got out of hand. Men just expect sex. Just like that. So you are damned if you do as with Alfred, and damned if you don't, as with all the rest of them. She laughed to herself. But I think Pocket

Prince is different. Arnold definitely is, and Simon is looking for a relationship. To settle down and take care of me. Just like he said. And of course he wouldn't be showing me those photos of his sons and houses if he wasn't pointing out that he was willing and able to take care of me. So no, well yes, I am right to be treading carefully this time, so I choose the right man for me. I can't do that without seeing them. So then I will choose and tell the rest that I am taken. Yes that's what I shall do. That's the right way for me and for them. Anyway, what am I feeling guilty about once you find out what they get up to? I am bloody, Snow White.'

She called Charlie.

"Hi there Charlie. How are you doing?" She breathed in deeply, as she wasn't looking forward to potentially upsetting him. He was a doll she thought and giggled to herself, when she realised her double entendre.

"Hi. Oh hi there Victoria. I'm fine. Well pretty much so. I didn't get to sleep until four this morning."

"Oh, sorry honey. Have I woken you up?" It was five in the afternoon.

"No, no. I've been up for ages. Just had quite a bad night, last night."

"Oh. What's that then? Are you okay?" Victoria did worry from time to time about Charlie's safety. As much as his world might be fascinating, it was a big reason for not running as fast into the relationship as she would perhaps have done otherwise. Looking from the outside into Charlie's world, was a heck of a different to living it on the inside.

"Nah. I'm fine. Always will be, me. Nah. It's just that, while I know it goes on, I've never been there when it has happened."

"What's happened?"

"An execution."

"A what?"

"Mmm. Sorry Victoria, perhaps I shouldn't have told you."

"A bloody what? Shouldn't tell me. What do you mean?" she interrupted and felt a little scared.

"Mmmm. Oh dear. I didn't mean to…"

"Mean to meant to what?" she interrupted again.

"I can't tell you, if you keep on interrupting." Charlie was pacing his kitchen floor.

"What? Oh yes. Sorry, but execution! What do you mean? You witnessed a murder?" Her eyes were frightened, she felt a little dizzy and sat on the bottom step of the stairs.

"No, not exactly."

"Not exactly?"

"Victoria. You have to be quiet. I can't get a word in edgeways. It's not as bad as you think, so please let me explain." He sighed, exasperated with her and not altogether comfortable with what he had witnessed.

"Sorry Charlie. Of course. Go ahead. I'm zipped." She adjusted herself on the step. At least the carpet was soft and yielding underneath her buttocks.

"Last night, in one of the clubs, downstairs where we're renovating for a VIP area."

"Mmmmm?" She gently acknowledged that she was listening to him.

"Well, it's a bit of a bunker down there. No windows and pretty much shut off from the rest of the club. You can only get in by one entrance and it's in the basement."

"Mmmmm?" she mumbled back. It sounds scary already, she thought. God, did he watch someone being killed? Please God, don't let him tell me that. She swallowed hard.

"Well someone needed to be taught a lesson." He laughed and poured himself a diet coke.

Victoria gulped her juice, blinked her eyes several times, and swallowed. Charlie had her complete attention.

"And?" she said, this time sipping at her juice.

"And, well, he got taught one. Victoria in my world, we are the law."

"Yeah, but…"

"Anyway. The poor bastard only pissed himself, but he won't ever be the same. I know that. And of course he won't get no work, nowhere, not ever over here anyways." Charlie drank half the glass of 'brown nectar' as he called it. "Gotta have a coke after a hard night out," he had told her.

"Oh that's good. Then he is alive. So why did he piss his pants then?" Victoria took off her shoe. All in all, it had been quite a day and she was looking forward to her bed. An early night would do her good. Just a book, phone turned off, and leave the circus alone for a while.

"Because somebody was holding a gun to his head." Charlie walked to the other side of his kitchen and put on some music from the amazing hi-fi set up that he had.

"What?" Victoria spat out the juice. Fortunately, she had only taken a small mouthful and it just dissipated in the air.

"Yeah." Charlie giggled. "Quite heavy really. Some guy had really cheesed off my partner, so he decided to put the wind up him. Poor git thought he was going to die. Jameel had him kneeling on the floor, hands tied behind his back. We were all standing around. Jameel was shouting at him, telling him what a stupid turd he was, and that he needed a bullet in his head to teach him a lesson, and how he would be first to see him in hell and teach him another lesson there. Holding this gun to his head. Shouting and circling him. That's when I saw he'd pissed himself. Gary must have seen it at the same time, cos he shouted it out. Jameel just kicked him and told him he was fucking lucky and to get the hell out of his sight. If he ever saw him again he wouldn't give him another chance and that he might be better off dead."

"Oh. Oh well. Really. I don't know what to say."

"Nothing to say." Charlie slugged back the rest of his drink. "Ah. I needed that."

"What? Needed what?"

"Only my diet coke Victoria. Don't get agitated." He laughed again. "You know, it ain't as bad as it sounds, but I guess it kept me up a bit late." He started to polish the kitchen counter tops.

"No probably isn't, but seems pretty bad to me. Anyway sweetheart, I am sorry, but Emmaline wants to come home for the weekend. Apparently, she is homesick and well I… you know how I feel about waiting until I have the right relationship before…"

"No problem Victoria. I fully understand. Guess I'll spend a bit more time with my kids, and the clubs still need a lot of working on 'em. But I was gonna ask you something."

"Yeah, sure. Fire away." Victoria toddled toward her kitchen and opened the fridge door. She was going to get a coke herself, when she realised yet another double entendre and giggled.

"I was with Trixie last night." Charlie had just given the job of strip club manager to Trixie. She had been the headline stripper there, but after Charlie and Jameel took over, the incumbent manager was promptly sacked. Trixie had been given the job strictly on a temporary basis, or until the guys could ascertain her ability to do it. After three months or so, they were so pleased with her and of her control over the girls and in particular their moves and lingerie. Charlie had said that their morals were all still as bad, but then what could he expect. One girl brought her baby into work, as the baby's father was in prison and she didn't trust any of her family as they had violent tendencies (her brother was also just about to go to prison for choking his girlfriend half to death because she wouldn't get a beer for him). Charlie had a lot of respect for the girls. They did their work, collected their cash and disappeared. Tidy. Nice and sweet. No problems. No bother. They took their problems home with them and left them there.

"Oh, really? Hope she wasn't at the, um, err, um execution." Victoria sipped at her coke.

"No, no. Course not. I was with her before I went around to the jazz club."

"Oh good."

"Anyway, whilst I was talking to Layla." Layla had taken over Trixie's old job and was now head stripper. "And when I was showing her your photo, Layla shouted out to Trixie, 'Hey Trix. You seen Charlie's new girlfriend?' and Trixie called back, 'Yeah, she is a real looker, ain't she?'"

Victoria was thrown by 'new girlfriend', but didn't say anything to Charlie.

"And anyway…" Charlie's voice faded away and he could feel his face colouring up. He really did like Victoria so much and he hadn't felt like this about anyone, ever. Not ever, he was excited and petrified. She was such a woman. He loved everything about her and would do anything for her. He had told all his friends. Jameel knew more than anyone that Charlie did not feel this way about women, so, whoever this Victoria was, had to be somebody special. He couldn't wait to meet her, which is why he had suggested to Charlie that he invite Victoria up to the clubs for his birthday. They would arrange for the limo to take them to dinner at the right good Indian and then onto the clubs. Right good, evening out. Nothing was too good for Charlie. Jameel owed him big-time, not only on the financial side, but Charlie had saved his life, well more or less. Charlie had got rid of the leach girlfriend of his. Blood-sucking bitch. Yep. Charlie knew exactly what to do and had got Jameel out of a right mess. He sure owed him, and this woman must be something else, never seen him so happy.

"It's my birthday soon and, well, I just wondered would you like to come up my way? Go out to dinner and well, just, erm, visit the clubs. The girls want to meet you too?" There, he had said it.

Victoria didn't know what to say at first. It wasn't staying over with Charlie, Victoria knew she was quite safe there, it was the 'girlfriend' thing. She didn't think they had progressed to girlfriend/boyfriend stage. And she certainly wasn't sure about the girls wanting to meet her. What had he told them? But she had second thoughts of it, as she liked Charlie's company and was very, very curious about seeing the clubs.

"I would love that Charlie. Thank you very much. When is it?" It was Victoria's birthday soon, but she decided not to tell Pocket Prince, as she wasn't quite sure with whom she would like to spend it.

"Oh right. Great. Great. I'll arrange it. Two weeks' time, roughly." He punched the air and did a little dance. Charlie was over the moon. He couldn't remember when he had been happier. His business was going great, his pal, Jameel, was the best and now he had found the love of his life, and he knew Victoria was straight, She would not have accepted his invitation, if she hadn't wanted to be with him. Charlie wasn't a hundred percent sure that Victoria loved him as much as he loved her, but he did know she loved him.

"Charlie. Sorry honey, but I am feeling quite tired and would welcome an early night. I'm going to leave the rest of this coke, swap it for a Lemsip in bed and just read a book. Can we talk tomorrow?" Victoria put the bottle back in the fridge, switched on the kettle and took the packet of flu cures from the cupboard. She had started to get a headache.

"What? No. Sure, of course night, night then."

Of course, Charlie was full of beans as this was his morning although it was unusual for Victoria to go to bed so early. They had had more than one or two midnight conversations and a good night's sleep would do her the power of good. She would just call Simon and then go to bed.

That was indeed true, but this evening was different. She was dog tired. Mmmm. Well, that will be interesting, she thought, whilst imagining herself dancing around the poles in her favourite lingerie. I bet that would make Pocket Prince's eyeballs stand out, she laughed and rang Simon.

The call to Simon went straight to voicemail. "Hi Simon. How are you honey? I am off to bed now as I need an early night. Looking forward to seeing you on Friday. Call me tomorrow or I'll call you. Sweet dreams." She ended the call and sighed heavily. After all the trials and activity of the day, she was drained.

Christopher? Forgot to tell his wife that they were separated! Gee-whiz. Where did they come from? She would take a nice long shower. She picked up her book and shoes, shook her head and made her way upstairs to doze off into what would hopefully be a nice, long sleep.

Chapter 22

Mr Right on the Horizon

She woke up to another batch of text messages. Stephen; the newest kid on the block.

Just recently, she had joined another site. This was predominantly for Americans, although it was a global site. She had found it quite interesting, especially the amount of American men that had contacted her and their difference in approach and general demeanour.

'Hi there beautiful. Have an absolutely, fabulous day.' He was supposedly a very successful man in IT, living in California. Victoria was quite interested, but wanted to concentrate on Simon now. She only returned casual, polite messages to those who either texted her, or emailed her through the sites.

After breakfast, she prepared her suitcase for the weekend and, while she was putting the finishing touches to her wardrobe selection, decided that she was going to have great and amazing sex with Simon. She packed some risqué lingerie. A black, see-through, fur trimmed, baby doll nightie with black, teeny tiny panties and a maids outfit in which she looked particularly fetching. She would perform some role-play. She would be in her maid's outfit, a dress with white, puff sleeves, synched in by a blue corset, tied neatly at the back, with a white, very short, lace skirt, topped off with a white lacy thong and white stockings. Obviously the skirt would be short enough to allow the stocking tops to show. She would carry some fluffy, white, soft towels and knock on Simon's bedroom door, as though he were a guest in a hotel. He would let her in to deliver the fresh towels and turn down the bed, and she would run a bath for him with aromatic oils and bubbles.

Simon would ask her if she was finished for the night and she would say, "Actually you are my last guest, Sir." Then Simon would approach her with a glass of champagne and suggest that, as the bath was so big, it would be a pity for it to be for just one person. Victoria would then giggle girlishly and say, "Why Sir. What an idea? I am not sure I could," and Simon would say, "But I am sure you could, my dear," laughing caddishly and handing her the champagne. Then he would grab her by the waist and kiss her passionately, taking her by the hand and leading her towards the bath "Wait, wait sir," she would cry ."I must take my clothes off first. The hotel would be furious if I damaged them. They would make me pay and I don't have that kind of money."

Simon would let go of her hand and rip her clothes off, pick her up in his arms, kiss her gently, and, as he put her in the bath say, "My darling, you don't have to worry about that anymore. I shall take care of you from now on, and you shall take care of me." He would disrobe and offer her his huge erection.

Yep. That sounded good, she thought. She was a little rusty as she had been out of the loop for a long time, but well, it would be like riding a bike really, just get over a few nerves and the rest would be history, as they say.

'Can't wait,' she thought excitedly, and packed her red devilette outfit just for good measure.

She wasn't looking forward to the journey, but was so looking forward to meeting Simon again. As she shivered in the taxi taking her from one station to the other, she thought she would give Simon a call to let him know her progress.

"Hi darling," he answered. "How's my girl?"

"Hi darling. I'm just on my way to the station in a taxi."

"Taxi? Why have you taken a taxi? The tube is quicker."

"Oh, err, well." Victoria hardly ever took the tube, and the size of her suitcase would mean she would find it difficult, if not impossible, to drag the case up and down the stairs and escalators, and then there was the thought of heaving it on and off the tube train itself.

"Mmm. Well, I'm in the cab now dear-heart, so I'll let you know when I'm on the train to Oxford. Can't wait to see you."

"Me too, my beautiful lady. I'll be waiting for you. Keep me posted."

"Will do. Bye, Mwah."

What did he mean 'quicker to take the tube'? She shrugged and didn't give it any further thought, especially as she picked up a text from Tom.

'Hi lovely lady. Can't wait to lift up your skirt and lick your sweet pussy this evening. ETA and postcode please hugs and stuff T xx.'

"Oh my God," she gasped. "I've forgotten all about Tom." She stared at the message and had a quick vision of him doing just as he described. Oh my. I hope I've chosen the right one, she smiled to herself.

God, what do I tell him? I don't think the truth will go down too well in this case. Mmm. Yes, run that by me again Victoria. We were looking forward to rampant, passionate sex, we've been texting all week about it and you have forgotten. Not only have you forgotten, but you are on the way to see another man to have mad rampant sex with him. No that wouldn't be good. God there are so many men. I am just going to concentrate on Simon now. He ticks all the boxes and he did get a definite four ticks when she first answered his response to her advert. Yep. Concentrate on Simon. Now what do I say to Tom? Beautiful, handsome Tom. Well maybe I don't have to switch him off completely. It's still early days with Simon, whatever I think.

Victoria texted Tom. 'I am soooo sorry dear one, but I cannot make it this evening. My aunt has taken a turn for the worse and I really have to visit her. I just got the news and I'm packing to go. Sorry baby, as I was looking forward to seeing you so much.' Victoria didn't have an aunt, but at least there was some truth in the message.

'Cripes! Me too. Can't believe we're not meeting. Had everything set to go. But okay I understand. Keep in touch. What about next week? X X X.' Tom was quick to text back. She could almost feel the disappointment, which actually, in many ways, she felt too. Oh well, she sighed. At least there could be another time maybe, but it would all depend upon this weekend. She typed, 'Yes that would be good. Will be in touch.'

'Can't wait to be in touch with you. lol,' he replied.

"Ditto." She placed her mobile back in her handbag, as the taxi pulled into the station's drop-off area.

The journey was fast and easy, and, as usual, she had lots of help on hand to help her with her suitcase. In fact, the very nice man who helped her off the train with her suitcase was so very charming indeed. When she had explained to him that she was going to see her boyfriend, he seemed to be a little disappointed.

"Simon. Oh, Simon." There he was waiting for her, all smiles with arms wide open to greet her.

"Here, let me help you with that." He glared at the helpful man, who, glaring back at Simon, shrugged, said his goodbyes to Victoria and how nice it had been to meet her.

"Who is he?" Simon demanded, picking up the suitcase.

"Just a nice guy that I met on the train. He was very helpful." She linked her arms around his waist and squeezed.

"Mmmmm, it is soooo good to see you. How are you? Have you had a good day?"

"Mmm. Yes, yes." The man had disappeared and so had the grimace on Simon's face, as he felt Victoria's arms wrapped around him.

"What have you got in here? Are you staying forever darling? I do hope so." He laughed, putting the very heavy suitcase in the back of his Range Rover Sport. He opened the door for her and she climbed in. Once he was in the driver's seat, he leaned over and kissed her.

"Where have you been all my life, darling? My beautiful darling." His fingers clipped her gently under her chin.

"Mmm you too, darling." She returned his kiss.

They were like a couple of teenagers. Giggling and cooing at each other. Victoria forgot all about Tom. In fact she forgot about everybody, except Simon. She was in heaven and he would be her guardian angel. She had found her knight in shining armour at last.

Simon narrated throughout the journey to his home. Eulogising about the amazing countryside, as though Victoria was some Townie, which she had been once upon a time, and hadn't seen a blade of grass ever in her life. He was a little on the tedious side and quite persistent. Whenever she wanted to change the subject, like where were they eating that evening, he would ignore her and continue with his knowledge of the region, like some tourist guide.

Oh well. She'd stopped interjecting and sat there like a good girl listening to Simon warble on about how beautiful the area was.

"And here we are. This is where I live." Simon pointed ahead.

She couldn't see anything apart from local stone walls and miles of fauna and flora. He turned left at the bottom of the road and then right, down a private road bordered on both sides by stunning pine trees. There were fields on either side, which seemed to go on for miles, and they did go on for miles. She later discovered that Simon had a working farm of over 3,000 acres.

When they eventually reached the house, Victoria couldn't help but marvel at the size of it. It wasn't a house more of a mini stately home or maybe even a major stately home. It was enormous.

"Darling, we are home. I hope you like it, as someday you will live here," Simon quipped as he got out of the car.

Victoria mused, 'Maybe, just maybe,' and got out of the car as well.

"It's beautiful Simon."

He was standing next to her now and lifted her up to kiss her full and hard on her mouth. "I am so glad you like it. I built it myself. You remember how much I am into architecture?"

"Yes. I do like it. I like it very much indeed."

"Let's go in and you can look around." He was ahead of her, wheeling her suitcase over the gravelly ground, humming a little tune to himself. He couldn't remember being this happy in such a long time. He thought that the old bag of an ex-wife of his had ruined his life forever after bleeding him dry and poisoning his sons against him. Well 'Fuck her' now, because he had his sons back, he had made far more money than he ever gave to her, built his own houses and the ultimate cherry on the cake was Victoria. Beautiful, gentle Victoria, with a figure that could be the eighth wonder of the world. Fuck his wife. Fuck everybody, who had ever said he wouldn't recover. He wished that his ex-wife would shrivel up and die, but, better still, he knew she was miserable and didn't love her third husband any more than she did her first and second. 'Fucking whore,' he thought as he heaved Victoria's suitcase up the stairs. He was so lost in his thoughts about his ex-wife that he had quite forgotten he'd left Victoria behind in the kitchen.

She didn't want to follow him, as she thought she would leave it up to him where he put her case.

"Victoria. Victoria?" Simon called from the top of the house. She walked across the kitchen, one which could happily be roller-skated around. The house was enormous. She continued through a passage way, dining room on her left, and into an amazing stairwell. It look as though they had come in through the tradesmen's entrance, as there was a huge door to her left, obviously the front door, and a massive hallway.

The floor was a tasteful, black and white diamond, marble affair with what looked like a lounge, directly to her left as she stood facing the stairs. She placed one foot on the stairs, an arm across the banister and looked up, and up and up to the pin-sized head of Simon looking down at her. There must have been at least four floors.

"Hi Simon. How are you up there?" She could have sworn she heard an echo.

"Oh great, darling. Do you want to come up and make yourself comfortable?" Simon couldn't wait to get his hands on her, but he first wanted to make sure she was relaxed and felt at home.

"Sure. Yes thanks." She continued up the stairs. She passed a gigantic stained glass window. Quite breath-taking, admired several of the paintings and sculptures he had on display.

"Come. Come here to me you gorgeous thing." He gestured for her to go into the bedroom smiling and flapping about.

Victoria couldn't imagine what she was about to see, but it wasn't quite what she had thought. The room was huge, in keeping with what seemed like everything in and about the house, but whatever she had imagined, and she didn't quite know what that was, it certainly wasn't this. Oh boy, this man had been alone for a very long time. If she needed any proof that Simon had been a bachelor for over fifteen years, as he said he was, then this was it.

She entered into a room with mahogany lined walls that would have been incredibly dark and grim, if not for the patio doors and large windows at either end. Both windows had balconies. Apart from the wood covered walls, the rest of the room was decorated in darkest green damask and flock.

'Ghastly, absolutely ghastly,' she thought. So what had happened to the fantastic interior designer that Simon had told her about and who apparently designed all of Simon's houses? She walked past a huge bed, feeling a little bit like Alice in Wonderland after she'd drank the shrinking potion, and stepped into the en-suite bathroom. It had a huge enclosed bath, recessed into the wall and framed by mirrors. All of the furniture was heavy and the wood was dark and morose. The only thing lifting the bathroom was the white ceramic basins and cream carpet. A separate shower loomed up in the corner, like some demonic statue guarding the place.

Masculine was not the word for it. Aggressive, testosterone overload, or 'oestrogen not allowed here' described it better.

"Wow!" she said, turning around to face Simon who was still grinning.

"What do you think then peaches?" He looked expectantly at her.

She felt like a deer when targeted by a huntsman, his rifle aimed and ready to fire.

She had to make a decision. Should she lie outright and be doomed forever more to live with this horrid, screamingly horrid, bedroom, or should she tell the truth? She would rather stick pins in her eyes than live with it. Her whole impression of the house so far was that it might well be big, and made of beautiful stone, but it was like a funeral parlour. She knew the house was warm, which she had discovered when she caught her bottom unexpectedly on the Aga. It was enough to know he had the heating set to 'extreme', but still the house felt oddly cold, as though nobody lived in it. With the exception possibly of a cleaner who came around to ensure the place was spotlessly clean. She asked about who used the bathroom in which she was now standing.

"No. I use the shower and cloakroom downstairs next to my study," he responded.

"Oh right." She nodded. "Why is that?" although she had a fair idea she knew what the answer would be.

"It's just me here. I live like a student." He shrugged. "Well. Let's talk about this over dinner, shall we?"

"I thought we might have a glass of champagne, before we leave. What do you think?"

"Yes. That's a great idea." They walked into the bedroom. "Why don't you unpack, while I open the champagne? Make yourself comfortable - *me casa, su casa.*" He skipped out of the room. Simon was deliriously happy.

Victoria opened her suitcase and started to unpack. She was very happy. She quickly finished unpacking, using all of the space Simon had set aside for her. I wonder where he put his clothes? How kind of him to move them for me.

She changed into an Yves St Laurent black cashmere, cowl-necked dress. One of her favourites, with black, fully fashioned stockings, black lace 'la Perla', matching bra and panties and her dark green, almost black, YSL court shoes, with light brown, wooden heels. Goes with the bathroom, she giggled to herself. God forbid! Victoria turned around as she left the room and shook her head. This had to go for sure, if I have anything to do with it, she thought and went downstairs, checking herself in the ornately framed mirror that Simon had hung on the wall just beneath the top floor.

"Hello baby." Simon handed her a glass of champagne in an ordinary champagne glass, which struck her as rather strange, but then she looked around the room and, apart from the fact that fittings that were of high quality, very little else was.

She took the glass of champagne from him and they toasted each other. "To health and wealth." Victoria cocked her head to one side and looked Simon in the eye.

"To us." He beamed back.

"Okay. To us, my lovely Simon."

"And you, Victoria, are my very own eighth wonder of the world. You see I consider myself a special package and I deserve a special lady in my life and I think you are very special." He hugged her with his free arm.

What a very strange thing to say, she thought, but said, "Yes. I think you are a special man, and I have to agree with you. I am a special girl." They sipped their champagne.

"Shall we go?" Simon pointed to the door. He was now getting very anxious to get her into bed. He was simply aching for her.

"Yup. That's fine by me, I'm starving and we can finish the champagne after we get back." She finished her glass and put it on the granite island counter top.

Simon placed his glass next to hers, kissed her cheek and led her to the door. It was dusk now and there weren't any exterior lights.

"For goodness sake Simon. Why aren't there any lights out here? I can hardly see a thing."

"Hold on to me. I told you darling. I live life like a student." This was a phrase with which she would become very familiar.

"Well I am definitely going to have to do something about it." She was a little peeved as she tiptoed across the gravel in fear for her beautiful shoes, as well as a possible twisted ankle.

"I do hope so darling. That's what this is all about. Stay there while I get the car out of the garage."

Chapter 23

The Great Lover

"And this is still my land." Simon addressed Victoria and lightly touched her thigh. Simon had started off the journey by telling Victoria 'This is the start of my land and what appeared to be ten miles, or so after observed that this was still his land. Victoria was impressed.

"How are you going to manage the farm when your manager leaves? Surely it's a specialised job."

Simon's farm manager was leaving after being with Simon for over twelve years, as he had a better offer from a recently established Irish gentleman, who had purchased an even greater acreage.

"Think of the money I shall save, plus I need to do something. I'll manage it myself until I find another building project to interest me."

Save money? Save money? she questioned herself. How odd. It was obvious that Simon was a very wealthy man. How much money would he save? £40,000 or £50,000. So he would be driving the tractors? Victoria counted herself out of that career.

"I hope you like this restaurant, but I don't want you staying here all night." He switched the engine off.

"I beg your pardon?" she coughed.

"You know. Going through the whole menu. We did agree on an early night."

"What?" she spluttered. "When was that discussed?" She opened her door and got out of the car. 'What a bloody awful thing to say,' she thought. 'Hmm, I suppose he is eager, but even so, do have some finesse, some decorum for goodness sake.'

She came around to the front of the car. "Simon. I am here all weekend. Thank you for wanting to well, um, err, be with me, but this is being with me as well!" What a thing to say. Quite off-putting really. "Please do remember you are a gentleman while in the restaurant. You can be a complete Casanova in the bedroom, but wait until we get there, honey-pie." She reached up and kissed him on his cheek.

"Oh. What? Yes, yes. Alright then, let's go. But you don't have to have a dessert, do you?"

"Simon," she hissed. "Behave or I shall have four desserts and copious cups of coffee." She pushed him to cross the road. Shaking her head. "I shall hear no more! Okay?"

"Well, Um, yes. Alright," he mumbled.

Simon opened all the doors for her, but she was beginning to think that something was very wrong with this special package sitting across the table from her.

The restaurant was lovely. A cosy informal, rustic setting, and by all accounts from the comment book, the menu and the dishes whisking by her, there was a very good chef.

"I'll have the *menu du jour*." Simon handed the menu to the waiter and looked at Victoria. She couldn't tell for sure, but she thought he was expecting her to choose from the set menu as well. Nothing wrong with set menus, but only if you genuinely want something from them. No point in eating what you don't want or like.

"I am not quite ready yet." She looked up and smiled at the young good-looking waiter and glared at Simon.

"Maybe you could choose some wine, whilst I am deciding darling?" She passed the wine list to him.

"What? Oh, yes. Right. Well what was that wine I had when I was here last time?" he asked the waiter.

"Sorry sir. I can't remember the last time you were here. I might not have been on duty, but I shall be happy to recommend some wine for you."

"No. Erm. No. Come back in five minutes and we'll let you know."

The waiter dutifully left, and Simon leant over the table holding the wine list up against his face.

"They only recommend the most expensive wines, you know?" he whispered to her.

"No they don't Simon. It's a restaurant myth, but anyway, I have chosen now. I'll have the warm duck salad and the rib eye steak. As you're having the wood pigeon, perhaps a nice red burgundy would be lovely? Is that what you had before?"

"What? Erm, no. I think it was a merlot."

"Perfect." Victoria gestured to the waiter that they were ready to order. "What a very lovely restaurant Simon. Thank you for bringing me here." The waiter arrived with their wine.

"Well I don't know it very well, but it does have a very good reputation." He looked down at his tie. "Do you like my tie?"

Victoria had noticed that Simon was wearing the same jacket and trousers as when they first met, which she had passed over, because at least he had a change of shirt, and the fact that the tie was dreadful was of no significance, as she could help out with all that later.

"Well Simon. Seeing as you ask." She took a sip of wine. "No. It's awful."

"Yes. I thought that as well, but I only have two and I thought you would prefer me in a tie." She had a vision of him sitting there wearing only a tie and she laughed.

"What? Oh don't you? I mean. I well, I'm not really one for clothes."

That much was clear. He leant forward to hold her hand and accidently tipped his glass of wine right in her direction.

"Aaargh!" Victoria jumped up from her chair, missing the blackish red onslaught by a whisker. The liquid ran straight over the table and onto the floor, while the glass bounced off the table.

Simon caught the glass as it fell, causing the table to jolt and the bottle of wine to fall over. Victoria simultaneously grabbed up the bottle together with her glass of wine, saving the situation from becoming a complete disaster.

"I'm sorry. So sorry," Simon said, steadying himself upright in his chair. The waiter had noticed what had happened and rushed over to Victoria's aid.

"No problem. Don't worry. No harm done," she told Simon. "Thank you. Thank you," she bid the waiter.

The evening continued, punctuated by more and more apologies from Simon for his clumsiness.

"It really is alright," she kept telling him.

During dinner, Victoria referred to Simon's bedroom.

"It's not that it's not a nice room now, it's just that well, it is rather masculine, and, well, really a bit tired and very dark. A little grim. I don't mean to be rude but -"

Simon cut her off. "No. No you are not being rude. You are right. I just haven't noticed. No need to until now." He held her hand, this time with success and no drama. "Victoria you are right."

Victoria was smiling, her eyes sparkling. Simon felt certain they had stars in them. She thought how wonderful of him. I am sure he will let me decorate and redesign it. Victoria was already imagining a stunning leather bed, with walls being torn down. He really was a wonderful man.

Walls weren't the only thing crashing down, as Simon said to her, "I'll call Steven, my designer, first thing on Monday. I'll get him onto it straight away." He kept stroking her hand, which Victoria hated.

She took her hand back from Simon's unwelcome caresses and wiped it on her napkin. "Oh, err, umm. Great. Yes. Great." She felt truly let down, especially as Simon was so complimentary about her home. Oh well, the main thing was that it was to be changed, and, to be fair, they hadn't known each other that long. He would change his mind after tonight, she felt sure.

"Coming home?" Simon grinned at her. "I want you so badly Victoria. Forgive me if I'm rushing you, it's just I can't wait any longer. Looking at you so close to me. It's all I can bear." He made a puppy dog look and pouted at her. He did look cute.

"Yes. Let's," she said and lightly dabbed her mouth.

Once they reached Simon's home, Victoria had to pick her way over the gravel in pitch black this time. It was positively dangerous and probably damaging her beautiful shoes. This was definitely going to have to change as well.

"Let's take the champagne upstairs." Simon was moving faster than a ferret down a rabbit hole and was beginning to resemble one in Victoria's eyes.

"For goodness sake! Where is the romance?" she sighed. 'I don't think I'll dress up this evening. I'll mention the subject tomorrow. Let's go for it then,' she thought as Simon raced up the stairs, bottle in one hand, two glasses in the other. She bet he had never gone up those stairs so fast since they were built.

"Bath!" Ping! The idea came to Victoria. He was going about this all the wrong way, and she had to slow him down.

Simon was pouring the champagne into the two ordinary glasses when Victoria entered the room. He had managed to at least dim the lights and put on some music.

"Simon? Why don't we have a bath together? I've noticed you have some candles in the bathroom cupboards and I've seen some bubbles around here somewhere."

"Bath?" Simon stood up bottle in hand.

"Bath. Yes. A bath together. It's relaxing and well I'm not going anywhere am I?" she brushed past him like a chinchilla cat, purring as she went. Her perfume filled his nostrils and he was gone.

'Okay. If she wants a bath, she can have a bath. Haven't ever used it anyway so might as well christen it,' he thought. He caught her hand as she glided by. "You can have anything you want my darling," he said, planting a kiss on her shoulder.

"Good. Well I'll just run the water and light the candles. Have you some matches or a lighter?"

The bath idea turned out to be a good one, as Victoria began to relax underneath the mountain of bubbles, and once she was absolutely certain that Simon was clean. Not that she doubted for a moment that he wasn't, but there is nothing like surety is there?

They drank some more champagne and both enjoyed the closeness, but not any intimacy, not just yet.

"You are so beautiful my darling. Your body is to die for." Simon leaned back and rested his back against the smooth white porcelain of the bath. Victoria did the same at the opposite end and lifted her shapely leg out of the bubbles and placed a pointed foot on his chest.

"Thank you, darling. I am glad you think so," she purred. "Is it me or have you lost a lot of weight in the last few days?" She was puzzled, as it seemed an inordinate amount considering the time.

"Yes, as a matter of fact I have. It's you. I haven't done a thing. No exercise, perhaps not eating as much. I have lost my appetite, but I can feel my body running at a million miles an hour. It's all because of you my darling. I am sooo happy and I think happiness is eating my body."

Victoria chuckled. "Simon, really!"

"Darling. Are we all ready, sweetums?" He placed his glass on the side of the bath and got out, his long body taking most of the bubbles with it. He grabbed a white towelling robe and belted it around his waist. Victoria remained sitting in the bath, glass in her hand, scooping up the remaining bubbles with her other hand.

"Yes baby, I think we are." She placed her glass beside Simon's and stood up. A veritable Aphrodite! Her slightly tanned skin, so smooth and soft. Her large, firm breasts dotted with foam. She had put her hair up and had arranged it around a large bejewelled clasp, some strands of her hair hanging down over her bosom. It nigh on took Simon's breath away. Victoria made to step out of the bath.

"No, no," Simon cried out. "Stop, darling. Stop. Please allow me. Allow me to help you."

Victoria was rather surprised and wondered what on earth he had in mind.

"Here. Here. Please just stay there a minute." Simon took a huge, soft, white, fluffy towel from the warm radiator and wrapped it around her shoulders. He had stepped up to the bath and kissed her. Then he took her is his arms in a movement meant to lift her out of the bath and to carry her to the bed waiting for them along with great pleasure to come in the bedroom.

"For Christ's saaakke," Victoria screamed as Simon stepped back from the bath and promptly fell over, carrying Victoria with him. It wasn't at all what he had in mind and, crumpled on the bathroom floor, Victoria's hair clasp barely missing poking out his eye. Simon's legs were twisted at one end, but there was a saving grace at least for Simon, as Victoria's breasts were now covering his face.

"Urgh!" He tried to wrestle his body around.

Victoria balanced her hands on his chest and managed to stand up, straddling his lower torso with her legs. This wasn't what she had in mind either.

"Oof! I think I've hurt my back," groaned Simon, helping himself up onto his elbows.

Victoria stepped back reclaimed her towel and wrapped it around herself.

Simon got up rubbing his back. "I am so, so sorry darling. Are you alright?"

"Yes, yes. I'm fine. Don't worry about me. What about you? You had quite a way to fall."

"I'm okay. Not bad at all, just a little shocked that's all. Come on lovely to bed, to love and beyond."

Victoria laughed. 'Oh well. There's more to him than I thought.' They ran to the enormous bed and launched themselves at it.

"Darling, come here. I have been longing for you from the first time I set eyes on you." Simon pulled Victoria to him and much to her surprise found herself being dragged to the edge of the bed.

"I love this. I need to taste you." He began to kiss her inner thighs and lick her labia majora.

"Mmmm, Simon. Oh yes, please. Simon, darling." Victoria closed her eyes and squirmed down onto Simon's face.

Simon lapped, and licked, and sucked, and licked some more, but never found her spot. There was a lot of slurping and snuffling, but evidently Simon had never been shown the way, and was in dire need of a map. Victoria was not in the mood for this, as she considered that her teaching days were over, and, in any event, she was used to her men knowing what they were doing and pleasing her. As things were not going well for her, to which Simon was quite oblivious. He seemed to be having a fantastic time, if all the mumbling was anything to go by.

Victoria started to pull Simon up by his shoulders, so that he could mount her. 'Let's see how this goes,' she thought, stroking his member. It was long and thin. Not the best of shapes, but, hey ho, she wouldn't judge too soon. Simon did make a big thing of sex being important to him. Maybe she would teach him the great art of cunnilingus later.

"Mmm, darling." He entered her, using his hand to guide him. Victoria caught her breath. She always loved that first moment of entry.

Simon thrust deep inside her and kissed her full on the mouth, his tongue going deep into her throat. He thrust again, and again, and again. Nothing happened. No earth movements. No inner ecstasy. No, not much at all.

"Simon?" Victoria's arms were wrapped around his torso, but she quickly moved one arm down to their loins that were joined together or were supposed to be and there it was in spectacular slithery limpness. He had lost his erection. Simon seemingly hadn't noticed or was ignoring the fact, as he just kept humping away.

"Simon. Simon, for heaven's sake!"

"Don't worry darling. This has never happened before. I am a great lover. Really I am." Simon continued trying to put his limp penis into her vagina.

"Stop it. Stop it. Stop it at once." Victoria moved out from beneath him.

"Darling, darling. Please don't worry. He'll be back, I promise. I am aching for you." Simon implored her.

"It's okay. It's alright." Victoria told him. 'It wasn't,' she thought. 'But let's limit the damage.' Victoria cuddled up to him. "It's okay baby. This isn't the first time its happened to a man and a woman. Sometimes it can be a bit too much. You know? For the first time. What with all the waiting, anticipation, Mr Willy can't always cope. Come on, let's get some sleep and work on it in the morning, best to forget it ever happened and start from scratch."

Victoria wondered why women did that. Why they were so understanding, so sympathetic. The reaction of a rampant, hot-blooded male in the very throes of embarking on a night of intense sexual pleasure and then getting refused would not be hard to imagine. Just like that. 'Sorry. I am no longer in the mood,' she says. Would he have said all that Victoria said to Simon? No way. No. Boy he would be hopping mad, angry as a rattlesnake that's been poked with a stick. There would definitely not be any cuddle or sweet words of understanding. Sadly, many men would just ignore the change of mind and carry on regardless.

Simon grasped the invitation with both hands, legs and any other part of his anatomy. He was just so bloody grateful, but he knew he could redeem himself. His last lover often told him how good he was. He was in fact a great lover. These things happen and, as Victoria said herself, anticipation and built up was too much. So he was glad she didn't notice he had a bout of acute premature ejaculation. Which is another thing of course she did notice! She just decided to bury the subject. Why didn't he wonder about why she had to go to the bathroom before she went to sleep?

Simon cuddled up to Victoria, so pleased she not only looked great but was a nice sweet person as well. He was falling in love, he knew it. She was everything he had ever wanted.

Victoria lay in his arms, eyes closed, but wide awake wondering that this may not be the 'one' after all.

Chapter 24

Showers and Fairy Godmothers

The next morning Victoria awoke to Simon stroking her pussy.

"Mmmm, darling." He gently started to rub her clitoris and nibbled lightly on her ear.

"Mmmmm. Oooooh. That's nice," she responded and wriggled her bottom into his groin. Hoorah! He was as hard as a rock.

"Darling. Darling. Come to me sweetheart." Simon made to enter her, using his hands yet again to guide him. Maybe this guy needed more than a map and a lesson or two, she thought. He continued to use his hands to help his penis enter Victoria's very wet and willing vagina, but it happened again, this time before he had even entered her. However, Simon continued trying to insert his penis. What did he think he was doing? He certainly wasn't doing anything for Victoria, whose arousal was disappearing as fast as it arrived.

She thought she would try and arouse him in another way and turned around to face him.

"Let me baby." She kissed him and slid her hands down to caress his cock and make him hard again. But, try as she may and she did try very hard to make him hard, her gentle, knowing ministrations were to no avail. Simon remained as limp and unattractive as a deflated soggy balloon.

"Never mind, darling." She repeated her soothing words from the night before.

"It's never happened before darling, I can assure you." he whined.

"Don't worry honey. We have all the time in the world. It's just a little first time nerves. Nothing to worry about. How about that breakfast you promised me?" She gently pushed him away.

"Yes, yes. Of course. Right away. Pineapple, natural yoghurt, and my fresh coffee. Sound good?" he said, getting off the bed and walking towards his dressing gown.

"Sounds fantastic, darling. Exactly what I would like." She sat up, displaying her marvellous breasts. She looked very lovely just sitting there naked with a little flush to her cheeks.

"You look lovely darling. I love you without your makeup. You look like a teenager."

"Mmmmm. Thank you, but I don't like me at all without makeup."

"Nonsense. In fact, go to lunch today without all that war paint. Just be my fresh faced baby doll." Simon left the room, still smiling, and feeling as light as a feather.

Victoria got out of bed and went straight to the bathroom. Yuk. She needed a shower. Why did he insist on trying to shove his limp cock up into her, as if that would make her feel sexy? She made a memo in her head to talk to Beth about it. In fact she hadn't looked at her mobile for some time now. She turned the shower on and then went to her handbag to see what was going on with her army d'amour.

There was a funny noise coming from the bathroom. She picked up her mobile and went into the bathroom to discover that the shower was having an apoplectic fit. It was hissing and coughing and spluttering. Spitting out brown water, it then managed just a dribble of water from its golden spout.

She looked at it in disgust. "God, this man needs far more work than I thought," she said to herself. 'I suppose I shall just have to have a bath for now and find out the story behind the shower later.'

She turned the golden taps and released a flood of hot water. "Thank God for that," she muttered. "I'll send Beth a text."

'Hi beautiful, Simon lovely man can't get it up, but not new for me as we know. Seems smitten. Going to lunch later today.' She pressed send, but was amazed to see the recipient was not Beth, but Simon.

"Crikey! how did that happen," she exclaimed. "Oh well. Not going to lunch after all. It looks like I shall be packing very shortly." She shrugged at herself in the mirror. "Can't believe it."

At that moment, Simon came bouncing into the room brandishing a tray with cups, plates and saucers, proudly holding golden cubes of pineapple and bright segments of oranges. The smell of the coffee was divine.

"Da, daaah!" he crooned. "Just for you sweetheart. Don't you look lovely." Simon's smile couldn't get any wider.

"Oh. Thank you darling. Just put it on the ledge over there." She pointed.

Evidently, he hadn't received the text yet. Oh well, she might as well eat before he threw her out.

"Simon, why doesn't the shower work?" She turned on the cold water bath tap waving away the steamy air.

"I live like a student darling." Where had she heard that before?

Wish you could fuck like one, she thought, having a flashback and fond memories of her first lover at University.

Victoria walked back to where the breakfast tray was balanced on the window ledge and picked a piece of pineapple from the plate. Simon must have given her a whole pineapple as the pieces were overflowing from the plate and piled high. Simon just stood there at the entrance of the door staring and smiling. Smiling and staring.

"Is there another shower somewhere?"

"Pardon? Ermm? What?" he seemed to be in a trance. "Another shower? Shower. Yes, shower, of course. I use the one downstairs next to my study. Why do you want one?"

"No. Not now, I've run a bath, but I'm more of a shower person than a bath person. Well, if it's by myself of course."

"Well, I'll just get on and have a shower myself." He saluted her and left her alone. As he went down the stairs, he punched the air. "Yes. Oh yes. Oh boy, she's fantastic," he pronounced.

Mmmm? If he is having a shower, then I might be able to find his mobile and delete that message. She wrapped a towel around her and proceeded downstairs in pursuit of Simon.

"Singing in the rain, just singing in the rain." A very croaky, but happy refrain was coming from the shower room where Simon was obviously doing his best to emulate Gene Kelly. She quickly found his mobile and deleted the awful evidence, then went to where Simon was showering, opened the shower door and stepped in. Simon was soaping his hair. Victoria pressed her breasts against his chest.

"What? Mmmnph? Oh, Victoria. Victoria, darling." She slid down on her knees, the hot water streaming down over them both.

"This is where my fairy godmother turns up and says 'Time's up,'" Simon said with a slightly delirious note to his voice. Victoria cupped his balls in her soft, small hands and continued sucking and licking until his hardness was able to lie between her breasts.

Aha. Time for 'me' time, she thought as she stood up for Simon to thrust his hard manhood into her aching, and horny little pussy. Unbelievably, as she stood up to welcome him into her body, he spurted all over her tummy.

"Arrrrrgh! Ummm. Emmmmm. Oh baby." Simon fell back onto the shower wall. 'Oh baby?' she thought. 'Bloody hell! This won't do, but at least the water is keeping me clean.' Victoria wasn't a fan of spermatozoa. Always messy, as far as she was concerned.

"You really are the eighth wonder darling." Simon kissed the top of her head.

'Yes and from where you are, I am,' she thought. 'So what are you?'

Simon finished soaping and left Victoria to finish her ablutions alone. She appreciated the space.

When Victoria was alone and finishing getting ready, she answered some of the texts that had mounted up since her arrival.

Charlie had sent one asking how she was and how her weekend was going.

Oliver, the international lawyer sent: 'Can't wait to meet you gorgeous. Let me know if you can make dinner in two weeks, as I am due to be in London. Have secured a very large account. So can have some pleasure as well as business. Soft soft soft kisses.'

Tom: 'I can't wait to take you from behind and fuck you senseless.' Victoria had never understood that phrase, but quite liked the idea, especially after the last twenty-four hours.

There was one from Irish Arnold wishing her well and looking forward to the weekend when she was going to see him.

'Oh dear. Yes. I had forgotten all about that,' she thought. She had been going to cancel that idea in favour of Simon, but from the performance, or rather lack thereof so far from Simon, she decided to leave Arnold in place for a while longer. There were numerous other texts from men who had contacted her one way or another simply asking after her wellbeing, and when could they meet up. Victoria couldn't keep up with the backlog on her texts, let alone meet all of them. Most were barking mad in one way or another, pretending to be somebody they were not, and apart from Mad Sam who, although barking, was at least very handsome. Most were less than average in the looks department.

There was a text from Sam too. 'Morning gorgeous. How are you today?' She replied that things were well and hoped they were with him as well. She called Berrie, her dear Berrie. She often wondered what sex would be like with him, but banished this thought as soon as it came. Berrie was her dear and wonderful friend, and they had agreed at the very beginning of their relationship that they would always be friends, but that was all. Just friends. She wouldn't want to do anything to spoil their friendship. She quickly called him, said she was fine and safe, then put her mobile away in her handbag and went downstairs.

Simon took her to lunch. A super country pub that was extremely popular with tourists and locals alike. They chatted about Simon's love of architecture and his hatred of his ex-wife.

"I wish her ill, you know," he told her. Victoria winced and told him that would bring bad karma upon him and that for goodness sake, it was over fifteen years ago. Simon could really hold a grudge. The discussion about his sons was much better. He loved them very much. This conversation made Victoria feel much better about Simon and she guessed that his ex-wife must have really hurt him and so she dismissed what he had said and mentally forgave him. He also openly admitted the feelings that he was developing for Victoria.

She blushed a little and told him that she thought she could feel the same way too.

He asked her when her birthday was.

"But that's only two weeks away," he announced to the whole pub.

"Simon! Shush. Yes it is." She put a finger over his lips.

"Would you like to go away? Madeira! It's lovely there and of course warm. I know an exclusive, very expensive hotel. It could be our little piece of heaven for a few days." Simon was very excited.

"Sounds wonderful." She could do with a break and this could bring Simon and her together. She could see Charlie for his birthday. She didn't want to upset Charlie, as she liked him very much. That would keep him happy and then she could have a little holiday for her birthday with Simon. Perfect!

Victoria decided that perhaps she should wait before dressing up for Simon. 'Let's keep it more low profile until he has time to get used to me,' she thought. That evening it was just as well she had come to that decision, because Simon fell asleep on the sofa while watching one of his numerous DVDs. It was only Nine o'clock. But he was a kind man even if he did have some strange habits, like not leaving a tip when the restaurant didn't have a service charge. Actually, he seemed to positively delight in it.

"They overcharge for the food anyway," he commented to her on their way home.

Victoria wrinkled up her nose with a mixture of distaste and embarrassment. Simon had just been discussing buying another villa in Portugal, which was priced at over six million, and he couldn't even leave a ten percent tip. Ludicrous! Something was wrong with this picture. But again she dismissed it. Simon had so many other positive qualities. One only had to see how generous he was with his sons, and what a kind gesture to take her home, and collecting Emmaline on the way. Yes, most men wouldn't do that, would they? It was three hours driving.

Victoria, like many women today, frequently forgot just what a prize she was. The fact was that most men would have offered to do that for her, and much, much more besides. She just hadn't found them yet.

Simon was delighted to meet Emmaline and, judging by the way Emmaline was laughing, joking occasionally and teasing him, she quite liked him too. However, Simon wasn't the wittiest of men. He had missed several of Emmy's quips, which had gone straight over his head, but again Victoria saw this as unimportant.

They arrived home all in good humour, but tired. Poor Simon had to go return home and he even refused a cup of coffee.

"No thanks, darling. I'm better off to go straight back, Get it over with." He kissed Victoria on the cheeks and said goodbye to Emmaline, squeezing her hand gently and saying how nice it had been to meet her.

"Likewise," Emmaline replied, smiling widely and revealing her perfect, beautiful, white teeth. Victoria was so proud of her. They waved him goodbye and went into the house.

"So, what do you think?" Victoria asked her daughter.

"Very nice. He seems very nice. It was kind of him to bring you home, and collect me too," she said, taking her heavy suitcase upstairs. Emmaline had inherited her mother's habit and could never travel light. Victoria was please that Emmy and Simon had hit it off, and delighted that she had Emmy at home for half term.

Victoria went into the kitchen to make herself a cup of coffee and for Emmaline her favourite, hot chocolate.

They talked long into the night. Victoria about the different men she had come across, especially Mad Sam, Pocket Prince and of course now Simon. Simon was the only man Emmaline had met and Victoria hoped that it would remain that way. Emmaline liked the sound of Pocket Prince.

"Oh, he sounds so sweet, but I do like Simon and, if his house is as big as you say it is, maybe I could have my birthday party there. I am sure he wouldn't mind."

"Emmy, sweetheart. It's far too early to be thinking about things like that."

"I saw the way he looked at you. He's already a goner Mummy. But it is what you think and feel that matters."

They talked about Emmaline's days at school and her boyfriend Zac. If a mother could choose a first boyfriend for her daughter, then they would choose Zac. He was such a lovely boy and adored Emmaline.

They went to bed that evening, tired, but both mother and daughter were very content. Emmaline was so happy to be home with her mother, and Victoria was so happy to have met Simon. She quite forgot all about the bad sex. It wasn't everything in a relationship and in any event she could make that better.

That was the problem with Victoria. She would never turn away when something wasn't quite right, she could always make it better. She should have learnt by now that it wasn't good to make this mistake time and again. She should have taken any opportunity to walk away from something that wasn't right. It was fine and, if it wasn't broken, there no need to fix it, but if was broken… She should have left it well alone, especially if it concerned middle-aged men.

Victoria woke to another deluge of texts. She would reply to them later, as she wanted to take care of Emmaline. She went to the kitchen to prepare their breakfast whilst Emmy still lay sleeping. She loved it when her daughter was at home. She also liked it when Emmy was at school. Yes. Life was wonderful. She only needed a man to complete her world and she was sure she had found him in Simon.

Chapter 25

The Gangster's Moll

Simon had been in touch every day and they chatted for hours, the same as with Pocket Prince.

Charlie was beside himself with joy that Victoria was going to stay at his house and meet all his friends, especially his business partner, Jameel. Charlie hadn't felt this happy in years. The kids were settling down really nicely. That old bitch hadn't been on his case for over a week now. The business was ticking over nicely and Victoria was coming. Could things get any better? Not that he could think of. Oh, only when Victoria agreed to marry him. Yes that would be the icing on his cake. His life would be starting all over again. This was his second chance to live a good and decent life. A happy life, not one stooped in misery and resentment. In Victoria, he would finally have what he had always wanted: a classy, beautiful, intelligent lady. Not like the other women that surrounded him. And certainly not like that cow who had suppressed him and made him live in the dark for all those years. No. Those days had gone, he was on the brink of a whole new world. Victoria was wonderful, and she would love him, and be loyal to him, and he would work hard to give her everything she wanted.

All these thoughts kept swimming through his mind while he was cleaning his house. His house. That's right. HIS. No mortgage, no nonsense house. It might be a little small for Victoria, but the business was growing rapidly and he would soon be in a position to buy her something bigger. No mortgage though. Charlie hated debt of any kind. If he wanted something, he would buy it. All of it. He had seen too many people get into too much trouble by borrowing. It's how he ended up with the clubs. No. If any loans were in the offing, then it would be him doing the lending, never the borrowing.

Charlie cleaned and cleaned the house, top to bottom, bottom to top. The oven was gleaming, with not a spot of grease. It looked like it had never been used. The taps positively shone like diamonds and the carpets were soft and smelt of oranges. The whole house looked brand new. A 'show' house, Charlie's house, soon to be Charlie and Victoria's house. He knew the children would adore Victoria, and what an amazing role model she would be for them, especially his twelve-year-old daughter, Louise. Perhaps not quite the same with his son, Damien. But Damien was a fifteen-year-old and Charlie would take care of all his needs. Oh life was so good and going to be better. He couldn't wait to see her. He couldn't wait to see her face when she saw the flowers he had bought for her. He had some trouble at first because he didn't quite understand her cryptic comment that all flowers should be stunningly beautiful and come in large bunches. But Jameel had been a great help, as well as the florist.

Victoria would be surprised when she saw them, because they covered almost all of the kitchen table and they were stunning. A mixed bunch of tropical and local: irises, lilies, proteas and roses. There were so many roses, blood red and snowy white, all laced together with ferns and long grasses. The flowers' scent was fighting rather unsuccessfully with the acrid smell of bleach from Charlie's cleaning efforts, which was a pity. But Charlie was happy with the smell of the bleach. It denoted everything was clean in every way. Victoria was going to be proud of him. Charlie was proud of himself. He couldn't wait for her to get here. He had given her good directions, and she should be here any moment.

Victoria was starting to get a little tetchy, as the directions Charlie had given her seemed to be wrong. She couldn't find his road and, out of the four people she asked, three hadn't a clue. Finally, she called Charlie, who said he wasn't at home as he had just popped out for something, but if she waited by the Co-op, he would come and fetch her. She parked the car and waited.

She knew that this was a big night for Charlie and so she had dressed in her leather strapped, black linen dress. It did show a lot of cleavage, but then Victoria did have a lot of cleavage. One of Emmaline's favourites, the dress flowed around Victoria in large folds of material. Her ensemble was accompanied by a blue, Swarovski necklace and matching earrings, and to top it off she wore her favourite rings, the 11.2 carat sapphire and diamond one and her 4 carat baguette diamond ring. She had had her nails manicured, along with a pedicure, and her fake tan had been carefully applied. She wore electric blue stockings, and her six-inch, Yves St Laurent black patent shoes. Well Charlie had told her that she must be herself and he had no problem that she was taller than him. Nearly everybody was anyway. So she had thought, I don't care either, which was a lie.

She thought Charlie would be pleased and proud to introduce her to his friends. She was fascinated to meet them. Who would have thought it, Victoria Moreton, a gangster's moll.

Charlie drew up alongside her. "Hello Victoria. Follow me. It's not far."

Victoria could hardly see his head. He looked like a small child behind the wheel. She made an 'okay' sign and did as Charlie instructed. They drove into a cul-de-sac of redbrick houses. Charlie parked and pointed to where she should park her car, next to his. The house had a double garage, so she parked outside one of them. Charlie leapt out of his car and rushed around to Victoria's and opened her door.

"Ooooh Charlie. You startled me. Where did you come from? Bloody difficult to find your house though."

"Milady." Charlie offered his hand in order to assist her from the car.

"Thank you, kind sir." She took his hand and got out of the car. They weaved themselves between the cars to Charlie's front door.

'One day I'll carry her over this,' he thought as he opened the door to Aladdin's cave. "After you." He indicated for her to go ahead.

Everything was bright. It seemed to Victoria as though some bright, white light was emanating from the very house itself. Amityville Horror.

"Wow!" Victoria turned around and then went into the kitchen where she was bowled over by the combination of bright lights, bright flowers, lots of them, and the pungent smell of bleach. All of her senses were being attacked at once. Charlie was standing right behind her, holding her suitcase. He was quivering with excitement.

"What do you think?" he asked nervously.

"Mmmmm." Victoria was still recovering from sensory overload. She felt sunglasses would have been in order. "Oh. Mmm? Pardon? Yes, lovely. Lovely and, oh my gosh, look at those flowers. They are beeeauutiful." She rushed over to touch and smell them. They smelt of bleach, which was unfortunate, but they did look absolutely beautiful.

"Just like you Victoria. Just like you." He put the suitcase down and walked over to her as she preened over the flowers. Charlie touched her shoulder. He loved touching Victoria and did so at every possible opportunity. His habit grated on Victoria's nerves, but she didn't have the heart to tell him so.

Charlie led her up the stairs to his bedroom and put her suitcase down in it. Even this blatant movement did not scare Victoria. She knew she would be safe with her Pocket Prince. They had had many conversations on the subject of sex and how they both felt about it, and there was no way that Charlie was ready to make love to her at the moment. He just wanted to be close and cuddle her. As she knew all this, it was remarkable that she didn't know how Charlie felt about her. But it had simply escaped her notice. Rather selfish perhaps, but certainly without any malice. Victoria genuinely liked Charlie.

"Oh, Charlie. The whole house looks brand new. Everything is bright and polished. I swear I couldn't find a speck of dirt, even if I looked all day."

Charlie's face beamed. "Shall I leave you to freshen up? There is a glass of champagne waiting for you in the kitchen, or shall I bring it up for you?" He was leaning on the fitted mirrored wardrobes, and she was looking at the bed. It was enormous. There was hardly any space left in the room to move around it. Charlie could have gone for a swim in it.

"Pardon? Oh no, that's fine darling. I'll be down in a jiffy." She went into the cupboard-sized en-suite shower and reeled from the smell of bleach. Charlie went down to the kitchen.

'I know cleanliness is next to godliness,' she thought. 'But this is taking it a bit too far. Never mind. What a very nice gesture. It must have taken him days to get it to this standard, or maybe he lives like this all the time? You wouldn't necessarily have thought of a gangster wearing an apron and rubber gloves would you?' She freshened her makeup, opened her suitcase, and took some perfume from it. Anything to alleviate the smell of bleach. She sprayed her perfume behind her ears and on her wrists, then returned it to the case all in one fluid movement, before going downstairs to give Charlie his birthday presents. She had bought him a Lanvin belt and a white shirt in the hope that he would wear that, rather than the frilly ones for which he obviously had a penchant.

"Hiya." She walked into the kitchen, where he was already waiting with champagne, poured into very pretty 'Marie Antoinette', gold rimmed crystal glasses. Very kitsch.

"Here you are darling. To you." He passed her the glass and raised his own glass to hers. She sipped the ice cold, brilliantly sparkling liquid.

"Mmm. Wonderful. Thank you Charlie. Everything is so wonderful. To you, you marvellous man." She sipped again. It tasted fabulous, the bubbles veritably danced over her tongue.

The sound of a car horn interrupted their joyous moment. "What's that?"

"Oh. Sorry Victoria. They must be a little early. Jameel and Gary have come to take us to the restaurant." Charlie went to the front door and Victoria followed, bringing her champagne with her. She was sure it was Cristal, it tasted so good. Not like that supermarket 'own brand' stuff Simon had given her.

"Hi there man. How's it going brother?" a very good-looking, tall, slim built, coffee-coloured man greeted Charlie.

'This must be Jameel,' Victoria thought. Charlie had described him to her as half Afganistani, half Iranian. He was in his early thirties, had a shaven head, and bright blue eyes. Quite striking. Victoria was surprised at how he looked. He was also dressed extremely well. A nice light weight, light tan coloured suit, with a white shirt left open at the collar, brown belt and shoes and a splendid Cartier watch. The only disappointing thing was that he was wearing a multitude of rings. 'One on every finger,' she thought.

"Hi man." Charlie returned his greeting and they high-fived each other. She could see a figure in the driver's seat of a huge, black, stretched limousine. Presumably that was Gary, as he was their driver for the night.

She backed off into the kitchen, leaving the them to do 'man stuff' greetings. Jameel entered the kitchen in front of Charlie and he was even better looking in the blazing lights than he had been in the darkness outside.

"And you must be Victoria?" he said, striding over to shake her hand.

"Yes, and I assume you are Jameel?"

"I have heard so much about you," he said, lightly taking her hand.

"And I about you. I hope it's all good?" Victoria looked over to where Charlie was standing, his chest all puffed out, as proud as a peacock. Charlie had never been this happy.

"See, Jameel. I told you she was beautiful, didn't I?"

"You did bro, you sure did." Jameel slapped Charlie on the back in a congratulatory fashion. Victoria felt like some prize cow at a country fair and not very comfortable at all.

"Not to rush, but are you ready? The table's all booked. Expecting you for eight, okay?" Jameel looked at Victoria and Charlie in expectation that they would immediately leave and follow his instruction, which is exactly what they did.

For the first time since meeting Pocket Prince, Victoria began to feel a little out of place. She was towering over him as they walked to the car.

They didn't look like a match made in heaven, more like the odd couple, a very odd couple indeed. Victoria felt ashamed of herself, because she wanted to stick a notice on her back saying, 'He is only my friend.' God, how awful. She was embarrassed to be with him. Charlie didn't deserve that. He was a very lovely man. She submerged the feeling and shook herself. She should be glad she was with him, and they were going to have a lovely evening.

Look at all the trouble he has gone to so far. But because of that Jameel rushing them so much, she had left his presents on the kitchen table. Something to look forward to when we get back. She would tell him once they were in the restaurant. It wasn't clear, but she wondered if Jameel would be dining with them.

After some general chit chat and small talk about the previous night's activity, they soon reached the restaurant. Apparently, it had been a great night at the jazz club and a new black comedian was especially good.

"You'll be seeing his act later this evening Victoria. You'll love him. He'll crack you up." Jameel looked back at her from the front seat of the limo.

"Oh great. Good. I'll look forward to it." Charlie squeezed her hand and looked at her lovingly, he was beyond happy. His time had come at last.

They drove into a crescent shaped driveway in front of a baby pink coloured Indian restaurant. It was probably the biggest and finest Milton Keynes had to offer.

Victoria was a little surprised, as she was expecting something a little more sophisticated, but what the hell, she loved Indian food.

Jameel opened the door for her, while Gary leapt out to open the door for Charlie.

"Everything has been done Chas. You don't have to worry about a fing just 'av a great time n' call us when yer finished. We'llll come and get yer, okay?" Jameel was clapping Charlie on his back and grinning from ear to ear, obviously very pleased for the both of them.

"Nice to meet you Victoria. 'ave a great time together. I fink you'll like what we've done."

"Oh sure. I'm sure we will. Thank you." She returned his smile and hoped that whatever it was they had arranged, did not include a 'surprise' birthday package, singing 'Happy Birthday Charlie' over the public address system.

They were greeted by a very tall gentleman wearing a pink and green, embroidered Kaftan and trousers, with a matching turban and gold, pointy shoes.

"Good evening Mr Smythes-Bowles." He bowed. "Please follow me. We have your table all ready for you. Madame, please." He bowed to Victoria and gestured towards the stairs. They went upstairs to a round restaurant and on a further level Victoria saw a solitary table, all set up with candles all around, and further surrounded by flowers.

"Sir. If you please?" He pointed for Charlie to go up the stairs to the table on the top floor of the restaurant.

Charlie drew a chair from under the table for Victoria. "If Modom pleases?"

She sat down, very happy to be with Charlie on his birthday. "Modom does please, and thank you," she said sitting down and marvelling at the setting.

Charlie sat down as well. He almost floated around the table to sit facing Victoria. "I've never had a birthday party, or any celebration before."

"Oh really? Sorry Charlie. That is sad." She felt a little embarrassed for him, but Charlie was not at all embarrassed. In fact he seemed elated that never having a birthday celebration was worth it if this was his reward. To be spending the night with Victoria in this palace.

Charlie waved to the waiter who was hovering at the top of the stairs. "Champagne Victoria?" He reached for her hand across the table.

"That would be lovely Charlie," she replied.

They drank delicious wines and ate delectable foods, and talked and laughed all evening. Charlie was regaling her with all sorts of anecdotes about his life, and how happy he was to have met her, and how their life was going to be together.

'Together? Life together? What? Where had he got that from?' she thought, alarmed and disconcerted. It was the first time that she had any idea where Charlie was going. It put a huge downer on the evening for her, but she didn't want to spoil this time for Charlie, and so she made no comment, but continued smiling, laughing and joking with him. She would deal with this later, at a more suitable time. He looked so happy, she wasn't going to do anything to take this time away from him.

"And are we ready to go Victoria? Would you like anything else?"

"I'm fine thanks Charlie. No I don't want anything else. It has been perfect."

Charlie looked over to the ever-present, but discreet waiter and signed in the air. The waiter approached and whispered something in his ear.

Charlie grinned and said, "Well thank you very much. Much appreciated.

Shall we, Victoria?" He got up from his seat and held his hand out for her. "Looks like Jameel has dealt with everything, including the bill. Great bloke, isn't he?"

"Oh that's lovely. What a lovely thing to do. Although I would have liked you to open your presents here, but I left them back at yours."

"No problem Victoria. No problem at all. We will open them when we get in. Don't worry. Everything will be fine. Let's go."

"Shall we call for Jameel?" Victoria said going down the stairs.

"No need. I did it already. Gary should be outside waiting for us."

Sure enough there it was, the very black and very large car. This time Jameel was not there, but Gary had on a chauffeur's hat. Victoria was touched by everything that had been arranged for Charlie. He was obviously well liked and respected. She thought it was super of Charlie to want to do this for her, she realised this wasn't his everyday transport, but she was worried about the many references Charlie had made over dinner to 'their life together'.

They parked outside The Parakeet, Charlie's strip club. The neon signs featured all of the colours of the rainbow, with a few extra just for good measure. At least no one would walk by and not notice. A huge man, probably over 6'7 and weighing over twenty-five stones, opened the car door for her. She climbed out, excited, and not without trepidation.

When she entered the club. Pow! The darkness hit her like somebody had just turned the lights from electric to ebony in a micro-second. The air was hot and acrid. She could see vague outlines of figures walking around.

"Come with me Victoria. I want to introduce you to Trixie and the girls."

"Fine. Yes, of course." She caught his arm, while her eyes were adjusting to the gloom. Moving through the hallway into the club itself the light got better and she could see the bar, the poles on the tables and the dance floor. There was one girl twisting and turning around a pole. She didn't seem very enthusiastic and neither did the men sitting beneath her. Most seemed more interested in their beer and conversation with their pals.

"Wow!" exclaimed Victoria, following on behind Charlie, as he led her across the room to where she presumed Trixie was standing.

"Hi Trix. This is Victoria. Victoria this is Trixie, our manager." Charlie touched Trixie's shoulder by way of greeting. He was obviously very proud to be introducing his 'girlfriend' to Trixie.

"'allo love. 'ow are yer?" Trixie moved toward Victoria and gave her an unexpected, great big hug.

"Oh. Err. Um. I'm fine thanks. Good. Yes, very good," she responded, somewhat startled by this very warm greeting from a stranger in a strange place.

"You 'av a good dinner then?" Trixie was all lit up with smiles and glitter over her face and body. She was about forty-five, long blonde hair, strappy, glitzy silver top that left nothing to the imagination.

"Mmm. Fine thanks. Very good really," Victoria said as she untangled herself from Trixie.

At that moment, another lady approached them. Marylyn Monroe red lipstick. The shortest skirt in silver lame showing a gold thong with the tiniest bikini top barely covering her breasts, black seamed, lacy hold-ups and black patent, gladiator stilettos. Her enormous, gold hooped earrings were sitting on her shoulder.

"'allo Chas. 'ow yer doing?" she gave Charlie a big hug. "Ooooooh this must be yer new girlfrien'." She looked directly at Victoria. "Nice. Even betta looking than 'er picture, eh Trix?"

There was that word again, 'girlfriend'. Victoria was not Charlie's girlfriend, but she decided to not inform anybody at this time. They looked nice girls, but Victoria thought that they would and could slit her throat at a drop of an 'I am not his girlfriend', so she decided, in this case, playing dumb would be the better part of valour, discretion or whatever for survival.

"She is lovely, ain't she?" the girl said to nobody in particular.

"What would you like to drink?" Charlie addressed Victoria and introduced the girl in gold as Layla, the dancer Charlie had spoken about before.

"Is it possible to get a glass of white wine?"

"Course it is," Trixie replied. "Anyfing for Chas's lady. Sancerre alright for you, or Meursault?"

You could have knocked Victoria over with a feather. "Um. Err. Yes. Fine. Well, I would like a glass of Meursault, please."

"What do you want Charlie?" Trixie said, bending behind the bar.

"The same Trix. Send a bottle over to a table for me. I'm gonna show Victoria around the place. How many girls working this evening?"

"Twenty, all in all," she replied, head popping up over the bar. "Sonya and Peaches can't make it. Sonya's bastard boyfriend beat her up again and Peaches is taking care of the kids while she is in hospital."

"That wanker. Why doesn't someone take care of him?" Charlie said, guiding Victoria through a beaded curtain.

"We did. Donch yer remember? Wines on table when yer want."

"Obviously didn't take care of the fucker properly," Charlie mumbled. "I'll see to it later."

Victoria pretended not to hear that last comment.

"Here we are. These are the private rooms." Charlie did a twirl on his heels.

"Private rooms? What do you mean by 'Private', Charlie?" Victoria's eyes were wide with interest. She didn't know if she wanted to know the answer, but was far too curious not to ask.

"Private. Just that, Private. You know. Get your own private dance," he said matter-of-factly. Surprised that she should not know.

"Private dance. Private dance? Is that all? Come on?" she replied, disbelieving him.

"Yeah. Course. The girls come in here and the guy gets twenty minutes for a hundred quid, or more if the dancer can get it."

"And that's it. No stripping. No, well you know, let's say touching?" She bit her lip.

"Definitely no touching. That's what we have Bruno and Zane for." Charlie nodded toward the corners of the room. There were two huge men standing straight as pokers, hands behind their back. She hadn't even noticed them until now.

"Oh right. Hi." She gave them a wave of her hand. They reciprocated with a simultaneous nods of their heads. 'Menacing. I want to get out of here,' she thought. "Charlie it's very nice, but shall we go outside and sit down and listen to some music?" She could hear Annie Lennox in the background.

"Yeah sure. G'nite boys. See yer later." Charlie waved at the two men who nodded back to him. Charlie led Victoria to the table that had been set up for them. A wine bottle was sitting neatly in an ice bucket. "Want to go to the Jazz club?"

"Yes that would be great. Do you want to tell someone to put our wine behind the counter. It would be a shame to waste such a good wine." She sipped at it and it was deliciously cool and smooth.

"No problem." Charlie waved in the air and out of nowhere appeared a little man of about thirty, dressed in Arabian red and gold harem pants, a tiny waistcoat, and a little fez.

"Wot can I do fer you Boss?" He was panting and so eager to please Charlie.

"Just look after the wine will you Oscar?" Charlie gave him a ten pound note.

"No probs boss. Whatever you want, Boss. I'll keep it just right fer yer."

She was in Aladdin's cave after all, she laughed to herself.

Chapter 26

Bonnie Meets Clyde

The lighting had now gone from the sublime to the ridiculous. Streaks of light tore itself between the people in the crowded room. Nearly everyone was coloured. More Rasta and Caribbean, than African. The music was so loud that it throbbed off the walls.

"What do you want to drink?" Charlie shouted into Victoria's ear.

'I suppose Meursault is off the menu here,' she thought and didn't bother to ask. "Vodka and diet coke please," she shouted back at him.

All of a sudden Jameel was up alongside Charlie. "Hi mate. How's it going? She's a bit of class alright. I'm well 'appy for yer." He draped his arm over Charlie's shoulder.

They stayed in the club for a couple of hours or so. Listened to the 'man of the moment'. A Jamaican in his early thirties. Very quick, very witty, very racist, and very near the knuckle. Victoria thoroughly enjoyed the show and the club.

"I love you Victoria," Charlie whispered to her, but Victoria pretended not to hear.

Jameel came and interrupted them, asking Charlie if he had a moment for some business. "Sorry to take him away from you Victoria, but I just need the man for a minute or two. Won't be long, I promise," he told her.

"Sure thing. No problem."

"You sure you'll be okay?" Charlie looked at her with such concern in his eyes that she wanted to kiss him and hold him tight. What was she going to do? She couldn't see any way that she could have a life with this man.

"Of course darling. Look around you. There must be as many security guards as people in the club," she laughed and his eyes sparkled.

"Well. Just as long as you're okay then. I won't be long. Jameel wouldn't ask unless it's important. Alright for drinks?"

"Yes and yes. Go. I'll be fine." No sooner had Charlie disappeared downstairs to the VIP room, or 'execution' room as Victoria recalled with a shudder, a fight broke out.

Victoria was pushed to one side by a large, coloured lady who was herself being pushed by another lady behind her. Victoria tried to steady herself with flailing arms, but failed and started to fall to the floor.

'Argh! Dear God. I am going to die!' she thought, as she fell. But she didn't hit anything hard at all. She was lifted up into the air and held aloft, out into the fresh, cold night air.

"Stay there. I'll be back. Sam, Togo, Jet. Come with me." It was Charlie. But she had seen him disappear downstairs. How could he have ever gotten back to her that fast. Amazing. Victoria was very shaken, but unhurt and was just getting things back together when Gary drew up in the limo.

"Victoria. Please get in." He held open the door for her.

"But, err, Charlie? He, err, um." She stood there, frozen with fear.

Crack! there was a gunshot. It split the night. Everything else happened in slow-motion.

"I thought I told you to get her out of here, you fucking idiot." Charlie came around the back of Victoria, while Gary just stood there. Charlie grabbed Victoria's hand and pulled her towards the car, slapping Gary in the face, as he passed him.

"Get in the car, you dummy." Gary didn't need to be told twice. "Victoria. Victoria, get in the car, darling."

Victoria didn't need to be told twice either. She virtually ran into the car. Charlie left her and went back to the melee in the club. "What the..." She was terrified.

Another gunshot. She couldn't believe how loud it was. People were starting to storm out of the club, spilling onto the street like a human tsunami. Just ahead of the onslaught was Jameel. Charlie punched his shoulder, turned around and ran back toward the car, Jameel hot on his heels. The two men raced into the car. Gary 's foot went down hard on the accelerator and the car took off, Jameel slamming the door behind him.

"Ha, ha, ha, ha. Well how's that?"Jameel turned and sat down laughing his head off. "Hey partner. Way to go." They high-fived one another.

"Anyone dead?" Charlie asked.

"Nah, nah. Eric lost an ear, but 'e'll be alright. Those fucking bitches! What they doing fucking around with guns?"

"The Old Bill's here," Charlie commented, as though he was reporting the milkman had arrived. The sirens could be heard all over Berkshire, harsh and piercing.

Victoria just sat there, frightened and aroused at the same time.

Gary slowed down to a respectable speed and the police whistled past them.

"Gonna have to clean up this mess with them an all," said Jameel.

"Mind ya. They owe us a few. We've 'elped 'em out sumfing rotten just lately." Jameel took a bite of an apple he'd stashed in the backseat of the car. "I'm fucking starving. Ooops. Sorry Victoria. Forgot ladies woz present." Victoria just nodded. So far, she hadn't said a word. So far, she hadn't been able to. She was literally scared into silence.

"Fancy a kebab mate?" Jameel nudged Charlie. "Oh sorry. Forgot. 'ow's your dinner then? Everyfing done for yer? 'ad a good time did yer, eh?"

"Yes thanks mate. It was perfect." They were acting as though the whole scene back there had never happened.

"You hungry babe?" Charlie looked at Victoria. "You okay sweetheart?" His voice was concerned. " Oh babe. Come here." He pulled her to him and wrapped his arms around her. "Don't worry darling. Everything is okay. It wasn't much. Nobody's been hurt, well not badly anyway. The cops will sort it out and everything will be back to normal. Lickety-split in the morning."

"Lickety-split," she thought, still shaking a little. 'My God this is Charlie's life. No one here is upset or shaken. It's all quite normal to them. How can Charlie be such a sweet man when he lives amongst all this, all day and every day? Even if I did love him, I couldn't live like this, always wondering if he would come home every night.' Then. Ping! The idea came to her.

"That's it!" She sprang away from Charlie's arms.

"What is it baby?"

"Oh. What? Um. Nothing Charlie. I just got the jitters from the scene back there. By the way, how did you get to me so fast? How did you know?

You were downstairs."

"I know honey. I guess I haven't told you, that I spent six years in the Far East. I learned a lot there, including martial arts. I heard you scream."

Victoria hadn't even noticed that she had screamed.

"I'd sensed trouble brewing while I was with you, but stupidly didn't take any notice of my instincts. I suppose, by wanting to have a good time with you, I almost let you down. Sorry babes. I'll never do that again. I promise. I would never forgive myself if anything happened to you." He tenderly stroked her long blonde hair. She wriggled over the seat and snuggled up into his firm, strong body.

"Don't be silly. I am fine just fine." but she was going to talk to him.

This was her way out, quite reasonable and justifiable really. Victoria smiled to herself and enjoyed the warmth of Charlie's body, and thought 'martial arts'? Was that before or after he was a radio thief? She wasn't about to bring that up. All gone, dead and buried, which under the circumstances, was an appropriate way of putting it.

"Anyone for a kebab?" Jameel piped up.

"Victoria. Would you like a kebab?" It was past three in the morning and she was a little hungry, but more tired than anything else.

She looked up at Charlie. "You?"

"I don't eat that stuff. You never know what's in it."

"Me either. Let's go home."

"Sure you don't want to go back to the Parakeet?"

Was he completely insane? Victoria replied. "No thanks, darling. A nightcap back at your place and a good night's sleep is all I want right now."

"Sounds wonderful." He kissed the top of her head.

"No thanks J, we're all in. Just drop us off."

Jameel issued instructions to Gary. "Sure mate. Know wot you mean, but there again I 'avnt 'ad a romantic meal for two," he chuckled. "And I'd better go back to the club, help the police and clean up the mess. Don't want them closing us down again, do we?"

"Course. Okay then." Charlie squeezed Victoria tightly to him.

Chapter 27

Breakfast at Tiffany's?

"Champagne?" Charlie held up the bottle. Victoria sat at the kitchen table, still a bit tense from the night's events, and struggling a little with the bright kitchen lights.

"Yes please. That would be lovely. May I have a cigarette?"

"Of course. I'll join you."

"I like your house," she said. She didn't, but did appreciate the efforts he had made to make it the cleanest house in Britain. Ever! She lit her cigarette and blew the smoke out into long trails. She certainly did get herself into some amazing encounters.

They chatted for an hour or so, mostly about his experiences in the Far East. Charlie was a fascinating man that was for certain, but she couldn't see herself being with him, and she was pretty sure that Charlie wouldn't just accept her as a friend, which was a pity. However, she knew it would be all or nothing with him.

Getting into bed, she had that same Alice in Wonderland feeling she had at Simon's. The bed was enormous. Pocket Prince was tiny, the room was small, and she felt as though she was bigger than usual. Time for sleep. Charlie slid over to her and enveloped her with his body. She backed into him knowing that Charlie wouldn't go any further than stroke her soft smooth body.

"I love you baby," he whispered to her, but she pretended to be asleep, which wasn't the case for Charlie's penis. It was up, full on and strong. He wasn't trying to do anything with it. It was just there, and to her utter surprise felt as large as a baby whale's cock. Huge! Who would ever have guessed?

They both nodded off, or, more correctly put, all three of them slept. She awoke to the smell of frying bacon and fresh coffee.

"Mmm. That smells so good," she said, getting out of bed and putting on her leopard spotted, soft shorty robe. She padded downstairs to a whistling and dancing Charlie.

"Morning darling." She smiled, cocking her head to one side.

"Morning, morning." He stopped swishing the bacon around in the pan and went over to kiss her. "Hello daarrrrling! How are you? Did you sleep well? Fancy some breakfast?" He held her by her waist and twisted her this way and that, beaming brightly.

"Good. Good. And great idea. Thanks." She kissed his pointy nose. He was cute and it was such a shame that she didn't feel the same way. Charlie longed to be loved, genuinely and deeply. She knew that he was going to be hurt enough after she told him she wasn't the one for him. But if she hung around with him for any longer, he might just be. She was genuinely very fond of him and liked his company, but that wasn't what either of them were searching for. 'Fond' just wasn't good enough. She gave a deep sigh.

"What's up babe?" he said, placing a plate of crispy bacon, fried eggs, tomatoes and beans in front of her on the table. It looked delicious.

"Nothing Charlie. Nothing." She picked up the sea salt grinder. He had remembered what she had said about salt, and by the looks of the coffee machine, the coffee as well. Great coffee was a must in her life.

"There we go. Here's your coffee." Charlie placed a Villeroy & Boch coffee mug by her side followed by a small milk jug.

"It's goat's milk," he said, his eyes were sparkling. His pupils almost filled the iris. Charlie was in love.

"Thank you sweetheart. You are magnificent, you really are. Where is your breakfast?"

"Oh, me? No. I don't eat breakfast."

"Well it could be lunch. It is one o'clock in the afternoon, after all."

"Well, I don't eat before four o'clock. I'm not usually up before four."

"Oh yes. I forgot, but still I don't fancy eating alone."

"I'll sit with you and drink my coke," he said.

"It's not the same." Victoria took her knife and fork and began to eat.

Charlie put some bread in the toaster for her. He was so happy. He would have dinner with Victoria later. Show her some of the countryside. Just having her around him made him happy.

Victoria showered and got ready to leave, having in mind to call Charlie and explain the dilemma she was in. Charlie was getting ready in the bathroom, ready to take Victoria out and show her off to all his friends.

Victoria took her suitcase downstairs and went into the kitchen. The flowers were beautiful, but life as a gangster's moll living in 'lego-land' was not what her heart or soul was searching for.

"Victoria," Charlie called as he came into the kitchen.

"Hi Charlie. I um…"

"Hi. You look great. Ready to see some of the countryside?" he interrupted.

"Oh, um. No, well I…"

"You will love it. We can go down by the river and have a drink, and dinner later."

"I am sorry Charlie, but you didn't tell me any of this. I have made other arrangements and I have nobody to take care of the cats."

"The cats? Surely they can look after themselves?"

"Well, not really." Victoria was anxious to get home to her own territory and to solitude. She needed to be by herself, and certainly out of Charlie's caresses. She thought she would go mad with the irritation. She knew he meant well, but all that stroking and touching, he couldn't keep his hands off her. "Charlie I would love to stay, and the river sounds nice, but the journey is long and, well, it was one heck of a night last night. It's not every day I get to see half naked girls whip around poles, laugh at racist comedians and then become embroiled in some gangster warfare."

"Gangster warfare? Ha, ha. That wasn't anything to do with the hood sweetheart."

"Well whatever it was. I need to go home Charlie. Please understand I have had a wonderful time. I suppose even the fracas was a little exciting, but not one I'd like to be repeated. Thanks all the same, but I really must go."

"Oh well. If that's what you want. That's what you want." The disappointed look on Charlie's face was heart-breaking.

"I am sorry sweetheart." She kissed him lightly on his cheek.

"It's okay. I just wanted to spend a bit more time with you. What about if I come down to see you next Friday?"

"Mmmmm. I think that will be fine."

"Great, great. Let me help you with your case and then I'll wrap the flowers," he said as he picked up her case.

"Wrap the flowers?"

"Yes. They are for you. You said you liked them."

"I do honey, they're beautiful. Thank you. It's very thoughtful of you."

Victoria followed Charlie out to her car. She got in and waited for him to return. The bunch of flowers was almost as big as him. He opened the back door and, as though they were a baby, carefully placed the wrapped flowers on the back seat.

"Thank you darling. That's just perfect."

Charlie leant inside and kissed her. "You smell great."

"It's probably the flowers coming up for air after all that bleach," she giggled.

"Sorry about that, I just wanted…"

Victoria shushed him and told him everything was fine. He was fine, the house was fine, and she would call him tomorrow, or he could call her.

"Okay. No problem then." He closed the car door for her and tapped the roof.

It was such a relief when Victoria was back home. "Lady, Leanader. Here babies. Where are you?" she called to her beloved cats. They came quickly, stretching their legs and mewing at her, as if they were scolding her for leaving them.

"Well, you won't believe what has happened to me," she told them. "I think I shall just get comfy and then see what's been happening whilst I've been out playing 'Bonnie' to Charlie's 'Clyde'." She went into the kitchen and made herself a cup of coffee. She then went upstairs and ran herself a bath. She needed to take five, relax and think. She was sure that Simon was her man and would call him later that evening after her bath. She would call Charlie tomorrow. He had sent her a text six pages long about how much he cared for her, his past life, and how he saw their life together, including the kids who would love her once they had met her.

It had to stop. It wasn't really her fault. She hadn't led him on. All this was a fantasy of his own making, so it was time to steer him in the right direction. She only hoped he would want to be friends. Although she doubted it. Then after Simon, she would call Berrie. She really needed to speak to him. She missed him.

After her long, delicious bath she had no need to call Simon, as he had text her to ask if it would be good to call after nine, which of course it was. Mmmmm. Her Simon. At last, she had found the 'one'. She mused, lathering herself in a creamy body lotion. She wanted to be perfect for him.

Arnold, Oliver, Berrie, and Mad Sam had all texted her, along with a few others from the past who were just catching up, or from the present where they were just getting to know each other. The quest was really rather tiring and finding Simon was no mean feat. But now she had to switch off the rest, but only after their time away together in Madeira. She was sure everything would be wonderful, but she may as well wait a little longer and spend a little more time together. The weekend away hadn't at Simon's been all plain sailing and she was still trying to get her head around the fact. Why would a man who has just spent another six million on another villa want to constantly eat supermarket 'price reduction' food, buy cheap wine, and always choose the cheapest courses on the set menu? She supposed the answer would be simple enough. Simon obviously wasn't a food or wine lover. And there was another thing. Maybe he loved the idea of sex, but nobody had ever taught him. He obviously hadn't taken his ex-wife's advice and read a book on the subject.

She returned texts, especially to Charlie, thanking him for such a lovely time and then to Mad Sam. 'What do u think u r doing to me?' and to the rest with just, general polite 'hellos'.

Simon called and they chatted comfortably together. He explained that he had booked the flights. It was an early departure, and Easyjet was 'easy', but it certainly wasn't Victoria's favourite airline. Having to leave at 6 a.m. was not her idea of fun either.

"Can't we stay at a hotel near the airport ?" Victoria pouted.

"Oh, snookums. It's not that bad and it does give us more time over there."

"Oh well. If you are going to pick me up. I suppose it's not so bad."

"Darling. It's really a long way around for me." They were leaving from Gatwick, almost half way between them. "Couldn't you meet me there?"

Victoria was starting to become pissed off. Leaving home at 6 a.m. was bad enough, but driving herself there as well? "Simon. It's bad enough that you chose to return on the day of my birthday and now you are asking me to leave so early in the morning, and drive myself there. I can't ask Sean to take me at such an early hour." She wondered why he hadn't offered to pay for a taxi for her, at least that would be something.

"I know darling, but I haven't forgotten its Valentine's Day while we are out there, and you are seeing Emmaline later on your birthday."

"Mmmm. Okay. I suppose so." But she wasn't thrilled by this trip so far.

"Listen sweetheart. I've booked one of the most expensive hotels in the world. We have all the luxury you deserve. We will have a fabulous time. I can't wait to ravish you, my sweet, dear Victoria." He was so sincere.

"Oh Simon. Okay. Sorry to be a bit demanding, but I am oh so not good with early mornings. You know I am a night owl."

"You will be just fine. We can relax in the spa."

"Oh, it has a spa? Great. Do you have to book the treatments in advance?" she brightened up.

"Treatments? Treatments? What treatments?" Simon hadn't any idea what she was talking about.

"Simon. Simon. Hellooo. Are you there?"

"Pardon? Yes, yes, of course. No. I don't think you will have to book for treatments, not this time of the year." Simon was thinking, 'And you can pay for them if you want them, whatever they are.'

They arranged to speak again tomorrow and then she would meet him at the check-in desk at 7 a.m.

Simon put his thoughts to the back of this mind. "Bye, sweet darling. I shall be dreaming of you. Can't wait to see you kisses. Mwah."

"Bye darling, speak tomorrow." She ended the call and felt quite flat. What was he doing booking a flight that early and what was so wrong with staying at one of the hotels at the airport? They wouldn't have to get up so early and they could have another day and night together. She was puzzled.

She would call Berrie. Have a glass of wine, some chocolate and call Berrie. That would make her feel better. She was beginning to feel a little uncomfortable about Simon. Please God, don't let him be mean.

No, of course he wasn't. He offered to buy her a car, remember, and he was taking her on a break to Madeira, to a very expensive hotel. He said so himself. No. Simon wasn't mean, just a little out of kilter when it came to courting and knowing how to treat his lady. She dismissed any of her misgivings about Simon immediately.

Victoria called Berrie and spoke to him for the next hour. She told him all about Simon, and how he could be the 'one' and the trip he had planned. Berrie wasn't very happy about the things she was saying about Simon. He didn't tip at restaurants. He'd booked that red eye flight. Bought 'best before' sale food all the time, along with cheap wine. He may have money, but that was probably because he didn't like spending it. He sounded like a real tightwad. But Victoria wasn't seeing it. He hoped she would be alright, and wasn't too put out when she returned, as he and Emmaline were planning a surprise birthday party for her.

And that was peculiar as well. Why didn't this Simon bloke want to be with Victoria on her birthday? Berrie hoped he wasn't planning a surprise party for her that would bugger up his plans. Maybe Victoria hadn't told Simon. Who knew? Who cared? He was getting to see her on her birthday. He couldn't wait to give her her birthday present. He hoped she would like it, as he and the kids had spent a lot of time choosing it.

They finished talking. Victoria made herself a cup of green tea, called the cats and went to bed. She would ring Charlie tomorrow and explain that they weren't going to have that life together after all. She wasn't looking forward to that one little bit. She really did like her Pocket Prince, but she could love Simon. He was her real Prince.

Chapter 28

Holiday Heaven

There he was standing by the check in waiting for her. You couldn't miss him, as he towered over nearly everyone. How he was going to fit into an ordinary seat on the aeroplane, she had no idea. At least the valet parking was good. She was tired and quite agitated. Simon was grinning from ear to ear as usual. Dressed in the same old jacket, but he had agreed to go shopping with her, so she could choose a new wardrobe for him. A new wardrobe to Simon was perhaps a suit, possibly two or three shirts, a pair of trousers and a new a pair of shoes, even if he had bought a pair only two years ago. His ideas and Victoria's ideas bore absolutely no resemblance to one another whatsoever, but she didn't realise that yet.

The flight was ordinary and Simon looked stupid with his knees up nearly to his ears, but it didn't seem to bother him. He did moan on about the cost of the flight though.

Victoria read her book through most of the flight and Simon held onto her arm. She was pleased that he was falling for her. He seemed a kind man and she would help him get the sex right, or maybe she needn't.

Perhaps it really had only been first time nerves.

She had never been to Madeira before and was looking forward to the spa in the hotel. She started to relax and look forward to being with Simon for a few days. She wondered what he had arranged for Valentine's day and if he had remembered her birthday.

'Oh my! I wonder if he has bought me the car he talked about?' Victoria sidled up to Simon and kissed his cheek. He positively glowed.

The hotel was nice, not great, nor fantastic, and certainly not the most expensive hotel in the world. Their room was also average, in fact it could really have done with refurbishing, as it was a bit tired.

"When were you last here?" she asked Simon.

"Late last year. I have some properties on the island and also some land that I'll show you later."

'So he knew what it was like and that it was fifteen minutes away from the town,' she thought, 'Oh well it's not too bad, but not as he described it.'

"I'll leave you to freshen up, whilst I go to reception. I've forgotten the name of the restaurant I want to take you to this evening."

'Oh good. I hope it's romantic,' she thought, turning on the shower tap. The water was lovely, very hot, with good pressure and cleansed and soothed her perfectly.

Simon returned to the room. "All done," he announced. "The taxi leaves in half an hour. Is that okay?"

"As it so happens, it isn't. Simon, I have been up since five o'clock this morning. I have just had a shower and I won't be ready for another hour. I have to dry my hair and I would then like to relax."

"Oh sorry. I should have asked. I forgot that ladies need more time than us gents. I'll go and change the reservation."

"Thank you!"

"I'll just go and take some photos of the hotel, as I want to pinch some of the architect's ideas for my next project on my land. Remember the old barn I told you about?"

"Yes I do, but you said you weren't sure of the two million the architect said you needed."

"Ah yes. Well, thought about it and the coffers can take it. Even if it is quite a dent. I should be able to sell it for three million."

"Oh well, that's great, so you're not buying the villa then?"

"Oh no. I think that villa is a great buy and investment, plus the location is superb."

"Okay sugar. Have fun with the camera."

"Let me take a photo of you. You look lovely."

"We've been through this before honey. I hate my photos at the best of times, but now with no makeup, wet straggly hair. You must be joking."

"Okay. As you wish darling, but you are wrong. You look divine, angelic and childlike."

"Be off with you." She laughed and returned to the bathroom.

Simon rang up to say he was in the hotel lounge waiting for her and that he had rebooked the taxi for thirty minutes time. Victoria asked if he could book for forty minutes to be safe. He replied forty-five minutes then.

"If you like," she said. 'What was that all about?' she thought shaking her head. 'He does seem to be set in his ways. Never mind, it is early days. I'm sure he means well.'

Victoria came into the hotel lobby looking stunning in a Hermes, halter neck, silk dress and Zinotti golden stiletto sandals. She thought she would save her sapphire ring for Valentine's night.

"You look absolutely stunning my dear." Simon got up from his chair as soon as he saw her approach.

"Why thank you darling. It's all for you." She linked his arm and he led her to the taxi waiting outside.

The mystery of the taxi times was soon solved. It was the free hotel taxi service. They only operated at certain times during the day so that guests had to come and go according to the these times. In truth it was very much like a bus service. Simon insisted on using the service regardless of the freedom to relax. She later discovered that the commercial taxi fare into town was only six Euros.

The restaurant was lovely. Victoria forgot about the taxi incident. It was nothing really.

"Darling. Please order what you want. Don't worry about the price." He leant over and patted her arm.

"Why thank you Simon, but I wasn't going to. What made you think I would?"

"Well that's just it, my sweetness. I know you don't concern yourself with the cost of anything."

"What does that mean?" she said, her eyes on fire.

"Nothing darling. Nothing at all. I am glad you like the restaurant."

Victoria let the matter drop and continued to choose from the menu.

The evening passed congenially enough, especially when Victoria turned the subject to buildings and Art. They had to leave in order to catch the last taxi back to the hotel. This was getting to be too much for Victoria, but she suffered in silence. He would change his attitude after tonight. She had packed her black, fur trimmed, baby doll outfit, with the sexy black string panties.

He opened the bedroom door for her. She went straight to the bathroom where she had previously hidden her naughty, sexy outfit. She quickly changed, sprayed some of her favourite perfume 'Caleche' onto her wrists and behind her ears, and took one last look in the mirror. She did look and smell good. You could just see her breasts through the sheer black net. It was very sexy. Simon would go wild. She was so ready for him. It had been a long time since she had had any sex at all.

She opened the bathroom door, walked across the room and slid into bed. She couldn't believe it. Simon was asleep. Snoring and with his mouth wide open. Yuk! Unbelievable.

"Simon, Simon," she cooed. "Simon!" She shook him.

He just turned over and snuffled, saying in his sleep, "What, what?"

For crying out loud. Would you ever believe it? A man in bed with a sex siren who was gagging for some sexual activity, even if it meant training him, and he falls asleep. It'd been a long day but… she got out of bed, went to the mini bar, poured herself a glass of wine, went out onto the balcony, sipped her wine, and smoked a cigarette. She was supposed to be doing this after the 'Act', not because it never happened. 'Where are those sleeping tablets?' she thought.

The whole trip went from bad to worse. She discovered that Simon hadn't chosen Madeira for romantic reasons, but business ones. He had arranged a meeting with his architect to agree what was to be built on the parcel of land he had bought. He just thought it would be convenient to have Victoria tag along.

He had arranged to go to dinner at the hotel on Valentine's Day and presented her with a card on Valentine's morning at breakfast. Victoria thought he would give her a present that evening, when she would give her present to him. But no. There wasn't anything else and the dinner was awful. There must have been two hundred people and guess what? There was a set menu!

She gave Simon his Valentine's present, a silver pocket flask for when he went hunting.

"You are such a sweetheart. It's lovely. Nobody has ever given me a Valentine's gift before." He admired the flask, then got up and gave Victoria a kiss.

He did not produce a present for her though. The attempt at sex that night was another series of fumbling, amateur, embarrassing experiences.

His cock went from rock hard to flaccid in a split second. Victoria was so frustrated and Simon didn't even seem to notice.

They went to a charming little restaurant in the middle of town on their last night. They were early, mainly dictated by the times of the hotel taxi service, and as the restaurant was so tiny, they didn't have room for them to wait. They were asked if they would like to go for an aperitif to a sister restaurant for half an hour, until the restaurant was ready for them. Of course, this was no problem, however Victoria ordered a glass of wine that was like enamel remover, so she left it and Simon ordered half a beer.

The staff were perfectly charming and eager to help. When they were told that their restaurant was ready for them, Simon said to the waiter, "I suppose those drinks are free?" The waiter looked at him incredulously. Shocked that a wealthy gentlemen with his beautiful wife could ask such a demeaning thing.

"If you wish sir," he said, shrugging his shoulders.

That was it for Victoria.

"Simon how could you?" she hissed, and left him at the table. She had no choice but to stay, so she went back to the first restaurant. The kind and winsome proprietor saw her to their table. She explained Simon would be joining her soon. Simon appeared shortly after and was also escorted to the table.

"What is it? Why did you rush off like that?" Yeesh, he didn't even know what he had done. But Victoria could take his meanness no longer. 'Meanie Murray', as she had named him, had gone far enough. She was so embarrassed. These people were so sweet. She was so angry she couldn't speak for a while. What was she doing sitting opposite this mean freak? He wouldn't change. Instead of what she had anticipated - a life of happiness, laughter, and love - she saw misery, and miserly times. Everything started to add up, the food, the wine, the early flight. Now she knew why they couldn't stay in a hotel the night before. 'Stingy Simon', who could easily afford it, couldn't see a profit in it, so that was that. No wonder his TV was out of the ark and the house looked like a mausoleum. The guy was a miser, simple as that. He was even mean with himself, ergo tatty old clothes. It's not as if his cars were that luxurious. Oh dear, Victoria was in a pickle. She did like him. He was actually quite good company if he didn't have to spend any money, but she knew he was too old to change. She would be doomed to watching every penny forever. She had held out so far, she would hold out some more. Her search would have to be on again, so she decided to tell Simon that she could not see him anymore after their return.

"Don't dump me, please Victoria. Don't do that to me." Simon's eyes began to water.

"Simon, I do like you, I really do. In fact, I was thinking that you would be my final destination, maybe even marriage one day, but I can't tolerate such behaviour. It just makes me unhappy, especially as it's so unnecessary. You are a wealthy man, are you not?"

"Well not that wealthy no, but I…" He wiped one of his eyes. He did look extremely sad and unhappy. "Victoria, I love you. Don't do this to me. I'll never find another woman like you. We get on so well."

'Not in the sex department though,' Victoria thought and replied, "Simon I don't know, I…" she sighed and looked down at her sea bream, no longer having any appetite. Simon was pleading so much, she started feeling sorry for the fish. Eventually, she gave in. "Okay Simon, but you must try and change. It's awful. I know you don't see it but it really is."

"I shall change darling." He took her hand with both of his and held it tightly. "I shall. You'll see. I don't think I can bear not to ever see you again darling. I want you to come and live with me when we get home and you can start turning my morgue into a home. You'll see what a good life we shall have."

His smile was back now and although Victoria was wary about Leopards and all that, she was happy too. It was horrible watching him crumble like that. She didn't know and never would, but Simon could crumble up in a heap at a drop of a hat. He had done it at least twice before. He knew he was miserly, but he also knew that he was right. It would just take a bit of time to convince Victoria. She wouldn't run off with her salsa trainer like that disloyal bitch Janice. Good God, what more did Janice want? He had taken care of her for years and wanted her to move into that beautiful property in Cheltenham, but, oh no, she had to have an affair with that jumped up Brazilian. He even forgave her unfaithfulness, but she still ran off with him. Simon had begged Janice to stay as well. But Simon's idea of taking care of her was going out twice a week and on holiday to Portugal every year.

Janice was also the lady whom he told Victoria had said that he was a great lover.

They were due to leave Madera on Victoria's birthday. Simon hadn't bought her a present. No car keys were dangling from the foot of the bed that morning. They never would, ever, because Simon also forgot to tell Victoria that he was renowned for not meaning anything he said. It was another unsavoury side to his personality.

At the airport, Victoria went off to do a little shopping for herself and Emmaline. She was so upset Simon hadn't even got her a card. She was at the check-out when Simon came up behind her.

"Darling, let me get that for your birthday."

'What!' she thought. 'How dare he. He knew about my birthday before we left.'

"No thank you Simon. It's quite alright." She didn't look at him and continued placing her shopping on the counter. Perhaps that should have been the death knell for Simon, but Victoria controlled her anger and reminded herself that it was only yesterday when he promised to try and change. Maybe she was wrong. Maybe she should have accepted his offer to buy the airport goods for her birthday. Well that was until she called Beth when they got home.

"What? He did what? How much longer are you going to take this abuse?" Beth was all riled up. She had heard all this baloney before. Victoria was a beautiful woman inside and out and she was still forgiving burnt up, bitter and twisted old men.

"Yes. Well you are right of course. I'll call him right now Beth and tell him it's all off."

"No you won't darling. Let him call you, because he will and then tell him. Victoria, darling this has to stop. From what you have told me, it isn't as if Simon is a handsome, young, six-pack hunk with the sexual appetite of a stallion left out on grass for weeks on end."

"You are so right about that," said Victoria.

"Well relationships are about deals, as well as love and sharing. Stingy Simon won't change. That comment he made about his e-wife! 'I wish her ill'. Yeeesh! And the tipping and the car comment. He has no intention of buying you a car. Not that you need, or want one. But this guy doesn't mean a word he says. He didn't even take you away for a romantic break. It was because he was going on business any way! There weren't any spa treatments either and that's because he would have to pay for them and he didn't want to. He is not thinking of you at all. No birthday present? I mean that's the last straw, honey."

"Yes I know. Unbelievable." Victoria was sagging and by now starting to realise.

"And he has the audacity to beg you not to dump him. For God's sake, I bet he has done that before. Forget him Victoria. Move on. There are plenty of really nice men out there and you deserve a good one. Stick to your guns don't let a schmuck like Simon bring you down, or make you think you are in the wrong. The mean old sonofabitch is in the wrong. Let him keep his money. You don't need it the way he dishes it out, or not, as is the real case."

"Okay Beth. Don't worry, I shall get rid of him. You're right. He is not worth the angst. But there are so many of them. It is very tiring and boring. I get fed up repeating the same old, same old. 'I like this,' 'I like that,' 'I can do this,' 'I can do that.' You know what it's like. The stupid prats think that just because they have contacted you and that you are speaking to them, sex is on the menu. I can't tell you how many conversations I have had explaining that one to men."

"Yes, I know. Sex is a powerful drug."

"I suppose so. But I wouldn't mind having some," Victoria chuckled.

"You could have as much as you like. You just have to be in love with them. Ha ha. Look at my gift of Max."

"Oh yes. I quite forgot about him. But look at what happened there."

Beth had thrown Victoria a bone a while back and introduced her to Max, a very handsome twenty-eight year old pilot. His body was fit and muscular. Quite the hunk. Anyway, the idea was to have sex, no strings. But it wasn't Victoria's way and she felt uncomfortable from the very first minute they had met. Aroused, excited, but still uncomfortable. They went to bed, Max cajoling her all the way. The sex wasn't bad, but in the middle of Max eating her sweet little pussy, he looked up and winked at her! It put her right off.

"Oh yes. I remember." Beth laughed. "You should have just let yourself go and not worry about silly stuff like that."

"Yes maybe, but afterwards, when we went to dinner, I felt I was with a child."

"Huh! Now *that* is funny. Don't you know most men are children? They never grow up. In fact, I swear they go into reverse the older they get. Sorry, but I've got to go now, hun. Chin up Victoria, at least he didn't smell." Beth laughed.

"Bye darling and thanks. I'll keep that in mind." Victoria hung up and resigned herself to spinsterhood.

Chapter 29

Time to Say Goodbye

"Hello?" Victoria answered her mobile.

"Hi there Victoria." It was Gino. She hadn't heard from him in a while. "I've been ill in hospital. I caught pneumonia." He explained.

"Oh dear. I am sorry to hear that. Is everything alright now?"

"Yes, I'm fine thanks, so why don't you do yourself a favour and come and see me? Get yourself a real man."

They had gone through all of this before. Gino was very macho. Very handsome, if his photos were to be believed, and a good conversationalist.

"I am not coming to see you. Why don't you come here? You said that you had visited a lady not far from where I live."

"Yes I know, but she wasn't what she claimed."

"What's that got to do with it? I am."

"Yeah and I believe you. Listen why don't you come up here? Right now. Just do it for impulse's sake."

'Duh!' Victoria thought he was nuts.

"Yes, come up here and we can go to dinner. Talk a lot. Sleep over."

"Gino you know…" She took a deep breath, completely fed up with the way that men concentrated on sex so much.

"I know, I know, sleep over in your *own* room. I have a very big house, so you can have your own bathroom and space. Then I'll drive you back the following day. Maybe have some lunch? Bingo! the beginning of a great relationship. Just you and me doll." Put that way it was tempting. She could do with some 'chill time'. He didn't seem like a psychopathic killer.

"I'll think about it Gino."

"No. Come now. Come on. Don't you ever do anything spontaneous?"

"Listen. If I come at all, that will be spontaneous enough for me. I said I shall think about it and I shall. But you can always come down here and take me to lunch."

"Okay. Then think about it and I'll call you later. Kisses to you gorgeous." Gino hung up.

Victoria went back to her mobile message box.

One from 'Tom Train'. 'Where are you? Can't wait to eat you and take you from behind. I keep thinking of your gorgeous body naked.'

One from Mad Sam. 'Gmng darling how's you?'

One from Irish Arnold. 'Hello Victoria when am I to get your ticket to see me?'

Plus others - Stephen in the USA. Steven the stockbroker. Ashley in the midlands. Darren the handsome young black guy and finally Karl from USA. 'You are very, very beautiful. I like what I see. Miss our chats.'

Simon was calling. "Hi beautiful, how's my girl?" she could feel him grinning.

"Hi Simon. I am fine and you?"

"Great. Couldn't be better, now I've found the love of my life." He laughed.

"Ha ha. Ah yes." She winced.

"Have you thought anymore about coming to live with me? Building paradise together, off into the sunset."

"Ah yes, Well yes. About that Simon."

"I can send removal vans for your clothes." He giggled at his own joke.

"Yeah sure. Right. Simon, it's not that I don't appreciate your offer, because I do. But well, really it's your meanness that bothers me. I know you said you would change, but I… Well I don't know. I don't think you will or could."

"Mean! Meanness! I don't know how you can say that darling. I've taken you away and bought you fifteen meals! That's hardly mean in anyone's book."

Simon was aghast. Simon actually thought that he was generosity personified. We all see ourselves differently. Some more differently than others.

"Well yes, I know. But sorry Simon, if I count up the dinners and lunches you have bought me and they add up to fifteen, I will rest my case and I am afraid I can't see you anymore."

"Darling, darling. No, no. Don't do that. I am only joking. Of course I don't know how many meals we have had. Who would know that?"

"Precisely Simon. That is what I mean. What sort of person would know that?"

"Victoria, I *was* only joking sweetheart." There was panic in his voice now.

"I know, I know, Simon. Sorry but I have to go right now. I'll call you later okay?"

"Victoria don't go, don't go. Let me explain, please."

"Sorry Simon. I will call you later, I promise. I'm just a little tired. Have a good day."

"Okay darling. You too. Love you."

"Bye Simon." Victoria hung up and, with it, her head in dismay. 'I wonder if there really were fifteen meals? He even said meals not dinners, or lunches, or dinners and lunches. Something wrong here,' she thought. She got out a piece of paper, took out her *Twilight* calendar and began to count the 'meals' they had had.

Fifteen. Bang on the money. There they all were. Drawn out before her.

It had taken her some time to recall all of the occasions, but she got there. Fifteen it was. Simon had to be counting. He wouldn't have had to go back over the times like she had had to though.

'Oh my God!' she thought. How could he have counted! How pathetic. How sad. Stingy Simon was aptly named. Beth was right. 'I deserve better than that.' She resigned herself to not speak to him again.

Chapter 30

Irish Eyes Are Smiling

Victoria was feeling really low after the reality check she had received from Simon, and the fact that she had to say goodbye to Charlie. She was right. He didn't want to be friends with her. He guillotined her as soon as she told him she didn't think they had a future together.

As a big fan of Nicolas Cage, she was sitting on her sofa watching the movie *Ghost Rider* for the second time, when her mobile rang. It was Irish Arnold. She had forgotten he had texted her earlier in the day to ask if it would be okay to call that evening.

She paused the movie and clicked on her mobile. "Hi Arnold, how are you this fine evening?" A little of the disappointment of the past few days reflected in her voice.

"I'm fine Victoria dear, but you don't sound so good."

"Oh I am just fed up with this dating palaver."

"Oh there, there. Don't let it get you down. Come and visit me. Come to my place in Donegal." Now Victoria's ears pricked up as Sean had told her about Donegal and how beautiful it was.

"You will love it. You can relax and be sure that you will be safe with me I'll treat you like my own sisters. Just like the lady you are. I'll email you the flight tickets."

She was warming to the idea. She could do with a real break and she loved Ireland and the Irish. "Well, Um, err, I…" She didn't know quite what to do, or say.

"Come on Victoria. I promise you will have a great time and you sound as if you need cheering up. I shall look after you like a queen and you'd have no fear of me."

"Okay Arnold. You're right. I would love that." Over the months of talking with Arnold she had come to like him and trust him. He was a kind man. Perhaps not for her as a partner, but then you never know. Look how certain she had been of Stingy Simon. On the surface marvellous, tall, good-looking, intelligent, fun, wealthy, and he'd turned out to be a miser. Scrooge could have taken lessons from him. Disastrous and, not to forget, awful in bed to boot.

She wouldn't have any of that nonsense from Arnold. Judging from his photo, she could knock him across the room if he forgot his manners. But she was sure that wouldn't happen and not to forget the flowers. The beautiful, thoughtful flowers. Stingy Simon hadn't bought her so much as a daffodil.

Of course she should go. He was offering her two nice days in a lovely country that she adored, and the Irish were so hospitable, and so much fun. She had enjoyed some great conversations with Arnold. He was into Art and antique clocks. Donegal had a coastline and, the way Arnold had described his house there. Well, it sounded very luxurious and she would have her own large bedroom with an en-suite. Fluffy warm towels and roaring wood fires if required.

"Thank you Arnold. That would be very nice and lovely to finally meet you as well."

"So this weekend then? I'll buy the tickets and send them to you somehow." Arnold had never been so excited in his life. He had a huge erection all the time he was speaking to Victoria. In fact, Victoria's photos had provided Arnold with a distinct source for his erotic fantasies and solo sexual pleasure.

"Oh don't bother Arnold. It would be easier if I paid for them and you reimburse me. Is that okay?"

"Sure. Sure. Whichever way you want Victoria dear."

" Will it be okay to include a taxi to and from the airport?"

"Of course. It'd be an absolute pleasure. Anything you want. It'll be just wonderful to cheer you up."

"Okay then. Well, I'll call you when I've booked the tickets."

"Absolutely. Fine, Yes, yes. Absolutely. Hear from you soon then?" Arnold was beside himself and unzipping his flies already. "Bye then

Victoria. Be safe." He couldn't get her off the phone quickly enough.

"Bye Arnold. Sleep well." She hung up and placed the phone on the thick cut glass and stainless steel coffee table.

She sighed and put up her feet on the sofa, turned back on the movie and snuggled down. She started to relax and enjoy the film.

'Good old Arnold. He is such a nice man,' she thought.

Back in the Emerald Isle 'Good Old Arnold 'was frantically taking down his trousers, staring at Victoria's image on his PC. He thought she was so beautiful. So pure. An angel of a woman. He masturbated over her picture, and, careful not to make any mess, he caught his semen in a handkerchief. He hated himself for this, but couldn't help himself. She was the loveliest woman in the world and just looking at her photo gave him so much pleasure. He would take great care of her and wouldn't succumb to his urges. But he was the best kisser on the planet. Maybe she would just close her eyes and forget what he looked like. Perhaps she would allow him to kiss her. Arnold shuffled himself back together again and went to make a cup of tea.

Victoria went up to bed feeling a little lonely, but looking forward to meeting her sweet Arnold.

The mobile rang. It was Gino.

"Hi Gino."

"Hi sweet thing. You still up?"

"Well technically, yes. I am just getting into bed. I am really tired."

"Well you should be here. I would give you a massage so you could enjoy the best sleep ever."

"Thanks Gino, but at the moment I am very happy to be where I am."

"When are you coming up here then? I crashed my Ferrari today so I need some comforting."

"You are in the wars. First hospital, now this. Are you okay."

"Yes, I'm fine, but it would be much better if you were here."

"Mmmmm. I'm sure, but I'm not, and now I am going to sleep. Speak to you later."

"Well hang on. Don't be rude. When are you coming? Come on. It could be the start of something fantastic for you." He was so arrogant, but funny with it.

"I'm still thinking about it Gino okay? Now goodnight, there's a good man." Victoria was very tired and looked a little drawn.

"Okay babes. Speak to you later. Offer's always open to you."

"Thanks. Goodbye." She switched off her mobile. That was a very rare thing for Victoria to do, as she always wanted to be available in case Emmaline needed her. But her mobile was becoming more of an intrusion into her life now, rather than the helpful instrument it should have been. 'Emmy can always contact me on the landline if she needs to,' Victoria thought. Right now, she needed rest and could do with just one morning without being woken up by the manoeuvres of her 'love army'.

This whole quest thing was not only physically tiring, but also emotionally draining too. She was still sad about Simon and wasn't sure if she had made the right decision regarding Charlie. And as for Mad Sam, who was still texting her and asking to meet, well nobody would have had the answer to that one.

She took a couple of sleeping tablets. It would be nice to go to Ireland and be pampered unconditionally by sweet Arnold.

She booked the tickets and taxi the very next day and called Arnold to give him her itinerary.

"No problem, Victoria. I shall be there to collect you. I have bought the Bollinger 1998. I thought I'd bring some caviar as well. Do you like it?"

"I love caviar Arnold, but I prefer ice cold vodka instead, if that's okay with you?"

It sent Arnold into a mild tizzy, as he wasn't prepared for Victoria to prefer something else other than he had suggested. He had taken so much trouble to get the champagne. Okay it wasn't Bollinger 1998, but she would never know. God's blood, the whole trip was going to cost him enough as it was, and with no guarantee of even a kiss. He hadn't expected Victoria to be as ungrateful as most of her fucking gender, grasping at anything they could get and giving nothing in return. No, Victoria was like his dearly beloved sisters. They had taken care of Arnold, always had and always will. He didn't have to beg for their kisses.

"Oh. Yes, yes of course, or maybe something else with the champagne?" Arnold said, frantically trying to find an alternative to Victoria's suggestion.

"Arnold. We'll be together for two days and nights. Surely we are not just going to have one bottle of champagne?"

"Weeeell, No, no, of course not. We will be going out. There are one or two lovely restaurants close by."

"Oh that's great. You do what you think is best Arnold. I just want to see you and enjoy the sea air."

He knew it. She was sweet and pure. There listen to that: 'You do what you want Arnold.' No grasping and grabbing there.

"Well, whatever you want Victoria. I'll see what I can do." Arnold was so happy. He wasn't going to change what he had in mind for her though. She might be the sweetest woman on earth, but she was still a woman.

They said their goodbyes and looked forward to seeing each other in a few days' time.

Victoria checked in at the airport, but this time at a reasonable time in the afternoon. Arnold had asked her to get Belfast before three o'clock. His house was around three hours' drive from the airport and he wanted her to see home before it got dark. She wasn't looking forward to the drive, but at least it would be in the comfort of an Aston Martin, so things could have been worse.

The flight was good and on time, but the weather in Belfast was foul. Ice-cold, rain and wind. Oh well, Arnold did say he had log fires and a central heating system that would make you believe you were in Brazil. She passed through baggage claim and looked around for Arnold, but he was nowhere to be seen.

'Oh no. Don't let the blighter be a no-show. For goodness sake. I don't believe it,' she thought, fishing her mobile out of her handbag. "Arnold. Arnold. Answer the phone," she said to her mobile.

"Victoria. Victoria is that you?"

'No, it's the chocolate soldier. Strewth, who did he expect?' she thought. "Yes Arnold. I am here in the airport. Where are you?" She was agitated.

"I am here too."

"Oh?" She immediately calmed. "Well, where is that?"

"I am near the exit."

The airport wasn't that big and there were hardly any people. Why hadn't she seen him? The answer came in the shape of a diminutive, middle-aged man wearing glasses and with very balding head, who emerged through the exit doors.

She had walked right by him!

She dropped her mobile as she saw the man, dressed in a lime green V-necked sweater, wearing beige trousers, walk towards her. This couldn't be Arnold ? Could it? This man didn't look like any of the photos that Arnold had sent to her. This man stood no more than 5'6, certainly not 5'11. And he was definitely in his late fifties, not the forty-three year old he had declared. He'd also had a full head of hair in the photos she had received.

'Fucking hellfire. It can't be him. He couldn't have been *that* deceitful! What the fuck was he thinking?' she thought, goggling in amazement.

But he wasn't the first guy she had met who had blatantly sent her photos of themselves ten or twenty years younger. One had even sent a photo of his friend! But this was the first time she had flown to another country and met one of them. Richard had been different. She was greener then and hadn't even seen a photograph, but now what was she to do?

"Victoria?" the little man asked tentatively, bending down to help her pick up her mobile.

They came face to face.

'Oh God,' she thought. 'It is him.'

"Yes, yes. I'm Victoria." She managed a weak smile.

"Oh you are too good-looking. Much too good. Oh my…" said a now marvelling Arnold.

"Sorry, I must have walked straight past you," Victoria replied.

"Yes. I saw you, but I was in shock," Arnold said, his mouth unable to close fully.

'Not as much as I am,' said Victoria to herself. "Why shock?" she asked, taking the mobile from him and uttering "Thanks," with as much of a smile as she could muster while suffering Post-Traumatic Shock.

Arnold was stunned by her. "Well, because you are so good-looking. You look very pretty in your photos, but you are beautiful, much too good-looking." He must have repeated 'too good looking' a further three, or four times, while taking her suitcase to the car.

'Oh well,' she thought, albeit not for the first time, She briefly recalled 'Pig Man,' but dismissed this immediately. 'He seems harmless enough and I am here now, so I might as well carry on.' She walked beside him, the wind and the rain seemed secondary to the shock of Arnold. Little weasely Arnold.

Victoria should really have known better. She'd had a similar experience before, for God's sake. Another man had misrepresented himself to her. She should have immediately turned around and caught the very next flight home, or found the nearest restaurant in which to wait. She should have known that with a beginning that was so bad, it just wasn't going to get any better.

They reached the car which evidently had metamorphosed into an Audi.

"Where is your Aston?" Victoria was holding her jacket tight against herself trying to protect herself from the biting wind.

"Ah yes. It broke down. This is a courtesy car," he said putting her case in the boot.

"Oh. Sorry about that."

"Get in Victoria, or you'll catch your death. The car is open."

She did as she was told and Arnold was soon sitting beside her.

"You want to go back now, don't you?" Arnold said, his left eye twitched a little.

Oh boy, did she want to go back home and, after the experience with 'Pig Man', that's exactly what she should have done. But no.

"Um, err. No Arnold. I am here now and you have promised me a relaxing couple of days in your own little paradise. I trust you will do just that. We shall have a lovely time."

"Oh Victoria. Yes we will. I promised you that and I intend to deliver. Of course, because you wouldn't get an earlier flight, we may not be able to see paradise in the light, but we can only try." He started the car and drove out of the car park.

The journey was long and, to make matters worse, was hindered by traffic, as someone had unfortunately had an accident. They chatted all the way. About Arnold's father and his sisters. About Emmaline and her school. About the world in general. About their likes and dislikes Arnold's job and his passion for Art and clocks. He had a collection of over two hundred, which was alarming in itself, as he kept them all at home in his house in Belfast, so at least Victoria wouldn't have to go through that ordeal. Although it was a long journey, and the weather was vile, and the night drawing in, she was comfortable and the conversation was flowing agreeably enough. Arnold was a nice, kind, little chap. A leprechaun all of her own. However, Victoria wasn't aware that leprechauns were known for their mischievous and malicious ways more than their kindness. They tended to err on the side of the bad, rather than side of the good. So there he was and she was sitting right next to her own little leprechaun.

"Here we are," Arnold said, as they parked outside the house. "I hope you like it." And he then seemed to mumble something that Victoria thought could have been, "You can stay in a fecking hotel, if you don't." She didn't comment, as she obviously wasn't used to his Irish brogue.

'He's probably just a bit nervous,' she thought.

As they had arrived at dusk and neither the coast, nor the outside of Arnold's little paradise could be seen, but once he turned on the lights, it was apparent that Victoria and Arnold had different perceptions of what paradise was like.

Clearly Arnold's paradise was set in the seventies and consisted of dark oak, heavy built furniture. The table and chairs in the dining room cum lounge looked like they needed a crane to move them. The crimson tasselled tablecloth did little to hide its hideous bulk.

He led her straight into the corridor leading to the bedrooms. Arnold's paradise also didn't have any stairs. It was a bungalow, built in utilitarian fashion and just plain square. Each room was similar to the other apart from size.

"Here is your room Victoria," he said proudly. "There is a nightgown for you, fresh towels, and here is the bathroom." He pointed to what resembled a broom cupboard.

The bedroom was bare, apart from a huge, unmade bed and some white MDF, plasticky looking drawers. And the whole house was freezing. Victoria was mortified. Not for the first time she asked herself, 'What am I doing in the middle of bloody nowhere, in the night, in a cold, tired, barren, tasteless house that didn't even have stairs? And along with that, standing next to a midget of a man, dressed in green who's a virtual stranger.' That was such a good question, but Victoria was incapable of providing an answer. However, she comforted herself with the knowledge that she'd had the forethought to leave his address and telephone number with Beth. Well that's if they weren't a figment of his imagination as well.

"Oh thanks Arnold. But why is the place so cold?" she asked.

"Oh yes, I'll light the fire straightaway. I called ahead for Mary to switch on the central heating, but I suppose she couldn't get here. Don't worry, it will soon warm up." He scurried off, leaving her deflated and more than a little disappointed. The place was dreadful. She longed for her beautiful home with log fires and beautiful modern furniture. However, she was not going to be daunted too much. She told herself that she had better make the most of things, as she unpacked her suitcase. She could hear Arnold scampering back and forth from the kitchen to the lounge. 'Well at least we'll have a fire,' she thought.

"Brrrrr." She rubbed her arms to get rid of the goose bumps. She went into the broom-cupboard bathroom. It was actually a shower room, but not as cosy and spotless as Charlie's had been. It wasn't exactly dirty, but it had seen better days. The taps had rust on them, the floor was covered in white small squared lino, the toilet seat had been left up, and the remnants of some blue liquid had congealed around the sides of the bowl.

'Nice,' she thought.

She decided it wasn't necessary to change out of her jeans and cashmere, midnight blue blazer. She had brought her cowl-necked, black cashmere

Yves St Laurent dress, and Kurt Geiger black knee-high boots. But she somehow got the impression that Donegal wasn't quite ready for that style at the moment.

"Victoria." Arnold called for her to come into the lounge and have a glass of champagne.

The fire was roaring away.

'At least he knows how to make a fire,' she thought, and then took a second look at what was burning in the small, brick built fireplace. It looked like chair legs.

"Hi Arnold. The fire looks good, What is that that you are burning though?" she quizzed him.

"Old furniture. Been meaning to get rid of it for ages. Does the job don't you think?"

"Splendidly." She walked over to where he was sitting birdlike, on a stool near the home made 'bar' area. Two glasses, filled with champagne stood straight and soldier like on the dark wooden counter, the 'bar' walls were made of brick, with the top half covered in mirror tiles.

'Well some mirrors in this house, but all broken up. Maybe that's why Arnold can't see himself straight,' she chuckled to herself.

"What's that? What are you laughing at?" Arnold almost snarled and hunched up even further on his stool and hugged his legs. Very still. He looked like a giant parrot perched on the ugly, wooden stool.

"Nothing Arnold. Nothing. Is one of these for me?" She took one of the glasses.

"Yes. Yes it is. Are you frightened?" he asked whimsically, his beady eyes all the while staring at her breasts.

A stab of fear ran through her. 'A nutter, a fucking nutter,' she thought. She had come across his type before. They were schizoid. Sort of Jekyll and Hyde. She would have to handle this very carefully if she was to get through the night unscathed and unharmed.

"No, no. Not at all. Why? Should I be?" She cocked her head and moved gracefully out of his gaze and around to his left-hand side ready, if necessary, to knock him off his perch.

"What? Oh, err. No! no! no! Of course not. You are safe with me. I told you I would treat you like you were one of my darling sisters." He seemed startled. He got down from the stool and reached for his glass. "To you, Victoria. You are even more beautiful than when I first met you." He turned and raised his glass in the air, moving toward hers.

They chinked and they drank. Arnold was animated once again. "Thank you, Arnold." she put down the glass on the counter.

"Actually Arnold, if anyone should be frightened it ought to be you. I am an expert in the martial arts and could kill you in a split second."

"Pardon? Oh sure. Yes of course. No need to be scared. Not of me. I wouldn't harm a hair on your lovely head. I bought you some sushi."

There was a clear plastic tray on the counter with tiny, vine leaf wrapped rice rolls. Victoria went over to examine the food. Arnold had left the supermarket sushi in its packaging and had forgotten, or simply not bothered to remove the 'reduced price' label.

"I am sorry Arnold. Obviously I never mentioned it, but I don't like sushi."

"No you did! You did! You told me you loved it!"

"Oh sorry. You must have misunderstood. I would probably have told you that I loved sashimi, not sushi. But don't let it stop you from enjoying it. It would be such a shame to waste it."

"Well, it's not my cup of tea either," he replied, rather grumpily.

'Mmmmmm. I didn't think so, and this champagne is about as vintage as a new born,' Victoria thought, as she ambled over to a grandfather clock that stood on the opposite side of the room.

"This is lovely," she said, stroking the clock case.

"Yes. It is early Victorian. I brought it down with me last time I was here." He came up behind her and breathed deeply. Her perfume was intoxicating. Her long blonde hair flowing down her back. She was perfect, but she wouldn't want him, no matter how good a kisser he was. Arnold sighed.

Victoria turned around to face him.

"Hungry? Shall we go? I am starved." She brushed past him adding, "I'll just get my coat, shall I?"

"Yes. Sure, sure. Let's go. The table is booked for eight."

The restaurant was built of brick and local stone its long and uninteresting rectangular interior was filled with ordinary tables and chairs. And yet, although plain and sparse, it was warm and there were people sitting, talking and laughing. For the first time since she had arrived in Donegal, Victoria felt human again.

"Hiya." Arnold stopped a passing waitress hands full of plates stacked with food. "I booked a table for two. The name's Arnold O'Mally."

"Great and what am I supposed to do about it?" she replied, smiling and moving smartly on. "Anywhere you want. Sit anywhere you want. I'll be with you shortly now," she said as she carried on to her destination, balancing the plates with great care and expertise.

"Let's go down here Victoria." Arnold set off to the left side of the restaurant, where no one else was sitting.

"No. Let's go this way. Look there's a cosy snug for two right there." She pointed.

'Oh no. That's near all those men sitting at the table. They are bound to interfere,' he thought.

"But Victoria…" he called after her. It was too late, Victoria was at her chosen table. She also knew that Arnold wanted her for his own, and was frightened that one of the men, who had all stopped talking when she'd passed by, would whisk her away from him. Victoria instinctively knew this and was determined to have the comfort of other people around her.

Creepy Arnold might look like a small wretch, but he may be a force to be reckoned with once he had made his mind up. And his mind was made up. To have Victoria. She hadn't come all this way just to have dinner with him. She was hot and gagging for it. He could tell and now the hussy was flaunting herself at any man she could.

"This is much nicer and warmer," she told him as he joined her.

"Yes, yes it is. You are right. Quite cosy really." He'd noticed that a view of Victoria by the ten men sitting at the next table was obstructed by a four-foot tall brick wall. It provided the security he wanted and gave him the feeling he had her all to himself after all.

Arnold beamed at her. "What would you like to drink?" he asked.

"Some wine please. Are you going to have some?" She looked around the place. Old and charming. She spotted the menu up on a huge blackboard on the wall.

"Yes. I surely am."

"How about some red? I think I might have the steak and kidney pudding."

The 'balancing' waitress took their order and Arnold regaled Victoria with all the facts and fantasies about Donegal.

Victoria relaxed and had a good time, with Arnold fussing over her and showering her with compliments and telling her how he wasn't good enough for her. He knew that, but he also knew women. They all wanted sex. Victoria had come over for sex and he knew it. He was such a good kisser. She would be so surprised. They were all surprised in the end.

"Let's go home then," he said, as he paid the bill.

It was only half past ten, but what the hell. She intended to get him dog-eared drunk. She had noticed that there was plenty of wine at the bungalow and the unfinished champagne. However, she had a feeling that getting her drunk was Arnold's intention, he might have fortitude and determination, but he hadn't reckoned on Victoria's constitution. The odds were more likely for Arnold to fall to the floor first, way before Victoria.

The rain hit the windscreen like shotgun pellets. The wind actually moved the car across the road as they travelled across the moors.

"Stay here until I open the front door for you. Don't want you getting all wet, do we?"

'He was alright. Quite pleasant company really,' she thought.

"Damn, damn, damn. What an idiot I am. I can't believe it." Arnold had returned to the car and was cursing and wringing his hands.

"What's the matter?" Victoria said, quite concerned for him.

"I've left the keys inside the house."

"Oh boy. Oh dear. What are we going to do?"

"It's not too bad. My sister Mary has a spare set."

"Oh good. No harm done then." Victoria smiled. But Arnold looked disproportionately unhappy. "Let's go then. It could have been far worse," she encouraged.

"Yes, of course it could and Mary doesn't live that far. I'll call her to see where she is." Arnold seemed to have relaxed a little.

"Good idea," said Victoria.

Mary was in the local pub with her husband and friends.

"I won't be long," Arnold said, getting out of the car outside the pub.

"Why don't we go in and have a drink with them. It would be nice to meet your sister. Take the chance whilst it is here. It would be good for our future." Over dinner, Victoria had realised that her safety and wellbeing lay in Arnold believing there could be a future for them both. She had begun to allude to their next meeting and how much she was looking forward to Christmas.

Arnold took the bait and said that he knew the best place in all the world to have Christmas. It was a castle in County Cork. Very expensive, very lovely. She would love it. She agreed that she would and asked him to enquire about any vacancies as soon as possible. They also arranged when he should come and visit Victoria at her home.

No wonder Arnold was anxious to get home and had a glowing face.

"Um, err. No, you wouldn't like it." He was out of the car, but he couldn't prevent Victoria from following him into the pub. It was heaving with people. Hardly any room to move. Wonderful. Two musicians were playing in the corner. It was small, warm and welcoming. Arnold introduced Victoria to his sisters, Polly and Mary, and their respective husbands and their friends. Victoria felt right at home.

They all had shocked and astonished expressions on their faces, although Victoria ignored this, but knew why. None of them could believe that Arnold was with someone like Victoria. Where had she come from? How did he know her? Maybe she was a work colleague, or contact?

Arnold was very agitated. All he really wanted was be alone, beside the fire with Victoria, discussing their future together, holding her and showing her what a good kisser he was. She could put a paper bag over his head if she wanted. She could do anything she wanted with him. He just wanted to be close to her. Arnold had fallen in love with Victoria over the telephone. Her voice was so sweet and she said such lovely things, not like those bitches from hell in Warsaw, or those harpies he had met in his life. No. Victoria was different. So pure, so good, so beautiful.

He loved her even more now that he had met her, but he still wished that he hadn't forgotten his keys. However, perhaps Victoria was right. It was a good opportunity for her to meet his sisters and family. He knew they would approve. Look how well they were getting on already. Chatting away like billy-o. Arnold started to relax and ordered the drinks for everybody.

"There you are darling." He handed Victoria a glass of wine.

Victoria was beginning to enjoy herself. Arnold's family were lovely people. Immediately very friendly, accepting her despite their curiosity. His sisters were interested to know where Arnold had taken her to dinner. What they had to eat, and if she liked Donegal. She insisted they'd had a delicious meal and that she would tell them later about Donegal, after she had seen more. But, so far, it seemed a wonderful place, especially the people.

They were enamoured with her and she felt safe and more than happy to talk with them, laughing at the men's jokes and listening to the music. This beat the pants of just sitting there with Arnold's eyes glued to her face.

But, as all things do, this time came to an end and they had to go. Victoria didn't want to antagonise Arnold. He wasn't going to do anything unpalatable now. She was almost one of the family, so much so had been her welcome. Mary handed over the spare keys and they said their goodbyes, all saying that they hoped to meet her again soon.

Victoria hoped so too, but knew she would not. Nevertheless, she was grateful to them for providing her with the security she needed. Arnold definitely had a split personality and, whilst he might not hurt her, Victoria believed he could be a spiteful creature.

Victoria was right about the spiteful part and that he would not harm her, at least not whilst she was able to make him believe there was a future for them, but sweet, darling Arnold had some very dark secrets he'd hidden in Warsaw and Prague. He was yet to add to these in his beloved Ireland, but how would Victoria now play her cards. It was very intuitive that she recognised the danger she could be in, but it was with a stroke of genius how she chose to handle it.

Arnold was so taken by her and had gone to so much trouble to make her happy that it would have been a huge mistake to antagonise him. She couldn't make him feel that she had teased him and encouraged him to believe she wanted sex with him and then snatch it away. Admittedly, it was a huge mistake to be in this situation in the first place, but once in the soup, she intended to swim calmly out of it. There was no way that Victoria would have been so calm and confident of her situation if she had even a fraction of an idea about Arnold's secrets.

So Victoria continued with the charade. She even enjoyed it a little.

The rain had stopped and the wind had died down markedly. The stars were bright and studded the black, velvet, night sky. All was quiet and peaceful around them as they arrived back at the dingy bungalow. Victoria hoped that the fire was still alight. Fortunately, it was. Arnold hurried into the kitchen to fetch more wood or old kitchen furniture.

'Oh good,' she thought to herself. 'He's comfortable with me and only wants to please. I'll get him completely drunk and there's a lock on my bedroom door. Everything will be just fine.' She didn't even dislike this creepy, half-maniacal man.

She wasn't aware of how psychotic Arnold really was. He had always been careful. The police were no match for him. He knew they all thought he was nothing but a nauseous little bean-counter, having a sexless, hapless life. But that wasn't true. He had shown them alright. He was a great kisser. He had shown them all. And he had been right all along. They deserved their punishment and look now. He was completely vindicated, because he was going to marry one of the most beautiful and gentle ladies in the world. Arnold couldn't be happier and couldn't wait to kiss Victoria.

When he returned to the living room, he found her sitting very comfortably on the ugly old sofa he had bought from a local farmer. Arnold had owned it for at least fifteen years, but it was comfortable and didn't Victoria look like she was right at home.

'We're going to be so happy,' he thought, content with imagining their wedding day as he gazed at her. He put more chair legs and what appeared to be half the seat of one onto the fire. It responded heartily, consuming its food for life. Great yellow and red flames leapt up, enveloping the wooden legs and giving out a very welcome warmth.

"Would you like a drink Victoria? Perhaps some champagne?" Her lips looked so inviting.

"That would be lovely Arnold. Thank you."

Arnold returned with two glasses and the bottle, joining her on the sofa. "Would you like to change into the robe I brought for you?"

'No I wouldn't. You stupid fool. It's old, tatty and very scratchy,' she thought, but said, "What a good idea, but I think I'll change into something more comfortable that I brought with me."

'Wow!' he thought, he couldn't believe his ears.

She jumped up and placed her glass on the nest of tables nearby and went to the bedroom. She needed to find those sleeping tablets. She returned after changing into a white, Juicy Couture tracksuit with a pink embroidered motif. She loved these designers as they used such soft fabric and the cut was such that it showed off her figure in a comely fashion. Not too sexy, but sweet and prettily. It was also extremely comfortable.

Victoria hadn't been the only one who wanted to change into something a little more comfortable. Arnold had taken the opportunity to change into a white towelling robe with blue edging. Her little leprechaun looked quite cute now, snuggled up on the sofa, the fire roaring its approval.

"Would you like some coffee darling?" she asked, walking into the kitchen.

"What? Oh, err. Yes. Let me make it please." He jumped off the sofa, but Victoria was already in the kitchen and had switched on the kettle.

"I intended to buy us a coffee machine, only I haven't been able to stay here for a while, so I am not that prepared for you," he whined.

"No problem. No problem at all Arnold, and by the way, I think you are very prepared. Are we having guests for breakfast tomorrow?" Victoria had looked in the fridge, which was bursting with all sorts of breakfast foods: beef and pork sausages, bacon, eggs, tomatoes, black and white pudding, yoghurt and a mountain of fruit. Packets of cereal adorned the counter top, along with two loaves of sliced bread, one plain white and one wholemeal.

"Oh yes. I mean, no. I wanted you to have a great breakfast. I thought we could take a walk on the beach like we talked about and that would build up an appetite so I could cook for you." His eyes had gone all beady and he was wringing his hands.

'And then you would let me kiss you,' he thought.

"Oh Arnold. You are wonderful. That would be great and how kind of you," she said, but thought, 'No way sweet cheeks. I am outta here asap. I am near the knuckle as it is.'

"Now go. Shoo. Check the fire, there's a good man and I'll bring in the coffee, or would you prefer cocoa? Let me take care of you for a change."

'Oh Mary, mother of Jesus. She's going to let me kiss her. And then bam. Yep I'm going to make her so happy,' Arnold thought leaving the room on a small cloud.

'Right. Quick where are they?' Victoria had put the sleeping tablets in a cup when she was disturbed by Arnold. She found the cup, grabbed a teaspoon and proceeded to crush them into a fine powder. She made Arnold a cocoa thinking the sweetness would cover up any sign of the tablets. These were good. Her doctor had prescribed them for her when she used to travel a lot. Two would be enough to have him knocked out and sleeping like a baby. He wouldn't know what had hit him. And she would get a good night's sleep, without having to be alert and worrying if the little weasel would creep into bed with her. She wouldn't put anything past 'Mr Innocent' out there.

"Here you are Arnold. Be careful it's hot, but I made it especially for you so drink it all up. It will help you sleep." She smiled and gave him the hot, steaming mug and sat down on the opposite him on the sofa.

"I've topped your drink up Victoria. Is that okay?"

"Sure, sure. It's delightful champagne. You really are the most thoughtful man I have met. I have a good feeling about us."

On hearing her words, his penis became instantly erect and he began to salivate. "Oh Victoria. Me too." He wriggled back into the sofa hoping she wouldn't notice. He didn't want to ruin anything by being too forward. He had to get the timing just right.

"Yes. I can't wait for you to come over to England and stay at my place. I would be interested in what you thought of it."

"I know it would just be lovely if you did it."

"Yes. Well I did, didn't I Arnold? I told you that." Victoria talked and talked about the way they would spend Christmas. How enchanting his family was and how much her daughter would like them as well. Arnold started to yawn.

"Oh Arnold. How selfish of me. It's late and time for bed. Let's go and take this up in the morning." She got up from the sofa and watched a rather dazed looking Arnold slide down the sofa and onto the floor.

'No. That won't do,' she thought. 'He must wake up in bed. I don't need him suspecting a thing.'

"Arnold. Arnold!" She shook him.

"Emm, err, whaaat?" He opened his eyes, only to shut them again. "Sorry Vic, feel so sleeeeepy," he slurred.

Victoria shook him again, shouting this time. "*Arnold* come on. This will never do. Come on now. Help me get you into bed." That helped.

Arnold got the wrong end of the stick. 'Ah, she does want me. But so blasted tired. I shouldn't have had that last drink,' thinking of the champagne rather than the cocoa. Victoria helped him stand up and then, with his arm across her shoulder, they staggered towards Arnold's bedroom. Now it was time for her to be thankful that there were no stairs.

Victoria flopped Arnold's limp body onto the bed. He was asleep, fast asleep. She noticed he had his pyjamas laid out on the bed. She would have to dress him in his pyjamas. He had to wake up as normally as possible. Hopefully with a mighty hangover, but no suspicions. He had to trust her.

She pulled his torso up toward her in order to take off his robe. "Oh my God," she said out loud, alarmed at the sight of Arnold's erect penis. "How could that be?" she gasped. 'Oh well it's not that bad. Bless the old sod. I'll look after you like you were one of my sisters. Yeah right. God alone knows how he looks after his sisters,' she thought as she tossed his robe across the floor.

She had managed to dress him, pull the blankets over him, gave the top of his head a kiss and tiptoed, unnecessarily, out of his room. But, there again, she didn't want to take any chances. Once back in the living room, she rested on the sofa and 'to a job done well' toasted herself with the champagne she had earlier left on the nest of tables.

"Ah. The things I get myself into! I am sure the old bugger doesn't mean any harm, but yeesh! I can't do this anymore. He is the last. I am hanging up my dating boots. I just can't go on anymore. If it means a life of man-less days, so be it. I have failed Emmaline, my darling baby. I am sorry, but the quest is over." She smiled and held up the glass in the air imagining Emmaline to be there.

All of a sudden, she was very tired. The fire was still very much alive and she would have liked to have snuggled up on the sofa and dozed off, but she decided to seek the security of her locked room just in case Arnold managed to sleepwalk. She pulled the blankets tightly around and as soon as her head touched the pillow, she went straight to sleep.

Chapter 31

Playing With Fire

Come the morning, she woke quite refreshed and was pleased Arnold hadn't turned the central heating off. The previously cold and unwelcoming shower room was warm and with a little heat not so bad after all. She could hear Arnold singing.

'Ah good. He has no idea, but no hangover either. Pity. The weasel deserves one. What do these men think? Just because I accept an invitation to meet a complete stranger in a different country and go away to his retreat. Where do they get the idea that that means I want to have sex with them?' she thought, vigorously brushing her teeth.

"Morning Arnold," she called to a very busy Arnold in the kitchen.

"Don't come in! Stay and make yourself comfortable on the sofa. I'll be with you in a moment," he shouted.

The fire was lit and beckoning to her to sit beside it and do as Arnold asked. He held no more apprehension for her now. It was daylight and she could keep up the pretence until she was on the flight home. So she was willing to play along with the game. She was the one in control now. She held the upper hand and thought it about time that they did what she wanted. She would go for a walk on the beach, because as she had come all this way she may as well see a little of Donegal, especially as Sean had recommended it so highly. But she was determined to have lunch on the way back to the airport. Her flight wasn't until seven in the evening, so they had plenty of time to enjoy a relaxing lunch, in a good restaurant, in one of those pretty towns they had passed through on the way here. She made her way over to the sofa, stopping at the window to take a look at the view offered from Arnold's paradise.

The day was cold, but now with sunshine instead of driving rain. A good winter's day, a good day for a walk on the beach. Victoria couldn't see much from the window, but enough to learn that they were in the middle of nowhere and winter's coat had given everything a silvery hue.

"Victoria. Victoria. Come on Victoria," she heard Arnold behind her. "Here you are. Yoghurt and fruit, just as you said you liked for breakfast," he said, excited as a small child on Christmas morning. He was balancing a large bowl on a tray.

"Oh thank you, darling," she replied, turning around and sitting down on the sofa as requested.

The bowl was enormous and full to the brim with natural goat's yoghurt and fruits, from bananas to pineapple and redcurrants. It looked delicious except for its gigantic size. The portion could have fed four or five adults. He presented her with the tray, which also had a bright pink napkin and spoon on it.

"And where is your breakfast hun?"

"I'll be in shortly. I just wanted you comfortable first." He toddled off back to the kitchen. "I'll just get your coffee."

"Well that's all good then. He hasn't noticed anything and seems in a fabulous mood. Now, let's taste the spoils," she said to herself, spooning some of the yoghurt into her mouth. She ate what she could sitting on the floor, while Arnold sat on the sofa eating some hot, buttered toast. They were both quite content. Victoria looking forward to her walk on the beach and lovely, Irish style lunch. Arnold looking forward to his walk on the beach, with Victoria by his side, and the brunch he was going to cook for Victoria and of course his kiss.

"I shall go and get changed to be ready for that walk. Did you bring me that weatherproof jacket I asked for?"

"Come here Victoria. Please. I want to give you a cuddle."

"Mmmmm. Alright Arnold, but only a cuddle. You know I'm not that kind of a girl. We have spoken about this." She sat down beside him.

'I don't suppose this will do any harm. It'll probably keep him happy,' she thought as Arnold wrapped his arms around her. Then he did it. Arnold kissed her. She didn't expect it, but she yielded to him. She didn't want a scene. Things were going so nicely. But to her utter and complete surprise, his kiss was quite pleasant.

"Oh Arnold. You are a good kisser." Arnold had told her this several times yesterday evening.

"I told you," he said very pleased with himself. "Just one more pleeeeease. You can pretend I am somebody else. I really don't mind. Just keep your eyes closed."

Victoria leant into him. For Arnold to give her his 'best ever' kiss.

"Oh Victoria. I could eat you," he said, at which remark Victoria jumped up, went around the sofa, told him what a naughty boy he was, that she was going to get changed, and that it would be a good idea for them both to dust off the cobwebs.

Arnold was sitting at the heavy set table waiting for her on her return. "I'll give you that cheque now. How much do I owe you?"

"A cheque? I thought we agreed cash. You told me you had brought it along with you."

"Well, you did say a cheque would be alright and I spent some of the cash last night."

"Oh! Okay then. Two hundred and ninety."

'Why did I agree to a cheque? I know I need him to trust me, but how do I know I can trust him?' she mused.

Arnold presented her with a £300.00 cheque for her air fare and taxi rides. Off they went to the beach and a guided tour of Donegal.

It was freezing. The sun had gone in and left rain and freezing, howling wind to charge at their wrapped up bodies. The wind was so strong at one point it whipped the scarf off from around Victoria's neck.

'Enough is enough, even if it is putting my head into the lion's mouth again, I can't stand this cold any longer,' she thought,

"Let's go back Arnold. It's too cold. I'm freezing. Brrrrr."

"Just let me show you the end of the bay. You can see where the Spanish Armada ships sheltered," he insisted, taking Victoria's arm and dragging her down the beach.

"There. Okay Arnold. I've seen the view. It's very nice, but I am soo cold, darling. Please let's go back."

"Okay, okay. Let's go then," he relented. Victoria's face had gone bright red from the wind chaffing at her skin.

Chapter 32

Revenge Is Mine Sayeth Arnold

"What do you mean you aren't hungry?" Arnold asked, tight lipped.

"I am sorry Arnold, but in a way it's your fault. It's only half past midday and breakfast that was only two hours ago. And you did give me so much to eat."

"You didn't even finish it."

"I know, but I'm sorry. I can't help it. I can't force food down myself."

'Force it! Force her more like,' he thought - she was beginning to get to him again.

"Please Arnold. Don't be angry."

"I am not angry, just disappointed that's all. Are you sure? Only I have organised everything."

"I am sure. What's wrong with giving the stuff either to your sisters or take it back with us. It's not ruined."

'It's not what I want,' he thought irritably. But what could he do? She was already in the bedroom packing. "How about a cup of coffee then?" he asked, standing at the door.

"No thank you, darling. I don't want anything but to be with you in a cosy restaurant on the way back to Belfast. It makes more sense and it is quite a way, so the nearer to Belfast we eat the better, and by then I'll be hungry and ready for it."

'All this woman wants is for me to spend money on her and give me nothing in return. Damn bitch. She *is* just like all the others,' he snarled to himself, walking into his bedroom. Arnold was very disappointed indeed, because the tempting treat he wanted to cook for her contained Rohypnol. The fucking bitch didn't deserve him. Arnold was throwing his things into a dirty green holdall. "I'll show her. Oh yes, I'll show her alright," he mumbled.

Arnold said goodbye to his little piece of paradise and they both got in the car. Time was getting on. Victoria was tired and started to feel hungry as the journey rumbled on.

"Arnold, where is this restaurant you know? It's getting so late. It may be closed before we get there."

"It's not long now. Promise." He was so angry. She could feel his anger, but kept him in the 'game' by talking about their future together and settling on a date for him to come to England.

Eventually, Arnold turned off the main road to Belfast and onto a small side road. He parked opposite what looked like a roadside truck stop.

"You can't be serious?" she said, looking at the filthy net curtains covering the windows.

"It's nice and they will have roast beef like you wanted." He smiled at her, getting out of the car.

"Arnold please. It looks horrid," she said, walking after him.

"I am so tired and I need to eat. This is fine, Victoria," and he walked off toward the restaurant door. "I'll show her alright. Roast beef. Nice cosy restaurant. Yeah, yeah, yeah, nag, nag, nag. Just spend more money." His face lit up when he walked into the cafe. "Yes. Just how I remember it when I came here with me Dad forty odd years ago." Arnold now made no attempt to be polite with Victoria, but just sat down at the nearest table for two.

On entering the café, she was totally aghast at the sight that greeted her. It was the cafe that time forgot. She was in a time warp. The sixties was everywhere, including the few people who were taking their lives in the chefs hands and eating there.

"Arnold. Please this place is…" She sat down and he cut her off.

"Is nothing good enough for you?" he growled at her.

"Well. I say!" she said very softly. She couldn't afford to anger him now, she was almost home. She also didn't know where she was and the people in the restaurant looked as scary as Arnold. No. She would pacify him. Put him back in good humour, get home safely and without incident. She ordered her food, roast beef and Yorkshire pudding, requesting that the vegetables be put on a separate dish and not piled up, as she had seen on another diner's plate. Also a glass of red wine.

Arnold ordered roast turkey with stuffing and a glass of water.

They ate in silence. It was awful. Victoria ate as much as she could. She didn't want to set Arnold off again. They left the restaurant, Victoria trying to be as affable as possible, still wittering on about Christmas, and his visit to London. She didn't make any reference at all to the revolting restaurant with its plastic flowers. She hoped she hadn't contracted food poisoning, but hoped Arnold had.

'Not far to go now,' she thought. Then Beth's words popped into her head. 'You've got this far, so get the money. He has no intention of paying you. As soon as tomorrow comes that man is down the bank stopping that cheque.'

Oh no. Why had she accepted that cheque? You could cut the atmosphere with a knife, it was so thick. Arnold's miserable, sinister side was manifesting itself, getting stronger as the journey progressed. He was pissed off. Really pissed off. Who did she think she was? Jumped up tart? Stupid whore, that's all! Putting on her airs and graces. Bitch. Just like all the others. Well, he would make her pay. He would make her pay alright.

As the journey progressed, Beth's words reverberated in her head more and more. 'Don't let him get away with it. How could you have been so stupid to settle for a cheque. It's not fair, you went in good faith, he offered to pay your fare and its only right he does. You are a very foolish lady. Don't let him get away with it. Go on and ask him,' she nagged away at Victoria 's subconscious until finally Victoria came up with a plan that might just work.

"Arnold, I have just thought. I could do with that money in cash after all."

"What?" He was startled out of his inner thoughts. "Pardon? Why? You said its fine and besides, I've spent it."

"Well, it's my gardener, Sean. You know, the one who told me that Donegal was so lovely, which it is. Well, he is coming over here next week and I owe him some money, so I know he would appreciate it if I could give it to him in cash. Surely. that's not a problem to you?"

"Well, I don't have it on me," he said, driving scrunched up so much his back appeared doubled up.

"We can stop at an ATM. That's not a problem."

"Well I would like you to see my clocks and paintings before you go and

I have some cash at home, so okay, we can have a cup of tea and I can give you the cash there." He smiled at her and touched her thigh.

Victoria shivered and began to think, hang the money with or without Beth. "Great. That's great. It would be nice. I'd love to see your collection," she smiled back at him.

The air tensed up a notch. Arnold could smell her fear. 'Good,' he thought.

They arrived outside Arnold's house. It was a dark, huge Victorian monstrosity with bulky bay windows. He parked in front of the house, by an old oak tree that grew up and covered the house from the road.

"Here we are then. I am afraid the house is in a bit of a mess and will be cold. But I wasn't expecting company, let alone you coming here. So please forgive me in advance." Arnold got out of the car and fished through his pockets for the house keys.

"Oh don't worry about the cold Arnold. It will just be nice to see your collection of clocks and paintings," she said over the roof of the car.

"Come on then. I'll make a nice cup of tea." He opened the door, switched on the hallway light and waited, allowing Victoria to go ahead.

The house had stood still in the sixties. She looked up to a great staircase. Dead straight and what looked like an old rocking chair on the landing, leading to what she could only presume were the bedrooms. A huge grandfather clock stood tall and austere to her right. There were doors on her right and left, both closed, hiding their secrets just like Arnold hid his. Arnold was taking her through a tour of rooms made and decorated in different decades.

A cold shiver ran through her. She felt afraid but was also strangely excited.

"Shall I go in here?" she turned left into a small room where the door was open. It led into the kitchen.

The room couldn't have been any bigger than ten feet by ten feet. There was a large, old, leather sofa just in front of her and large, matching dull brown, leather chairs, one in each corner. A fireplace which was evidently often used, but not cleaned often, as the ashes were piled high. A small electric radiator stood in front of one of the chairs. Everything was brown including the huge, closed, velvet curtains, which, judging from the threadbare patches, must have been there since the house was built.

Dirty teacups with dregs of brown liquid in them sat on the old, mosaic tiled coffee table. Newspapers were strewn everywhere. A standard lamp stood by the chair in the far left corner. The lampshade was brown and tasselled around the bottom. It reminded Victoria of a skinny old lady and only gave out the dimmest of light. The place was a mess, just as he had described.

"I am sorry Victoria. Like I said, I wasn't expecting you to come here." He was genuinely apologetic, but he had been planning this after she had said that she wanted the cash. She didn't trust him. How dare she. She deserved all that was coming to her. He wanted Victoria so badly though. He loved her. He wanted her with him all the time. "Shall I make some tea? Please sit down, I won't be long." He walked across the room to the kitchen entrance.

Victoria sat down on the sofa and was very glad she was wearing jeans and not a skirt, or dress. The atmosphere was sickly, old and musty.

Her eyes adjusted to the gloom and there they were, the paintings he had told her about. Beautiful works of Art, punctuated here and there by his clocks. She counted ten clocks. Some small, some large, all working and ticking away. How could he sit in this room? They were already beginning to send Victoria crazy.

They were lovely though. She could understand why he had bought them, but the presentation was diabolical. Despite the wonderful paintings, one of which covered a whole wall, the room had a sad and lonely feel.

"Milk. No sugar?" he called.

"Mmmm? Pardon? Oh, yes, yes. Thank you Arnold." He loved the way she said his name. "Is there another light?" she asked.

"Yes. On the wall." He entered the tiny room with a tray on which were two cups and saucers.

"I'll get it. Oh sorry Victoria. I'll take those back into the kitchen." He picked up the old cups that had been left on the table. Placed the tray on the coffee table, and switched on the light. A burst of brightness made Victoria blink. The paintings glared back at her.

"Arnold. Oh my. Arnold they are wonderful. Simply magnificent."

The huge painting, which really should have been displayed on a wall at least ten feet tall and fifty feet wide, was of a clown peddling a unicycle, and holding a bunch of flowers in one hand.

"Is this by the Irish artist you were telling me about?" she asked.

"Yes," he said returning to the room. He stood next to Victoria who was now looking around in wonderment. Arnold had his hands on his hips. He was so proud of them. He looked at Victoria and was so proud of her too.

"May I see the rest of them? I take it you do have other exciting treasures for me to see."

'Why doesn't she just love me?' he wondered. 'I only want to please her. Then I wouldn't have to do what I have to. She's so beautiful and just look at how she loves my things. Nobody else knows about my treasure. I can't let her go now.' Arnold's thoughts were ricocheting across his brain.

"What? Oh, err, yes. Of course. Let me show you," he replied, casting off his thoughts.

She followed him out into the hallway and into the room on the right. Again it held a veritable treasure-trove of antique furniture, along with more clocks and paintings. It was like walking into a Chelsea antique shop. It was the same with the room on the other side of the house. Victoria estimated the hoard at about one million pounds, or maybe two. Staggering.

"Wonderful Arnold. Simply magical and wonderful. I am lost for words." She hugged him.

Arnold blushed and hugged her back. What was he to do? He loved her, he couldn't harm her. But he had to do what he had to do. She had refused him and didn't trust him. He would do anything for her and she didn't trust him.

"Oh. We had better get a move on. I don't want to miss the flight. Oh I do wish you were coming with me, Arnold." Victoria flurried off back to the tiny brown room.

"Don't you want to see the rest of the house?" Arnold asked in astonishment.

"I'd love to, but let's have tea first." Victoria sat down again on the tatty old sofa, perching herself on the edge and swapping the tea cups without Arnold noticing.

"Have you got the cash darling?" Beth was still nagging inside Victoria's head and she also thought, 'Fuck him. Why should he get away with it?'

"Yes, yes. I'll fetch it." Arnold went to a small desk that was propped up against the chair next to the radiator. He opened a drawer and got out a fistful of money. Victoria could see that there was a lot of cash in the drawer.

"Three hundred pounds, did you say?" he said turning and counting out the notes.

"Actually it was two-ninety to be precise," she corrected him.

He sat on the arm of the sofa. "You haven't drunk your tea."

"Oh, sorry. I got caught up with all your lovely things." She sipped from what was Arnold's cup. "And you haven't had any of yours either."

"You don't trust me, do you?" he said with just a hint of menace in his voice.

"What? Don't be silly, of course I do. It's just that Sean will appreciate it, and he is so good to me, and it just helps me out."

"Well, it's in Irish pounds. That won't be of any help to him in Donegal."

"Who said he was going to Donegal?"

"You did."

"No, no. I said he thought Donegal was beautiful. He is coming here to Belfast to visit family. But anyway, its currency isn't it? It's not monopoly money."

"Yes it is currency."

"So good then. No problem."

Arnold reluctantly counted out the cash. "There you are then, two hundred and ninety pounds exactly." He reached for his cup and drank at least half of its contents.

Victoria looked on, fully expecting him to keel over. Nothing.

She put the money in her handbag. "Time to go Arnold," she said, looking at her watch. "I'll have to see the rest of the house some other time. It will be something to look forward to." She got up brushed by him and went to the front door.

Arnold couldn't believe how quickly she could move.

Victoria opened the door and breathed in the fresh, cold night air. "Oh please God. Get me out of here," she mumbled, walking towards the car.

She had no idea just how much God had taken care of her so far.

She got in and waited for Arnold to drive her to the airport. Five minutes later Arnold got into the car, reversed it into the road, and followed the signs to the airport.

"What will you do this evening?" she asked.

"I think I'll go and see my dear old dad," Arnold said distantly.

The lights from the other cars kept flashing into Victoria's eyes, but nothing could have been more welcome than when the airport passenger drop-off sign loomed into view. Arnold stopped the car and they both got out. Both of them were in a hurry. Arnold handed over her suitcase from the boot. Victoria hesitated, but decided to kiss him goodbye. 'Let's keep up the pretence to the end,' she thought.

Arnold was astonished, but kissed her back.

"You are a good kisser, Arnold."

"Yes. I told you. You could still put that paper bag over me head and imagine I was someone else."

Victoria only laughed and shook her head. She walked away from the car towards the departures door, wheeling her suitcase behind her. As she was crossing the road, she turned and waved to him.

"Smart move Victoria. The cash was a smart move," he shouted. Arnold was hanging off the car door. She knew it. She had been right. He had intended to stop the cheque. The old bastard. What she didn't know as she went through the automatic doors, was what Arnold whispered to himself as he got back in the car.

"Yes very smart move my beauty, but I know where you live and I am a patient man. We shall see who has the last laugh Victoria, my dear. We shall see."

Now safe in the airport, Victoria was so relieved to be rid of the monster, Arnold, that she almost burst into tears when she looked into the mirror in the ladies' room. She decided to cheer herself up and went shopping for her and Emmaline. She perked up immediately, forgot all about Arnold for the moment and enjoyed herself testing perfumes and makeup. The flight left on time, was smooth, and even the cabbie in London was pleasant and chatty. Spookily though he was from Belfast, a place Victoria knew she would never see again, or at least, she thought so.

Chapter 33

Just One Last Chance

Victoria woke the next day full of energy and cheery. She was so glad the dating scene had come to an end. She could go back to normal. Maybe she'd have a short break with Berrie and basically get her life back together again. Start a new business. Forget all about men. First thing to do is disband the army d'amour. She went barefoot downstairs to make a cup of coffee and check her emails and texts. There was a bucket load of texts and over a hundred emails to go through, but first she would have her coffee and then call Beth.

They chatted for over an hour on the phone examining the pathetic Arnold.

"I'm so glad I stuck out for the money. Do you know Beth, I think he actually expected sex."

Beth rolled her eyes to the ceiling. "Yes Victoria, of course he did."

"Yes, but we went through all of that. You know me."

"Yes I do, but he didn't and hope springs eternal. It's how he was after that's so creepy. Taking you to that dreadful restaurant as punishment and then the money business. Why you agreed to a cheque I'll never know."

"Yes I know, but I had you in my head. I imagined a conversation with you and you saying, 'You did what?' So I wasn't going anywhere without the cash, however embarrassing the whole episode was. God I'm so glad that's over and my dating days as well."

"You will find someone. Don't worry. Oh. What about that agency? What are they doing?"

"Oh yes. I quite forgot about them. I'll deal with them later." They arranged to meet for lunch for a good talk and catch up.

Victoria picked up her mobile and went through her messages. There he was. 'Victoria I love you. Marry me. Please let me see you. Let's talk.' Mad Sam. He had also forwarded a photo of himself pretending to be crying. Sam was really something.

Against all her own self advice and instincts she text him back. 'What is going on? Why should I see you again. You only let me down.'

He replied instantly. 'Because we love each other.'

'Oh please, Sam.'

'I don't want anybody but you.'

'Call me this evening.'

'Okay xxx'

Victoria pressed on with her day.

Sam rang that evening, which surprised Victoria, as he hardly ever called. She had fully expected him not to call. Sam pleaded with her to see him. To give him one last chance. He wouldn't let her down, as he knew she would never see him again if he did.

"Come on Victoria. Please. We could be so happy together, we are good together."

"Well, what have you in mind?"

"I don't know. Take you to dinner? Talk? Get our lives together."

"Well, you can't stay here."

"No problem. I'll hang out at the local pub."

"Oh well. Okay. Is Friday good for you, because I am going to collect Emmy the next day?"

"Perfect. I'll get there for six o'clock. Okay?"

"Fine. Just let me know when you have left the office."

"Will do."

"Sam?" She hesitated.

"Yes darling?"

"You won't let me down, will you? Only it's upsetting. If I look forward to you coming and you don't show again. Please don't do that, will you?"

"I promise Victoria. I really do want to be with you."

"Okay then. I'll see you on Friday."

"Yes. I can't wait."

"Okay. Bye."

Victoria sighed. Was she doing the right thing? She'd bet that Beth and Emmy would be mad at her. He was a very strange man. She had first met him over a year ago now and things couldn't have been slower, so why was she agreeing to see him again? She didn't really know, but if she kept her expectation level low, as in not expecting him to turn up at all, then what the hell. She had nothing to lose and maybe everything to gain.

The days went by pleasantly enough. She called an old business colleague, Colin, and arranged to meet him in London, with a view to maybe doing some online business together. He had been talking with her recently about purchasing an internet business and working together with her. The timing couldn't have been better.

Friday came and, although she tried not to care, Victoria was on edge most of the day. Sam had texted her in the morning.

'Gmng gorgeous, looking forward to seeing you Xxxx'

'U too baby xxx.' She was looking forward to seeing him, but wouldn't believe it until he was standing at the door.

About four o'clock she texted Sam, as she hadn't heard anything else all day to ask if he had left the office.

'On my way,' he texted back.

Victoria began to become hopeful, but the memory of his past behaviour was firmly in her mind. She decided to prepare for the evening ahead, just as if he were going to turn up. So, all showered and made up, dressed in skin-tight stretch trousers, white blouse and peach coloured, box jacket finished off with a wide black patent YSL belt cinching her waist, she waited for her elusive lover. And she waited. She texted again.

'ETA please xxx.'

'Only 20 mins xx'

'Oh, so he is coming,' she thought, looking at herself in the mirror again. She always looked great, but somehow Victoria never truly saw that.

There was a knock at the door. 'Sam?' she hoped. 'Or at least not a wrong delivery address again.'

"Hi." She smiled and blushed slightly. It was Sam.

"Hi Victoria." He smiled back.

"Good. You are here?" She opened the door for him to enter the house.

"I said I would be," he replied, with a surprised inflection in his voice.

'What you say and what you do can be two very different things,' she thought, but didn't reply. She wanted things to start afresh and bringing up his past behaviour would not be helpful to that cause.

"Would you like to look around the house? It's mostly finished now. I just need to give Emmy a quick call and we can go?"

"Yeah, that's just fine." Sam went upstairs.

"Emmy. Hi darling it's Mummy. I'm just going out for the evening, but will collect you tomorrow at noon. Is that okay?" Victoria was in the kitchen running her hand through her hair talking to Emmaline.

"Hi Mummy. Yes, that's great. Can't wait to see you."

"Me too sweetie."

"Are you seeing Berrie?"

"Um, err, well no. Not exactly."

"Not exactly?"

"Well it's Mad Sam actually."

"Oh Mummy why? He is mad. I don't like him."

"You haven't met him."

"I mean I don't like the sound of him. Just look at what he has done so far. You can't trust a man like that." Emmaline had more sense in this direction than her mother would ever have.

"I know baby, I know, but, well, we shall see. He isn't staying here, so that shows he is a gentleman at least."

"Yeah. Gentle 'madman'." Emmy sighed.

"Well. You started off all of this for me."

"It didn't include dating mad hatters. I thought that the whole idea was to steer clear of the nutters?"

"He is not a nutter." Victoria's mind went straight to Arnold. "No, no Emmy. He is not a nutter. I'll let you know how it goes."

"Okay. Have a nice time then. I suppose he is there, but I still don't like him."

"Bye baby. See you tomorrow. Love you."

"Love you too. Bye Mummy."

"Hi there," Sam said has he strode into the kitchen. "It's come on a lot since I last saw it. It's really lovely Victoria. You've done really well."

"Oh great. You like it then?" She was pleased. Since they last agreed to meet, she had been thinking of Sam moving in with her. She couldn't help it. She was trying to think positively and she so wanted a man to love and cherish. She wanted a man to want to do the same with her and Sam was young and attractive.

"Yes, it's really beautiful." He walked over and kissed her cheek. "Good to see you."

"Mmmm, you too. Shall we go?" she liked his kisses. She liked Sam. They went to the restaurant to which they had gone to on their first date.

"Still sauvignon blanc?" he asked, sitting down on the stool at the bar.

"Yes please," she said, slipping onto the stool next to him. They ordered and sat down at their table.

"Victoria." Sam held Victoria's hand and looked her straight in the eye. "I've missed you."

"Mmm. Me too, but you know…" She began to go over the reasons for his behaviour, as she still didn't understand. Furthermore, there was no sign of the birthday present he had promised, and neither of the Valentine's card.

"Come on Victoria. We agreed. Fresh start. Let's talk about the future, not the past." He leant over and lightly kissed her lips.

"Err, yeah, sure. Sorry. No, you are right. There's no sense in going over the past. Here's to the future." She raised her glass.

"Here's to *our* future," he corrected her, raising his glass to meet hers. But there was still a nagging doubt inside her. They talked cordially enough, but not in the straightforward way Victoria had wanted. She wanted him to give her some idea of how he saw the relationship going and how they would come together in a practical way.

The only practical thing he mentioned was that he had an idea of renting a place halfway between Victoria's home and where he worked, and of them spending the weekends at the 'halfway house'. It was hardly what Victoria had in mind at all. Why would she be interested in that mad idea? What was the point in that? Sam had said that he wanted to be with her and to take care of her. But then Sam had said a lot of things and not done a lot of things.

The conversation didn't really go any further about how he proposed to bring their lives together. Victoria found herself not willing to bring up what she had in mind for fear of misinterpretation. Besides, it was the man's place to say how he thought things should go in the first place and Victoria would take the lead from there. Sam gave her no such lead. He seemed happy enough to talk about nothing in particular and she went along with that choice.

"Shall we go for a drink at the pub where I am staying? They seem a friendly bunch," Sam asked her, putting his arm around her waist on the way out of the restaurant. "The night is still young and I won't have far to drive."

"Sure. That would be nice." But she didn't think it would be nice. She only thought that, as he had made the effort to take her out and stay overnight at the pub, he deserved more than a quick kiss goodnight at her front door. The pub was full of the local population. It was very noisy and Victoria felt uncomfortable and very disappointed in the way the evening's conversation had gone. It was all going nowhere yet again and Sam had put on weight again. In fact, he wasn't looking that desirable in the least.

The removal of rose-tinted spectacles always has that effect and, unwittingly, this was what Victoria had done. She looked at the real situation and saw it for what it was. A lost, half decent looking man, getting fat with not a romantic bone in his body. He didn't bring any flowers and those that he had once sent were only after she had asked for them, and they had not been exactly memorable.

Sam had lied. Even if he couldn't or wouldn't recognise it. It was a fact. With the exception of tonight, Sam hadn't fulfilled one promise he had ever made.

"It's noisy here Sam, can we go please? We can have a drink at my place."

"Yes of course. It is a bit noisy. Let's go."

They drove the whole five minutes' drive in silence, listening to The Black Eyed Peas' 'Gonna Be A Good Night' and Victoria's smile was ironic indeed.

"Would you like a drink, or a coffee?" she asked, opening the car door. Sam rarely opened the door for her. She hadn't complained, because she thought he made up for it with his looks.

When was she ever going to learn? Victoria and every good person walking on earth deserved to be with good people. The nasty ones should be left to themselves. If people who have been abused dealt with it by abusing others, then they deserved to be dumped immediately. Walking away from the control freaks and standing up to liars and time thieves in the hope that they would change, was a waste of time. They wouldn't.

"Err, no thanks darling. I'd best be getting back."

'Back to what?' she thought, but was secretly very glad she didn't have to be with him any longer.

"Okay sweetheart." She got out of the car and he followed her.

"Victoria? I, err… I, um. Thanks for a lovely evening."

"Oh and thank you too, Sam." She had no idea why he'd wanted to see her again. No idea why he had gone to such effort to not say, or gain anything.

They kissed. Lovers' kisses. Pleasant, but not passionate. He made no attempt to disrobe her, or feel her breasts, but she felt his erection on her thighs.

"Victoria I am nuts about you." He pulled away from her, took both her hands and kissed her cheek. "Night, night babes." He let go and turned back to his car. She waved him goodbye and turned to go inside.

"'Nuts' is the operative word Sam, but I don't mean it like you do." She heaved a heavy sigh and unlocked the door that stood between her and sanity. She was desperate to get back to her world. A world that might at times be lonely and left her with a hole in her heart, but a world that was honest and straightforward. Victoria slept soundly that night.

She woke with a surge of energy and sheer joy. She had crossed her Rubicon. She was going to collect her precious daughter. They were both in great health. She lived in a spectacular house. She earned enough money to be comfortable. She sang in the shower that morning, something she hadn't done in a long while. She put on her makeup and dried her hair. She dressed in her skinny, stretch, light blue jeans, a dark blue, Armani t-shirt that she had bought over ten years ago and her blue open-toed Louboutin high-heeled shoes. She took one last look in the mirror before leaving the house.

"You look great!" she said to her reflection and gave herself a huge smile. She skipped down the stairs, gave a little shimmy whilst picking up her keys to the house and car and danced out of the house to the car.

She texted Emmaline. 'Just leaving be with u in an hour, love Mummy xxx.'

'Great cu soon love you too XXX,' came the immediate response.

Victoria started the car and drove up the drive feeling light and bursting with love and excitement.

The sun was shining. The day was great, her life was great.

She didn't need a quest to find happiness. She had it here all the time. She couldn't think of anything else she would rather be doing right now than collecting her daughter and then driving them both back home.

The quest hadn't been to find a man. The quest had been to find herself, and she had.

'I love you Emmy,' she thought, a clear, sparkling tear spilling down her cheek.

She couldn't stop smiling.

THE END

Printed in Great Britain
by Amazon.co.uk, Ltd.,
Marston Gate.